HOLLEN THE SOULLESS

DOKIRI BRIDES SERIES

DENALI DAY

CONTENTS

1.	The Dragon Submits to None	1
2.	Better Forgiveness Than Permission	11
3.	Bride by Right	19
4.	Joselyn Helena Elise Fury	31
5.	Bonded	41
6.	Bloody Savages	52
7.	Obsidian Wings	60
8.	Starting Fires	76
9.	Brothers and Brides	89
10.	May the Mountain Fall	107
11.	Mu Saliga	119
12.	A Wild Night	136
13.	Huntress	154
14.	Veligiri	167
15.	Duty First	172
16.	Little Sister	186
17.	Stoking Fires	199
18.	Leaning Back	214
19.	Fools Rush In	226
20.	Out of the Frying Pan	236
21.	Hollen's Wrath	244
22.	Twice Wronged	251
23.	The Strongest Among Us	265
24.	The Soulless	276
25.	Small Steps	286
26.	The Glory of the Gods	292
27.	Judgment Day	306
28.	Playing Games	319
29.	Confessor	328
30.	Gegatudok	343
31.	The Shoulders of the Mountain	351
32.	A Feast for the Gods	364

33. Brother of My Heart	371
34. Hard Choices	382
35. The Gameboard of Lords	390
36. Kept Vows	405
37. Mark of the Captive	418
38. The Butcher of Brance	428
39. Wings in a Snare	442
40. For the Love of a Savage	452
41. A Beacon of Hope	463
42. Knitting Scars	472
43. Mu Hatu	477
Want more?	481
...And more?	483
Also by Denali Day	485
About the Author	487
Glossary	489
Acknowledgments	491

Copyright © 2020 by Denali Day

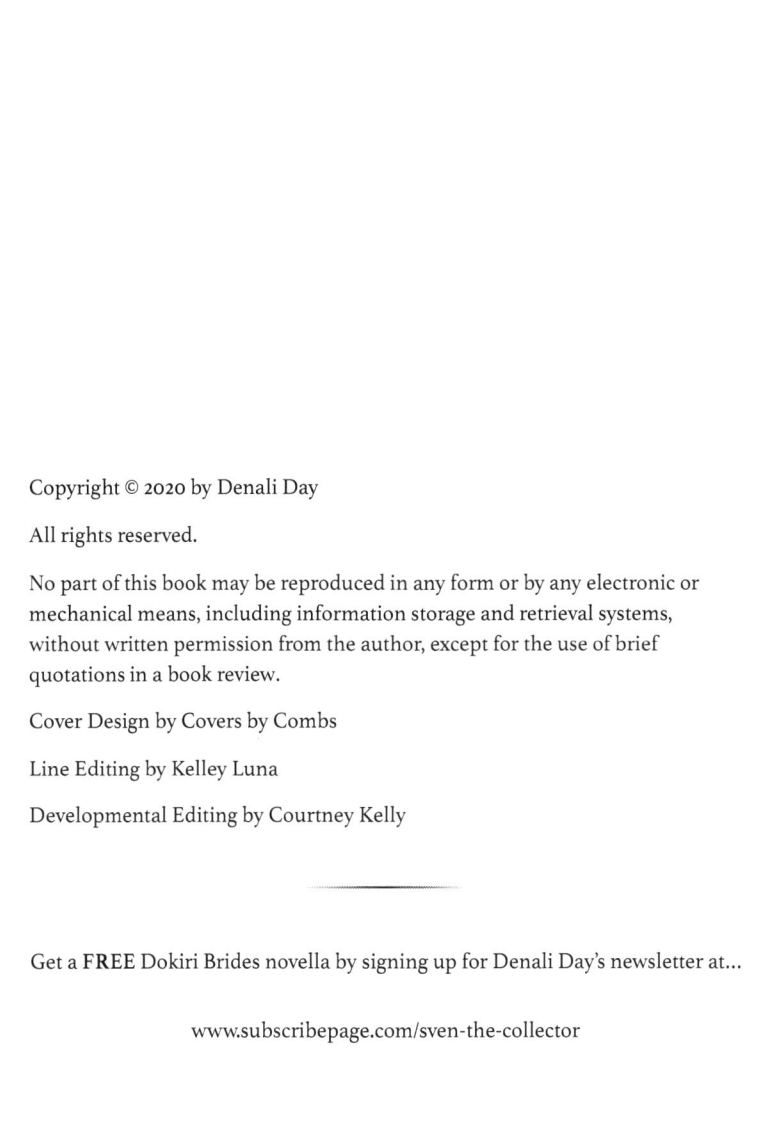

All rights reserved.

No part of this book may be reproduced in any form or by any electronic or mechanical means, including information storage and retrieval systems, without written permission from the author, except for the use of brief quotations in a book review.

Cover Design by Covers by Combs

Line Editing by Kelley Luna

Developmental Editing by Courtney Kelly

Get a **FREE** Dokiri Brides novella by signing up for Denali Day's newsletter at...

www.subscribepage.com/sven-the-collector

For my husband

My alpha in more ways than one.

1

THE DRAGON SUBMITS TO NONE

"He's a monster! The man your father wants you to marry, he's the foulest sort of depraved!"

Joselyn stiffened at her nurse's words, her slender fingers wrinkling the page she'd been about to turn. Outside, torrents of rain pelted the study windows. "Tansy? Calm yourself. What's wrong?"

Tansy, a stout, middle-aged woman with graying hair, clutched at Joselyn's arm. She leaned forward to catch her breath. "Milady, I ran here as fast as I could. Straight from the council chamber."

"They let you in?" Joselyn set the logbook down on her lacquered desk. It bumped against an untouched dinner tray. The area was a mess of quills and parchment, a testament to the long nights she'd spent ensuring everything at Fury Keep was in order. Ready for winter and her own final farewell.

Tansy ignored the question. "I heard it all! Every word. Dante Viridian has a heart black as soot. He's not a man, he's a demon. A demon born of the dirt at the bottom of the sea!"

"Tansy!" Joselyn took her beloved nurse by the arms. "Slow down. Tell me what happened."

Through the window, a thick storm cloud shrouded the last of the sun's rays, darkening her nurse's reddened eyes. "Your father was meeting with your fiancé's representatives, discussing the terms of your nuptials, when Lord Ellis barged right into the council chamber."

Joselyn gasped at the mention of her former suitor, the man Joselyn had *thought* she would marry. "Lord Ellis? What did *he* want?"

"He wasn't alone! There was so many men about, I thought surely the guards would flash steel, but he had a woman with him."

"A woman? Who?"

"Just some peasant woman from Brance. A pretty little thing, or at least"—Tansy choked on her tears—"she used to be. Maybe. Before he got to her."

Joselyn's heart thrummed in her chest so hard it burned. She forced herself not to squeeze her nurse too tightly as she waited for the rest of the story. Tansy swallowed, her voice cracking.

"She'd been cut up. That monster carved up her face like a slab of raw meat. It was awful, Joselyn! I don't know how the girl survived."

"You're saying my intended did this? Dante Viridian?"

As Tansy nodded, a crack of thunder shook the stone keep and the vibrations rumbled up Joselyn's buckling knees. She gripped the desk, steadying herself as Tansy rushed on.

"Lord Ellis brought the girl to your father as proof. Swore there's a dozen more victims just like her, but he only had time to hunt down the one. He begged your father to break off the marriage negotiations, or at least to slow things down. Begged him to reconsider."

"And"—Joselyn licked her lips—"what did my father say?"

Tansy broke into an agonized sob and pressed her gray head into Joselyn's shoulder. Hot tears soaked through the blue silk of her dress, onto her freckled skin. Joselyn swallowed hard.

What are you doing, Father?

She'd been shocked enough when her father had initiated marriage negotiations with House Viridian. Apart from their wool trade, Viridian was a house teetering on the edge of total obscurity. Not like her own house, whose lord was second in line for the throne. And now *this*? It couldn't be true.

Joselyn stroked Tansy's curls, reveling in the old woman's love, the affection she gave so freely. Unlike the woman who'd borne Joselyn. Unlike the man who'd sired her.

"Hush, now, Tansy. All will be well. Lord Ellis is an ambitious man. He'd do anything to secure the alliance between his house and ours. It's not so hard to imagine him staging the whole affair."

Tansy tore out of her charge's arms, sobering. "I'm an old woman, Joselyn. I know a kettle of tripe when I smell it. Those scars wasn't fresh and they wasn't staged. Where there's smoke there's a fire, and I tell you, Dante Viridian is the Butcher of Brance."

Joselyn's stomach dropped. She'd heard the rumors. Everyone had. The Butcher of Brance, a beast of epic brutality, had plagued the lands of House Viridian for the better part of the last decade. Dismembered stable boys, children lashed to death, women mutilated in such ways that Joselyn's maids would not repeat the details. That the fiend had not yet been identified and brought to justice was brow-raising to even the most skeptical gossip. According to rumor, all victims had been serfs, and very few had ever survived.

"You can't go through with it, milady. You mustn't."

Joselyn frowned. "What would you have me do?"

"Tell your father no, child. Just this once. Refuse him!"

Joselyn squeezed her nurse's hand. Tell Lord Fury no?

Refuse him? Like the useless, petulant daughter he was always waiting for her to turn into? The one he expected her to be?

No. I think not.

Joselyn would get to the bottom of this. It made no sense. Lord Fury was no fool. If this was the decision he'd made, there was a good reason. And she'd be damned if she left her home behind without knowing what it was.

Tansy continued on in a panicked frenzy. "The barons will support you. Your father's own steward disapproved of the match, and that was before we knew you were to be wed to the Butcher of Brance." She whispered the title as though it would bring a curse upon them.

"I must speak with my father."

"Yes, child, tell him! Tell that miserable bastard you won't be his—"

Joselyn released her nurse. "That's the Lord of Tirvine you speak of, Tansy. *Your* lord."

Tansy stiffened, choking back her words. No one spoke ill of her father in front of Joselyn. Not even Tansy. Joselyn wouldn't have it. If *she* had to show him respect, then, by the gods, so would everyone else.

"Despite what you think, my father has my best interests at heart," Joselyn said.

The familiar lie slipped out, and Tansy, bless her heart, was wise enough to let the subject drop. The old woman's lip quivered, and Joselyn's heart ached for the only person who had ever shown her loyalty. She pressed a gray curl out of her nurse's face. "No matter what happens, I will survive it. I'll survive it and come out stronger. You believe me, don't you?"

Tansy shook her head. A tear rolled down her plump cheek. "You can't mean to go through with it. Surely you wouldn't submit yourself to a beast."

Joselyn fingered the golden pendant she'd been given the

day she was born. One side depicted a great dragon, spewing fire. The other was engraved with her family's credo.

"There is no greater beast than the dragon, Tansy"—she swept her thumb over the words and released the pendant—"and 'the dragon submits to none.' "

JOSELYN'S slippered footsteps echoed down the sweeping stone halls of her lifelong home. Shadows flickered in the torch light of a hundred iron sconces. The effect gave her a sense of vertigo as she hurried to her father's chambers.

Thunderclaps shook the corridors, as if the storm were threatening to collapse the stone walls around her. Let it try. Fury Keep was as indomitable as it was cold. Nothing so wild and scorching as a bolt of lightning would master it.

Joselyn was just ordering her father's guards aside when his steward exited through the heavy doors. A haggard, frustrated expression dominated his battle-scarred face.

"Sir Richard." Joselyn greeted the tall man with a curtsy. "I trust today's negotiations weren't too exhausting."

Richard hesitated when he saw her, the corners of his mouth pulled into a frown. "Milady Joselyn. I am indeed as tired as I must seem. You, on the other hand, glow radiant as ever."

Joselyn flashed him a polite smile.

He continued, "It's no small wonder that you stand before me now, proud and fierce as ever."

"And why would I not? Is this not a happy day for House Fury?" Joselyn asked. *Go on. Tell me why I should be afraid.*

Sir Richard regarded her. For a moment she thought she saw a flicker of regret cross his features. Or was it shame? In the end he only sighed. "As you say, milady."

Joselyn watched him go, wondering what the man thought

of the day's events. Had he been like her father's other knights, begging him to reconsider the alliance with House Viridian? Had he begged on her behalf? Not that it mattered. No one told a man like Marcus Fury what to do.

She turned to the door, blinked, and sucked in a steadying breath. A guard knocked for her. After a long moment, Lord Fury answered. Joselyn let out the breath, and her shoulders relaxed the barest of inches. The guards pushed the doors open.

Courage.

As she stepped over the threshold, her eyes struggled to adjust to the darkness. She scanned the cavernous room. The hearth lay empty, and Joselyn shuddered at the autumnal chill. Silken blankets were smoothed down to pristine perfection across the massive bed.

A bolt of lightning lit up the room, and Joselyn's gaze landed on her father. His back to the window, he sat with his legs crossed upon a great carved chair, upholstered in rich crimson. To his side rested a lamp which provided the room's only light save for the sconces at the entrance.

"Father?"

Marcus raised a hand, beckoning her.

Joselyn glided across the room with practiced grace. Beneath her swooping sleeves, she clasped her balmy hands together. His eyes stared her down as she approached.

Marcus Fury was a man early into the second half of his life. The years had not robbed him of his good looks, however. The lines upon his face were shallow. His hair, though faded, still contained brilliant streaks of red which, in addition to the cleft in his chin, were the only features Joselyn had inherited from him. His gray eyes held a constant severity that inspired men to obedience. That severity rested heavily upon her now as she waited. She knew better than to speak before he'd given her permission. Finally, Lord Fury arched a brow.

"Did you know?" Joselyn's nails dug into her palms.

After a long moment, "Yes."

Of course he knew. Marcus Fury was as shrewd as he was cunning. He would not enter into a marital alliance with another house without first knowing everything about its lord and people. Her legs began to shake. At least he'd spoken truthfully. It must suit him tonight.

"Your intended's reputation for violence will not do."

Joselyn's heart withered at his flat tone.

Lord Fury went on, "When you marry you'll mind he takes more care to clean up after himself. You may take his name, but the son you bear him will take our house. House Fury must not suffer for your husband's perversions. Put him in check."

"Yes, Father."

"Are you prepared to do your duty, Daughter?"

Duty was Joselyn's god and master, and she was the highest of priestesses. Her father knew this well. She swallowed. "Haven't I always?"

"You're a woman. Until now nothing significant has ever been required of you."

No? Joselyn's gaze dropped to her fingers, covered in black ink stains. She felt the throbbing ache in her neck from hours bent over one account book or another. All to ensure that Lord Fury was never troubled over affairs he deemed *insignificant*.

"I manage your estate, reconcile your logbooks, entertain your guests, give—"

"Any backwater lady can run a manor. Your mother was an expert in such things. You of all people know how little it meant in the end. Are you like your mother?"

Joselyn gritted her teeth. How could he ask her that? How *dare* he? "No."

Her father huffed. "We'll see."

Joselyn shook her head, despair getting the better of her. "But, why?"

Marcus cocked his head. "Why?"

Dropping to her knees, she grasped at his hand. "Yes, Father, why?"

Lord Fury eyed her with irritation and Joselyn shrank. She folded her hands in her lap. Her father had a way of waiting people out until the silence had his opponents blathering over themselves. By the end of the discussion, he would have inevitably won whatever he was after, having said almost nothing at all. Joselyn would not be fooled into a one-sided conversation. Not this time. She remained totally still.

For once in your life, Father, take pity on me.

Marcus heaved a sigh and clicked his tongue. "As Lord of a dying house, Dante Viridian would do anything to preserve his legacy."

Joselyn broke in. "Yes, a blood alliance between Viridian and Fury would no doubt give him what he desires. But what can *you* possibly stand to gain, Father?"

His lips thinned. Joselyn battled the urge to cringe.

Skies, Joselyn! Be silent.

"We *gain* nothing. What we *avoid* is the destruction of our house."

Lord Fury turned toward the nightstand and poured himself a glass of wine. He swished the burgundy liquid in the jewel-encrusted goblet before taking an agonizingly slow sip. "Four weeks ago, Dante Viridian sent a missive to our keep. It contained a list of dates and locations as well as a number of anonymous testimonials lending credibility to the letter's contents." A few more languid sips and he continued, "The dates and locations correspond with the occasions I have met with Queen Arabella over the past three years."

Joselyn choked as though she were the one drinking the

wine. Her gaze tried to connect with her father's, but he was pointedly ignoring her in favor of his cup.

"Father?" she whispered, her question unspoken.

"Yes, Daughter," Marcus answered, still not meeting her eyes. "I've been plowing the king's wife."

Joselyn swayed. Had she not already been on her knees she would surely have fallen. When Marcus finally met her gaze it was Joselyn who looked away.

"I see," she murmured. Her shoulders slumped, and she pressed a hand to the carpeted floor, trying to remain upright.

As a woman, Joselyn wasn't privy to most of her father's activities. Had she been the son her father longed for, she might have guessed that proud Lord Fury would only have considered such an alliance under the threat of blackmail. And what a great threat it was.

Should King Travaran learn of her father's indiscretions, Marcus Fury's head would be lopped off immediately. Possibly without a trial. There was more at stake than the sanctity of the royal union. Though healthy, King Travaran was an old man, and his only heir was a son too young to rule. Should the king suddenly die under tragic circumstances, Queen Arabella would rule as regent in his stead. And Lord Fury, as her consort as well as third in line for the throne, would hold more power than any other man in the kingdom.

The very worst detail of all, was that the young Prince Cyran was not the son of Queen Arabella. Rather, he was born of the king's first wife who'd died in childbirth. Should both King Travaran *and* Prince Cyran die, Marcus Fury would become king of all Morhagen. An affair between her father and the queen reeked of both treason and conspiracy.

"Is there nothing . . ." Joselyn broke off. *How to ask about an assassin?* " . . .to be done?"

Lord Fury raised a brow. "Do you *really* suppose I haven't

considered that?"

Of course he had. The testimonials were likely arranged to be sent out in the event of Lord Viridian's sudden death. Joselyn's gaze dropped to the floor. "No."

"Do you know what this dilemma means for our house?" he asked. "For our people?"

Joselyn nodded, fingering her necklace. Should her father's activities be made known, Marcus would be executed and the lands and titles of all his family would be stripped. It would be the end of House Fury. As for its people? No lord's people were better fed or protected. Though Joselyn might have wished for a warmer father, her people could never want for a more effective lord.

Her eyes stung as the full weight of her duty settled upon her. This wasn't about Joselyn, or her happiness. She was grateful for the darkness of her father's chamber, grateful he couldn't see the tears welling in her eyes. She blinked them back and rose shakily to her feet. She smoothed her gown and resumed a dignified posture. The posture of a noblewoman, a persona she'd perfected over eighteen years.

"I am prepared to serve you, milord Father, as only a *daughter* can."

"Indeed. You'll do your duty for the good of your house. And you'll do it without complaint. This world owes you nothing, Joselyn. Remember that."

Her stomach clenched. *As if I could ever forget.*

"Would you know anything else?" His eyes were clouding over with that familiar haze, the one that said she'd been taking advantage of the great honor of his time.

Joselyn knew what she wanted to say. What she wanted to ask. *Is this enough for you, Father? Am I enough?*

"When do I depart?" she asked instead.

"In three days."

2

BETTER FORGIVENESS THAN PERMISSION

The crisp autumn wind blew against the shutters of the rocking carriage. Golden sun streamed through the cracks in the limber, though it put off no warmth. Joselyn drew her ermine lined cloak more tightly around her shoulders and tried to ignore her maid's constant chatter.

"He favors knives, you know? That's what the cook said. I'll bet he's sharpening his favorite ones right now. Big curved ones with jagged teeth!"

"You have quite an imagination," Joselyn muttered, pressing her head against the lattice window. What she wouldn't give for an hour of peace. She had already sought out every rumor about her intended *before* leaving Fury Keep. In the three days since then, she'd heard them all over and over again. Even her maid must have been getting bored, because her retellings had devolved into morbid speculation.

"Do you think he'll wait until we're alone to start cutting at us? Or will his attendants be invited to watch?"

"Enough, Dina!" Joselyn whipped toward the little maid. "We're not obscure peasants tucked away in his hamlets. Even if everything you say is true, the Lord of Brance will not harm us. It gains him nothing and loses him everything."

"Won't harm you, of course! You're too valuable. But what of me? I hear The Butcher favors blondes." Dina clutched at her yellow braid.

Joselyn rolled her eyes. "You volunteered to come."

"Of course I did. To be first maid of Lady Fury as she establishes her new household? How could I turn that down?"

"Then listen well, Dina. I've had enough of your doomspeak. If you can't think of anything uplifting to say you'll keep your silence for the rest of the journey."

The maid crossed her arms and pouted in the corner of the carriage. Not five minutes passed before she began humming the tune to "Pray Ye Maidens, Fair," a ballad about noblewomen being ravaged by blood-crazed marauders. Joselyn gritted her teeth and kicked open the carriage door. She pointed at the guard riding closest. "You! Bring me my white."

"Milady?"

"I'm riding," Joselyn snapped, jumping from the carriage.

The man frowned. "Milady, if you wish to rest—"

"No, Captain," Joselyn cut him off. "We will continue. I simply require some air."

The man hesitated, then whistled, waving to those at the back of the procession. Joselyn's mount, a pale vision of speed and grace, was led up to the carriage side where she paced. Joselyn ran her hand over his withers and some of the tension eased from her body.

"Hello, boy."

So long as he received his oats, Morningstar wouldn't plague her with anxious prattle. Joselyn climbed into his saddle. The guard glanced at the carriage. "Surely you'd like your maid to attend you. I'll have another mount brought."

"I'm sure I would not," Joselyn said. "I'm going to ride at a distance. I'll be gone but five minutes. Ten at most."

The captain was opening his mouth to reply when Joselyn spurred her horse into a canter. When cowing someone to your will, it was better to say less and do more. Her father had taught her that much.

Better forgiveness than permission.

Still, she shouldn't push the men too far. They had a duty of their own, to protect her. She urged her horse along the top of the hill where she could easily be seen by her guards.

Her ancestral lands were breathtaking. The autumn season was early and the hills still rolled green. The land was kept fertile by streams of sweet water said to be blessed by the gods. Forests of brilliant red and orange trees sent their leaves sailing upon the wind like burning embers. The backdrop to all this was the snowcapped Crookspine Mountains. No matter how far they traveled, the immense mountain range never seemed to move.

When she'd reached a good distance and felt adequately alone, Joselyn steadied her mount. They swayed together as he shifted their weight, nickering. Joselyn breathed the cold air and closed her eyes, reveling in the peace. It took only moments for a new voice to invade her thoughts.

"The deficiency of your sex has put a target on my back. It was only a matter of time before something like this happened."

Her father's words echoed. Joselyn had spent the past three years since her mother's death wondering why her father hadn't yet taken a second wife. After the accident that claimed Lady Fury's life, Joselyn had expected him to make begetting a proper heir his greatest priority. But he hadn't. And now she knew why. He had a lover, and not an easy one to scorn. Now he may never be free to take advantage of his wife's death. How justly ironic.

Her father was right about one thing. If she'd had a brother, this would never have happened. She wouldn't be riding off to marry the Butcher of Brance and she'd never have this chance to demonstrate who she was, or what she was willing to do. To prove her parents wrong.

That was something for all this misery. Her fists tightened around the reigns. Joselyn was not deficient. She'd fulfill her duty as well as any son. Better. And her father would live with the knowledge that, for all his imperious lecturing, *she'd* been the one to save their house from *his* recklessness.

She opened her eyes. Fixed on the mountains ahead. So distant, cold, and silent. Joselyn hadn't cried the day she left Fury Keep, and neither had her father. Only Tansy had wept. If the old nurse had been a spinster, Joselyn had no doubt she'd have picked up and followed. As it was, Joselyn would meet her future husband—her fate—with her father's guards, an insufferable maid, and no one else.

She'd never felt so alone.

Morningstar nickered, his white ears flickering back and forth.

"What is it, boy?" Joselyn leaned down to stroke at his strong neck when the horse reared on his hind legs. She gasped, clutching at the reins.

A violent gust bore down on them, and Morningstar, who'd been battle trained by the finest horse masters in Morhagen, let out a whinny that sounded more like a scream. Joselyn's heart skipped a beat. She caught the bit in her hands and urged Morningstar back down. Just as she managed to ground him, a great shadow swooped up from the valley below her.

What was she seeing? Was that? No. It couldn't be! A massive black dragon hovered not twenty feet above them. Its mighty wings sent a cyclone of wind all around. Joselyn's mouth fell open. Her red hair whipped about her face as she stared up at the winged horror. The scaly beast shrieked, snapping its fang-lined jaws at her.

Morningstar bolted before Joselyn could think to spur him on. She barely managed to keep her seat as the animal raced back toward the procession. Ahead, her guards were scrambling. Some appeared to be forming rank and the rest were notching arrows.

Joselyn leaned low on the horse's back, willing him to run faster. The blasts of air intensified rather than diminished, and Joselyn risked a glance above her, only to see wicked claws extending in her direction. The sun was totally eclipsed by the giant creature's raven scales. She couldn't even manage a scream.

The dragon seized her; its talons encircled her waist and yanked her off her steed. Morningstar bucked as her weight left him. Joselyn's body folded in half as the monster changed directions and began a rapid ascent.

Her guards scattered below; some fired arrows. Stretching her hands toward the earth, she cried out to them, "Help me!"

The howl of the wind drowned out her voice. Another breath and her escort was so far away, they appeared as tiny dots scurrying around the carriage. *No. This can't be real. Can't be happening.* The dragon shrieked, sending a shot of ice down Joselyn's spine. When they burst through a cloud, Joselyn knew she was on her own.

She flailed. Her first instinct was to attack the beast. One touch of its iron scales destroyed that hope. Next she tried to pry the creature's grip open. She strained against its inky claws before understanding that, even if she could free herself, she would plummet instantly to her death. She forced herself to breathe against the creature's crushing grip and craned her head backward.

Its belly was covered in plates black as onyx. If it bore any other coloring, Joselyn couldn't tell from her low vantage point.

It appeared to have only two legs, both of which held her to its body. Its wings were each composed of five long spines which connected a thin layer of flesh together. She could almost see the sun through that skin, the light illuminating the beast's spidery, obsidian veins. There was no doubt she was being carried by a dragon. She steeled herself against the urge to faint.

She'd heard tales of such beasts. The dragon was the sigil of her house after all, but never had she actually seen one. Precious few had. Joselyn despaired. She was unarmed. Even had she been the greatest of warriors she'd stand no chance against this monster when it finally released her. The thought sent fresh terror through her body.

Will it drop me? Devour me as it hovers above some foul nest?

A flash of something dark caught her eye. Was that leather? Joselyn squinted. The beast was entwined in a wide band of some sort, like a saddle strap laced under the belly of a horse. A vague memory tried to surface, but Joselyn was too panicked to call it up.

Beneath her, the earth was gone. In its place was a shining sea of golden clouds. The sensation of looking down at what her mind told her should be above, made Joselyn's stomach blanch. Icy mist saturated her cloak and her flesh stung with cold. As they soared past another vapor, Joselyn caught sight of their destination. Mount Carpe, the tallest peak in the Crookspine Range, loomed ahead. The mountain was said to hide great riches and be home to all manner of ancient devils. She knew now that at least one rumor was true.

The mountain's terrible stone face glared at them. They were at least halfway up. The earth below was gray rock. Its blanket of snow grew thicker as it climbed toward the peak. Her heart pounded in her chest as the beast began to circle a gradual descent. They spiraled and a wave of nausea rolled over her. The contents of her stomach rose into her throat. Joselyn gripped the dragon's claws for support and willed the bile back down.

What's happening? What's it going to do to me?

They were nearly to the ground, but instead of landing, the dragon leveled off and picked up speed as it soared across the earth. So close to the ground, Joselyn could see how fast they were moving, and it was all she could do to hold on.

They were headed straight for a stony cliff face. Joselyn's eyes widened. Just as she thought she would die, plastered to the side of the mountain, a dark crag came into view. A cave waited, suspended hundreds of feet into the air. Joselyn let out a sob of relief.

With incredible grace, the dark creature sailed deep into the cave's opening. For a moment, she was totally blinded by the sudden darkness. She could hear the dragon's wing tips gliding along the rocky edges, though they didn't catch. At last, the dragon landed with the soft crunch of gravel beneath its feet. Joselyn's ease was short lived as her eyes adjusted.

The dragon held her parallel to the ground. She was suspended several feet above it, arms and legs dangling awkwardly to the side. Whimpering, Joselyn pried at the creature's talons. Hysteria loomed as she jerked and bucked, desperate to get free. The beast let out a deep growl, and the cavernous walls reverberated with the sound. Joselyn stilled. Her mouth went dry.

Back home, in a moment of weakness, she'd briefly considered if death would not be a better alternative to marriage with the young lord Viridian. A lifetime of misery and possibly violence. She knew now, however, beyond a shadow of a doubt, that she did not want to die.

Please, gods! Please!

A thud echoed through the cave. Joselyn listened over the sound of her heart hammering in her ears. Heavy footsteps.

Where were they coming from? She swept at the pieces of red hair that had slipped their elaborate coif and blocked her vision. The footfalls were nearly upon her now. Her fear pulsed like a living thing, threatening to consume her. Unable to do anything else, Joselyn squeezed her eyes shut.

"*Velsa lagi.*"

A deep male voice spoke in a language Joselyn didn't recognize. Her eyes sprang open just in time to see a massive man staring at her. Suddenly, she was released. Joselyn fell into his waiting arms. She clutched at them, steadying herself, then looked into the darkest gaze.

A gaze that threatened to consume her.

3

BRIDE BY RIGHT

He was the wildest thing Joselyn had ever seen. Standing well over six feet tall, he wore leather, studded armor over layers of rich pelted fur. A double-bitted axe hung belted at his side. His dark hair was pulled tightly into a bun, away from his bearded face.

He stared at her with such intensity that Joselyn wondered if she should be more afraid of him than the dragon standing behind him. His grip on her tightened ever so slightly. She had her answer. She planted her hands against his broad chest and began to thrash. "Put me down!"

The man merely stood there holding her, as though the monster at his back was of no concern to either of them.

"Are you hurt?" he asked in the trade tongue. His deep voice was cool and even.

Joselyn barely processed what he said, her attention fixed upon the dragon who was turning to face them. She gasped. Its face came into view, and the beast was all the more terrifying with its yellow eyes fixed upon her. Though smaller with its wings closed, it was easily the length of three stone cottages and as tall as two. Its skinny tail swayed back and forth. Three razor-sharp barbs whipped with it. A serpentine hiss passed through its monstrous teeth as it tasted the air with a forked red tongue.

"Please." Joselyn whimpered.

The man set her feet down and let her go. The moment she was free, Joselyn bolted. She made it all of three strides before a wave of vertigo had her skidding to the ground. She just caught herself with her hands. Those same heavy footsteps from before approached. Joselyn felt through the black gravel for a rock. She wouldn't be trapped again.

His hand wrapped around her arm and Joselyn swung back. Her own hand crashed into the side of his face. The impact sent him groaning back on his heels.

Bleeding skies!

Joselyn's hand throbbed, but she didn't hesitate. She released the rock and turned to run deeper into the cave.

Cracks in the stone ceiling sent yellow light pouring to the ground, illuminating her path as she went. The moss-covered walls grew closer together the deeper they stretched. She had no idea where she was going, only that she had to find somewhere small to hide. Behind her, she could hear footfalls in pursuit. Joselyn was already running as fast as she could.

Ahead, the path disappeared before a great stone wall. It sloped back slightly before reaching a plateau some twenty feet high. Her pursuer was nearly upon her now. Without slowing to search for a foothold, Joselyn threw herself upon the rock. Her hand caught a small crevice, and for a moment she clung to the wall. But seconds later she lost her grip and slid back to the ground. Behind her, the footfalls halted. Joselyn spun and backed into the wall.

The man stood panting. A trickle of blood trailed from his left temple into his beard. The dragon hadn't followed. She could no longer see it around the twisting path that had narrowed nearly to a tunnel. That gave her some comfort, but now her attention was fixed upon the man before her. Joselyn had to tilt her head up to see his face. She knew there would be rage burning in his dark eyes. Violence. But . . .her brows drew together. There was no anger in his expression. The man stood with his palms open, extended in a placating gesture.

"Shh! It's all right," he said.

Is he concerned? For me?

"Don't touch me!" she spat, and cast her gaze around for a way to escape. There was none. The savage man had her cornered.

"Don't run," he said, his voice thick with a guttural accent Joselyn didn't recognize. "I won't harm you."

Had there been anywhere for her to run, Joselyn would be gone already. She was a caged animal, her nails scraping the wall behind her as she flexed her fingers to strike.

"What is your name?" the man asked. He lowered his arms and leaned backward, as though trying to lend her space without giving up ground.

Joselyn frowned, still panting. The man sighed and licked his lips. He spoke again. "I am Hollen the Soulless. *Salig* of Bedmeg of the Dokiri people. I—"

Joselyn lunged to the side, trying to dart around him. When he stuck his arms out to catch her, she ducked low and slipped past.

"*Va kreesha!*" The man swore when he grasped at empty air.

Just like that, he resumed the chase. Joselyn ran back the way she'd come, searching for an alternate route. She didn't make it far. An arm swept around her and pulled her off the ground. She screamed, and the sound echoed off the craggy walls. She thrashed and kicked, but her blows didn't faze him as he wrapped both arms about her waist and held her to him.

"Peace, woman!" he pleaded. He turned his face away from her flailing hands.

"Let me go!" she screamed, as he brought them both to the ground. He settled her on his lap, her back to his front. He caught her wrists and held them out. Joselyn bucked, trying to get back to her feet. It was no use. The man was too strong. She let out a pitiful cry.

"Shh! Easy! Easy!"

Eventually Joselyn stilled. She could not free herself. No man had ever laid his hands upon her. No man would have dared. Her father would have ordered him imprisoned or worse. Her virtue was a commodity worth far more than any one man's life. Sitting here now, pressed against his knees, Joselyn was utterly helpless. She squeezed her eyes shut, awaiting her fate.

Nothing happened. A long moment passed, her breaths gradually slowing as the adrenaline subsided. What was happening? Who was this man? Why had the dragon carried her here? Fear twisted inside her as she remembered what she'd tried to recall in the sky. An old legend, one of great dragon-riding demons who stole unsuspecting maidens from the lands below their mountains, raped them, then fed them to their winged steeds.

"What do you want?" Joselyn whimpered. She strained away from the close contact.

The man's grip around her wrists relaxed, though he didn't release her. "I won't hurt you."

"Please, let me go!"

"If you keep running this direction, my mount will see you alone and devour you." It might have been a threat except for his coaxing tone.

"I'll not run—I swear it. Please release me." She fixed her eyes down the shadowy tunnel ahead.

After a moment, his massive hands eased their grip. Joselyn snapped her arms forward and jumped from his lap. She landed on the ground in front of him, turned, and scrambled backward until she reached the edge of the tunnel. Walking her hands up the wall, Joselyn got to her feet and stared her attacker down.

He remained on his knees, staring back just as intently. He was so large, even on his knees. What could she do? Would he rise? Lunge at her? Command her to approach?

He said nothing. Did nothing.

"What do you want with me?" Joselyn asked.

"What's your name?"

She didn't answer.

"I'm Hollen the Soulless," he said again.

"Why didn't that beast attack?" she demanded. She itched to confirm her suspicion.

"He's already eaten today." A corner of his mouth twitched. "He's broken to my will, and I didn't want him to attack you."

Joselyn's mouth fell open. "A dragon cannot be tamed."

"He doesn't bear me upon his back out of good nature, I promise you."

Joselyn blinked. So the legend was true? How much of it? "You ordered that thing to steal me away?"

He nodded.

"Why? What do you want from me?" Her body stiffened, preparing to bolt again. As if sensing this, he shifted forward on his knees.

"Yourself."

"You have me! What are you waiting for?"

How could her life have come down to this? When she still had a duty, a purpose to fulfill? Fear turned to rage in her veins. She wouldn't die without a fight. Joselyn searched for a vulnerable spot to sink her claws.

The man's mouth fell open and he shook his head. He extended his palms to her again in that pleading gesture. "Easy, woman. I'll not harm you. I brought you here to be my bride."

Joselyn gaped at him. She waited for him to laugh, to grin,

even to attack her. Anything to indicate his obvious insanity. Instead he watched her, waiting, she realized, for a response.

"Why me?" she blurted.

"I've been watching you for days, waiting for the right opportunity to bring you to the mountain. Today I got my chance."

"You saw a strange woman from the sky and just"—she shrugged—"decided to make her your wife?"

The man, Hollen, was silent.

"You're mad," Joselyn said, more to herself than to him.

He straightened, his expression darkening. "I am *Na Dokiri*. It is my right to claim you."

"Dokiri." Joselyn tested the new word on her own tongue.

"It means 'He Who Conquers,' " the man explained, an edge of pride in his voice. "My people are the Dokiri of the Bedmeg clan. I'm the eldest son of Sven the Collector and I have claimed you as my bride. So you shall be."

Joselyn strained for words. Be it owed to madness or pride, he was so brazen that she was almost impressed. But it wasn't to be borne. Indignation roiled up. "How dare you?"

"It is already done. I have chosen you by right."

"By what right?" she demanded. "Who do you think you are? Who do you think *I* am?"

The man rose to his feet, taking a step backward. Joselyn stiffened against the wall. Some of her nerve wilted.

"This mountain is stained with the blood of my people. The Dokiri guard all the earth below from the many evils which lurk within. My own blood mingles with those who have fallen protecting you and the other lowlanders."

Joselyn listened, her trepidation remounting. This man was deluded. Likely unstable. He continued his speech.

"By the right of Earth and Sky I claim you as my reward. You will be the mother of my sons and *Saliga* of my people. I would know your name."

She stared at him, stunned. "Joselyn. My name...is Joselyn."

He smiled. Creases lit the sides of his cheeks, and a tingle of awareness crept down her spine. He was beautiful. Strikingly so. She'd been so overwrought she'd failed to notice. A wild, beautiful, madman. And his smile was for her.

Focus, Joselyn. Command this situation.

She forced herself to step away from the wall. "I am Joselyn Fury, Lady of House Fury," she said, her voice much clearer than before.

Get his attention. Introduce the stick.

"My father is an heir to the throne of Morhagen. He will have you killed when he learns what you've done. For a crime such as this? A swift public beheading will be in order."

The barbarian listened, his attention rapt as though she were the most fascinating thing he'd ever laid eyes on. Joselyn swallowed.

Now for the carrot.

"But," Joselyn said, recalling her father's many passive lessons in leveraging, "if you return me to my men, I'll see that you are paid your weight in gold as your reward and a symbol of goodwill toward your people. I can guarantee the payment out of my own dowry settlement."

Hollen tilted his head. "I'm not surprised you're a woman of esteem. But your title, and that of your father, mean nothing to me or my people."

He was dismissing her? Just like that? Joselyn gritted her teeth. This never happened. Joselyn wasn't one to hold her nobility over others, but she'd always been treated with the utmost respect by default. Now she realized just how great her privilege was. How vital. Joselyn snapped to gain the advantage.

"I'm to be lady of *two* great houses in less than a fortnight." Joselyn stretched the truth of House Viridian, trying to inspire fear in this wild man who seemed so unruffled by her threats.

"My husband would have you bled in the square for all to see! You would be wise to—"

"—You're married?" he asked, his voice dark and tense.

"I . . .not yet," she said, faltering at the hint of temper in his voice. "Soon. Very soon."

His face softened. "Yes. Soon. Today I will join you to myself, and you shall be mine."

Joselyn shook her head. Her breath ratcheted. "Impossible. I'm to be married in eight days to Lord Viridian. That cannot be undone."

"That life is passed for you." A hint of remorse rang in his deep voice.

"You don't understand!" she cried. "I have to go back. You must take me!"

Was this really happening? Was she truly pleading with a barbarian not to carry her off and make her his concubine, bride, whatever? How could she stop this?

Calm yourself, Joselyn. Reason with him.

"My father would find a dozen willing women to service you. I am for the Lord Viridian. Please, find another woman to be your bride."

The man frowned down at her. In her earnestness she'd taken several steps toward him. They were but a foot apart now, close enough to notice his fingers fidgeting at his sides.

"I'm sorry," he said. "But I will not."

"I will *not* marry you," she said. She drew upon every thread of courage to face him as she spoke.

"You will," he said with equal resolve. There was no malice in his voice, just a statement of fact. "I have conquered wyverns, I have conquered all manner of demons beneath the earth, and I shall conquer you."

Joselyn's stomach lurched at his determined words. The savage meant them. Every one. What to do? She knew what she couldn't do. She couldn't give in to fear. Her freedom, her life depended upon her wits. She glared at him.

The man reached for her bruised hand, the one she'd used to strike him. Joselyn snapped it away.

"Are you hurt anywhere else?" he asked.

Joselyn's lips parted as she studied him. "No."

"Think it over. You're not likely to notice until you've calmed."

Joselyn obeyed, despite herself, and shivered. She was cold. Freezing. The clouds had left her cloak drenched and her gown heavy with moisture. Her damp hair clung to the sides of her face.

"Come," he said, holding a hand out to her. "I have dry clothes for you."

Joselyn stepped back and scowled at the hand he offered. He lowered it before turning away toward the cave entrance.

"Come," he said again. He started down the tunnel.

Would he just leave her here? Then why had he chased her in the first place?

He wasn't trying to catch you.

A sinking suspicion settled low in her gut. Was she already trapped? Beyond hope of escape, of rescue? She could keep delving deeper, find out for sure. She considered it. Another round of chills had her clutching at her arms. She had no idea where she was, except on a mountain said to be home to unimaginable demon terrors. For now, she'd follow the one she'd already met. At a distance.

The tunnel air was dank and musty. She had to squint to see clearly in some spots. All the while she searched for some alcove to slip into. There were none. When they made it back to the wider entrance of the cave, Joselyn was surprised to see the dragon lounging upon its belly, planted in the spot most exposed to sunshine. Somehow it looked almost serene.

Hollen casually approached the beast. It ignored him as he climbed onto its back and began unlashing a pack from its saddle. So it *was* a saddle. The man hadn't lied. He really had mastered the dragon. Joselyn fingered her pendant as she watched him work.

Maybe he's not a man at all. Though he does look like one. A very large, fierce man.

He leapt to the ground and unwrapped a magnificent gray fur coat from the pack. He shook it out as he approached her.

"What sort of creature produced this garment?" she asked. She leaned away as though it held some foul magic.

"Dire wolf."

Joselyn eyed it, barely able to keep her mouth from falling open. Dire wolves were ferocious creatures, and only the greatest of hunters could boast of killing one. But then, such a feat probably meant little to a man who could command a dragon.

"Your cloak is wet. Take it off."

Joselyn wanted nothing from this man. When she didn't move, he reached for her broach as though he meant to remove her clothes himself. She jerked away and hastily unclasped the drenched garment. He swung the dry pelt over her narrow shoulders. It swallowed her up, instantly warming her.

"Come, I'll make us a fire." He hoisted a large pack which he'd removed from his mount and started back down the tunnel. Joselyn stayed where she was. Should she keep following?

Hollen glanced back. "Unless you'd rather spend the evening with Jagomri."

At the mention of its name, the great serpent cracked a single yellow eye. Joselyn shivered when its gaze rested on her. Without a word, she skittered after her captor. Her eyes bored into his back. Was he truly mad? He didn't seem so, but then, she barely knew him. They were silent as they moved, and Joselyn considered repleading her case.

No. Not yet. "The man who understands his opponent best, wins." Her father's words played in her mind. She needed answers.

They reached the place where he'd cornered her, and Hollen led her along the wall until they reached an inlet. A crude natural staircase had been cut by ancient ice and they followed it to the plateau above. Up and over they trekked until they were hiking downward again. As the minutes passed, the air grew warmer and the moss upon the walls thicker.

She swallowed. "Where are your people?"

Hollen glanced back at her, his expression neutral. "They live on the mountain, in a cave system called Bedmeg."

"Are any of them here?"

"No. Just you and I tonight."

Tonight. Joselyn's step faltered. "Where are you taking me?"

"*Amo Tanshi.*"

Surely he knew those words meant nothing to her. "For what purpose?"

"Bonding."

"What does that mean?"

He slowed and Joselyn had to stop to keep from walking into him. The tunnel was so narrow now, his broad shoulders brushed the sides. A soft glow appeared ahead as he turned to her. He scratched at the back of his head, his face drawn like he was searching for the right words. Joselyn's wariness flared.

"I'll give you my *tanshi* mark of bonding. You'll bear it upon your flesh just as I will. Then we'll go to my people and live as one."

At his words, Joselyn's throat grew tight and she reached up a hand to clasp it. Hollen grimaced, then continued down the tunnel. Joselyn stood frozen.

Bear it on your flesh? What in the swiving hells did that mean?

Fresh light filled the tunnel as Hollen stepped through the passage and disappeared from view.

What grim fate awaited her? Joselyn considered scrambling back up the tunnel, away from this savage man. She couldn't go back to the dragon. If she tried to hide, the barbarian would find her. Even if she could outrun him, which he'd already proven she couldn't, there was nowhere else to go. She'd kept an eye open for alternate routes on their way down here. There'd been none. Heart pounding, Joselyn crept toward the light. Her eyes widened at the sight before her.

A wide, grassy cavern lay stretched out. The air smelled sweet, and a waterfall burbled as it trickled into a nearby shallow pool. Though the cave was covered, holes let in enough light to feed a verdant, twisting tree near the center of the meadow. Joselyn marveled at the dreamlike scene, the fertile beauty hidden away so far above the earth.

Hollen must have jumped down from the little ledge at the entrance because he stood there, waiting for her. When he held up a hand to assist her, she pulled back and clutched the tunnel wall. Without a word, he continued to the tree and dumped his heavy pack to the dirt. He busied himself with unrolling it, seeming to pay her no attention at all.

Joselyn stood, her feet rooted to the stony ground. What a coward she must look like. If the barbarian glanced at her now, he'd see her cringing like a terrified rabbit. How would that serve her? How would she reason with him then?

She jerked away from the wall and clenched her fists. She'd been robbed of enough this day. She'd be keeping her pride.

4

JOSELYN HELENA ELISE FURY

Hollen's pack hit the earth with a dull thud. He removed his axe from its holster and set it gently against the tree. Across the knoll, his bride remained fixed at the entrance. Unwilling to follow. He wanted to look at her, wanted to take advantage of every opportunity to know her more deeply. He thought of her red hair, the freckles scattered across her pale flesh, the pink glow of cold upon her nose, and the pleasing dimple in her chin. She was more beautiful than he could have hoped for, but she was afraid of him. And for that reason he set about building a fire, pointedly ignoring her until she decided to approach him. After all, there was nowhere else for her to go.

The meadow held sacred meaning for his people. Since the birth of the mountain, it played host to the joining of all Dokiri unions. Helig herself, Goddess of the Earth, had planted the joining altar beneath the tree he now sat beside. It was a shining sheet of black granite, set several paces above the ground. His heart raced at the thought of laying his bride upon it and making her his.

Will she fight me?

He hoped to Regna she would not. There was no going back now. He'd chosen Joselyn from the multitude of women in the lowlands to be his bride. It was a choice he'd only make once, and now she must bear the consequences. It was his duty to carve his unique mark into her flesh and make her acceptable to his gods. If not, he'd call a curse upon his people too terrible to imagine. She was on his mountain now. She was his responsibility. His reward.

Though Hollen had always known this would be the way of his bonding, he realized now that he'd spent very little time over the years considering what it would actually be like. He couldn't be different from most Dokiri riders in that he'd spent the majority of his time thinking of the many nights *after* he'd won her heart.

Hollen's blood heated as he pictured what it would be like to have her beneath him, shaking from want instead of fear. The image was so much more potent now he knew what his bride looked like. He grimaced. Thus far, reality had been far less enticing. She thought him a monster. He could hardly blame her, and the worst was yet to come.

After a while, Joselyn came marching across the knoll. As she neared, his heart sped up and he forced himself to wait before fixing his curious gaze upon her. What would she say next? What would she do? He looked up to see her eyeing the altar with suspicion. As though she could feel his gaze upon her, she turned her head to face him. She stared him down, a defiant glint in her blue eyes. His lips curved into a smile.

So fierce.

Folding her legs beneath her, she took a seat on the opposite side of the firepit, as though this were her meadow and he, her humble servant. He chuckled and struck his flints together. Perhaps this night would not be too frightening for her. The kindling sparked to life.

Hollen uncorked a water skin made from a ram's stomach and wet a rag. His bride's face was covered in a fine layer of dust and sweat. He held it out to her and she sneered, turning her face away. He sighed, dropped the rag onto her lap and walked away. As he knelt to his pack, the cloth smacked him in the back of the head with a wet slap. Hollen shot his bride a look of reproach, but she was turned toward the fire, as though nothing had happened.

Hollen rolled his eyes and plucked the sagging cloth from his neck. He returned with enough dried ram meat and cheese for the two of them. He took his seat across the fire from his bride, portioned out the food and passed over her share. She scowled at the offering.

"You should eat," he said, and took a bite of his own food. "Too much fear in a day makes the body weak."

"Do I seem afraid to you?"

He stopped to regard her. To her credit, she didn't shrink from his gaze. He pursed his lips. "Less than most women, I'm sure. But I doubt you'll find the bonding to your liking, so you'd do well to care for yourself."

His bride's imperious expression wavered at that. "You're making a mistake."

"No, *mu hamma*," he replied, voice gone husky. "I don't think I am."

Hollen thought of their conversation in the tunnel. *"Why me?"* she'd asked. *"Because you remind me of someone,"* he'd thought.

When she'd struck him with the rock, Hollen's first coherent thought was of pure pride. Or at least, it was once the stars had cleared. Though there was little about his own bonding he'd anticipated as a youth, the one thing he'd hoped for was a woman as strong and fierce as his beloved mother. In that moment, he was sure he'd found one, and nothing could have pleased him more.

Joselyn sat staring into the fire, her mouth pressed into a tight line. Regna, he wanted to know more about her. He fed twigs into the fire. "How old are you?"

She ignored him.

"Do you like to ride?"

Nothing.

"Do you have any brothers or sisters?"

"If I did, I suppose I would never see them again," she snapped.

Va kreesha. Hollen swore inwardly. He'd only just met his bride and already he was making an epic mess of things. After so long alone, after waiting so long for her, this distance was torture.

Patience, Hollen.

He picked up the damp cloth she'd rejected and pressed it to the wound on his head. "You have a quick mind. Lucky for me it was only a stone."

Silence.

"Were you armed with a knife I might have shared my father's fate."

Her gaze snapped up at that, and Hollen turned to hide his triumphant grin. He mopped the blood from his beard. Would she take the bait?

"What happened to your father?" she asked.

Hollen turned to answer. "My mother stabbed him before he had a chance to bond with her. He nearly died."

"Why didn't he?"

"My mother saved his life," he answered honestly.

Joselyn gaped. "And your father stole her away just as you've stolen me?"

Hollen nodded.

"Then why would she save his life?" Her brow creased with suspicion.

He shrugged. "I guess she felt he was worth saving."

Joselyn scoffed. "Your mother sounds like a fool."

Hollen stiffened. His father and mother's bonding was a story they'd shared proudly with their children over and over throughout the years. Each time they did, one or the other would remember a detail they hadn't mentioned before. Hollen remembered sitting around the campfire as they spoke, feigning indifference. In truth he'd committed every detail to memory.

He watched Joselyn's face pale and realized his fists were clenched. He relaxed and managed a tight smile. "As are all women who choose to love us men. Thank the gods for foolish women."

She frowned. He'd surprised her. If the gods were on his side, he would manage it many more times.

THE SAVAGE'S *mother is off limits. Good to know.*

Joselyn watched the wild man from across the fire. She remained stock still, her head held high.

"What do you think of your new husband?" he asked, continuing to eat as he crouched.

"You are not my husband," she said flatly.

"Soon enough, *mu hamma*."

"You look like a savage." Her voice was laced with contempt.

The man stopped eating and looked up, with a twinkle of amusement in his dark eyes. All at once he rose, sucking the last of the grease from his fingertips. He stared down at her and wiped the fingers dry against his furs.

Joselyn tried not to shrink. He began pulling at the straps of his leather armor, and her wariness ascended to outright alarm.

When his studded cuirass was hanging loose, Hollen stripped it off and dropped it to the ground next to him. He met her eyes and Joselyn prayed he was simply over-warm and would presently sit back down. Instead, he reached for the bottom of his furs as though to pull them up.

Joselyn's gaze flitted across the ground as she searched for a weapon. In her periphery she saw him draw first the furs and then a wool undershirt over his head. With that temporary block, she snatched a stone from the ring of the firepit and pulled it deep into the sleeve of her own cloak. Pain flared in her hand. She'd used the bruised one. Skies!

When she looked back up, she sucked in a breath. Her captor stood across the tiny fire. He watched her as her eyes fell over his bare torso. His towering body was a mass of well-formed muscle. No one would accuse this man of idleness. A light brush of hair covered his chest and much of his belly, growing thicker as it disappeared beneath the line of his pants. Joselyn had never seen a man so indecently exposed, and certainly not one so appealing. But that wasn't what caused her breath to catch.

"I hope you have a stronger word than 'savage' at your disposal, woman. I think you'll be needing it."

Indeed.

Scars covered him—along his arms, across his broad chest, and all down the lengths of his sides. These weren't the variety which covered Sir Richard's face. Her father's steward bore many marks, a testament to long years earning glory on the battlefield. Though they'd robbed Sir Richard of beauty, they were badges of great bravery and fortitude. There was a dignity in them that lent Sir Richard instant respect wherever he went. Hollen's scars weren't the sort that inspired respect. Hollen's scars inspired wonder and fear.

A labyrinth of raised white flesh crept down his body in

elaborate sweeping patterns, a sophisticated web of inscribed skin. There was an order to the designs that Joselyn couldn't make sense of, but each mark had obviously been chosen with care for shape and position upon the masculine canvas that was his body. Though there was artistry to them, Joselyn couldn't quite call them beautiful. They conjured bloody images of someone carving those marks into naked flesh.

"Who . . . did this to you?" she asked, unable to tear her gaze away.

"I did."

"You?" she squeaked.

"Many of them." He held out his arms and turned his back to her. It, too, was fully adorned. Someone had assisted him with these. He turned back.

"Why?" she asked, breathless.

"My *idadi* tells my story and prove my place as a Dokiri warrior. One has only to look at me and know I am worthy."

"Worthy of what?"

"That depends who's looking."

He was watching her watch him. Her face flushed, but before she could look away, he pointed to an area on his right upper arm. Along the bulging curve of his bicep was a row of little cross marks with a line above each. They spanned from his inner elbow to the pit of his arm before disappearing. A similar trail marked his other arm.

"Each of these tells of a blood-seeker which has fallen by my hand."

Joselyn's eyes widened. She'd heard blood-seekers were foul creatures with black eyes, four legs, and rows of saw-line teeth. They made their dens in the dark places of the earth, spurning the sun. It was said they only left their fetid caves when the scent of blood tempted them beyond resistance. A good thing, for blood-seekers could destroy an entire herd of cattle and its shepherds, too, before enough fighting men arrived to drive them off. They were more easily frightened than killed. Joselyn gaped at the sheer number of marks.

"You mark yourself for every kill?" she asked.

Hollen nodded.

How? He must have hundreds of scars, some large, most small. This was indeed a wild man. She imagined other Dokiri men comparing their marks, blustering for dominance over one another. Were there many with more marks than Hollen? She frowned. Why should she care?

"What's to keep you from giving yourself extra marks?" she asked.

Hollen's face darkened. "Such a thing isn't tolerated among the Dokiri. Few crimes carry a steeper penalty."

"What is the penalty?" Just how barbaric were his people?

"Exile, and denaming."

Less than she imagined, though she didn't know what 'denaming' meant. It was beside the point. She had greater questions. "Every one of those marks represents a creature you have killed?"

Hollen shook his head and pointed to an area beneath the hollow of his neck. "This one tells of my rank within my clan."

"And what rank is that?"

"I am *Salig*, Chieftain."

Joselyn appraised him. "You're young to have such a title."

"Yes," he muttered low like she'd said something both true and terrible.

"And now you mean to make me a chieftainess? A . . ." Joselyn's tongue struggled over the foreign title he'd used in the tunnel. ". . .*Saliga*?"

He nodded.

Joselyn was beyond the point of laughing. Her father would be outraged when he received the news of her disappearance.

She could see him doling out punishment to every guard present at the time of her abduction. She could hear the wrath in his voice as he dictated an explanation for Dante Viridian.

Would her intended believe him? Would he be merciful and bury his threats to destroy her father? No. He wouldn't. When she didn't arrive in Brance at the appointed time, Dante would assume Marcus had tried to outwit him. Were he to receive a missive with the outlandish tale of Lady Fury's abduction by a dragon, he would surely burn the letter and pen his own tales for the king.

Joselyn's stomach hardened as she rose. She had to make this man, this Hollen, understand. She spoke in a cool, even tone, keeping the stone hidden beneath her cloak.

"I am a Morhageese lady of high breeding. I have been trained since birth in the management of households spanning half a league. I speak four languages. I can make any guest feel at home, no matter how foreign he may be. Commerce and politics are subjects upon which I speak with authority. I dance as a lady dances and ride as a lady rides. I am everything a nobleman could hope for in a wife..."

Hollen said nothing, listening. She sucked in a steadying breath and willed every shred of conviction into her voice.

"But you are not a nobleman. You are a barbarian. I am Joselyn Helena Elise Fury, of House Fury, and you shall have no use for me."

Still half-naked, Hollen stepped around the fire. It took all her courage not to cower as he towered above her, so close she could feel the heat from his exposed flesh.

"You shall dance with my people upon the shoulders of the mountain. As for riding, you shall glide above the earth on obsidian wings. You are Joselyn Helena Elise Fury, *Saliga* of Bedmeg, and I shall treasure you above all others."

A long moment passed between them as Joselyn contemplated the gravity of his words. They were spoken like an oath, and he didn't seem the type of man who took his oaths lightly. She could take no more. Joselyn inched backward.

An unmistakable flicker of disappointment flashed across his face, and she couldn't understand why. He sighed, casting his gaze to the ground by the fire. "Will you not eat?"

She'd surely retch anything she put into her belly. She shook her head.

He held his open palm out between them. "Let's have it, then."

"Have what?"

"The rock," he said, dispassionately.

Joselyn tensed. She could deny she had one. But then, he must have noticed one missing from the ring. Would he punish her? Was she better off striking him and making a run for it? There was nowhere to go. Resisting the urge to cry, she returned the makeshift bludgeon to her captor.

He took it, brushing her fingers as he did. He leaned down and replaced the stone.

"My head aches enough as it is," he said, tapping his skull as though it were an intimate joke between them.

Joselyn frowned. Again, this primitive man had surprised her. Damn him. She crossed her arms over her chest.

Hollen inhaled, his broad chest expanding wide. "It's time, *mu hamma.*"

5

BONDED

At his words, her spine went rigid. She took several hasty steps away, as though she were making up her mind to run. Hollen bit the inside of his cheek.

This was one part of the claiming rite he'd put some thought into. In quiet moments, he'd sought out a few of the elder men who were not given to mockery. Hollen had asked how he might perform the necessary tasks without frightening his bride. So close to his claiming, they'd all smiled with sympathy and said something akin to, *"Accept that she'll hate you for a while, then get it over with."*

That had *not* been what he wanted to hear. His only comfort was that each of those men now possessed a bride whose great love for her husband was obvious. Of course, each was also old enough that the years had grayed them. Hollen needed his bride to forgive him before then.

"There's nowhere for you to go," he said, measuring his voice for gentleness.

"Listen to me." She held her palms up to him. "There's more at stake here than your need for a wife, or even my desire for freedom."

Hollen sighed. She wasn't going to make this easy for either of them. Still, he could be patient. Whatever she needed. Whatever it took to keep her from panicking outright, from fighting him.

"What's at stake?"

"My father is depending upon my marriage to secure an alliance that will keep my house from total destruction."

Va kreesha. As excuses went, that sounded like a good one. Too bad for her house.

"My father is a powerful man, but right now his enemies have the power to destroy him. If I don't make an ally of Lord Viridian through marriage, my father will perish. My house will be undone. And it will be my fault."

Hollen raised a brow. Her father was being threatened and the only way he could defend his house was by selling his daughter for allies? Pathetic. What sort of leader, after landing his people in such a position, was unwilling to fight for them? And now Hollen's bride wished to give herself up as some sort of payment, so her new husband would help save her house? Hollen shook his head.

"If a man can't protect his house without the help of his daughter, it's no fault of hers. You burden yourself unjustly."

His bride's voice went high. "Do you understand what I'm saying? My father will die without me."

Glanshi. Could this situation get any worse? The back of his neck began to itch. He'd be gray for sure. And rightly so.

"I'm sorry," he said, forcing himself not to look away.

"Then return me."

When the mountain falls.

His jaw tightened. "No."

For the first time since taking her, Hollen saw hatred glow in her deep blue eyes. His fingers fidgeted.

"You can't keep me. I swear to you before all the gods, I *will* get away from you."

Hollen's heart seized in his chest. That was the worst thing she could have said. He'd considered how much he should say, how much to explain. Now he knew he could tell her nothing. He'd indeed claimed a fierce bride, one he'd have to master as well as claim, by *any* means necessary.

"After tonight, we'll be a part of each other. Nothing can change that."

That hate in her eyes blazed white-hot, and Hollen actually bristled.

Accept it. Get it over with.

Hollen sighed. "I'm going to start now. I won't touch you yet. You need only watch."

His bride swallowed, but raised her chin. "Watch what?"

Hollen stepped away from the fire and toward his pack. Though several feet away, he was careful to face her as he kneeled down to rummage. Occasionally he glanced at her, making sure she didn't pick up more stones. Her eyes scanned the perimeter of the meadow, probably looking for an escape that didn't exist. Perhaps Helig had designed the bonding place in such a manner for a reason.

Hollen rifled through his pack for the *gneri* blade. He found it within seconds, but paused to appraise it. The hilt was made of ivory. He'd spent many painstaking hours carving an image of the sun onto one side, its hazy rays sweeping along the edges. He turned it in his hands to see the reverse, an image of the moon and five pointed stars within its deep crescent.

He was no artist, but he'd worked the images to his satisfaction, and the result held a crude beauty that he hoped his bride would come to appreciate. The blade itself was razor sharp. He'd seen to that. Few things hurt more than a dull blade, and when used to perform a rite, the resulting scar was often mottled beyond recognition.

Hollen continued to dig through his pack. He withdrew a wine skin, a wooden bowl, squares of cloth, and a tiny clay bottle sealed with wax. Though he had everything he needed, Hollen lingered on the ground, pretending to search for additional items. He was stalling.

Don't be a coward.

With a steadying breath he rose to his feet, the five items in hand. Joselyn's eyes took stock. He saw panic there, though she tried to conceal it. He took care to give her a wide berth as he walked back. Still, she took a step away. He continued toward the trickling stream of water that poured from the cave's ceiling.

The edge of the pool was mossy where he knelt and set the items down. He removed the knife from its leather sheath and dipped the steel blade into the pool. Joselyn's gaze regarded him as he recited the first portion of the *tanshi* rite in his father tongue. The words were memorized from an early age and they came smoothly.

Helig, mother of the earth
Regna, father of the sky
As water is the tie that binds you
Let it bind me now to my bride.

Before rising, he filled the wooden bowl with water from the ancient pool. He turned, stood, and placed his items on the black granite altar's shining surface.

Joselyn stood like a doe caught in a predator's sights, poised to run. He looked her in the eye and recounted the rite in trade tongue so she would understand. Her lips parted as he brought the blade tip to his chest, just above his heart.

THE SAVAGE DREW the blade tip down upon his own flesh. The area he'd chosen was conspicuously bare, as though it had been reserved for this specific purpose. A scarlet line appeared along his path as he carved upon himself.

Joselyn gaped. She checked Hollen's face for a reaction. His expression was neutral, his chin pressed into his chest as he focused on his task. Blood trickled down to the top of his pants. Had years of such savagery trained him not to feel the pain? Her stomach churned even as a thrill of hope fluttered to life. Had she misunderstood him? Perhaps he'd never meant to mark her, only himself?

It was over before long. He put the knife down and cupped his right hand beneath the dripping stream of blood. When he'd collected enough, he flicked the dark drops onto the altar's surface, muttering something in his language. He'd referenced gods she had never heard of, and Joselyn wondered if his people only worshiped the two.

She watched as he poured half the bowl's water down his chest, washing away most of the blood. His new mark glowed pink. It was just smaller than her palm and had a delicate quality that set it apart from the others. She squinted to make out its details. He'd used maybe a dozen lines in all, each crossing the other like a braid of corded rope.

He turned toward her, holding out his dry hand. He curled his fingers and beckoned her forward. "Come, *mu hamma*."

Joselyn's heart seized and her knees locked. She shook her head once. Dropping his hand, he sighed, took a step toward her. Joselyn took one back. He stopped and cocked a brow.

"Do you mean to run from me?"

Joselyn worried her lower lip between her teeth. Running was pointless. He would catch her, just as he had in the tunnel. She'd once seen a wolf stalking a deer through a meadow. The deer had frozen when it noticed the wolf creeping forward. It wasn't until the stag sprinted away that the wolf's complete ferocity was awakened. She didn't want to incite the full measure of this man's violence upon her.

And yet, she *couldn't* make herself go to him. If he intended to mark her as he had himself, Dante Viridian would have questions. No natural accident could cause such a scar. If she told him the truth, her virtue would be instantly called into question, jeopardizing the alliance and her father's life. She could think of no reasonable explanation that might lay a husband's curiosity to rest. Within the cloak, her hands grew damp.

Hollen approached with slow, steady steps. Joselyn stood erect, her arms plastered to her sides. When he stopped, she had to tilt her head to look into his eyes.

"Please," she begged, "don't." Joselyn had never begged for a thing in her life. Not even for her parent's love. But here she was, pleading for this barbarian's mercy, if indeed he had any to give.

Hollen frowned down at her. "I must. We are both cursed if I do not."

She didn't believe in any curse. But *he* did. He wouldn't be dissuaded. A cold sweat broke out across her flesh.

This is going to happen. You can't stop it. Only survive it.

When he took her by the elbow, she jerked away and fixed him with a glare so icy he stilled. His eyes widened with the barest hint of surprise.

Dignity, Joselyn.

Inclining her chin, she marched toward the altar. As she peered down at the ivory hilted knife, Hollen's footsteps came up behind her.

"It is a *gneri* blade, for performing rites. It will become yours in time."

Joselyn said nothing. She wouldn't give him the satisfaction of her interest. Still, what circumstances would lead him to provide her with a knife? How foolish. Were she confident of her speed, she might turn it on him even now. But, no. She would have to be more careful than that.

Her thoughts were interrupted when he offered her the wineskin. She shook her head, not trusting whatever lay inside. She wouldn't put it past him to drug her. He laid the sack in the grass. A moment of hesitation and he began pulling at the cloak he'd given her. As he peeled it back, it caught on her elbows.

Breathe, Joselyn. Just breathe.

Closing her eyes, she relaxed enough to let the sleeves slide off her arms. Hollen dropped the garment to the ground behind her. The cool air sent a chill over her body and she crossed her arms. Her dress was rich crimson velvet with a gold embroidered hemline. The colors of House Fury. Far from her best, it was still a fine gown easily worth years of a servant's wages. The neckline rose to a few inches below her collarbone.

Hollen turned her toward himself, and she opened her eyes to see him studying her hard. He wasn't looking at her so much as her dress. His eyes scanned back and forth, a puzzled expression on his face. He was trying to figure out how to open her gown.

Later she might appreciate that the mark was placed somewhere intimate and out of sight, but for now, her cheeks went hot with dread. Hollen brought his hand up and hooked two fingers around her neckline, then pulled to see if it would give. She slapped his hand away, temper flashing.

"What is it you're trying to do?" she snapped.

Startled, his mouth dropped open. An enormous measure of satisfaction surged within her, until he regained his composure and pointed to the fresh wound he'd given himself. Still uncovered, half-dried blood oozed.

"Your mark must match my own. Above the heart."

The heat in her cheeks set her eyes to stinging. She bit her lip. She would shed no tears in front of this man. She turned her back to him and untied the binding which held a layer of velvet over the dress's opening. Joselyn pulled her long hair over the front of her shoulder and exposed the lacing which bound the dress together. The tight weave stretched from the top of her spine to just below the small of her back. Joselyn's maids were responsible for helping her in and out of her clothes, as most of them were made in such a manner. She wouldn't be able to undo her gown alone.

Reaching over her shoulder, she pointed at the top of the crisscrossing ties. He seemed to understand and reached to undo them. His calloused fingertips brushed the nape of her neck as he pulled the cords loose. He worked in silence, and the dress hung looser the farther he went. Joselyn held the material to her chest. There was nothing she could do. Her cotton under-shift would preserve her modesty, for however much longer.

When Hollen reached a point halfway down her back, he stopped and circled around to face her. His breath had gone thready as though he were the one being disrobed by a stranger.

"Is that enough?" His voice was hoarse.

Joselyn blinked. Dare she believe he'd allow her to remain mostly covered? She'd hoped but hadn't expected. She dipped her head once, tentative.

Hollen bent down and swept her up in his arms. Joselyn gasped. It was all she could do to keep her clothing anchored to her chest as he set her immediately down upon the altar. The back of her dress gaped fully open as she leaned forward, pressing her body into her knees. She grimaced at the sight of his blood soaking into her gown.

"Lie down." He directed her with a palm against her shoulder.

Joselyn's unbound tresses spilled out around her upon the altar's gleaming surface. She began panting, her fear evolving into panic. The ancient tree's green canopy hung overhead, and she searched for a part of it to focus on.

Hollen walked around the altar to her left side. He took one of the fists that clutched her dress to her breasts. He pulled at it with a gentle, but growing determination as she involuntarily resisted. When her hand came away, it was still gripping the fabric and Hollen had to use both his hands to uncurl her fingers. She released the material, shaking wildly.

Hollen pressed her palm to the cool stone and stroked his thumb over her knuckles. He shushed her as one might a frightened child and murmured soothing words in his own language. Joselyn didn't look at him. It took every bit of her composure to remain where she was. She loosened her right hand's grip, but couldn't bring herself to set it at her side. He didn't try to make her. Instead he reached for the ivory blade.

When he pulled down the neckline of her under-shift, Joselyn cursed the tear that slipped from the corner of one eye. Her gaze flickered down, and she saw that her breast was not totally exposed, only what was necessary for his task. She willed herself to keep still, hoping to stay covered. Her golden pendant hung to the side. The engraved dragon glared up at her captor.

I am Lady Fury of House Fury. I am a dragon.

Yet here she was. Helpless. Submitting, if only in the flesh. Her spirit burned like the fire spewing past her dragon's fangs.

This isn't the end, Joselyn. You're not defeated yet.

Hollen pressed his fingertips into her collarbone and walked them down her chest. Counting her ribs, she realized. He stopped in the soft flesh of her upper breast. Joselyn's shoulders tensed. She'd never been touched so intimately. Hollen brought the blade tip to her skin and spoke smoothly in his language, then translated.

"In blood I claim you.
In blood you receive me."

She looked at him then. His dark eyes were fixed upon her. His gaze was neither troubled nor triumphant. Rather it was filled with longing, as though she held in her hands the power to grant or deny him everything he'd ever hoped for. Though she lay against her will, half exposed before this man, she had the sudden impression that it was he who was at *her* mercy.

When he pressed the cool point into her flesh, every muscle in Joselyn's body tightened. She gasped through gritted teeth and nearly came up from the altar. Only his massive hand lying solidly upon her chest kept her in place, and her own hands at bay. Unable to stop herself, she whimpered.

"Shh, *mu hamma*," he coaxed. "It will be over quickly."

Joselyn returned her focus to the leaves above her. She willed herself to be still. Writhing would cause greater damage and prolong this horrific ordeal. Hollen's dark head hung low over her body, his gaze intensely focused on his task. As her captor worked her over, Joselyn was somewhat relieved. The pain was not as great as she had anticipated, though she still trembled beneath his touch. A stream of warm blood rolled across her chest and over her shoulder.

True to his word, the rite was over in minutes. The knife clattered against the stone surface as Hollen reached next for the wooden bowl. He poured the remainder of its contents over the burning wound. The water cleared away the blood, soaking into the dress as well as her hair.

Could she look down? Confirm that now, whether she escaped or not, she would never fully rid herself of this nightmare? In her periphery, the savage grabbed a small bottle. A strong, earthy fragrance wafted from the container as he worked a bit of green sludge onto his fingers. Joselyn winced as he smoothed the concoction over the mark. At once, the stinging heat of the cuts subsided.

He set the bottle down and Joselyn finally gathered the

nerve to inspect his handiwork. Her blood was already congealing, perhaps aided by the thin layer of green poultice. Though obscured, Joselyn could see that the bonding mark matched Hollen's in shape and size. It appeared slightly larger on her small frame. She blinked. This was it. It was done. She would have to find a way to explain this to her intended if she were to save her house and her father's life.

Joselyn's chest heaved with fury. How dare he? This man had threatened more than her body. He threatened her father, her house, her future. At last she met his eyes, cursing him with her own. He didn't shrink away, the demon.

"Now we are bonded," he breathed, the ghost of a smile upon his face.

6

BLOODY SAVAGES

Hollen stared down at his bride. So defiant. He decided then, she was the most beautiful thing he'd ever seen. Her long hair spilled out around her in a fiery halo. Freckles smattered her face and spread down her throat, across her pale chest. Her breasts. He'd never touched anything softer. It had taken every shred of his willpower to refrain from sliding her dress down just a bit farther. Had his bride been even a bit less terrified, he wasn't certain he could have resisted.

"You are so beautiful." Regna, he wanted to touch her, to brush his thumb across her cheek and over the pink swell of her parted lips.

Her glower vanished, and startled confusion replaced it. Then she narrowed her eyes. "Is it over?"

"Yes." She wore his mark. The one he'd designed years ago. Their lives would never be the same.

Without thinking, he reached for her hand. She rolled away and stretched the bodice of her dress up high as she did. She struggled and Hollen reached across the altar to help her sit up.

The moment his hands touched her she recoiled. Hollen let go, fingers curling.

"You did well." He willed her to respond.

His bride sat with her legs dangling over the side, still and silent. Gooseflesh broke out across her bared shoulders. It was the push he needed. He stepped around the altar and went to his pack to dig for the clothing he'd brought her. Few Dokiri brides were appropriately dressed for the harsh climate of the mountains upon their claiming. Riders came prepared with everything a woman would need to clothe herself.

Joselyn's head hung between her shoulders. She kept an eye on him as he approached, clothing in hand. He placed the violet wool dress and furs next to her, as well as a pair of lambskin boots made to reach the knee.

"Your fine gown will not warm you here."

Joselyn leaned away from the offering. "I'm fine."

Hollen huffed and pointed at her wet attire. "You'll freeze come nightfall. You have to change."

"I would rather freeze," she said, her mouth pressed in a hard line.

Irritation welled. His bride was being unreasonable. The clothes he'd brought her were of exceptional quality and would protect her from the dangerous frosts. Her own gown was thin, wet, and now had blood on it, though that was invisible against the red velvet material. Surely she had sense enough to know she must give in. Why would she refuse?

"I'll not watch you dress," he told her, even as his mind whined in protest.

She cocked her head as if to say, *"Do you really expect me to believe that?"*

"Your old life is gone, Joselyn. You must survive this new one."

Once again, she looked away, her refusal plain.

Hollen sighed, his jaw working. He stared hard at her and considered his next words. "You'll dress yourself or *I'll* dress you."

Her head snapped up at that. Her cheeks glowed red. Hollen raised his brow in a dare.

"Give me an excuse, woman. I'm dying to know what my bride looks like."

He reached for the pile of folded clothing. Joselyn snatched them up and hugged them to herself. Hollen smirked. She glowered in return.

Hollen busied himself with building the fire back up. He could hear soft rustling as she slid the materials around her body. He itched to sneak a glance over his shoulder, but something told him his bride's eyes were fixed in his direction, and that she would know instantly if he did. Her trust in him was already abysmal. His curiosity could wait.

When she'd finished, Joselyn approached the fire and sat upon her knees. She kept her focus on the flames before her. Clad in the garb of his people, she looked every bit a Dokiri bride. Her woolen dress was fitted over a long-sleeved undershift and was secured along the sides by lacing cord which allowed it to adjust for varying sizes. It fit her well, as did the leather boots which poked from beneath her skirts. Hollen smiled. Her hair was a mess.

He handed her a comb carved from bone he had traded for with his brother. She took it and began working at the tangles of her long mane.

"Do *you* not fear freezing?" she asked, her eyes skirting across his bare torso.

"Not here," he said.

"Then why should I?"

"You're a lowlander. It will be a long time before you're accustomed to the cold of the mountain."

When she'd formed a long braid, they sat a while in silence. Again, Hollen offered her food which she continued to refuse. What to do now? The sky, which could be seen through cracks in the cavern's ceiling, was growing dark, and the fire he'd built cast wildly flickering shadows upon the ground and on the tree above them. Since he could not make her eat, he turned his attention to preparing their sleeping place for the night.

He felt her eyes upon him as he unrolled the thick bear pelt sack which would keep them warm through the evening chill. That, and the heat of their bodies pressed together. Should that excite him? No. Probably not. It would likely be a long, uncomfortable night for him.

When he finished, Hollen turned back to his bride. Her gaze jerked back to the fire. He regarded her. Her eyes, though stubbornly avoiding him, drooped with fatigue. She sat upright on her knees, determined to appear poised, but her shoulders sagged with weariness. This day had exhausted her. Not surprising. On top of her claiming, she hadn't eaten in hours, and he could only imagine how exhausting being carried underneath Jagomri was.

"You need sleep," he said.

"Am I to stay here, then?"

"Tonight we sleep beneath the *Tanshi* Tree. Tomorrow we go to my people."

She looked at the furs he'd arranged and blinked. "Where will you sleep?"

"With you."

She scoffed and turned back toward the fire. "I'll sleep when you do."

Hollen could understand her apprehension. After all she'd been through she must now think he'd throw himself upon her the moment she let her guard down. He held out a hand.

"Come, *mu hamma*. It's late, and you're tired."

"Why do you keep calling me that?" she snapped. "What does it mean?"

Hollen paused. "There's no perfect translation in the trade tongue. It's what a *Na Dokiri* calls the one he's claimed. It means 'my mated woman.' "

Joselyn's chest fell and she stared hard. "And now you mean to mate with me? Like a stallion upon a broodmare?"

Hollen scowled. He didn't care for that comparison. Not because of the ridiculous image it conjured, but rather because it implied a certain carnal impurity that tainted everything he'd ever wanted his marriage bed to be. Worse yet, she'd compared herself to a broodmare. She, the woman who, thus far, was everything he'd hoped for, likened to an animal. Indignation stirred within him.

" '*Mu hamma*' also means 'my only.' " His voice was a low rumble. "You are not chattel, to be used and traded away at my whim."

Her breath was coming faster now. She swallowed before muttering, "Only hunted and broken."

She's afraid of you, Hollen.

He took a breath, wrestling with the passion in his voice. "You are my bride. My *Saliga*. You are my purpose for all the blood I've spilled, and all that I will yet. You are my precious one . . ."

She frowned at him, perhaps unable to accept his words.

He sighed. ". . .and I will not have you this night."

Her eyes widened in surprise, then narrowed in suspicion. She glanced again at the furs behind him.

"Come to bed. Or I shall carry you."

That got him what he wanted, though he would have been more content to have a reason to hold her again. She wobbled to her feet, moving a little too quickly. He lunged forward to steady her. She caught herself on his bare chest then froze. Her hands dug into his skin. All at once her body went slack, and Hollen had to catch her before she hit the ground.

Va kreesha!

He scooped her into his arms and hurried her to the furs. Hollen dropped to his knees beside her. He brushed the strands of hair that had slipped from her braid out of her face. He didn't want to press his ear to her heart, which had only recently stopped bleeding, so he leaned the side of his head to her mouth and listened for breath. She was alive. She'd merely fainted.

He sighed. Mountain sickness took many forms. Some *Dokiri hammas* vomited for days, while others suffered fainting spells. He had a sudden image of her falling into the fire, her freckled skin scorching black. Hollen shuddered. Thank Helig it usually passed in a matter of weeks. He would have to keep vigilant watch over her until he was certain she was strong enough for her new home.

Hollen took advantage of this moment to brush his thumb along the delicate line of her jaw. When he reached her chin, he stroked a fingertip over the dimple that lay there. He longed to press his lips to that tiny hollow, to explore every inch of her. She smelled distinctly feminine. So sweet. He'd chosen well.

Joselyn moaned, her eyelids fluttering open. She stared at him blankly, as though she didn't know who he was.

"Are you all right?" he asked, his face inches above hers.

She blinked, then gasped, shooting upward. The top of her head smashed into Hollen's nose. Pain exploded. He reared back and swore. He climbed to his feet and brought his hand up to his face. Warm blood trickled from his nostrils. He turned back toward his bride who was watching him with wide eyes.

"Wha—what did you do?" she demanded.

Irritation shot through him at her accusatory tone. "Nothing! You fell and I carried you to the fur. Then you rammed your head into my face."

He pulled his hand away and confirmed that he was, in fact, bleeding. Heavily. He staggered over to his pack and removed a water sack to clean his face with. He might have plunged his entire head into the nearby pool; its icy water would have been soothing. But the pool was sacred to his gods and not to be sullied with his blood.

"Why would I fall?" she asked, sounding more confused than skeptical.

Hollen dabbed a wet cloth at his chin to mop up his blood. "Mountain sickness."

"Mountain sickness?"

Hollen returned and she drew her knees into her chest as he approached. "It's common," he said, dropping down next to her on the furs. She leaned away from him as he settled himself.

"The air here is too thin for lowlanders. It'll pass. Until then you shouldn't stand too close to fires . . . or ledges. Maybe rise a bit slower." Propping his elbows on his knees, he pinched the cloth over his nose and waited for the bleeding to stop. "Sleep, woman."

She didn't move. Hollen turned to face her, his face still half covered.

Her gaze jumped from him to the furs. "Where will you sleep?"

"I told you, right here." He pointed down at the bedroll.

Her shoulders tensed and her expression hardened. She started to speak when Hollen cut her off. "Even if I'd planned to force you this night, my desire would be well away by now." He pulled the cloth from his face and showed it to her.

She winced at the gory sight, her eyes skipping back to him in retreat. He raised his brow in silent chastisement for her blunder, though his irritation was fading.

Joselyn's expression cooled and she shrugged. "What's a bit more blood to a savage?"

Was she...mocking him?

Just as he opened his mouth to retort, she flipped to her other side and ducked into the furs. She made herself comfortable, then fell silent.

Hollen scoffed, shaking his head. He was beginning to understand why his father's hair had gone thoroughly gray so early.

7

OBSIDIAN WINGS

Someone was shaking her arm. Joselyn swatted at the offending party, eyes still squeezed shut.

"Wake up, *mu hamma*," A male voice said. The shaking continued.

Joselyn forced her eyes open, squinting at the soft glow of light filling the room. No, not a room. A cave. She was in a cave. Memory came screaming back. She was a captive. The proclaimed wife of a barbarian who'd laid hands upon her and carved his mark into her flesh.

Hollen the Soulless crouched over her, his enormous hand still gripped her upper arm. "It's late. We must go before the sun sets."

Joselyn cringed and pulled her arm from his grasp. She glanced around, wiping the dust from her eyes. "You said we would sleep here tonight."

"We did. You slept through the night and more than half the day."

She shot up and Hollen jerked back, his hand rising protectively in front of his face. His nose was a size larger than it had been before. In addition, he had a dark bruise at his temple from where she'd smashed the rock into his face. Good. Neither attack had been fully meditated, but it was gratifying to know that, despite his strength, she could still manage to hurt him.

He could hurt me far worse.

She fingered the space above her heart, confirming that no part of her ordeal had mercifully been a nightmare. The sting was sharp, and the ache went all the way down to her pounding heart. She swallowed. What would he do with her now?

When she'd woken the night before, with him hovering above her, she'd assumed the worst. But her clothing hadn't been disheveled, and he himself was quick to order her back to sleep. He hadn't raped her last night. At least the brute was honest. This was a new day, though, and he'd made no more promises to leave her unmolested. Her stomach was queasy. She had to find an escape, and soon. The first step would be getting out of this cave. She began to rise.

"Slowly," Hollen warned.

She obeyed, not wanting to give him an excuse to touch her. Once she was standing steady, she eyed Hollen as he rolled up the furs. He was fully clothed again, a fact Joselyn was grateful for. She didn't want to look at those grisly scars. More than that, his bareness made her uneasy, as though he were halfway to claiming her virtue as well as her freedom.

Joselyn scanned the meadow. It appeared her captor had already packed everything up for their departure. Even the altar's black surface shone again, wiped clean of their collective blood. The furs she'd slept on were the last bit to be gathered. When they were secured, Hollen turned and offered her more of the same dried meat and cheese from yesterday. Now that she was no longer in a state of full terror, she snatched the food from his hand. It wouldn't serve to be weak with hunger.

"Let's go," he said.

"I would like my comb," she said, fingering her braid which was bedraggled from sleeping.

"*Your* comb?" A mischievous smile lit up his face.

Joselyn's ears went hot. "The comb you let me use last night."

"Peace, woman." He lifted his palms in mock surrender. "I did mean to make it yours. It's put away now. Besides, it would be pointless to bother before a flight. You might as well wait until after we arrive."

"I'd prefer to fix it now." Joselyn's nerves were frayed enough at the thought of meeting more men like this. She'd *not* be presented to them like a wild animal, frightened and unkempt.

Hollen belted his axe, then swung his heavy pack over his shoulder. He turned away. "No."

Brute.

When they reached the meadow's edge, Joselyn refused his assistance in scaling the ledge at the opening. She regretted it at once. She had to pull her skirts up high in order to climb over. She must have looked ridiculous, heaving herself onto her stomach and then half crawling up the stone surface. Her humiliation peaked to see Hollen smirking down. She glared, her only weapon. He shook his head with a smile and led them on through the tunnels.

When they reached the tall and narrow cave that let out into the sky, Joselyn slowed her pace. Where was the wicked creature who'd carried her into this mess?

"Jagomri."

Joselyn caught sight of the beast as it responded to its master's voice by lifting its serpentine head. It'd been huddled in a dark corner, completely camouflaged by its inky scales. Its horrible yellow eyes appraised her, and Joselyn's breath seized in her chest. She stopped walking. Hollen glanced back at her.

"Come. You need not fear my mount while I am near."

"And when you aren't?"

"Never approach a *gegatu* without its master." His eyes fixed upon her. He was giving her an order that carried a grim warning.

She shuddered and looked back at the monstrous creature. "What kind of madness possesses a man to pit his will against a dragon?"

"Wyvern."

"What?"

"The *gegatu* are wyverns, not dragons," he said. "Wyverns only have two legs."

Joselyn had never heard the term 'wyvern' before. The sigil of her house was a golden, four-legged dragon. When the great beast abducted her she hadn't put much thought into the specifics of its anatomy. It crawled about using its spined wings like additional feet.

"Does it...breathe fire?"

Hollen looked like he wanted to laugh. "No. He prefers his meals raw and breathing, the bastard. His tail is barbed with paralytic venom."

Joselyn gaped. "Why would you ever approach it?"

"The Dokiri are masters of the sky and mountains. We are charged with no small task in keeping the lowlands safe from the underground. The *gegatu* make our duty possible."

Joselyn kept her distance as Hollen climbed up and secured the pack to the beast's saddle. The creature barely seemed to notice, preferring instead to keep its icy gaze on her. She shuddered. At any moment she'd see its forked tongue wet its lips in hungry anticipation.

Hollen jumped down and landed with a dull thud in the fine gravel. He walked the length of the great serpent until he reached its head, then clicked his tongue. The wyvern lifted its skull to the height of its master's chest. Though Hollen's hands were massive for a man, they were dwarfed by the creature's scaled jaw as he hooked his fingers beneath, taking hold. Hollen extended a palm to Joselyn, and beckoned her.

She shook her head more from fear than defiance. She didn't like his beast. Every instinct told her to run, to hide, to do anything to avoid its attention. Still, after everything that happened last night, Hollen couldn't mean to feed her to his mount.

"Come, Joselyn." Hollen's tone brooked no argument.

She crossed her arms and crept forward, stopping just out of Hollen's reach. Hairs stood up on the back of her neck as the wyvern let out a vibrating hiss.

Hollen shot forward, keeping hold of the beast and catching Joselyn by the arm. He pulled her in front of him and suddenly she was chest to nose with the terrible creature. The monster's mouth cracked and fangs the length of her hand came into view. She tried to lunge away, but Hollen wrapped his other arm around her, then hooked it to the other side of his mount's jaws.

Now she was locked in, a savage at her back, a monster at her front. Her instincts placed their bet on the savage. She straightened, locking her knees and digging her heels into the gravel. She pushed into her captor's chest. She needed space between herself and the serpent.

"Be still," Hollen ordered, his tone calm but forceful. "I want him to scent you."

"Why?" she cried. She craned her head backward. Hollen stared into the beast's eyes.

"He must know that you belong to me."

Joselyn tried to slink below Hollen's arms, hoping to slip out underneath. "Please let me—"

"—Shh." Hollen squeezed her between his arms. "He won't harm you, *mu hamma*. Not while I'm here."

The beast sniffed. Hot air blew over Joselyn's breasts. The warmth penetrated even the heavy wool of her dress. A dry, snakelike tongue jutted through its teeth, vibrating bizarrely. It ran from the hem of her skirts up to her neck, and Joselyn squeezed her eyes shut in disgust. She cowered and pressed her face into her captor's leather armor.

Hollen made a peculiar clicking noise with his throat, and Joselyn's eyes popped open. The beast no longer looked at her, but rather at its master. Hollen's hands, which still gripped the wyvern's jaws, began a sort of massage in the space just behind bone. The black slit pupils in the creature's eyes dilated widely. It answered its master's clicking with a stuttering trill of its own.

Hollen pressed Joselyn snugly up against the creature's snout, and she sucked in a breath. Her arms shot to the sides, eager to get as much of herself away from it as possible. Hollen continued his curious rubbing for several long moments before he finally released his mount.

"Wait for me at his side." Hollen nudged her. She needed no further prodding. She darted away.

Hollen continued to hold his beast's gaze a few moments and its eyes, black with dilation, eased back to their normal, yellow state. This man was a savage to be certain, but he was so much more than that to be able to stand so confident next to this winged monster, to expect its obedience. He released it and walked back to Joselyn.

"What was the point of that?" she asked, temper rising.

"To make him understand that you're my equal, not his prey." He tested the tension of the saddle straps.

Joselyn scoffed. "I suppose he might be confused on that point, considering our introduction."

Hollen laughed. "That's what I was thinking."

Joselyn crossed her arms over her chest. His flippant attitude wasn't charming. It *wasn't*. "If you're certain he won't harm me when you're here, and I'm not to go near him alone, then why try to reason with him now?"

"So he'll allow you on his back." He tossed her a pair of gloves, then held his arms out to her. "Come. It's getting late."

Joselyn hesitated. Were the beast a horse she'd have mounted alone, refusing his help, but the saddle sat well above her head. A sudden image of it whipping its long neck around to snap at her came to mind. Also, the saddle wasn't made like that for a horse. It had stirrups, but they didn't dangle beside the understraps like she was used to. These stirrups comprised adjustable leather loops corded next to each other like a tunneled cage pointing back toward its barbed tail. The beast wore no bridle.

Hollen was waiting for her to take his arms. The wyvern was her only way out of this suspended prison, so she stepped into her captor's arms and he hoisted her up, settling her into the leather.

She'd expected him to guide her up its back, not to lift her entirely. Joselyn wasn't a large woman, but she wasn't petite either. How easily he'd lifted her. Later, if he tried to force himself upon her, she'd be doomed. She couldn't think about that now. First she had to survive another flight, this time *astride* the ancient creature.

Hollen climbed up the serpent's body in two long strides, practically jumping into the saddle behind her. She stiffened as his front pressed into her back. There was nowhere to wiggle away. He spent a few moments adjusting the straps, and Joselyn kept her attention fixed in front of her.

Easy, Joselyn. Don't Panic.

Finally, Hollen threaded his arms on either side of her waist, his hands covered in thick leather gloves. He bent forward, which pushed Joselyn's belly flat against the beast's back. His chest pinned her to the saddle. She was about to buck in protest when Hollen's hands stretched above her to reach two black ridges at the base of his mount's long neck.

"You'll be glad of my nearness in a moment," Hollen murmured into her ear. The sensation tickled, and she pressed her ear into her shoulder.

It suddenly hit her that she was really about to go flying. She'd done so yesterday, but that was different. She'd been so terrified. Was she any less so now? Maybe. If only a bit.

She glanced behind them and saw that Hollen had secured his legs from foot to knee inside the narrow cage-like stirrups. He began to massage the underside of the wyvern's scales in a similar fashion as he had below its jaw. The beast's body tensed as it stood from its belly. Half its weight was supported on the spines of its massive folded wings. It made that alien clicking noise again. The vibrations reverberated down the creature's neck and up Joselyn's body. She shivered.

They started moving; the beast crawling its way toward the bright light at the mouth of the cave, some hundred paces away. Hollen and Joselyn swayed with the rise and fall of its giant shoulders until they reached the precipice.

Joselyn risked a glance over the beast's side, then instantly wished she hadn't. They were hundreds of feet into the air, far out of reach for any natural creature on land. The sun was lagging on the horizon, perhaps an hour from twilight. It illuminated the jagged peaks below them. Bile sloshed about in her stomach.

"How far is your home?" she asked, praying to the gods it wasn't far.

Her captor leaned even closer to whisper in her ear. "When you have wings, everything is nearby."

Hollen pressed forward on the creature's ridged scales. Suddenly they were plunging toward the earth. Joselyn might have screamed, but the wind whistling violently past her ears deafened her to everything else. Hollen pressed so hard into her back that she lay completely fixed against the monster's saddle.

The wyvern opened its massive wings, and Joselyn's breath caught in her lungs. A current of air caught them, whipping them backward, and their rapid descent halted. Joselyn strained to suck in a breath. They were gliding together, away from the stony gray cliff.

Now they were in full flight, Hollen lifted his body a bit. She could breathe again. He'd been right; she was grateful for his proximity. If he could hear, she might have begged him to cover her even more tightly. Instead she clutched the leather edge of the saddle.

She'd never imagined she'd be flying. That anyone could. In the past she'd compared galloping on Morningstar's back to flying. How wrong she'd been. There was *nothing* like this.

Hollen continued his strange massage on the creature, pressing firmly with his right hand as the creature banked toward the mountain. Realization dawned. He was directing the wyvern with his touch. How could such wicked creatures be tamed in the first place? Perhaps they were bred in such a manner. She would ask later.

As they flew, Joselyn allowed herself to relax. Hollen's great chest expanded into her back as he breathed, and she felt the line of his thighs fitted against hers. Her neck tingled. At least she wasn't in danger of plunging to her death.

Eventually, they began circling a slow descent. Hollen lifted a bit from her back and let go of one scaled ridge to point toward the earth. She gasped, startled to no longer be encircled in the safety of his arms. After a moment's reassurance that she would not be torn into the air by a gust of wind, Joselyn peered over the mount's wings in the direction of Hollen's fingers.

Far below them, a valley opened up at the juncture of two towering spires of rocky mountain. It was covered in snow, but Joselyn thought she could see the dots of several people against the stark white background. The ravine seemed to disappear into the darkness of the mountain behind it, and as they came closer, Joselyn saw that a settlement resided in the mountain itself. Fires shone under the sloping canopy of a curved cliff face, which provided natural shelter.

More interesting than what lay behind the village was what lay before it. Miles and miles of open snow descended into a sea of jagged gray stone. Beyond that, the beginnings of a thick fir pine forest, which eventually leveled off into what her captor had called 'the lowlands.'

Her heart sank in her chest. Escape from this place would be no easy feat, and far less so if she were pursued by those who could seek her out from the sky. Her only chance was to safely reach the dense forest below before she was found missing. How in the skies was she going to do that?

A gust of wind spun around them from the right. Joselyn jumped, and Hollen clamped his arm back down around her, tucking her into himself. A wyvern, smaller than Hollen's, blew past them. Joselyn almost lost sight of it as it ducked low beneath them. Its solid white coloring was difficult to track against the snowy earth. She distinguished it only by a large clump of dark furs that clung to its back. Another rider.

Joselyn watched the graceful beauty of the white creature's flight. Unlike Jagomri, it dove toward the ground, racing with no one in particular as far as Joselyn could tell. She wondered why anyone in their right mind would choose to fly so fast. Maybe the rider had lost control? In seconds, the white beast opened its great wings and caught the current, then glided the last hundred feet to the ground.

Hollen continued a steady pace, and Joselyn scanned the ground for any further details she might gather from her high vantage point. Just before Jagomri touched down, Joselyn caught sight of the white wyvern's rider dismounting and marching in their direction.

Jagomri's talons disappeared into a powdery blanket of snow. Hollen released him and reached backward to loosen the straps which secured his legs. Joselyn didn't straighten when he lifted himself off her; she focused on the blond man plodding through the snow. His gaze on Hollen, he pounded his right fist upon his leather cuirass, over his heart. His smile was barely visible in the distance. He halted. Was he looking at her?

"Forgive me, brother," Hollen called out in trade tongue. "I would return the greeting, but I find myself freshly blooded."

"Brother," the newcomer answered, also in lightly accented trade tongue. "Shall I approach?"

Hollen waved him over and the man resumed his march. Hollen tapped her on the back, and she walked her hands down to her hips, pushing herself into a seated position before him. Her rear slid into his hips and Joselyn jumped when he groaned. She glanced up, but he avoided her gaze. Hollen swung out of the saddle and jumped to the ground, kicking up snow as he landed.

Eager to be away from the winged serpent, Joselyn slid into Hollen's waiting arms. She stepped away from him and yanked up her hood. If only Hollen had allowed her to make her hair presentable before bringing her. She didn't want to look like a feral animal in front of these savages. Clad in foreign clothing and disheveled after the hair-raising flight, Joselyn did her best to appear confident in her unfamiliar surroundings. In her experience, fear had a way of painting a target on one's back. It would not do to appear weak. She pressed her shoulders back and proudly inclined her chin.

The man whom Hollen had called 'brother' stopped a few feet away. Joselyn was forced to tilt her head back to meet his pale blue eyes. The light-haired man regarded her with curiosity, and she stifled the urge to look away. He was dressed in the same furs and studded leather armor as his brother, and he too wore his long hair pulled tightly back, though his was in a braid. His gaze was gentle, and a shy smile played at his bearded face. He was handsome too. Unusually so.

"Are you well, brother?" the man asked, his brow raised.

He must be looking at the pretty marks I gave him. Joselyn bit her lip.

Hollen put a hand to Joselyn's back and guided her to stand before him. "I've never been better. Brother, meet Joselyn Helena Elise Fury, *mu hamma*."

Joselyn stiffened when his fingers brushed her hood, as though he meant to pull it down. At the last moment, his hand fell away.

Hollen's brother touched his fist to his blond head and drew it down toward Joselyn, opening his fingers as he went. He smiled. "Welcome to Bedmeg, *mu Saliga*. We have waited a long time for your arrival."

"Forgive me. I had no idea I was expected." She didn't bother hiding her contempt. If he took offense at her sarcasm, he didn't show it.

"No. Of course you would not. I am Erik the Tempered. Second son of Sven the Collector."

Joselyn bobbed her head in a makeshift curtsy. His soft manner took her by surprise. She reminded herself that this man hadn't been the one to take her against her will. If she was going to survive and eventually escape, she could make use of allies. At the very least, it was wise to avoid making enemies wherever possible.

Behind them, Jagomri growled impatiently. Joselyn jumped despite herself, and Hollen steadied her with his hands.

"What news for me, Erik? My bride is tired, and I want to take her to our *bok*."

"No news, *Salig*. It seems Helig favors your bonding."

Hollen turned to his wyvern and began working at the

saddle fastenings. "I'm glad you were here to meet us. If others ask, tell them I'll speak with them in the morning."

Joselyn moved out of the way as Erik came to stand at Hollen's other side. "I'll do this for you."

Hollen gently touched his fist to his heart. "Thank you."

Erik laughed, returning the gesture much more forcefully. He flashed a quick smile at her, stroked a hand over Jagomri's side and began working at the trappings. The beast stretched in relief as the bindings loosened.

While Hollen retrieved his belongings from the saddle, Joselyn squinted toward Bedmeg, trying to make out its details in the waning light. She stood at the bottom of a plunging, snow-covered ravine which led up into an enormous open cave. The cave's ceiling hung at least fifty feet above the floor and as far as she could see, the open area beneath it served as a common area for Hollen's people. A half-dozen fires lit the interior, and the tiny silhouettes of people passed around them. Joselyn shivered. The flames might have looked inviting under any other circumstances. Her face stung from the biting chill of the wind, and she'd lost all feeling in her fingers. At least her toes were warm thanks to the well-made boots Hollen had given her.

He came up beside her after swinging his pack over his shoulder. "Come, *mu hamma*. Let's get you warm."

Joselyn threw a glance over her shoulder at Erik. "I thought you said the wyverns were too dangerous to be handled by anyone but their masters."

Hollen guided her forward. "Yes. That's true of everyone except Erik. My brother has a way with the *gegatu* unlike any other. He can swat a brooding mother off her eggs and come away untouched. It's remarkable."

They passed Erik's white wyvern, and the beast ignored them. Still, Joselyn was glad to have Hollen between her and the winged creature. She kept quiet as they approached the edge of the cave. A dark-haired boy clad in furs noticed them first. He called excitedly into the cave, gaining the attention of some thirty men, women and children.

Joselyn's step faltered as curious eyes shot first to her, then to Hollen, before returning to her. Her captor stopped too. He stroked a thumb across her back in subtle encouragement. Her eyes darted to him. He was fixing his people with a hard, sweeping stare. When Joselyn looked back into the cave, she was surprised to see nearly everyone resuming their previous activities. A dark-skinned woman shushed the boy who'd alerted them, taking him by the arm and shooing him deeper into the cave.

Hollen's hand pressed her forward. They passed under the sloping roof of the cave. Joselyn felt the people's covert scrutiny as she and Hollen followed the smooth stone path which wound around the scattered camp fires. Each was surrounded by men as large as or larger than Hollen, all clothed in furs or wool tunics. The women wore woolen spun dresses dyed scarlet, and a few the same brilliant shade of purple as Joselyn's. The women were a diverse lot, with skin shades ranging from freshly fallen snow to blackest night. Their eyes featured every shape she'd ever seen in her father's many foreign guests.

The men, however, were slightly less varied. Their skin fell into a milder range of tones, from light cream to warm brown. Many were shirtless, and Joselyn had to work not to stare at the patterns of scarring that Hollen had referred to as his "*idadi.*"

Although the people kept their eyes to themselves, they were unnaturally quiet, and Joselyn had the distinct impression they hoped to catch a bit of conversation between her and their chieftain. They'd be disappointed, since Hollen was completely silent as he ushered her.

The stone wall that rose into the back of the cave reminded

Joselyn of an enormous honeycomb. It was covered in dozens of man-sized holes, which Joselyn was intrigued to see people exit or disappear into. They were scattered at varying heights up the wall, some several stories high with natural winding staircases leading up to them. Hollen ushered her up one such path after pulling a torch from a nearby fire. She walked in front of him, but hesitated when an auburn-haired youth exited a hole, blocking their path.

The young man looked to be about Joselyn's age, perhaps eighteen years old. He was shirtless, bare of much scarring, though he sported thousands of freckles much like her own. When he spotted the pair of them, his look of surprise morphed into what could only be mischief. He opened his mouth.

"Don't speak, Sigvard," Hollen ordered as though he were trying to race the younger man for the first word. "I'll address you in the morning."

The redhead grinned and turned his roguish face upon Joselyn. He wiggled his brows suggestively. What was this boy playing at? He turned back toward Hollen and bowed so low his forehead almost brushed his knees. He held his hands to the side, gesturing for them to continue. A corner of Joselyn's mouth twitched. He was teasing them, or perhaps only Hollen.

The mockery seemed to work. Hollen snorted and rolled his eyes. He pressed Joselyn forward, up the path. As they passed the bowing boy, Hollen flicked him hard on the head.

"Who was that?" Joselyn asked. The boy groaned and rubbed at his skull.

"My *podagi* little brother, Sigvard."

"*Podagi?*"

"Idiot," Hollen said, loud enough for the redhead to hear.

"How many brothers do you have?"

"Four. You'll meet the other two tomorrow."

Joselyn thought a moment. "No sisters?"

Hollen hesitated. Joselyn nearly missed it before he shook his head. "No. No sisters."

Somehow Joselyn wasn't surprised. She couldn't imagine how a man with a younger sister, or any sister at all, could bring himself to behave so barbarically toward an innocent woman. Of course, Joselyn had no siblings of her own. Perhaps it was childish fancy to assume sisters trained decency in male hearts toward the fairer sex. If she'd had a brother, Joselyn would have taught him tenderness toward women. A years-old bitterness coiled in her gut.

Don't think about that now.

They continued up the slope in silence. Hollen steadied her the few times she lost her balance on bits of debris. When they were a few stories in the air, he stopped them. They stood at the opening of what she now realized was a smooth winding tunnel. Air whistled inside.

"Go on. This way leads to our *bok*."

Did everyone in this village sleep inside these tunnels? She glanced back down into what she now recognized to be the common area, and caught a few people below jerking their inquisitive stares away. She looked at Hollen who was waiting patiently for her to move.

"Will we be alone in there?" she asked. She prayed to the gods they would not.

"Yes." The torch cast a glow on his face.

Joselyn swallowed. The last time he'd led her through a tunnel, he'd carved his mark into her flesh, forever scarring her body. She wondered what he had planned for her this night. Hollen prodded her forward.

Joselyn sucked in a breath and stepped into the darkness.

8

STARTING FIRES

The glow of Hollen's torch flickered through the tunnel. A current of air blew from behind them, giving Joselyn the faint impression she was being sucked inside. She crept through the curving channel. Her apprehension grew with each step. She needed a distraction.

"Why were your people so"—she tried to put a word to the forced inattention they'd exhibited—"silent?"

"When a warrior claims a *hamma*, it is up to him to decide when others may speak to her."

Joselyn's nostrils flared. "Of course."

"Would you have preferred them to rush you all at once?"

In truth, Joselyn was relieved she'd been given time to adjust to her surroundings, but to learn it was the result of her captor's ownership was too much.

"So when will you decide I'm free to speak to someone, besides you, of course?"

"You may speak to whomever you wish, Joselyn. It's others who must demonstrate their respect."

She didn't know what to say to that. Maybe she'd misunderstood the sentiment behind the tradition. Maybe not. It didn't matter. He was her captor and she had every right to think ill of him. She allowed herself to seethe. Anger was more useful to her than fear.

They continued down the tunnel before stepping through another opening. The light of Hollen's torch filled in around them, illuminating a gray, dome-shaped room made of porous stone walls. The diameter of the circular pocket was maybe thirty feet and the center of the room measured perhaps twelve feet high. Hollen dropped his bag near the opening and circled the perimeter. He set to work lighting torches that rested in chiseled notches in the walls.

"This is our *bok*," Hollen said, setting the torch he'd carried with him into the wall. "Each family has one of their own."

"Will the torches not starve us for air?" she asked as she pulled her hood back.

Hollen shook his head. He pointed to the center of the ceiling, which hung over a carved fire ring. A large cluster of pores provided natural ventilation, and Joselyn suddenly understood what pulled the current of air through the tunnel.

She watched as Hollen unraveled his pack and began resettling the room as he must have had it before he left to claim her. His axe was the first to be set aside. He hung it on a hook on the flattest part of the curved wall. Next, he shook out the bear pelt. He walked it to a small hill of furs on the room's massive bed. Hide pillows lay stacked against the wall.

"If you're cold, you may light the fire." Hollen nodded toward the pit in the center of the room. He tossed her the flints from the pack. Joselyn impressed herself by catching them both in one hand, and Hollen nodded in appreciation before turning back to his task.

Joselyn stared at the pit. She'd never made a fire before. That was the sort of thing her chambermaids saw to. How had she gone her whole life without performing such a basic task? She approached the pit. It was already stacked with wood and kindling.

How hard can this be?

Joselyn dropped to her knees at the pit and squinted at the sticks which were laid against each other in an upward pointing fashion. She rolled the flints about in her hands, considering. She shifted her gaze to the torches on the wall.

Would it not be easier to simply light the fire from one of them?

Last night Hollen had struck the little rocks together, feeding sparks into the ring until it danced with gleaming heat. Her lips thinned in determination. She squatted down and bumped the stones against one another. Nothing happened. She did so again, a bit harder, and a spark jumped before her. Smiling triumphantly, she continued striking the flints as sparks poured out over the broken branches.

A minute passed. Joselyn hissed in frustration. The flames wouldn't take. A tingle crawled up her spine. Hollen stood over her. She gritted her teeth in disgust at her own ineptitude. Pretending not to notice him, she continued striking the flints.

Hollen said nothing, but crouched beside her. Joselyn stiffened, unable to feign obliviousness. He reached into the tiny pyre and plucked out a tuft of bark thread, which he set beneath her hands. He waited.

Swallowing her pride, Joselyn struck the flints again, and this time, the spark devoured its offering. Her eyes widened. She snatched a palm full of twigs, lit them like candlesticks, and fed each one into the pyre until it glowed. From the corner of her eye she could see Hollen regarding her with a tilted gaze, his lips pursed. She refused to look in his direction until he returned to unpacking.

Across the fire, he stuffed his empty pack into a wooden chest beneath the hanging axe. She warmed her hands, watching him.

When he dropped the lid back down, he set the sheathed *gneri* blade upon it. Then he walked away as though he meant to leave it there. Her eyes flicked toward the bed. Despite the fire's heat and her cloak's warmth, a cold sweat broke out across her body.

"*Mu hamma.*"

Joselyn jumped as Hollen addressed her. He held out the comb from the night before. Joselyn took it, glad to have something to fidget with. She unraveled her braid and worked at the windblown tangles as Hollen began pulling at the ties of his leather armor.

"You should undress," Hollen said as he pulled off his furs. Joselyn straightened. With his torso bare, she could again see his scars, both old and new. His latest work was covered in a dry square of bloody cloth.

"I need to make sure your *tanshi* mark is healing." Hollen gestured to his own wound.

"It's well," she lied, not wanting him near her in such a manner again. In truth it ached like burning skies.

Hollen huffed. "I'm sure it is, but it must be re-dressed. Take off your cloak."

Joselyn ignored the order, watching him tend to his own wound from across the room instead. He peeled the old cloth back and wetted a new square with water. He dabbed at the cuts before covering them in more of the green paste he had used the day before. Finally he re-covered the area with a new square of cloth. When he finished, he strode over to where Joselyn sat before the fire. His *idadi* scars glared ominously down as he plopped to the ground next to her. Propping a knee beneath one elbow he stared hard into her eyes.

"Why aren't you obeying me?" he asked, voice even.

Joselyn shot a quick glance toward the *bok's* entrance. "You're not my master."

"And yet what I asked of you was perfectly reasonable, no?" Hollen cocked a brow.

"No," Joselyn whispered. If only she sounded more confident.

"So, you would have me allow your wound to fester then? Come all this way to die of a fever?" His accent grew thicker as the tension in his voice ratcheted.

"I expect I would be easy enough for you to replace," she shot back.

His dark eyes narrowed at that. There was a moment of strained silence before he spoke, "You're afraid of me."

Terror and indignation roiled within her stomach, sickening her. She could deny it, but what was the point? Her lie would be obvious. Instead she poured every drop of condemnation she could into her voice. "Of course I am."

He regarded her. Slowly, he reached into her lap and pulled one of her hands away. Uncurling her fingers, Hollen fitted her freckled palm against his calloused one. She stared at them, noting the vast disparity in their sizes. Her nail tips barely reached the point of his second knuckles. She looked back at her captor who held his iron gaze upon her

"If I want you to move, I can move you. If I want you to stay, I can make you stay." He spoke slowly, deliberately, willing her to understand him. "If I want you to undress, I can undress you myself. I am not your master, *mu hamma*, but I can master you, make no mistake."

Joselyn's mouth went dry. He was right. She dropped her hand from his palm, her eyes retreating to her lap. She clenched her hands around the comb to keep them from shaking.

"That's not what I want," he murmured.

He stroked two fingers across the back of her hand, leaving gooseflesh in his wake. Joselyn risked a glance back up at him, worrying her lower lip between her teeth.

"But I will do what I must to keep you safe because, despite your taunts, I cannot replace you, Joselyn. My only."

Joselyn swallowed, her brows drawing together.

"If I give you an order that you can explain to me is unreasonable, I'll not force you to obey me."

Joselyn's chin jutted forward. Should she take him seriously? "And, if we disagree on what is reasonable?"

Hollen was thoughtful. "Your new world is strange to you. If your safety is in question we will rely upon my judgment for the time being."

"And what if the matter at hand does not concern my...safety?" Joselyn's eyes trailed toward the bed.

Hollen sighed, dropping his hand away. "I have no interest in forcing my body into yours."

Joselyn flinched, cringing at the image those words conjured.

"You will sleep in my bed where it's warm and where I can keep you safe, but I'll not claim your body until you ask it of me."

Then you'll not claim me ever, savage.

Relief washed over her. Perhaps she'd survive this ordeal with her virtue intact, assuming he could be trusted. She wouldn't take that for granted. Joselyn brushed a strand of red hair behind her ear. Shifting under the weight of his gaze, she nodded.

"Now, let me clean your wound."

Joselyn set the comb aside and unclasped the bone broach holding her cloak together. The heavy fur fell to the ground behind her, still holding its warmth to the small of her back. She climbed to her feet so that she could loosen the cords at her sides while Hollen retrieved his supplies.

Joselyn peeled off the purple dress, leaving her in the long-sleeved shift. Its neckline had a deep slit in the front that was laced together with a thin cord. Hollen set his things on the ring of the firepit and settled himself back to the ground. He tipped his head, watching as she unlaced her shift. Joselyn felt heat creep up her chest and into her face as she undressed. Even this felt intimate. She dropped to her knees.

Too late she heard her pendant clink on its chain. Would he take it from her? Cite some nonsensical tradition about brides not being allowed to retain any belongings? When Hollen saw it, her fingers itched to hide it away. He hunched forward and swept it over her shoulder and out of the way. Joselyn relaxed even as he wetted the cloth and began pulling it from her mark. Once again he had been careful not to fully expose her breast.

She watched him as he worked. His movements were steady and meticulous, as though he'd done this a thousand times before. She studied the mass of tiny scars on his shoulders and down the center of his back. He'd done this a couple hundred times at least.

His dark head bent before her, Joselyn breathed in a bit of his scent. Surprisingly, it wasn't offensive. She couldn't imagine that people living on mountains were eager to bathe on a regular basis. But his skin and hair were clean. A hint of pine and sulfur was all the odor she could detect. It was pleasant, and that ludicrous thought made her nose wrinkle. She leaned away from him, anxious to get his heady scent out of her nose. He paused, raising a brow.

"Am I hurting you?"

"No," she said, too quickly. "I mean, yes."

Swiving hells, Joselyn! Stop stuttering.

His brows drew together and Joselyn willed him to ignore her. He began again, even more gently. He worked the green sludge into the fine lines before covering them with a clean square of cloth. "It will need to be changed like this daily for a week. Then it should stay dry. If it begins to weep, or burn, or stink, you must tell me."

Joselyn nodded her agreement, clutching her shift closed. Hollen rose and put his belongings in the trunk. He withdrew a long piece of cloth.

"To sleep in," he said, bunching it up and tossing it over the fire to her.

She caught it. It was a pale shift without sleeves and with a much lower neckline than her current shift. It was soft to the touch and she imagined it would be comforting against her skin. But it was indecent. Growing up, Tansy had given her many a lecture about the sexual appetites of men. Her warning had been clear: "*give 'em too much to see and they'll have you on your back the minute you're alone.*" Thoughts of Tansy made the backs of her eyes sting.

Focus, Joselyn.

What of his other declaration? That he wouldn't force her to obey him on matters which didn't concern her safety? Time to put one of those oaths to the test.

"I'll sleep as I am," she said, folding the shift as she stood.

Hollen regarded her from across the room. "You've been in that one since yesterday."

"Yes, it's quite warm," she said, moving to place the shift back into the trunk. She folded her hand over the *gneri* knife to keep it from sliding as she lifted the heavy wooden lid.

Hollen pursed his lips, pointing to his bed. "The furs are warm. I gave you the shift because I doubt you wish to join me there naked."

Joselyn bristled. Was he implying that he slept in the nude? Gods, she hoped not. Ignoring him, she lowered the trunk lid back down on his offering.

"Furs aren't easy to clean. We don't wear dirty clothes inside them."

Joselyn turned. "Are you ordering me to change?"

Go ahead, show me now if your little speech was sincere or not.

Hollen narrowed his eyes as if sensing her dare. She returned his glare. He shrugged then grabbed a stone bowl for dousing the torches.

Joselyn's shoulders relaxed. She retrieved her comb and finished reworking her hair into its braid. When it was considerably darker, Hollen propped a boot up on the wooden bedframe, bending to work at the laces. When his foot was free, Joselyn saw he was missing his three outer toes. She meandered closer to the bed, trying to make out what had happened to him. She froze. He was about to yank his pants off.

Turning at the last minute, Joselyn barely avoided laying eyes on the now, fully naked man. Her cheeks glowed as she clutched the end of her braid. His footsteps padded around the bed in her direction. She skittered forward, turning sideways so that she could tell where he was in her periphery.

Instead of approaching her, he dropped into bed on the side closest to her and the *bok's* entrance. Joselyn stood there, fidgeting with her hair. She jumped when he spoke.

"Come to bed."

Sighing, Joselyn mustered the courage to turn around. Hollen was lying beneath the covers, eyes closed, his hands laced behind his head. The fire cracked and popped, throwing its warm glow across the black-brown furs. Fingering the comb, Joselyn went to set it on the trunk's lid. When she got there, her gaze brushed the *gneri* blade, sitting conspicuously in the open.

In one smooth motion, Joselyn set the comb on the lid as she picked up the knife. Carefully, she turned. Thank the merciful gods that Hollen's eyes were still shut, his bearded face serene.

She hurried to the bed, her eagerness to hide her weapon strangling her misgivings about crawling under the blankets with a naked man. Turning her back to Hollen, she tucked the knife deep beneath her hide pillow and plunked her head upon it. She would have to return it in the morning, before he had time to notice it was missing. That was, assuming he didn't force her to make use of it before then.

Joselyn's gaze dipped to the fire in the center of the room. Once it burned out, they would be suffused in total darkness. Without the sun, would her body know when to wake her? She'd slept through half the day just last night. Her blood went cold. Perhaps this savage was a fitful sleeper. Perhaps his arm would sweep around her in the night and find its way to the knife's cool ivory hilt. Her stomach lurched as she imagined what he would do to her. He would punish her for certain. Or worse.

Despite the warmth of the furs, another cold sweat broke out across Joselyn's body. One of her problems was solved. She wouldn't be sleeping tonight.

LONG AFTER THE FIRE DIED, Hollen lay awake. Concealed by darkness, he no longer bothered to keep his eyes closed. He rested on his side now, facing his bride's back across the bed. She hadn't moved since slipping beneath the furs. Scooted so far against the edge, her limbs must be dangling over the side.

He hadn't been tired when he went to bed. He would have spent several more hours enjoying the company of his brothers, except he was unwilling to leave his bride alone on her first night in her new home. Now he wondered if she'd have been better off had he simply tucked her in and left.

His bride wasn't sleeping. She'd not slept a single minute. He listened for the same even breathing that'd lulled him to sleep the night prior, but it never came. Hollen suspected that had much to do with the knife she'd brought with her to their bed.

He'd left it out on purpose, anxious to see what she'd do with it, if anything. Hollen didn't relish the thought of spending the next weeks or even months wondering if his wife intended to kill him the moment he let his guard down. When he heard her move a little too quickly to join him, he knew she'd swiped the blade. It was just as well. Better she show her hand sooner than later.

However, after hours of nothing happening, Hollen began to think she hoarded the weapon less from a desire for early widowhood and more from desperation to retain her virtue. He knew he shouldn't be frustrated. But what was it going to take to make her understand that she was safe?

Of course, her wariness was rational. In her mind she'd been kidnapped and mutilated by a savage bent only on having what he desired. The longer he thought about it, the more he decided he'd have thought less of her had she left the knife alone. He'd not claimed a weak woman.

Still, she needed to rest. And eventually, so did he. Not bothering with the pretense of yawning or stretching, Hollen rose from the bed. His bride, who had been stone still all night, whipped around in the blankets as he moved. Hollen scoffed, his suspicions confirmed. When the dim glow of his torch filled the *bok*, Hollen saw his bride was sitting up, her face pale with alarm. She seemed to notice too late that he was still naked and her freckled cheeks burned.

Adorable. Disappointing. But adorable.

A corner of his mouth twitched. Unabashed, he rejoined her on the bed, pulling the edge of the furs into his lap for her sake. Joselyn looked ready to bolt, every muscle of her body tense. He let her squirm a moment before speaking.

"Where would you put it?" he asked, voice casual.

"What?" Her brow furrowed in honest confusion.

"The knife," he said, nodding at the pillow near her fidgeting hand. "If I were to attack you right now, where on my body would you put it?"

"I—" her voice cracked.

Hollen slid his hand under the pillow and retrieved the *gneri* blade. He saw panic in her eyes and she flinched when he reached for her hand. Though he was gentle, Hollen had to tug at her arm to bring it up between them. He pressed the hilt into her palm and closed her fingers around it. "Show me."

Joselyn swallowed hard. Hesitantly, she brought the tip to his ribs. When she pressed it to the flesh beneath his lung, Hollen was careful to remain still. He met her wide, blue eyes and waited. She was trembling.

"There," she whispered.

At least she'd turned the flat so that it would fit between his ribs. Hollen pursed his lips, nodding in appreciation. "Painful. But not deadly. Not deadly enough, anyway."

Joselyn frowned as he pinched the blade tip between his fingers and drew it up to the deep hollow of his throat. Her lips parted when he dropped his hand to his side.

"Stab a man here, and he won't have time to make you join him in death."

He looked her in the eye, and she stared back. Hollen waited for her to move, to speak, to do anything. She squeezed the hilt, the blacks of her eyes dilated. Her breath came in shallow, stuttering gasps, the only sound save for the crackling of the torch behind them.

She lowered the blade.

Hollen blinked, careful to show no reaction. Finally, Joselyn looked away, dropping her gaze to the bed beneath them. Hollen's heart thumped in triumph.

My first victory.

"Keep the knife if it comforts you, *mu hamma*. It's yours anyway."

In truth it wasn't the proper time to present the *gneri* blade to his bride. But so long as she kept it hidden from others Hollen saw no harm letting her have it. Joselyn's frown deepened, her eyes sparking with some emotion.

"Only, you must sleep. The mountain sickness will overcome you if you don't." Hollen turned away from her and settled himself back down into the furs, not bothering to dowse the light. He could practically feel her stare upon him.

"Aren't you worried I'll kill you?" she squeaked, incredulous.

Hollen yawned, tucking his arm beneath his head. "I'm not afraid of a woman who can't start her own fire."

9
BROTHERS AND BRIDES

"Are you ready?"

Joselyn was about to be introduced to the people of Bedmeg. She'd taken Hollen's word that it was morning. Without torch light, the *bok* was pitch black. It had taken a long while for her mind to convince her body it was time to rouse.

Joselyn nodded at her captor before following him through the smooth winding tunnel toward the common area. Though he'd allowed her to keep the *gneri* blade through the night, he'd bid her leave it in the *bok* during the daytime. If only she could keep it on herself at all times. There were stories from across the sea, from the ancient lands of Primoria, of savages who would breed women out in the open, for all their tribe to see. But surely a man who would follow through with his vow to leave her untouched in his bed would not suddenly decide to rape her in the snow. Surely.

Last night had been exhausting. She'd lain awake for hours, clutching the ivory hilt of the knife. Her mind and stomach had been in turmoil as she wrestled with the decision to keep the blade in case he should attack her, or return it before he noticed it was missing. Her heart had leapt into her throat when he'd suddenly stood from the bed to light a torch. In that moment she hadn't known what to expect from him, but what happened couldn't have left her more bewildered.

He'd known that she lay with the blade, and instead of applying some brutal punishment, he'd given her a lesson in self-defense. More than that, he'd given her an opportunity to kill him. Could she have done it? That is, if she were confident of escape afterward? She'd never killed a man before. She'd never killed anything at all. Hollen had terrorized her in ways she previously couldn't have imagined. Yet, as she'd held the blade to his throat, the intensity of his dark eyes boring into her, something had whispered that he wasn't quite deserving of death.

At least, not yet.

Joselyn had slept afterward, her hand wrapped around the knife. Now she stepped into the shaded light of the massive cave. It was like one of Sir Richard's war camps. Except there were no tents. And there were women. And children. And the people, more than twice as many as the night before, were smiling. They milled around the fires, talking and laughing with companionable ease. Beside her, Hollen scoffed.

"Nice to see everyone decided to wake early today." His eyes scanned the scene below. "Word in Bedmeg spreads quickly. They're anxious to get a look at the new *Saliga*."

Joselyn frowned and clasped her hands in front of her. She wore a red wool overdress now. It was nearly identical to what most of the women below wore, though some sported purple clothing. Her hair was freshly plaited. She was as presentable as she could hope to be, given the circumstances. Were the Dokiri as prone to judging appearances as civilized people? She straightened. It was a universal rule that few things made a better impression than a brave face and proud shoulders.

A woman below tapped her friend on the shoulder, then

nodded at Joselyn and Hollen. All eyes turned on them. An awkward moment of silence made Joselyn's heart skip a beat, but within seconds, everyone was back to minding their own business.

Hollen offered his arms for support should she lose her balance on the winding slope. A faint sense of vertigo had assailed her since being stolen away to the mountain. When would it fade? The smell of eggs and roasting mutton filled the air, and Joselyn's stomach rumbled. When they reached the stony floor, Hollen guided her through the throngs of people toward a fire near the mouth of the cave. The villagers stepped out of Hollen's path, as though they knew where he was headed.

Joselyn studied those around her as they walked—in particular, the women, with their varying colors, sizes, and face shapes. Joselyn had never witnessed so much diversity in one place. The only thing they had in common was the thin leather belts they wore about their hips. Each held a sheathed knife with a carved, ivory hilt. One woman tended to her young sons, while another sat grinding a dark fungus into paste. Still another perched across what Joselyn assumed was her husband's lap, whispering something into his ear that made the large man smile. His arms were wrapped about her waist, his thumb stroking at her hip. Joselyn blushed and looked away.

They reached a clearing around a firepit much larger than the one in Hollen's *bok*. Hollen led Joselyn to carved stone benches, where he indicated she sit. Three men looked up at her. She recognized the two on the right: Erik and Sigvard.

The one on the left was so tall, he sat nearly a head higher than anyone else in the cavern. Were she standing before him, she'd have to lean back to look into his eyes, and he was sitting down. He had long, sandy brown hair that looked as though he had shaken it out upon waking and then come directly to breakfast. His nose was slightly crooked, as though it'd been knocked out of place one too many times. He looked Joselyn up and down once with an appreciative arch in one brow. She swallowed.

"Brothers," Hollen greeted, touching his fist to his heart. The men mimicked the gesture with more force. "I have claimed a *hamma*."

"About time." The red-haired boy, Sigvard, snickered. He was silenced by Erik's elbow to his ribs. Sigvard clutched his side and continued to smirk.

Hollen's gaze flicked upward before he continued, "Meet Joselyn Helena Elise Fury, *atu Saliga*."

"*Mu Saliga*," they acknowledged her in unison. All three men drew their pinched fingers down from their foreheads, opening them at the end. She'd seen Erik do the same thing the evening before. She didn't want to acknowledge the title Hollen had given her, but unsure how else to respond, Joselyn nodded, careful to look at each of them in the eyes as she did.

"Where is Ivan?" Hollen asked. He shot a glance at Erik.

"On patrol," Erik answered.

"It's not his day."

Erik's gaze dropped from his brother's. "He volunteered."

Hollen blinked. His mouth pulled into a tight line. A brief silence fell over the ring before Hollen settled beside her. He reached over the fire and took a bit of roasted meat from the spit that hovered above and tore it along the sinews. Joselyn took the offered portion, then glanced around the firepit. Was she to eat in front of these men with her bare hands?

Everyone else is.

She nibbled. The mutton tasted sweet and smoky. Her mouth watered as her appetite flared.

"Good to see she didn't stab you," The redheaded brother said to Hollen.

"There's still time," The largest brother added, winking at Joselyn.

"*Mu hamma*, this is Magnus the Vast." Hollen inclined his head toward the sandy-haired man on the left.

She inclined her chin, and the giant nodded at her.

Sigvard's voice went high, cracking. "Red hair and freckles, Hollen? Really? I didn't know you liked my look so much."

"She looks like mother, you *podagi*," Erik said.

"That's even worse!" Magnus laughed.

I look like his mother? Joselyn shifted on the bench, unsure what to make of that.

Hollen smirked. "You're just so pretty, Sigvard. I couldn't help myself."

Sigvard tapped a finger to his temple in the same place she had struck Hollen. "I'd take you down a peg except, it looks like your *hamma's* already done the job."

"And I'd take you down a peg but you're already at the bottom." Hollen huffed. He turned to Joselyn. "You've met Sigvard. The *youngest*."

"And the smartest," Sigvard added.

Erik rolled his blue eyes and muttered something in Dokiri.

"Just . . . Sigvard?" Joselyn asked, noting the lack of title with the youngest brother's name.

"Yes. *Just* Sigvard," Hollen confirmed. "That is, assuming he didn't shut his mouth long enough to master a *gegatu* while I was gone?"

"Impossible," Magnus said, tossing his sandy hair over his massive shoulder as he reached for more food.

"A Dokiri warrior is named after he kills his first *veligiri*," Hollen explained. "But first he must master a *gegatu*."

"What's a *veligiri*?" she asked.

"Underdweller," Erik clarified. "Any creature from beneath

the mountain will do. Just ask Magnus." He shot a mocking look at the much larger man.

Magnus shrugged. "It's not my fault an imp was the only thing stupid enough to show itself for three months. Besides, I think it's fair to say my *idadi* is catching up with yours these days, Erik."

Erik scoffed, dismissing him. "You're growing too old for fanciful notions, little brother."

"Little?" Magnus reached over and shoved a fist into his older brother's shoulder. The force pushed the smaller man crooked in his seat. Erik laughed, apparently pleased to have raised his brother's hackles.

Despite her status as a captive guest at this primitive table, Joselyn watched the exchange with wary amusement. Warmth emanated from the teasing between these brothers. A familiar pang of loneliness pinched in Joselyn's chest. What must it be like to have brothers? Siblings? Allies bonded in blood? Some of her appetite faded.

Focus on gathering information, Joselyn.

"So, you choose a title for yourselves after you kill a creature from under the mountain?" she asked, trying to work out the barbaric culture of these men.

"No," Hollen answered. "The title is chosen by a rider's father. Or an older male relative if necessary."

An air of solemnity fell upon the men seated around the fire. Joselyn didn't have to ask if their father was dead. It would have been clear from their somber faces even if her captor hadn't declared himself to be the current ruling chieftain. Joselyn looked down at the mutton in her hands.

"Your titles are ... interesting."

Both Magnus and Sigvard tried to speak at once. The redhead yielded to his older brother.

"Our titles can be given for any reason. Sometimes they refer to a notable deed during the *Veligneshi*—the slaughter.'"

"Thank Helig Ivan isn't here!" Sigvard said. He threw his head back in mock relief while the other men chuckled.

"What's his name?" Joselyn asked.

"Ivan the Bold, and he's keen to let everyone know it. *Everyone*," Magnus said.

"How did he earn it?"

"We'll let him be the one to tell you," Hollen answered. "Regna knows it's his favorite pastime. Just let it be known that, regardless of whatever he claims, the true number was *five*. And it was *not* mating season at the time."

Joselyn bit her lip, baffled. Erik's soft voice broke into her thoughts.

"A title can also be chosen to describe the one who bears it."

That's right. Erik had introduced himself as 'Erik the Tempered.' It suited the light-haired man with his gentle, unassuming presence. Curiosity prickled. She turned to Hollen.

"Which is the case with you? Deed or nature?" What could have inspired a name like 'The Soulless?'

Hollen stopped eating and returned her gaze. "Guess."

He fixed her with an expression that dared her to answer. There was a pregnant silence around the fire as the men waited for Joselyn's reply. She shrugged and changed the subject.

"How is a . . . *gegatu* mastered?" Joselyn tested the Dokiri word for 'wyvern' on her lips. Subtle disappointment marked the sag of her captor's shoulders.

"Perhaps Sigvard will be good enough to show you?" Hollen suggested, with mockery evident in his voice as he glanced at the freckled brother.

Sigvard puffed out his chest. "All in good time." He stuffed an overly large bite into his mouth and chewed noisily.

"What about you, Joselyn?" Magnus asked. She stiffened. "Tell us about where you come from. You sound Morhageese."

Joselyn considered how open she should be. It couldn't hurt to let her captor and all his people know who she was, that she had a life and a purpose apart from being a savage's little bride. Who knew? Perhaps one of them would take pity on her.

"I am lady Joselyn Fury, of House Fury, a noblewoman of Morhagen."

"So was mother," Magnus said.

Joselyn's head snapped up. Their mother had been a noblewoman? Surely not. She opened her mouth to speak, but Magnus went on.

"You probably know all the same songs she did. I always wanted to learn more. Do you sing?"

Savages sung songs from her homeland? She stuttered, "I . . . no."

"Play?"

"No."

Magnus frowned. "Too bad. I can teach you to play the *kild* if you want. It's a little like the *crwth*."

Joselyn looked down at the food in her hand. This wasn't the sort of conversation she'd expected to have with a seven-foot tall barbarian. In fact, these men were nothing like she'd imagined Hollen's people would be. She was totally out of her depth here. She swallowed.

"I'm afraid I won't be here long enough for that."

Three pairs of eyes pinned her. Hollen swallowed hard on the bit of food he'd been chewing. He cleared his throat and dipped his head low to catch her eyes. "And why is that, *mu hamma*?"

"Because I can't stay. I'm needed at home." Returning his gaze, she took an easy bite of her meal.

Across the fire, Hollen's brothers snorted, stifling laughter. But they weren't looking at her. They were looking at Hollen.

He fixed her with a hard stare. "This is your home now. You're needed here."

Joselyn's brow rose in challenge as she swallowed. "You lot seem to have been doing well enough long before I arrived. My father, on the other hand, won't survive if I don't return soon."

His brothers' mirth seemed to dampen at that. Satisfied that she had their attention, Joselyn turned toward the three other men and straightened to her full seated height.

"I am The Lady of House Fury. My father is Marcus Fury, second heir to the throne of Morhagen. If any of you should be willing to return me to my father, he will see that you are rewarded so richly you would never need to return to this mountain."

There was silence around the fire. Joselyn waited for someone to volunteer. She'd potentially put her captor in a tenuous position. Her father's words rang in her mind. *Nothing motivates a man like the promise of a heavy purse.*" Though Hollen was their chieftain and they, his brothers, Joselyn doubted their loyalty was so absolute that they were beyond temptation. That is, if she could convince them she spoke the truth.

Finally, someone moved. Magnus leaned forward and rested his hands on his knees. His voice came low and serious. "Do you mean to tell us"—his eyes darted from side to side as though he were conspiring with Joselyn—"that we could be rich enough to ride horses, too?"

The laughter that followed from the three brothers was so loud they drew the eyes of half the clan around them. Magnus neighed convincingly, which was rewarded with another round of approving laughter. Even Hollen joined in, though his eyes betrayed his displeasure.

"Hear that, Sigvard?" Magnus asked. "No need to risk your spotted neck—you could just buy your mount!"

Sigvard flashed what must have been an obscene hand gesture, and the chortling continued.

Joselyn's nails dug into her palms. Nothing about this situation was humorous. Were they really mocking her plight?

What else were they to do? They aren't willing to help you.

How appealing the power of flight must be to a man who could wield it. But could it really be so tempting as to make a man immune to the lure of wealth? It seemed these savages believed so. What could she do now?

If they're willing to betray their brother, they won't do so openly.

She would have to wait. Joselyn's stomach soured as she swallowed the last bit of her breakfast. Her house didn't have the luxury of time.

"Your *hamma* doesn't seem any happier to be claimed than mother was at her claiming," Magnus said with his voice still full of mirth.

"That should please him." Erik laughed.

Joselyn's brow furrowed.

Sigvard chimed in, "Let's see how cold his stones get before she finally—"

"Enough!" Hollen rumbled, glaring. The ring quieted and Joselyn fought the urge to squirm in her seat. Apparently, her captor's patience had a limit.

Magnus mumbled something in Dokiri to Sigvard, who snorted so hard his face turned red. Erik also seemed to struggle reining in his delight. Hollen's eyes flashed and he opened his mouth to speak.

"F-forgive me, *mu . . .S-Salig*," came a feminine voice from behind.

Joselyn turned to see a tall woman with black, tightly curled hair standing at Hollen's back. She wore the same scarlet, woolen attire as the rest of the women in Bedmeg. A half-dozen carved ivory bangles lined her arms. Her soft eyes gleamed the same golden-brown color as her flesh, giving them an almost ethereal glow. When Hollen turned to her, she pursed her full lips in an apologetic expression. She was stunningly beautiful.

"What is it, Lavinia?" Hollen asked, clearly working to tamp down his impatience.

"I'm s-sorry, *mu* . . . *S-Salig*, but b-before Soren left this morning, he asked me to tell you . . . t-tell . . . you . . . " The woman's eyes darted between Hollen and Joselyn. Lavinia shifted her weight from one side to the other while her hand picked at a white bangle. Joselyn stared at the stuttering woman with dawning realization.

I'm making her nervous.

Joselyn was about to avert her gaze when Hollen took the new woman by the elbow and gently pulled her toward himself. As though this were common, she bent forward and whispered whatever she'd been trying to say into his ear. Joselyn watched, uncertain what to make of them. Men didn't touch women so casually, at least, not where she came from. She glanced around the ring, but no one seemed the least bit interested in her captor's exchange.

Hollen sighed. "Then I'd better go." He stood from the bench, sucking the last bit of grease off his fingers as he did. "Lavinia, *mu hamma* has not yet bathed. I wonder if you might show her the springs?"

Lavinia crossed her hand over her hips and bobbed her head. The gesture instantly put Joselyn in mind of the Golden Court of Ebron. She eyed the woman's dark, twisted hair and wondered. As she straightened, Lavinia brought her hand to her forehead and drew her opening fingers downward in what Joselyn was beginning to recognize as a feminine greeting.

"W-welcome to . . . Bedmeg, *mu Saliga*." Joselyn heard it then, the faint Ebronian accent, faded from years of disuse, and muffled by the stutter. How long had she been on the mountain? Joselyn smiled, nodded. Was she about to get a moment alone with a fellow captive? She tempered her eagerness as she stood from the bench.

Hollen touched Joselyn's arm lightly. "Will you be all right on your own?"

"I'm already on my own," she said, stepping away to get around the bench to Lavinia. The other woman's smile faltered at Joselyn's cold words, her eyes shifting to Hollen as though searching for a reaction. Hollen said nothing, electing instead to sign his farewell to the women as Lavinia led Joselyn from the ring.

"That one needs no knife to draw blood, *eh* brother?" Erik's sympathetic voice faded as they walked away.

Joselyn followed Lavinia, who cut smoothly around the clusters of people watching them. Lavinia's presence must have been taken by the clan as a sign that Joselyn was available for conversation. Many of them greeted her as she passed. At one point a small group of much older women flanked Joselyn. She jumped when one of them caught her braid in a wrinkled hand, and ran it down the long stretch of hair.

"So red!" the old woman exclaimed.

"Like flame," another added with an appreciative nod. "But does she have the spirit to match?"

"If so she'll have our *Salig* on his knees within days," The one holding her hair said with mischief in her eye.

"All the better, I'll wager she pups before her year's up," said a third woman. Her voice buzzed with enthusiasm.

"No doubt! No doubt!" a fourth agreed.

Joselyn, shocked into silence, was just opening her mouth to respond when Lavinia took her by the hand and tugged her free of the women's excited pawing.

"L-ladies, please! *Atu*...*Saliga* has only just arrived. Allow h-her a bit of...peace." Lavinia's spine straightened as she spoke, raising her yet another inch above the other women.

Joselyn sighed in relief when they took a few begrudging steps back. She gathered her composure and curtsied to the group of women who watched her with intense interest. One teetered precariously as she attempted to return the unpracticed gesture. The old woman's friend reached a hand to steady her as the rest giggled.

"Forgive me, ladies. I am Lady Joselyn Fury, of Morhagen. I should like to be formally introduced to each of you just as soon as I have made myself presentable."

Before anyone could protest, Lavinia took Joselyn by the hand and continued leading her toward the back of the cave. "Forgive u-us, *mu S-Saliga*, the claiming of a *h-hamma* is an exciting event...among the clan. The claiming of a new *Saliga* is even...more so."

"Thank you." Joselyn breathed, feeling as though she had an ally for the first time since being stolen away. Joselyn looked at the hand Lavinia gripped. She wasn't usually comforted by the touch of strangers, but in this moment, connection to the warm woman was lending her strength.

"How long have you been here?" Did she really want to know? A long stretch of captivity didn't bode well for Joselyn's own chances of escape. This woman obviously wasn't native born. Despite her apparent ease in her surroundings, Joselyn sensed an air of trained nobility in her, with her tall posture and graceful movements. A shame about the stutter. Royal courts could be mercilessly cruel about such things.

"Nine y-years," Lavinia said.

Joselyn's eyes widened. "Nine years? Did no one come to rescue you?"

"I was alone at...the t-time of my c-claiming. No one saw me taken. Even if they h-had . . .it's unlikely they could have t-tracked me here. The *g-gegatu* leave no trails."

"You were alone?" Then maybe she hadn't been a noblewoman. Though the Crookspine Mountains formed an impassable barrier between the Lands of Morhagen and Ebron, she was familiar with the ways of the dark-skinned people of the south.

The Ebronians were well known for their radical ideas about the appropriate roles of women. Whereas most of the world limited women to positions of motherhood or celibate piety, Ebronian women enjoyed a great number of freedoms. One or two female generals had even been known to command their armies. Even so, if her suspicions about Lavinia's background were correct, she couldn't imagine a noblewoman being left to go anywhere without the benefit of an armed escort.

Lavinia sucked in her lips and threw a sheepish expression over her shoulder. "Yes, m-much to my . . .uncle's dismay."

Who was her uncle? The question stalled on Joselyn's tongue. Lavinia didn't look comfortable with the direction of this conversation. Joselyn changed course.

"How often is a *hamma* claimed?"

"When our r-riders complete the *Veligneshi,* they may claim a bride anytime a-after."

"You mean after they kill an underdweller?"

Lavinia nodded. "Yes, a *veligiri*. M-most years two or three . . . *hammas* are claimed."

Joselyn looked around, trying to work out how many men must live here. It was doubtful that the women of this clan also abducted their mates from the lowlands. The unbalance would surely leave a surplus of unmarried women. "Do your warriors take multiple wives then? What of your daughters?"

"We don't have any daughters, *m-mu Saliga*."

Joselyn's step faltered at that. Lavinia stopped walking as

well. She stared patiently at Joselyn, who was searching for words.

"What do you mean?" A vague sense of dread settled over her. Was it possible that these barbarians cast off their female children? The elements in such a high place would surely kill an infant.

Lavinia's mouth opened a beat before she actually began speaking. Her voice was slow and careful. "The Dokiri cannot sire female children. Only...males are born to them."

Stunned, Joselyn looked around the cave at the many children occupying themselves with games. She turned and took care to examine each tiny face in the crowd. Every one of them was male. How had she not noticed before?

Joselyn blinked. She'd never heard of such a phenomenon. Could it be possible? An entire race of men unable to breed daughters? How could such a society be sustained? A thought occurred. She scrutinized the women in the common area. They were as lovely as they were varied. Black, white, brown, and red, they were each exquisite in their own right. Even the elderly women held a degree of beauty that seemed immune to the cruelty of time. All at once, the answer to many of Joselyn's questions became clear. Her mouth fell open.

"You've *all* been claimed?"

"Yes." Lavinia nodded. "All of us."

Joselyn's mind spun. Had Hollen told her this before, she'd have been brought to Bedmeg prepared to meet a mob of women riled to indignant hatred for their captor-husbands. Either that or a throng of broken, hopeless domestic chattel. Joselyn brushed a hand over her hair. There were no slaves here. Only happy couples and cheerful children. Families. She frowned and released Lavinia's hand.

"Why? How can you all be so..." She trailed off, unsure how to articulate her question.

"C-content?" Lavinia offered with a raised brow. She smiled at Joselyn's stupefied nod. "It's true that f-few of us were pleased when we first . . .arrived. But our *hatus* aren't like other men. I was f-fairly well traveled before coming to Bedmeg . . .nowhere on Earth are brides treasured in such a m-manner."

Joselyn frowned. "You're captives."

"We were." Lavinia nodded. She turned and continued to lead. Joselyn hesitated, allowing a bit of distance between them. Lavinia went on. "Now we-w are wives and mothers to the . . .mountain guardians. It's a noble thing."

Joselyn choked back a scoff. She remembered how Hollen talked about guarding the earth from the 'evils of the mountain.' At the time she hadn't given it much consideration, had dismissed it as an ill-conceived excuse for his barbarism. Apparently the bluster was enough to persuade an entire village of women to be content with their own enthrallment. Temper roiled with Joselyn's gut and rose up out of her throat.

"So because these savages kill the occasional pest that sneaks into the sun, you think it justifies that they help themselves to any woman in the world, regardless of her will?"

Lavinia smiled. She seemed unruffled. "I'm g-grateful to hear that the . . .lowlanders may still take their security for g-granted. I w-was the same before . . .coming here. As for my personal will, the world . . .never paid it any heed before. At least now I am h-happy."

"Surely there are those among you who know better!" Joselyn demanded, drawing the attention of several people around them. She needed to speak to someone who would understand her need to return home. She needed an *ally*.

Lavinia's pace slowed. Her back stiffened. She glanced backward and met Joselyn's furious gaze. Somehow, the other woman's stutter got even worse.

"P-perhaps, *m-mu Saliga*. Though if...they exist, I-I'm afraid I c-cannot identify them for y-you."

A pang of guilt wormed its way into Joselyn's chest, swallowing her rage. She was unfamiliar with this sort of guilt. Joselyn was usually too careful with her words for regret. But weariness and fear had gotten the better of her. She kept her gaze to the ground in front of her as she followed.

Lavinia pulled a torch from a nearby fire and led Joselyn into a wide tunnel that descended gradually downward. The air hung thick and damp. Joselyn's skin warmed as the temperature steadily rose the further they traveled into the darkness.

Before long, the ground grew slick with moisture. A wave of steam rolled into Joselyn's face as they stepped through a natural doorway into a large black cave. The faint scent of sulfur permeated the air, and something bubbled in the distance. Lavinia used her torch to light several more half-burned torches set into wall notches similar to those in Hollen's *bok*.

As the cave grew brighter, pools of various sizes came into view, stretching into the blackness. One of the pools was vast, with boiling water popping in the middle.

"These are the hot springs, a gift from Helig, the earth mother," Lavinia said.

So that was why Hollen was so clean despite living on snow-capped mountains. In her world, hot bathing water was a comfort reserved only for the very wealthy, who could afford not only a tub to soak in but also servants to fill it. Joselyn had craved the bone-deep heat afforded by steaming water since she'd been captured.

"G-go ahead and b-bathe, *mu Saliga*. It will c-comfort you." Lavinia gestured to a wooden rack that Joselyn assumed was for keeping her clothes off the wet floor. "There are s-seven pools and each is a different...temperature. I suggest you start cool and work your way up. T-take care to stay well away from any bubbling. The w-water grows hot enough to boil in certain . . .places."

Though longing pulled at her, Joselyn peered into the darkness of the tunnel's entrance. "Do you all bathe here?"

"N-no, only the women, though usually in the evening. The men . . .have springs of their own."

Joselyn fingered the collar of her dress and worried her lower lip between her teeth. Did she dare disrobe and leave herself vulnerable if a man were to wander in?

"I will stay with you, *mu . . .Saliga*." Lavinia said, surprising Joselyn. "Please, allow y-yourself to rest."

Joselyn bowed her head at the woman's generosity. Surely her guide had better things to do than to stand around watching her bathe. Another twinge of guilt pinched for her prior rudeness.

"Thank you, Lavinia. And—" Joselyn faltered, searching for the right way to apologize.

"Yes, *mu Saliga*," Lavinia said, holding up a silencing hand. "You are . . .most welcome."

The older woman smiled and Joselyn hurried to remove her dress.

10

MAY THE MOUNTAIN FALL

"*Mu S-Saliga*, please meet *m-mu hatu* . . .Soren the Lightfooted."

Joselyn stood from her bench in the common area to meet Lavinia's *'hatu,'* her husband. Perhaps *he* would be the reasonable soul to finally help her?

Soren drew his fingers downward from his head. "Welcome, *mu Saliga.*"

Joselyn fought the urge to sigh. By now her patience was threadbare. She was tired of being welcomed. What she needed to hear was 'farewell.' She nodded despite herself, unwilling to be impolite.

"Thank you, Soren. Your wife has been most hospitable."

Though tall, Soren was a good deal leaner than most of the Dokiri. He had a jagged scar that sliced through the center of one slanted eye, though his vision appeared to be intact. He was shirtless, revealing a toned expanse of warm bronze skin and thick, dark hair. Joselyn's cheeks warmed. What did these men have against wearing shirts?

Like all the Dokiri men, he was very handsome in his own,

uncivilized way. She supposed it was to be expected of a race that bred only with women who were chosen primarily for their beauty.

Soren stroked his hand at the small of Lavinia's back. She leaned into her husband with a contented smile on her round face. "She is a credit to the clan and to me, just as I'm sure you will be to Bedmeg and *mu Salig*."

"I'm certain I will not," Joselyn said.

When Soren frowned, Joselyn sighed. The comfort of bathing had been short lived. After Lavinia led her back to the common area, Joselyn had taken it upon herself to make as many introductions as possible. It had been difficult to approach the men at first. On the whole they were far larger than those in her homeland, yet they would shift uncomfortably as she spoke, finding anything and everything around her a more appealing target for their eyes.

How ironic. These beastly men seemed almost afraid of *her* as she planted her hands on her hips and her feet in the dirt, demanding their attention. Still, they listened patiently while Joselyn submitted all the reasons they should assist her. In the end, however, no one seemed interested in either her promises or threats.

"I'm afraid I cannot stay," Joselyn explained, trying once more. "I'm sorely needed at home. It's a matter of life and death."

Soren looked down at his wife, who turned her face up to him. "*Mu Saliga* is d-distressed. She has been unsuccessful in . . . .securing an escort off the m-mountain."

The women had been even worse than the men. They seemed deathly determined to defend their husbands for having claimed them, and by extension, their *Salig* for having claimed her. Each woman made similar references to the creatures beneath the mountain known as the *veligiri*. Their voices were threaded with an almost religious fervor as they spoke of how their husbands were all that stood between the dangers beneath the mountain and total destruction of the lowlands from where they'd all come. At most, a few of the older women would pat her on the hand and assure her she'd come to accept her new life, in time. Joselyn wanted to pull out her hair.

What was she going to do? Would no one take pity on her? She'd never been in such a position of weakness. Her will had always been the will of her father. In her world, no one stood against Marcus Fury.

No one until Dante Viridian. Damn him.

Hatred suffused her. Hatred for Lord Viridian, hatred for the barbarian, and hatred for herself. House Fury needed her, and because of her selfish desire for a moment alone on a hilltop, she'd rendered herself useless. Worse than useless. If she were dead, her father could present Viridian with a body, and thus prove himself innocent of foul play. But here she was, trapped on a gods-forsaken mountain.

"Please", Joselyn said, weary of begging. "If there is anything men like you desire, ask it of me. I swear that I will see it yours."

Soren returned Joselyn's haggard expression with a look of patient understanding. She cringed and her neck went hot.

I swear to the gods, I'd strip off my clothes if you people would but cease with your pitying smiles.

Soren didn't seem to notice her inner turmoil. "It would be easier to ask the mountain to fall than to persuade a Dokiri rider to betray his *Salig*. What you ask would require a warrior to give up his life on the mountain, for he could never return. Without the mountain a Dokiri has no purpose."

"There are a great number of warriors in the lowlands who find their purpose in serving men just as worthy as your *Salig*," Joselyn said.

Soren grimaced. "I doubt that."

"You could find a new purpose elsewhere, as a rich man, and held in the highest esteem by the greatest lord in Morhagen."

Soren shook his head. "For the Dokiri, there is no other purpose than guarding the world at the throat of the mountain." Soren squeezed his arm around Lavinia, who leaned her head against his chest. "And I am already a rich man, *mu Saliga*. What could I want that *mu hamma* has not already given me?"

As if to punctuate his point, two boys came running toward the embracing couple. "*Kano! Kano!*" The boys, whom Joselyn guessed were somewhere between six and ten years old, skidded to a halt and began chattering at Soren.

"Trade tongue, boys! *Atu Saliga* is new and does not yet know your father's language." Lavinia's voice was far clearer than Joselyn had heard it before. Her golden eyes lit with affection. These were her sons.

The boys stared at Joselyn with rampant curiosity. The smaller of the two began to mutter something in Dokiri before his father nudged him on the back.

"If you're here, does that mean Ivan can claim a *hamma* now?" the older one blurted with a hopeful expression.

Before Joselyn could process the question, Lavinia was scolding him in Dokiri. It was impossible to say, but she didn't seem to trip over her words so much in that language. The older boy's shoulders sagged, his face sheepish.

"Forgive me, *mu Saliga*," he said, obviously directed by his mother. "My name is Volo."

"I'm Brodie!" the younger boy added.

Despite her frayed nerves, Joselyn managed a genuine smile. "Hello, Volo and Brodie."

"Our s-sons," Lavinia said, bending to rest one hand on each shoulder.

Their black hair was curled like their mother's, pulled back from their faces. They were darker than their father and shared the slant of his eyes. Those brown eyes stared at Joselyn. Brodie didn't have to look up far. Volo barely at all.

"Do you think Ivan will claim his *hamma* now?" Volo asked. "He says *mu Salig* should have claimed his *hamma* years ago. Will she be pale like you or will she look like *Matha*?"

"She will be pretty like *Matha*!" Brodie cried, facing his older brother who nodded his agreement.

Lavinia's mouth fell open. Her eyes shot apologetically to Joselyn, who smiled back. She was about to excuse the childish remark when she heard Hollen's voice.

"Ivan will have to wait a while longer, Volo."

Joselyn turned to see Hollen and Erik. They looked as though they'd been working hard all morning. They were shirtless, their bodies smeared in dirt.

Volo and Brodie whispered conspiratorially to one another before turning to Erik. "Then we'll have to prey on you next, Erik! Why don't you find a bride so Ivan can have his turn?"

Erik grunted and wiped at a smudge of dirt on his face. Hollen slapped him on the back. "Better you than me, for once."

Hollen directed his gaze at the boys and then on Lavinia and Soren. Joselyn had the distinct impression that he was pointedly avoiding her.

Soren murmured his permission and the two Dokiri children laughed as they chased Erik outside the cave. Joselyn watched them go. In a few years, those sweet boys would grow into blood-obsessed savages. A shame.

"Thank you for guiding *mu hamma* in my absence, Lavinia," Hollen said.

Lavinia ducked her head. "Of c-course, *mu Salig*. *Atu hamma* seemed most gratified to make use of the springs."

"Good. I'm sure it's been the only gratifying experience for her this morning."

Joselyn's mouth twitched, noting the displeasure in his voice.

It was likely he'd caught wind of how she'd spent the last few hours of her time. But surely he couldn't be surprised. She'd propositioned his own brothers right in front of him, for all the good it had done her.

Soren nodded to his chieftain. "*Salig.*"

Finally, Hollen turned his solemn gaze upon her. "Come. I would speak with you."

Joselyn considered telling him he could speak to her where she was, but Hollen caught her by the hand and tugged her toward the open end of the cave. Not wanting to give onlookers the impression that Hollen could command her obedience, she threw a quick word of thanks toward Lavinia and followed after Hollen.

The Dokiri watched them go, their faces rapt with curiosity. Joselyn was loath to leave the safety of witnesses, but she had no choice as they plodded through the snow. Hollen's large boots plowed a trail for her. They hiked past rows of tanning racks, stretched with fresh hide. Down they went into the open ravine, which grew wider the further they descended.

They ended up a good way beyond the place they'd landed the evening before. The sun beat down and reflected off the snow. Joselyn shivered in the late-morning air, which was heavy with moisture. They slowed their pace as they approached another cave carved into the right wall of the ravine. This one was much smaller than the common area and its purpose appeared far more specific. Rows of weapons hung on iron bolts nailed to rocky wall. More noticeable were the dozens of massive *gegatu* saddles. The smell of aged leather filled Joselyn's nose, even at a distance.

A man sat at a raised, stone forge, where hot embers blazed. He looked up as Hollen and Joselyn approached with surprise etched on his deeply lined face. He saluted Hollen with that same, chest thumping gesture that Joselyn was growing familiar with. Hollen nodded but didn't stop. He pulled her beneath the cover of the cave ceiling and into a dry open area. All around, giant saddles were perched on wooden racks.

Hollen released Joselyn and she wrapped her arms around herself, now shivering with cold. He faced her, the tension in his expression gone. Relief turned to suspicion. Why had he brought her here?

Hollen unsheathed a knife from his belt. Joselyn sucked in a breath as he held it out.

"Take it."

Joselyn frowned at the blade, but obeyed. She cradled the hilt in her half-open palm. "What am I to do with this?"

"You're going to fight me."

Joselyn glanced over her shoulder at the only other person present, the old man hammering at his anvil. He threw them a tentative glance over his work. Seeing he'd been spotted, his head snapped back toward his work. Joselyn turned to her captor, and dropped the knife to her side.

"Don't be ridiculous," she whispered. "I can't fight you."

"Why not?" Hollen didn't whisper. "I told you. My own mother nearly killed my father with a knife. She would have succeeded, too, had she not changed her mind. If she could do it, so can you."

Joselyn hesitated, thinking of what she'd learned at breakfast. "Your mother . . . was a noblewoman?"

Hollen nodded. The corner of his mouth pulled upward. "You're not the first to have lived in Bedmeg."

Joselyn tried not to look too surprised. He seemed so damn satisfied with himself, she had to wonder if he'd baited her into this conversation. Curiosity got the better of her.

"Who?"

"Colette Vivian Selma Potrulis."

Joselyn's lips parted. So it was true. How else could a barbarian, so sequestered and secluded in these mountains, know the name of the missing daughter of House Potrulis? It had been years. Decades. Colette Potrulis had gone missing on a fox hunt. It was a fact that Joselyn's father had been quick to point out on the one occasion she'd mustered enough courage to request her own hunting expedition.

Lord Potrulis' men had scoured his lands searching first for the lady, and then for her body. Neither was ever found. It was supposed that some foul creature had dragged her off her horse and into the deadly forest at the foot of the mountains known as The Twist. No one had ever been willing to search for her there, not even her father.

Why would a lady of Morhagen stay here by choice?

Perhaps she had stabbed her husband at the bonding place. Perhaps saving him had been her only way down from the cliffside prison.

As if sensing her thoughts, Hollen spoke up. "My mother was clever. She tricked my father into landing before he'd even made it to the mountain. When he landed to check that she was safe, she sliced a knife across his chest." Joselyn listened, torn between horror and fascination. Hollen smirked. "My father always said my mother would be the death of him."

Joselyn frowned. His mother had been a captive. A prisoner. What did he find so amusing about that? Maybe he didn't care so much for his mother after all. "Oh? And that pleased your father, did it? That his wife meant to kill him?"

Hollen's smile faded. "Yes. Until she succeeded."

Joselyn's brows rose. "She...killed your father?"

"In a way." He took a breath. "When my mother died, he fell ill. His vision in one eye disappeared overnight, and his axe arm failed him. Even words were beyond him most days."

Joselyn had heard of such an affliction. It mostly affected the elderly though, it had been known to strike a healthy few under severe circumstances. "What happened to him?"

"He went on like that for four years. He ruled as *Salig* even when the elder council was ready to name his successor. He led us well. And then he died."

His explanation seemed blatantly void of many hard, ugly details. Joselyn swallowed. She imagined what it must be like to watch one's parent, a former leader of men, slowly deteriorate to an invalid. And all for grief of his wife. Joselyn marveled at that kind of devotion. Wondered that it could exist here, among these primitive men who were not above stealing their women from far-off lands below.

Joselyn thought of her parents then. Thought of how her father had spent years tormenting her mother with his infidelity, and of how low her mother had stooped to spite him. Joselyn's jaw tightened.

"So you see, *mu hamma*," Hollen broke into her thoughts. "Even a lady of Morhagen can kill a *Na Dokiri*."

Joselyn glanced awkwardly at the knife. "If you're waiting for me to attack you with this, we'll be standing here a long while."

Hollen huffed and took two long strides to close the distance between them. He reached for the hand with the blade and brought it up to his chest. "You're not tall enough to reach my throat while we both stand, so forget what I told you in our bed."

Joselyn's throat clenched and she shot a startled glance toward the elderly man at the forge, praying he hadn't heard. He was still ignoring them. When she looked back, Hollen was smirking.

"Do you think it surprises anyone here that you slept in my bed?"

"Apparently the only one shocked by that fact is me," Joselyn spat. Her wrist twitched. She could plunge the blade into his arrogant chest.

Hollen's smirk turned to an outright grin. "Yes, Joselyn, only you."

He folded his hand over hers and gripped the knife. "At this level there are two places you can easily reach to put me down." He brought the blade tip down to the center of his belly just over his navel. "Pierce a man here and he will bleed out more quickly than anywhere else, though you must strike deep."

He turned his back to her and Joselyn sucked in a breath, amazed at his nerve. Had he no fear of her?

Not until you learn to build a proper fire.

She glared at his scars. Tonight, she'd get intimately acquainted with those swiving flints.

Hollen reached both his arms back to point at the spaces below his ribs. "Either side will drop a man, but you must be low enough to avoid the bone. That shouldn't be too hard for *you*."

Joselyn ignored his mockery. "A knife is no weapon for a lady."

"What weapon *would* you use?"

Joselyn thought for a moment. "*If* I were to make use of any weapon at all, it would be a bow."

"You know how to use a bow?" Hollen turned. Interest lit his face.

Joselyn didn't answer right away. In truth, she was very skilled with a bow, and had been told by Sir Richard that she had remarkable aim for a woman. A part of her wondered, with some irritation, what difference being a woman might make in one's aim. But, she'd never argued the point.

"A bit." She wouldn't let on the full extent of her abilities. At some point she might need her captor to underestimate her in that regard. And when he did, she'd be ready.

"Good. I'll take you hunting with me."

Then again, maybe it was better she show him she wasn't *totally* helpless.

Hollen continued. "But the time may come when all you have to protect yourself is a knife. You ought to know how to use one. It's the way of Dokiri women."

Joselyn shook her head. "I'm not a Dokiri woman. Why are you so intent on teaching me to use a blade?"

Hollen's expression sobered. He waited until Joselyn looked him in the eye to answer. "Because your fear pains me, *mu hamma*."

Joselyn's lips parted. What to say to that? The intensity of his gaze made her want to squirm. She glanced around the armory, fidgeting with the knife hilt.

"You say you want to return to your father?" Hollen asked.

Joselyn's gaze snapped to his. She nodded.

He crossed his arms over his broad chest. "If I bargain with you to return you home, will you cease trying to persuade my men to betray me?"

So he *had* heard of her useless escapades. "What sort of bargain?"

"Train with me every day, and learn how to fight with a sparring knife. If you manage to best me, even once, I'll take you back to your father's house."

Joselyn scoffed. Why had she entertained this conversation? He was playing with her. "No. I will not agree to that."

"It's a far better offer than you'll receive from my riders."

She knew he was right. Though she loathed to acknowledge it, Hollen's people hadn't shown even a hint of disloyalty. She hadn't spoken with every member of the clan, but she'd been coming to an understanding about these people. They were as incorruptible as they were wild.

Joselyn scowled at the knife in her hand. She'd never be able to best this man. It was laughable. She recalled the colloquialism Soren had used earlier. "You might as well have said to me, 'when the mountain falls I will return you to your father.'"

Hollen shook his head, grinning wickedly. "No *mu hamma*, for even the mountain may fall one day."

11

MU SALIGA

The bastard had been right. Damn him.
Three days had passed and none of Hollen's people had offered Joselyn a way off this mountain prison. She'd spoken with all of them. Every last one. It was official. No Dokiri would be escorting her home.

So here she was, a barely willing participant in yet another knife fighting lesson from a half-naked savage. They were rarely alone. Often the eyes of men, women, and children played distant audience to Hollen's lessons. Tansy would be appalled, her father disgusted.

They aren't here. Don't think about them now.

How could she not think of them? Time was running out. In just three more days she was due to have arrived in Brance. In just three more days she would be missed. And she was no closer to escaping than she'd been the day she'd arrived.

Joselyn's shoulders rose and fell. A light sheen of sweat had collected over her brow and now drops rolled down the side of her face. Her captor stood a few feet away. His massive hands opened wide as he leaned forward, posturing to attack.

Joselyn gripped the knife hilt in her hand. Her breath rose in front of her face as she panted in the late afternoon air. At least she wasn't cold. An hour's worth of sparring with Hollen had cured her of that. Hollen smirked. His breath mocked hers with its slow and even pace.

"Don't run away this time, *mu hamma*."

Joselyn's blue eyes narrowed. They'd been over this before. "I didn't run away last time."

"Don't pull away. Lean into your knife hand."

Joselyn wanted to growl. They'd been running this drill over and over. Every time Hollen rushed her, she would strike out as she'd been instructed, but her instincts would force her body to lean away and he'd disarm her. Joselyn's palm was growing a callus from where the hilt had been so frequently ripped away.

"Widen your stance," Hollen said.

Joselyn huffed and ground her boot into the dirt. She held the blade level with her chest and waited.

Hollen lunged. Joselyn blinked. She struck at his stomach even as she tilted back. This time, instead of tearing the knife away, Hollen batted her arm upward and let the momentum carry her back. Her arms swung, trying to right herself. Too late.

Hollen went with her. Joselyn squeaked as he caught her around the waist and broke the last few inches of her fall. Her breath came out in a huff as she landed in the dirt. The sparring knife dropped from her hand.

Hollen hovered over her. Though he supported his own weight, Joselyn could feel the length of his body pressed against hers. His massive arm was still laced under her back, forcing her body to arch into his. Joselyn stared up into his dark eyes.

Her lips parted and her breath caught. He was so close. Every muscle tightened as he leaned his head down toward hers, until the end of his nose practically brushed her own. She should push him off, kick him, scramble. She lay still. A shiver worked its way down her spine.

Hollen's lips parted. His voice came out in a low murmur. "Stop leaning back."

Joselyn could smell the sweetness of his breath. She blinked. What had he just said?

All at once, he was off her, drawing her up by the arm. She took a hurried step away, heaving a shaky breath. What was that? Every nerve in her body was alight.

Quick! Find something to do.

She swallowed and cast her gaze around for the knife. Hollen found it first. He held the wooden hilt out in his hand. Joselyn reached to snatch it from him, but he pulled back. She finally looked up. Her cheeks stung with warmth.

"Enough for today. You should get cleaned up."

"For what?" Joselyn tugged on the ends of her braid, vaguely aware of distant sets of eyes upon them as they spoke. She prayed they'd be back to minding their own business soon.

"There's to be a feast tonight in your honor."

Joselyn's brows knitted together. "Why?"

"This will be your third night since being introduced to the clan. And you are *Saliga*. I expect it will be an especially wild night."

Joselyn's mind spun to imagine what a man like Hollen considered 'wild.' "What do you mean by that?"

He smiled. "You'll see."

THE COMMON AREA, typically lit in the soft glow of a half-dozen fires, was now illuminated by an enormous pyre in the center of the open cave. Joselyn's face burned from the heat. She took her seat a good distance away upon one of the many stone benches rearranged around the bonfire, making it the new focal point of the enormous space.

Joselyn threw her damp braid over her shoulder as she sat, glad to have washed the day's grime away in the hot springs. She watched as Dokiri men, women, and children filed their way into the common area from their *boks* or from outside the cave's sheltering roof. The amber glow of a hundred torches filled in the periphery of the cave, making the faces of the clansmen as easy to see at night as they would be in the day. Joselyn nodded to the many who greeted her, though she didn't return the feminine gesture they used.

Where was Hollen? In the time since she'd arrived, Joselyn hadn't been left alone for more than a brief moment, a fact that made planning her escape inconvenient, to say the least. Though he was a busy man, Hollen was relentless in his attentions.

His hours were filled with introducing her to clan members, offering her a variety of new foods, explaining the rules to various games the Dokiri children played, and guiding her on tours of the village's complex tunnel system. When Hollen's duties drew him away, he always made sure to assign her a "companion" who'd pick up wherever he'd left off in teaching her about Bedmeg and its people.

More like a guard.

Joselyn sighed and leaned on one propped hand. If she was going to escape, she'd need provisions, weapons, and privacy. None of these was forthcoming. She was going to have to be crafty.

"*M-mu Saliga.*"

Joselyn looked up to see Lavinia and another woman named Rosemary. They greeted her in the Dokiri fashion. Joselyn smiled.

"Ladies. Please, come sit with me."

Rosemary, who was as boisterous as she was beautiful, plopped down to Joselyn's right, leaving enough room for

Lavinia to sit between them. Rosemary was a Morhageese peasant woman from a province south of Fury's lands of Tirvine. When Joselyn met her, she'd been hopeful that a woman like her, one who understood what a man like Marcus Fury could offer, would be willing to provide some form of assistance. She couldn't have been more wrong, and Rosemary was quick to let her know it.

"Maybe a fancy lady like you don't see it this way," she'd said, her hands planted on her hips, "but the world down there don't hold anything for a woman like me. If it did, I'd be long gone by now."

The brunette woman held herself with a sort of defensive pride, as though she were afraid Joselyn might be tempted to look down upon her. Joselyn had put a soft hand on the other woman, who'd raised her chin stiffly.

"I'm glad you've found your home in this place. It's just that Bedmeg isn't mine. Please, if you know a way that a woman might leave this place, share it with me."

Rosemary's brow had wrinkled and she was silent a moment. "I imagine a lady like you could barely get along without servants and the like. But give it time. You might surprise the both of us."

Her response had been as helpful than any other Joselyn had received from the Dokiri women. Apparently no one in the damned place was capable of pity. Still, it would do no good to make enemies. As Lavinia settled on the bench, Joselyn did her best to engage them both in companionable conversation.

"Tell me, what does a Dokiri feast consist of?"

"Dancing of course!" Rosemary said, "And drinking."

Lavinia nodded, smiling. "Yes, *mu Saliga*. The . . .men will take up the call to begin the dance. Afterward there will be a s-sacrifice and then the women will take their t-turn."

"Gotta take turns to start with, or we'll all end up back in our *boks* before the moon rises." Rosemary laughed. She gripped the bench and leaned a little too far across Lavinia's lap to speak. Clearly she'd begun the night's drinking a bit early. She wasn't the only one.

All around people were filling their horns with wine malted from fungus. Hollen said the mushroom also produced the purple dye that adorned many of the wool dresses the Dokiri women wore. She'd yet to taste it herself—she doubted it could be all that appetizing. Still, the women seemed to think so. Many an ivory bangle was already stained purple from the enthusiastic sloshing of overfilled horns.

The children were in just as high of spirits as their parents. As though unable to contain their excitement for the night ahead, most were busy either engaging in, or spectating wrestling matches. Several fathers sat at a distance, appearing to gamble upon one boy or the other, their heads nodding appreciatively at the victor of each round. Soren was among them. He stood with his arms crossed, eyes fixed upon Volo as he grappled with a slightly larger boy. Another man stood with him, one Joselyn hadn't seen before. She would have remembered. The jagged scar stretching across his cheek would be impossible to forget.

At the edge of the cave Joselyn watched as several men, including Magnus, carried in what appeared to be drums. Two were wider across than Magnus was tall. With help, he arranged their surfaces to face each other and then stood between them. He took up two bone stick batons as thick as Joselyn's arms and struck the hide stretched across one of the deep barrels. The cavern echoed with the thundering noise.

A thrill of excitement rose among the people as all eyes shot to the natural platform where more drummers took up their positions. They, too, struck their drums once. The men were all shirtless, as though they anticipated some great labor ahead.

They stood with their bare feet spread wide in an unbreakable stance.

Joselyn jumped when she heard a masculine voice scream into the night. It was a long, drawn-out cry that rose in pitch before plummeting at the end. All around her, the Dokiri cheered. Many thrust open palms upward as they shouted, "*Mu Salig!*"

Joselyn looked up. Hollen stood near the drummers on a raised piece of ground several feet above the general crowd. He, too, was shirtless and barefoot. Again he screamed, and this time a string of Dokiri words poured out of his mouth as he did. Beside her, Lavinia and Rosemary joined in the answering call. Magnus and his fellow drummers began striking their instruments in a steady rhythm. Slow at first, then gaining momentum.

"What's happening?" Joselyn asked, shouting to be heard by her bench mates over the rising din.

Lavinia leaned close. "*Atu hatu* is m-making the call for his warriors to b-begin the dance."

Sure enough, the men gathered at the center of the cave around the great fire. Those whose chests were not already bare, stripped their garments before joining in. Each warrior's *idadi* was on full display, dozens of intricate scar patterns glowing in the flamelight.

Hollen called out again. His deep voice somehow managed to climb over the clashing drums. The Dokiri men cried out their answer and, in unison, they began a dance like nothing Joselyn had ever seen. Like the drummers, the men took wide stances as they beat their fists against their chests near their shoulders. Together they squatted toward the earth, hissing as they did.

Joselyn shook as a great lowing noise bellowed throughout the cave. She could feel the vibration through her boots. The noise was so foreboding that for a moment, it seemed like the booming voice of some vengeful god. Lavinia took hold of her arm and pointed to a place high up, near the roof of the cave. There stood a Dokiri man blowing into an impossibly large horn that coiled along the roof of the cave and opened at the center just above the firepit.

The dancing men reclaimed her attention as they called out to Hollen in their guttural language. He answered them in turn, beating his fists upon his chest. He was pointedly avoiding his *tanshi* mark. Joselyn brought her hand up to finger the area above her own healing mark.

The women and children cheered from the sidelines, frantic with enthusiasm as the men leapt into the air, then landed on their knees upon the packed dust below them. They pounded their fists into the ground as they shouted, their voices rising in time with the drumming that was now so loud, Joselyn felt it in her chest.

"What are they saying?" Joselyn shouted into Lavinia's ear, hoping the other woman could hear.

Lavinia leaned in. "*M-mu Salig* . . .calls to the Dokiri. He a-asks, 'Sons of R-Regna, who among you would ride by . . .my side even unto the throat of the . . .e-earth?'"

Lavinia strained with the effort it took to translate. Joselyn could tell from the frantic sweeping of her gaze that she was falling behind. Beside Lavinia, Rosemary stood from the bench and took a spot on Joselyn's other side. She grabbed Joselyn around the arm and tugged her away from Lavinia so that *she* could speak in her ear.

"His warriors answer, 'To the throat of the earth and into its bowels I would follow my *Salig*.'"

Joselyn glanced at Lavinia. The Ebronian sat, back straight, and stared into the crowd with a tight expression. Had her feelings been hurt? Maybe she was relieved? Joselyn leaned back toward Rosemary and strained to hear as the dance and its accompanying doxology continued.

"*Mu Salig* replies, 'And as the mountain purges its darkness into the world, how will you stem the tide?' His warriors say, 'My wings I pledge. My axe I pledge. My bow I pledge. My fists I pledge.' "

Again the horn above them bellowed. Upon the stone dais, Joselyn watched as the drummers slowed their pace a moment, only to resume with heightened ferocity once the horn's last echoes had faded. The musicians did more than simply play. They danced along with the rest of the Dokiri in a style all their own, banging their heads with each mighty stroke of their powerful arms. Magnus's long hair whipped in every direction as he alternated between the massive drums on either side of him. Joselyn wondered at the energy required to keep up such a display.

" 'Would you wash the earth clean with your own blood, even unto death?' " Rosemary continued, translating first for Hollen and then for his men, " 'My own blood I would let flow, even until my body runs dry.' "

" 'Be there anything you would withhold from your mother, Helig?' " Joselyn almost missed the last bit. She pressed her ear against Rosemary's mouth to hear, " 'The blood of my sons will stain the mountain red before the mother be defiled.' "

Joselyn's eyes widened and she yanked away from Rosemary, bumping into Lavinia. All around, the Dokiri boys shouted in eager acknowledgement of their fathers' pledges. Their fists pounded into the air. Even their mothers ululated their approval. Joselyn's mouth hung open as she watched the spectacle, which had taken an unimaginably morbid turn. And yet the riotous cries only grew in ferocity and fervor.

Joselyn missed the next several lines exchanged between her captor and his people. It wasn't until Rosemary wrapped her arm around Joselyn's shoulders to pull her in close that she resumed listening.

" 'And will you serve my *Saliga*, even as you serve me?' "

All at once, a hundred pairs of eyes fell upon her. The mass of Dokiri warriors turned to face her end of the cave. They jumped to their knees. Their shoulders pulsed heavily as they hovered half-bent over the ground. " 'My life is my *Saliga*'s, even as I am pledged to my *Salig*.' "

Joselyn went straight and still as a statue, bringing Rosemary up a few inches as well. She held her breath, shocked to be the subject of the savage display. Mercifully, Hollen was making the next call within seconds. With that, his warriors were back to facing their *Salig*. Joselyn let out the air she'd been holding.

The dance went on for several more minutes. Despite her never-ending shock at these people's obsession with blood, Joselyn listened to Rosemary's translations until at last, the drummers sounded a final, thundering beat. The clan cried their appreciation for the musicians, dancers, and their *Salig*.

The echoing din subsided, and the warriors who had brides returned to them for horns of water and wine. Those who'd yet to claim a woman retrieved their own refreshment. Beside her, Lavinia and Rosemary stood as their husbands approached. Their *idadi* scars shone brightly beneath reflective layers of perspiration. They grinned at their wives, who tilted wine past the men's parted lips.

After three days, her shock at such displays of intimacy was beginning to wane. They were constant in Bedmeg, so unlike her life at Fury Keep. Joselyn was certain she'd never seen her own parents touch, let alone kiss or pet. Warmth gathered in her belly. What would it feel like?

She forced her gaze away. It fell instead upon the blade that Lavinia wore at her hip. Up close, Joselyn noticed the elaborate level of detail carved into its ivory hilt. She squinted, trying to make out the tiny images. The men moved back toward the fire and the women took their seats.

"It's a beautiful blade." Joselyn gestured to her new friend's *gneri* blade. "May I see it?"

Lavinia smiled and pulled the dagger from its leather sheath. She folded the edge into her arm and handed Joselyn the hilt. A fine image of an openmouthed *gegatu* graced one side of the hilt, with its expansive wings and winding tail covering the reverse. Joselyn brushed a fingertip over the tiny ridges. She'd have known by touch alone what the image was.

"Exquisite." Joselyn gave an appreciative nod.

"Soren is a very s-skilled carver. He could put the artisans of the G-Golden Court to sh-shame."

Rosemary leaned hard against Joselyn's side. "My Ragnar couldn't carve a straight line to save his own life. I haven't let him add to his *idadi* in years. That'd be my job now, it is."

Joselyn edged away as Rosemary drew out the blade she wore at her own hip. "Anyway, guess I'm stuck with this ugly thing now. Pity he didn't have your Soren work the handle for him."

Rosemary held the knife out toward Lavinia as if to show her. It veered, of course, nearly slicing Joselyn's arm. Lavinia snapped up Rosemary's wrist. "P-put that away before you take...someone's nose off!"

"Well, well, the stuttering stark be quicker than a slithering snake!"

Joselyn tensed. Stark were a type of white bird whose call indeed sounded like a shrill stutter. Would Lavinia be offended? Both women laughed. An easy smile shone on Lavinia's round face. Perhaps not.

Joselyn thought of the *gneri* blade she'd spent the past three nights sleeping with. Earlier that morning, she had asked Hollen if the celestial scenes etched into the surface were of his own design. He'd smiled, pleased by her interest, and confirmed her suspicion before putting the blade away, just as he had every morning before leaving the *bok*. He hadn't yet forced her to make use of the weapon.

Why would a barbarian, who considered himself wed, not take his pleasure inside her body? Surely he thought he had every right to do so. Perhaps there was some rule of his backward culture that prevented him? Perhaps every Dokiri warrior presented his bride with a weapon for that very reason. It seemed far-fetched, but then so did everything else about this place.

Joselyn scanned the open cave. Her eyes fell upon the belted *gneri* blades of each Dokiri *hamma*. From the corner of her eye, she stared at the drinking women next to her. How to broach this subject?

"Perhaps Hollen received instruction from your husband, Lavinia. The blade he gave me is quite lovely, as well."

Rosemary choked on her wine, spitting half the drink back into her horn. Lavinia turned to her and patted the brunette woman's back. Still coughing, Rosemary locked her watering eyes onto Joselyn, her expression incredulous.

"He gave you a *gneri* blade?" She reached across Lavinia's lap to bat at the knife Joselyn held. "One of these?"

Joselyn nodded. What was so upsetting about that?

"T-time for some water . . .Rosemary. Tomorrow you'll complain if you're too d-drunk for dancing." Lavinia stood the woman up and ushered her toward the water trough. Rosemary grunted, but obeyed.

"I thought it was the Dokiri way to give their brides a *gneri* blade," Joselyn said as Lavinia retook her seat.

"Yes, *mu Saliga*. That is c-correct." Lavinia appeared unsettled. Her eyes fell on her blade and Joselyn quickly returned the fine item.

What did I say?

A sick feeling crawled into her belly as she considered the possibility that their husbands had not been so quick to supply their brides with a means to defend themselves. Perhaps Soren and Ragnar had not been so willing as Hollen to take a chaste vow for the benefit of their brides.

"You . . . didn't receive your blade for some time after arriving?" Joselyn asked, her voice low and careful.

Lavinia's eyes didn't meet Joselyn's. She shook her head as she resheathed the knife. "No."

Joselyn's skin went cold as she imagined sweet Lavinia being dragged into Soren's *bok* night after night until she'd come to accept her fate. The thought didn't seem natural when compared with the many moments she'd seen the two embracing, as though they couldn't have dreamed of a better life for themselves. But then, after nine years of captivity, who could say what a woman would begin to believe of the man who held her? Who could say what she would begin to believe of herself?

Joselyn put a hand over Lavinia's, which rested on the bench between them. The Ebronian woman shot Joselyn a dubious look just as the beat of the drums resumed their swell. The cheering drew Joselyn's attention back toward the fire. Hollen was now dancing along with his warriors. Joselyn sucked in a breath.

He was a spectacular dancer. His body moved with as much grace as it did ferocity. He would leap high into the air, only to land so smoothly upon his knees that the following rise looked like one fluid motion. As the other dancers, he held his open palms high near either side of his face, shouting as he pumped them forward and back, his head rocking in time. Joselyn had been amazed before. Now she was transfixed.

No one moved quite like him, and she wasn't the only one who noticed. At some point, the other warriors stepped away from their *Salig*, eager to give him space to display the full extent of his skill. The area they'd opened was conspicuously in front of where she and Lavinia sat.

Hollen caught her eyes near the end, and it was all she could do not to shuffle her gaze away like a guilty voyeur. He grinned, every bit aware of his appeal.

Smile back.

Joselyn stiffened. Her eyes narrowed as the absurd notion entered her mind. No. She would not encourage him. She was a decent lady. And decent ladies didn't smile at half-naked men. No matter how appealing.

When the drums finally died back down, the dancers didn't immediately break off for water like they had before. Most of those who'd been sitting now stood up. Their faces turned in the direction of the cave's open side. Joselyn straightened as Hollen approached.

"It's time for the feast, *mu hamma*," Hollen said. He stopped just in front of her knees and held a hand down to her. "You must make the sacrifice."

"Sacrifice?" Joselyn looked at Lavinia.

"Yes, *mu Saliga*. The honor is y-yours tonight." Lavinia rose and walked toward Soren, who stood waiting in the crowd with an outstretched arm. They, like everyone else, began filing out of the cave into the moonlit snow, torches in hand.

Joselyn stood, ignoring Hollen's offered arm. "You didn't mention a sacrifice. What does that even mean?"

Hollen grinned. He snatched her by the hand and tugged her behind him. "It means you'll slaughter the ram we feast upon."

Joselyn swallowed and jogged to keep up with Hollen. She shivered as they exited the warmth of the cave and stepped into a layer of freshly fallen snow. The waxing moon above provided a great deal of light, as did the stars that numbered in the millions. Again, she was struck with wonder that her captor, like all his warriors, didn't seem bothered by the cold. Hollen cut a path for them through the crowd. The clan gathered beneath a stone ledge, possibly ten feet above the sloping ground. The torches glowed, illuminating the area all around in flickering gold.

Joselyn heard lowing before she saw the giant beast being led up to the natural platform. She would have faltered were it not for Hollen's enthusiastic guidance. The animal was like nothing Joselyn had ever seen. It was the size of a bull, though it had the narrow face and bulging eyes of a mountain goat. Its long white hair hung off its body in thick, wooly locks.

Erik and Magnus walked on either side of the creature with their arms looped in the curve of its winding horns. Magnus seemed to feed off the excited energy of the crowd. He led a song in his father tongue that those around him took up. Erik stroked at the beast's powerful neck, murmuring something into its twitching ear.

"Hollen, I—" Her voice was drowned out as the rest of Bedmeg joined in the jubilant song. The two of them hurried up the ledge, coming up behind Hollen's brothers and the creature that was about to feed an entire clan. Joselyn was pulled forward to stand in front of her captor, with her feet but a few inches from the platform's snowy edge. The faces of those below her were difficult to see behind the glow of their torches.

Hollen laced his left hand in hers and, if only to be certain she wouldn't stumble off the edge, she returned the squeeze of his fingers.

"People of Bedmeg!" Hollen began, raising his right arm into the night air. "Tonight we put aside old sorrows and celebrate a new beginning!"

The people cheered as he continued, "We welcome into our clan Joselyn Helena Elise Fury."

Another cry of approval.

Joselyn was beginning to regret telling him her full name. The fact that he'd remembered it in its entirety after only hearing it once was impressive, though she wished he'd stop announcing it at every opportunity. Something about it seemed so official. So dignified. As though her presence here were every bit as legitimate as her marriage to Dante Viridian would have been.

"Tonight Bedmeg will want for nothing. Tonight we are whole. We have our *Saliga*!" Hollen thrust her hand up with his as those below shouted their pride.

"*Mu Saliga!*"

Joselyn stood tall. If there was one thing she was accustomed to, it was public scrutiny. She'd been the subject of both social and political attention since before she could remember. She inclined her chin. If these people would not help Joselyn of House Fury, perhaps they would acquiesce to Joselyn of Bedmeg.

Hollen released her hand, and she turned to see Magnus passing him a long, curved blade. Joselyn's gaze fell upon the giant ram. Puffs of smoke poured from its nostrils. Its ears moved back and forth at the commotion all around it. A pang of sympathy welled up inside Joselyn, quickly replaced by a stab of adrenaline as Hollen put the blade in her hand.

Hollen guided her to stand before him at the creature's shoulder. He took Magnus's place at the horn and held the creature's massive head steady.

"First push into his neck, *mu hamma*. Then pull back quickly."

Joselyn stood there. She looked at the blade in her hand as she made up her mind. She'd never killed an animal before. She'd never killed anything at all. She glanced at the gathered crowd. What sort of message would she be sending if she shrank from what these people considered to be an honor?

You wanted to hunt someday. This is no different. At least you're not chasing the poor thing first. Master yourself, Joselyn.

She brought the blade up, aligning it with the creature's wooly neck. She would have to put a great deal of force behind the stroke. Thankfully, the handle was long, which allowed her to use a second fist to steady the trembling edge. Perhaps sensing her fear, the ram nickered and reared its horned head. Joselyn jumped.

Hollen and Erik firmed their grip to hold him still. "Hurry Joselyn. Don't prolong his fate."

Swallowing hard, Joselyn realigned the razor edge. Drawing a breath, she pushed out any thoughts of sympathy for the doomed animal and sank her weight into the bulk of its tensing muscle.

The creature howled. Instinct made her jerk the knife away. A fan of blood sprayed as she drew it backward. Warm iron mist filled Joselyn's nares as the beast buckled first to its front knees and then to its rear. The animal's weight tore the knife from her hand as it fell to the snow. All around, the people cheered.

Joselyn brought a bloody hand up to her lips. Her stomach turned over.

Run. Hide.

She darted back, but barely made it to the creature's rump. Joselyn had indulged in not a drop of wine that night. And yet, somehow, she was the first to retch.

12

A WILD NIGHT

Hollen grimaced as his bride heaved the contents of her stomach into the snow behind the fallen ram's body. He released the fallen animal's horn. The clamor of the crowd remained deafening. Most weren't able to see why their *Saliga* had bolted.

"Joselyn?" Hollen put a hand on her back. She stiffened and pulled away from his touch. Still hunching over, she glanced backward at the cheering crowd. Hollen followed her gaze.

She's afraid they saw her sicking herself. Help her.

Hollen pulled her up by the shoulders and shuffled her off the back of the ledge, away from the clan. He nodded over his shoulder to Magnus. His brother nodded back and, picking up the fallen blade, began butchering the ram. The people cried their anticipation for the feast to come.

His bride held the back of her hand over her mouth, as though trying to avoid another bout of nausea. Her dress was covered in blood, as was her mouth from touching her face. She would want to change. Fast. At least her dress was already dyed red.

"Come." He ushered Joselyn up the sloping ravine until they

were back in the warmth of the empty cave. The quiet set his ears to ringing after the past hour of celebration.

"They saw," Joselyn said, her jaw tight. She wasn't looking at him. Instead her gaze was fixed on the ground to her side. She was still panting. From fatigue or unease?

He stopped them by a bench at the back of the cave. "Only a few saw. And it's nothing out of the ordinary."

She still wouldn't look at him. Guilt squeezed in his chest. He should have better prepared her. He was an idiot. He dropped his head low, putting himself in her line of vision. "Some Dokiri *hammas* are sick for weeks after arriving on the mountain. If they ask what is the matter, that's what we'll tell them."

Joselyn raised a brow at him. A blood-soaked strand of hair dangled in front of her freckled cheeks, and Hollen felt a sudden urge to brush it behind her ear. He clenched his fists, forcing himself to resist.

Don't. You'll remind her she's covered in blood.

His bride was a woman who cared about appearances, especially, he'd noticed, in front of the clan. And why not? She was *Saliga*. Proud. It was her prerogative, her duty to present herself well. It reflected on all of Bedmeg. It'd been years, and Hollen still hadn't grown comfortable with that constant scrutiny of leadership. His bride was a step ahead of him in that regard.

"You did so well, *mu hamma*. You didn't shrink away and your stroke was clean. Did you hear how the crowd praised you?"

Joselyn broke her gaze. She went to wipe the blood from her mouth, but scowled at the crimson soiling the white sleeve of her under-shift.

"Wait here," he said.

He left her in the common area and sprinted up the winding pathway that led to their *bok*. Hollen returned with her comb and a set of clean clothes folded in his arms. Joselyn's brow rose in surprise.

"Come." He led her deeper into the cave. She followed, breaking off in the direction of the women's springs.

"No, this way." He jerked his head in the direction of a different tunnel.

Joselyn's lips parted. She looked from the women's springs to the unknown path. "Where does that lead?"

"Come with me and find out." Hollen grabbed a torch to light his way.

Behind him, Joselyn muttered under her breath, "Come here. Come there. Come do this. Come do that."

Hollen couldn't resist. "I could just tell you to come, and leave it at that if you prefer."

"You don't need to command me for every little thing, you know. I can be accommodating all on my own."

I'll bet you can.

He coughed to cover his laugh. "I'll take your word for it."

For now.

Her soft footfalls followed. He smiled to himself, glad that, for once, she hadn't argued with him. They walked in silence as Hollen thought of his bride's extreme reaction to slaughtering the ram. Everything, from the grace of her gait to her inability to start a fire, indicated she was gently bred. Still, a sacrifice shouldn't have shaken her so. He glanced over his shoulder.

"I thought you said you liked to hunt." His voice echoed down the smooth stone walls as they went.

"I conceded that I have some skill with a bow." Joselyn's tone was defensive.

"You're a woman. What use is a bow to you if not for hunting?"

"Sport."

"Sport?" Hollen tested the unfamiliar word. He stopped, turning to give her his full attention. "What is sport?"

Joselyn stared at him with disbelief in her eyes. "When you do something for fun, just to prove that you can."

Hollen's gaze strayed to the wall of the tunnel. Lowlanders were a strange lot.

She spoke slowly, as though she'd never had to explain such a thing. "Like . . .how your boys wrestle each other, despite having no quarrel?"

Understanding struck. He turned and continued down the tunnel. "Our boys will be warriors one day. What you call sport we would call training. What's the point of learning the bow if you never intend to use it for anything useful?"

An indignant edge laced her words. "I *had* intended to go hunting at some point."

"So why didn't you?" Hollen jumped down a ledge. Though his hands were full, he held a steadying elbow out to her. His skin tingled where she touched him, as it did any time his bride touched him, for any reason.

Joselyn was silent another moment as they advanced. "I had more important things to concern myself with."

"Maybe I shouldn't take you hunting then?" Hollen turned backward and arched a brow at Joselyn. "Who knows? A few more years of begging, and maybe one of my riders will finally agree to steal you home."

Not bloody likely.

Her eyes sparked, and Hollen had the sense that half a dozen scathing remarks were hanging off the edge of her tongue.

Always ready to do battle. It's too bad for you I have things you want.

He intended to give her every one of them. Even those she didn't realize she wanted. Yet.

In the end, her gaze dropped to the ground. Her voice came out in a mutter. "I would like to go hunting."

Hollen grinned. He hadn't misread her. Her face had brightened when he'd made the offer three days ago. It was the first thing she'd seemed genuinely pleased about since he claimed her. Still, her comment about having better things to do gave him pause. Something about the subject had made his bride uncomfortable. Better to discuss it later, when she wasn't covered in the stench of her own bile.

"If you're well tomorrow, I'll take you with me to hunt." His voice lowered. "Forgive me, *mu hamma*."

She frowned. "For what?"

"If I had known before, I wouldn't have pressed you to make the sacrifice." Hollen's stomach hardened as he remembered her expression after vomiting.

Joselyn's face softened. She clasped her hands in front of herself, looking downward. Hollen looked down too, waiting for a response.

Finally, Joselyn gave him a single nod. Relief swept through him. They continued down the stone path.

After a while, the sound of rushing water reached them. The ground beneath them grew slick with moisture. They passed several natural openings to one side or the other of the tunnel they were traveling through. Hollen glanced back. Joselyn was peeking into the open spaces. Her eyes squinted in the darkness.

"They are springs. Some of them are hot. Others are cool. But they are much smaller than the ones you've been to."

"What's that noise?" Joselyn asked.

"The water pours from the ceiling in some of the alcoves."

"Why did you bring me here?"

"I thought you would like to be alone. And there are enough private pools for you to bathe in peace."

He stopped them in front of one of the openings. The sound

of splashing echoed from within. Though small, it was one of the warmer pools, and it contained a stream of falling water that he imagined would make it easier to wash the blood from her hair. Hollen began hanging the fresh clothing on hooks at the entrance which had been hammered into the stone. He turned. Joselyn was watching him. She shifted uncomfortably from one foot to the other.

"Go inside. I will wait here."

Her lips pressed into a thin line. "I'm sure I can make it back on my own."

"Yes." Hollen said. "But I'll stay all the same. I want to make sure no one else comes down here."

"Who else bathes in this place?" She looked back in the direction they had come.

"Couples, mostly."

Joselyn's head snapped toward him at that. He'd spoken truthfully. While the larger springs were segregated between the sexes, these springs were most typically used by those seeking a private interlude.

"Wha-what if someone thinks we're down here having . . .that we're . . ."

"Yes?" He just stifled the urge to grin.

She glared at him, her cheeks going red. "Nevermind."

The temptation to keep teasing her was overwhelming. Hollen resisted. Barely. He'd learned by now that Joselyn was profoundly modest. She'd still been insisting that he leave their *bok* entirely so that she might change into a sleeping gown. Hollen might have argued except she'd already proven that if he refused, she would simply sleep in her long-sleeved under-shift as she had her first night.

Even now, coming down here with her, he was pressing against the boundaries of his bride's comfort. Yet the need to prove himself demanded he give her this opportunity to trust him. Joselyn opened her mouth to speak. Hollen beat her to it.

"I don't think anyone else will be here for several more hours. Take your time. We'll rejoin the clan when you're ready." With that, Hollen pressed his back against the tunnel wall, facing away from the private alcove. Torch still in hand, he crossed his arms over his chest and made himself comfortable.

In the corner of his eye, Joselyn's lips parted. After a few seconds, she clamped them shut and peered into the darkened space. Hollen brushed at a bit of dirt on his arm.

Joselyn turned back to face him. *Here comes the argument.*

"Thank you."

His stomach fluttered. Keeping his eyes fixed on the tunnel wall ahead of him, he gave a curt nod as she stepped into the alcove. When she was out of sight, he allowed himself to smile.

When they re-entered the common area, the air hung heavy with the heady scent of roasted mutton. Joselyn touched a hand to her belly, willing herself not to think of the gruesome spectacle she'd participated in. Could she have imagined a more disastrous outcome than emptying the contents of her stomach in front of the same people she was trying to inspire respect from? Hollen claimed only a few had witnessed her shame. As they rejoined the throng of celebrating clansmen, she prayed he'd spoken truly.

There was no music in the cave, but it buzzed with excitement as hungry Dokiri men and women picked the roasted carcass of the slaughtered ram clean. Hollen directed Joselyn to sit where she'd been before and then left to retrieve a portion of the feast for them.

Joselyn sat tall and scanned the faces around her, searching for signs of pity or contempt. Her gaze fell upon Lavinia and Rosemary across the cave, who grinned and raised their hands in greeting. She returned the gesture with a relieved smile.

Joselyn sighed as she smoothed a hand down the length of her damp braid. She'd surprised herself by taking her time bathing. When she'd exited the alcove, the heat of the water had flushed her skin into a pink glow, and her captor stood exactly where she had left him, his eyes closed in peaceful meditation. Irritation gnawed even as a wave of gratitude welled in her chest, a chest still healing from the savage's handiwork.

Hollen returned, food in hand, with a stranger walking alongside him. It was the scarred man she'd seen with Soren. The right corner of his mouth stretched into a gruesome hash that trailed through his dark beard and up the side of his face, disappearing into his hairline. Despite the man's apparent youth, the injury was old.

What could have happened to a child to cause such a horrifying disfigurement?

Hollen took his seat next to her and nodded up to the new man. "Joselyn, this is Ivan the Bold, our middle brother."

He looked almost exactly like Hollen. He featured the same deep-brown eyes and serious expression. His dark hair was even clasped into a high bun just as Hollen seemed to prefer. His gaze upon her was direct and, on instinct, Joselyn leaned ever so slightly into Hollen's side. She licked her lips.

"So it's Hollen, Erik, you, Magnus, and then Sigvard?"

"Only by birth, *mu Saliga*," Ivan said as he held out a horn of wine to Joselyn. She took it, working hard not to stare at the freakish pull of his scar as he spoke.

"By significance the order goes Hollen, Erik, Magnus, me, and then Sigvard . . .because that little *podagi* outranks no one." He winked at her.

Joselyn's mouth quirked. So he had a sense of humor. But then, had she also detected a hint of bitterness?

"How are you adjusting to your life in Bedmeg, *mu Saliga*?"

"Well enough for a temporary stay."

"Oh? *How* temporary?" Ivan's eyes sparked with interest.

"As temporary as possible."

There was a moment of silence as Hollen and Ivan exchanged looks.

"Well, I'm sure you'll figure something out, though it might take you a while." He leaned back on his heels and scanned the ceiling above. "I'd give it a year tops."

Beside her, Hollen cleared his throat, eyeing his brother. Ivan returned his gaze with a tight smile. She'd been right. There was definitely *something* going on between the two men.

Ivan turned back to Joselyn. "I hope, for your sake, either time or your unhappiness passes quickly."

Joselyn nodded, and the scarred man walked away. Hollen took her gently by the arm.

"You'll not discuss leaving with Ivan again."

A flash of temper and hope danced in her belly. "Why? Because he might be the only man in this place to take me seriously?"

Hollen's face went hard as stone. "No. I swear to Regna he'd be the *last* person to take you from me. But he won't hesitate to make things harder on us."

"You mean," she took a guess, "on you?"

A muscle in his jaw tightened.

I see.

Maybe Hollen was telling the truth. Maybe. He'd sworn on Regna, his sky father. Joselyn had sensed the antagonistic glint in Ivan's eyes, but was it strong enough to inspire betrayal? She would find out. For now, she changed the subject.

"How did he get that scar?"

The set of Hollen's shoulders eased. "A *gegatu*."

"He must have been young."

"Yes. Barely more than a child. He didn't respect the danger they presented. Let that be a warning to you where the *gegatu* are concerned."

Joselyn thought of Volo and Brodie's questions from a few days prior. "Must each of your men wait to marry until their older brothers have claimed a *hamma*?"

He shook his head. "Not strictly. But it would be an insult to do otherwise. Why do you ask?"

Yes, Joselyn. Why do you ask? Why do you care?

"Your brothers often remark on how long you waited to claim your bride."

Hollen grunted, chewing another bite. "Yes, some of them"—his eyes flicked across the fire to where Ivan stood with Soren—"are quite impatient to claim brides. They'll survive."

"How old are your warriors when they claim a *hamma*?"

"It depends. Most of our boys complete the *Gegatudok*, the 'wyvern mastering,' when they are sixteen to twenty years old. That's when they become men. Then they complete the *Veligneshi*, the 'slaughter,' whenever they get the opportunity."

Joselyn recalled what she had been told on her first morning in Bedmeg. "And that's when your warriors are named by their fathers?"

Hollen nodded and gave her a smile.

Beautiful.

Joselyn's breath caught as the intrusive thought crossed her mind. Her gaze fell into her cup as he answered.

"Yes. Once they're named they are recognized as true *Na Dokiri*. Then they may claim a bride, but many riders spend a year or more adding to their *idadi* before doing so."

Joselyn counted to ten in her head. "How old are you?"

Hollen didn't answer right away. The space in the conversation prompted Joselyn to look up, only to see Hollen focusing very hard on shredding his meat into narrow strips. Finally, "Twenty-six."

Joselyn's lips parted. That was a great deal older than the usual age of claiming. Hollen glanced at her from the corner of his eye.

"I'd already waited longer than most warriors when I was preparing to search for a *hamma*." Joselyn nibbled at her food, staring more at his shoulder than his eyes.

"But then my mother didn't wake up the morning I meant to leave."

Joselyn stopped chewing. He wasn't looking at her, but rather into the fire at the center of the room. She remembered what he'd said about his father falling ill the day his mother passed. That he'd slowly deteriorated over four long years.

"I knew the elders meant to name me as my father's successor." In his hand, Hollen's food was now a mess of stringy sinews. "It didn't seem right to bring the next *Saliga* to Bedmeg while the prior's mate slowly died for the absence of her."

"And so you waited." Joselyn masked her awe with the smoothness of her voice.

Hollen nodded. "And so I waited. As did my brothers."

Despite their mutual teasing and mockery, Hollen's brothers must possess a strong sense of respect for him, that they would all await their own right to claim a wife. From everything Joselyn had seen of the Dokiri people, their family units were the source of all joy and pleasure. Surely Hollen's brothers had been eager to establish their own households. And what of Hollen's own restraint? He'd denied himself not only for the sake of his father's grief, but also for his mother's memory. Joselyn's heart swelled. Loyalty was no insignificant trait. Despite herself, her opinion of Hollen rose.

"And now you have a bride who's vowed to escape you," she said.

Maybe he deserves happiness. Just not at House Fury's expense.

Hollen shrugged. "She'll come around."

"Do you regret waiting so long?"

He shook his head. "Everything happens for a reason. If I hadn't waited, I wouldn't have met you."

He'd said it like it would have been the gravest of misfortunes. As if claiming someone else would have been his sole regret. *Even now? After everything?* Joselyn's stomach fluttered. Where could she take the conversation after that? She fidgeted with her horn of wine. "Will you not have some?"

Hollen smiled softly. "No, thank you. I don't drink."

Joselyn eyed the contents of her horn, even more wary of the "mushroom wine." She took a tentative sip. She gasped.

"How can you not? This tastes divine." She licked her lips, savoring the sweet aftertaste of the fermented fungus.

"Yes. It does. But a *Salig* cannot afford to have his wits dulled."

Joselyn regarded him, incredulous, which only seemed to heighten his amusement.

"Not even on a feast night," he added, inclining his head toward the stone dais where Magnus and the other drummers were taking their positions.

Joselyn's mouth dropped as all around, the women began unthreading the ties of their overdresses and stripping down to their white under-shifts. Their faces shone with excitement as they scurried to surround the great fire where the men had been dancing. Joselyn scanned the perimeter of the cave. Now only the men and their wives' cast off clothing occupied the stone benches.

Joselyn's ears echoed with the rising pulse of the drums. The Dokiri *hammas* joined hands, their faces to the fire, and began skipping in time with the beat, changing directions in perfect unison so that they appeared as one living entity. Hair of every color and texture whipped back and forth as they danced, and the echo of their laughter rose above the din.

All at once, their hands broke apart to perform a pair of sharp claps as they turned out toward the men. Bangles clattered together, adding to the music. They smiled as they rejoined their neighbors and began the circle anew.

From the sidelines, their husbands watched with avid enthusiasm, toasting and calling their approval. Joselyn peered at Hollen from the corner of her eye. Was he affected by the sight of so much feminine flesh?

Apparently not.

Hollen was finishing the last of his food, sucking the meaty flavor from his thumbs as he always seemed to do. He turned to face her, and Joselyn jerked her horn to her lips.

"I'm thirsty. Do you want water?" He stood.

Joselyn shook her head and Hollen started in the direction of the water trough.

When the music changed, the women broke off from one another. A new instrument that Joselyn hadn't yet heard began playing in the background. She followed the sound to a trio of men sitting on the ground below the drum line. In their laps sat shallow wooden boxes with strings stretched tightly across the middle. Each man held a sort of bow in his hand, which he drew across the strings. The enchanting melody sent the women into passionate displays of rhythm.

Hollen was heading back with a new horn when Rosemary threw her hands upon Joselyn's arm. Joselyn jumped, nearly spilling her drink. The brunette pressed her smiling lips to Joselyn's ear.

"Come, *mu Saliga*." Her breath was sweet with wine. "Let's show them what we Morhageese women can do with a little music to move about to." Rosemary tugged at Joselyn's sleeve, half pulling her from the bench.

"No, Rosemary. I'm sorry, I cannot." Joselyn pulled against the other woman's shockingly firm grip. She broke free and plopped back into her seat.

Rosemary reached for the sides of Joselyn's overdress. Her drunken fingers fumbled with the laces. "Too damn hot for all this nonsense."

Joselyn gasped as her freckled hands shot to stop the other woman's. "Rosemary, please!"

The brunette laughed as though they were playing some coy game, barely managing to untie the leather cords hanging at Joselyn's hip. Purple liquid splashed onto the ground as Joselyn was forced to release her horn in favor of retaining her clothing.

"Bad luck, *mu Saliga*!" Rosemary laughed, still wrestling with her. "Not supposed to put a horn down before it's empty. That's Dokiri tradition, it is."

One you must observe with religious fervor.

Hollen stooped over Rosemary's shoulder. "I think *atu hatu* is searching for you, Rosemary."

Rosemary paused long enough for Joselyn to snatch the cords of her own dress away. From across the cave, Ragnar stood from the bench. His sharp gaze flitted away from Hollen and fell upon his wife. Rosemary turned, spotting her husband, who began crossing the distance.

"He's so impatient." Rosemary huffed, with a pleased glint in her eye.

Ragnar was there in seconds. He reached for his wife, catching her about the hips. "Come, *mu hamma*. Let us dance."

Rosemary swayed and planted a hand against his broad chest. "It's too early. Let me dance with *mu Saliga* first. You can wait like everyone else."

Ragnar tangled his hand in her brown waves and pulled

Rosemary close enough to whisper something in her ear. The woman grinned, revealing deep dimples in either cheek. She leaned her head away, pushing the side of her neck into his lips. Joselyn stared while still trying to catch her breath.

"She's too fancy for us anyway," Rosemary muttered while staring dreamily into her husband's eyes. He ushered her back into the throng of dancing women.

Even as she was grateful for the peace, Joselyn's chest stung at Rosemary's comment. She'd never had friends before. She had maids and attendants. But no friends. Her position in the hierarchy of court had put her too far out of reach for things like that. It had been a lonely way to grow up, devoid of connection. But maybe it hadn't been all bad. She'd also been immune from mean, dismissive comments. Ones that reminded her just how alone she was.

Hollen took his seat next to Joselyn, bending down to retrieve her wine horn from the ground. "I'll get you more."

"No." Joselyn smoothed the wrinkles from her dress. She inhaled, scraping her composure back into place. "Thank you."

Hollen watched her a moment, his lips pursed. Joselyn turned her attention back to the crowd, ignoring the concern etched on his face. Eventually, he too went back to watching the dancers.

One or two at a time, the men from the benches rose to join their brides around the fire until Ragnar and Rosemary were only one of dozens of entwined couples. Joselyn sat straight with her hands folded neatly in her lap as she watched the scene before her.

They were practically mating as they moved. The men pulsed and hovered over their brides, sometimes from before and sometimes from behind. The women were led by their own hips rocking in time with the mighty beating of the drums, their hands swaying along with the lilt of the stringed instruments.

Joselyn's gaze locked upon Lavinia, whose back was pressed firmly into Soren's bronze chest. A 'v' of her own golden-brown skin glistened with sweat beneath the precariously open front of her shift. Soren's chin hung low over her shoulder, and Lavinia pressed her parted mouth into his temple as she swung her hips beneath his petting hands.

Was this normal? She looked around. No one else seemed the slightest bit discomforted. Even the children casually occupied themselves with games or third and fourth helpings of ram meat. Her eyes returned to the couples locked in sensual revelry.

For the briefest of moments, an image of herself swaying wantonly in Hollen's embrace projected itself in her mind. A surge of nerves tingled down her chest and deep into the hollow of her belly. Her skin went warm, and she licked her lips, regretting her refusal of a drink.

A sense of nakedness washed over Joselyn. Hollen's eyes were upon her. She stiffened, her toes curling in her boots. Surely he didn't think she would ever participate in such a carnal display *with* him. That she even could.

Did he? What would that be like?

Her skin went even warmer. She had to get away.

"I'd like to walk." Joselyn's head whipped to face Hollen, whose gaze darted away from hers before returning.

"I'll go with you." He stood.

"No." She yanked him back down. Hollen looked at the place where she gripped him. His brow rose in amusement.

"No, thank you," she repeated, a bit softer. She rose from her seat and skittered away from the ring of benches.

She spent the next hour milling about with the children and unmarried men, observing her surroundings at a relative distance. She glanced from time to time at Hollen, who'd been joined by Erik and Sigvard. The corners of his eyes creased as he laughed with them in easy companionship.

Once in a while, some of the men would approach and ask him to join in a game of *vokmadi*, which, from what she could tell, was a sophisticated version of tug-of-war. Each time, he'd glance around, searching for her. Joselyn would take care to appear busy, and Hollen would go with the men. He'd won every game he played. Not that she was keeping track.

An hour went by, and one by one, couples broke off from the crowd to return with clasped hands to their *boks*. As Hollen had predicted, more than a few made their way down the tunnel leading to the private springs. The youngest Dokiri children also began disappearing as the night grew late.

The music dampened and Joselyn yawned. She was uncertain which had been more exhausting, her entire day or the past few hours of such a wild night. She pressed a palm to her forehead. Large hands covered her shoulders and Joselyn spun to see Hollen.

"Come, Joselyn. Let's go to bed."

Joselyn's heart skipped a beat. She knew what he meant, but those words, after watching men and women join all but their most intimate flesh, sent a wave of heat curling in her belly. She wondered if the wine was laced with an aphrodisiac. It would account for the clan's lascivious behavior and her body's own inexplicable reactions.

She nodded, allowing him to steady her as they traveled up the winding path that led to his *bok's* tunnel. Hollen didn't bother to build the fire. Instead he set the torch into the wall, stripped, and tumbled into the furs of his bed.

It was on the tip of Joselyn's tongue to demand he exit so she could change into her sleeping shift. But after their time in the springs? It seemed silly. She watched him a moment, noting his peaceful expression as he closed his eyes and propped an arm behind his head.

With her mind made up, Joselyn went to the chest and

pulled out the thin white gown. Hollen's heavy lashes never fluttered as she changed, and she was grateful to be falling into the bed *that* much sooner. Her hand slid beneath the pillow, ensuring that the *gneri* blade remained where Hollen had bid her leave it. She fingered the ridges of the celestial scene he'd carved into its hilt.

For the first time since being sequestered to this godsforsaken mountain, Joselyn slept with an empty hand.

13

HUNTRESS

The fir pine forest was awash with golden light that streamed between ancient branches, bowing beneath the weight of freshly fallen snow. With every step Joselyn took, the earthy aroma of their snapping needles wafted into her nose.

She and Hollen had risen early. They'd stepped around more than a few sleeping figures in the common area whose lips were stained purple with wine. Before departing, Hollen had gone to the forge, which doubled as an armory, and selected for Joselyn the shortest bow he could find. Her ears had burned hot when she realized the weapon was meant for children. Even so, her captor was forced to rewind the bowstring so that she'd be able to draw it back.

The flight down the mountain had been short, and Joselyn had kept an eye out for possible escape routes. The slope leading away from Bedmeg was actually quite flat. Perhaps descending to the forest could be possible after all. But how would she cover enough ground to make it to the tree line before being spotted from the sky? She'd have to come up with something. Soon.

Her awareness of the date was an ever-present storm cloud looming in her mind. In two days, Dante Viridian would see that she'd not arrived in Brance. Time was running out. At least she could use this hunting trip to learn how to feed herself in the wild. She followed behind her captor, creeping through the snow as he'd instructed.

They were tracking a large mountain bird Hollen had called a Cerulean Storen. When her captor stilled, she knew they'd caught up to their quarry. Hollen crouched down and bid Joselyn come up behind him. Joselyn peeked around the tree they hid behind.

In the distance, three storens strutted, pausing intermittently to scratch at the earth. Joselyn's eyes narrowed. Their proportions were ridiculous. Their heads were bulbous and much too heavy looking for their bald, skinny necks. They sat upon stilted, feathered legs that looked like they might buckle beneath their considerable girth. The feathers were gray and white, lending them natural camouflage. The largest bird sported a bright blue plume. He flashed it at no one in particular. Hollen pointed at the colorful bird. His eyes met hers in silent directive.

Joselyn nodded and removed her gloves. She swung the bow around, held it parallel with the earth, and notched an arrow. Hollen scooted further behind the tree, giving her plenty of space. Joselyn stretched the bowstring backward and lined up her shot, right in the center of the storen's chest. It was perhaps twenty yards away, close enough to make her feel confident. Relaxing her shoulders, Joselyn let the arrow fly.

It missed. Barely.

The wooden stake whistled just behind the male bird, taking a few of his feathers with it. All three fowl startled into a frenzied panic. Joselyn gritted her teeth and hurried to notch another arrow. The birds noticed her then, and they scampered deeper into the forest. Joselyn let the second arrow fly. It, too, missed by mere inches. She growled, bolting to her feet. A staying hand gripped her arm, and she turned to see Hollen's wry amusement.

"Don't give chase. They'll settle much closer if you follow at a distance."

Joselyn's arm tingled where he touched her. The sensation was fast becoming familiar. Her body had been abuzz beneath Hollen's weight during the flight down the mountain.

"You have excellent aim." He brushed past to lead her after the fowl. He swung his own unused bow over his shoulder.

Joselyn followed after, scoffing. "I missed twice."

"No." Hollen shook his head. "You didn't miss. Your target moved."

Don't patronize me, savage.

"What's the difference?"

"Missing would be if you'd aimed too high or if you'd mismeasured your force." Hollen stepped around a root, and Joselyn followed suit. "Your arrow would have struck true had your quarry been a stationary target."

"If we were depending upon *my* skills to eat tonight, we'd be going hungry," Joselyn countered. How was she going to survive this wilderness alone?

"Perhaps." Hollen flashed a devilish grin over his shoulder. Joselyn scowled. Hollen's physical attractiveness had become increasingly difficult to ignore. Her traitorous mind seemed to catch everything: the shade of his eyes when he looked at her, the curve of his lips when he smiled. It had become all she could see. Joselyn kicked up a puff of powdery snow as she walked. Hollen chuckled.

"I think you'll surprise yourself today. You must have 'sported' often before."

Joselyn huffed with amusement at his misuse of the term,

but didn't correct him. Her mind recalled hundreds of afternoons practicing archery by the old oak tree. Her father had spotted her there once. He'd come home after three months at court when she was thirteen. She'd run to him, begged him to watch her, boasted she could hit her target's center every time. If he only took the time to see, he'd be so proud of his daughter.

"I wouldn't give a damn if you hit a coin as it flew through the clouds, girl. Go find your tutors and learn something you can put to good use someday."

After that, her afternoons by the oak tree had grown fewer and farther between. Knowing how much she'd loved archery, Tansy had often begged her to practice when Joselyn felt discouraged and alone. She'd always brushed her nurse off, citing her ever-increasing roster of responsibilities as excuses. She'd thought learning to be the perfect lady might finally be the thing to earn her father's love. In the end, that too, had been a waste of effort.

"Not so often as I wanted," Joselyn muttered. *Not so often as I should have.*

Hollen continued his march, but turned to regard her with an arched brow. "Why not?"

"A lady has more important things to occupy her time with."

"Like what?"

This savage really knew nothing about her world. Odd, since his mother was a lady. Had she taught her son nothing? "Like preparing for marriage to a *lord*."

Hollen's step went out of rhythm at that. They walked along, weaving around trees.

He whirled to face her. Joselyn bumped into him. What was he doing? He planted his bow into the snow, and stood apart from it as though it were a walking stick. Hollen stared down, his expression flat.

"Were you in love with your intended?"

The shock of his question was like cold water being splashed in her face. In love? With Dante Viridian? Of all people! Years of social training kept her from reacting. "Would it matter to you if I was?"

His body tightened. "Yes."

"Why?"

"I mean to claim you, *mu hamma*. All of you. Mind, body, heart."

Joselyn's breath quickened. He wanted her *heart*? No one had ever staked a claim on that. Not that she'd ever expected to find love with anyone she married. Warm regard had been the deepest extent of her hopes. Hollen's eyes heated. Joselyn didn't think "warm regard" was in this savage's vocabulary. For some reason, that didn't seem like a bad thing. He leaned forward.

"If someone has already staked their claim on any part of you, I want to know *who*."

Joselyn's blood heated. He was jealous. Why was that so damn pleasing?

"I don't love him."

Hollen's shoulders relaxed. "Then why did you agree to marry him?"

She cocked her head in honest incredulity. She answered slowly, as if he might not clearly understand her language. "Ladies like me don't marry for love. We marry into whichever house will bring our own the greatest advantage. Surely your mother explained *that* to you."

Hollen shrugged. "By the time I was born, my mother was a Dokiri *hamma*. Not some lord's bargaining chip."

Joselyn narrowed her eyes. Bargaining chip? She was all that stood between her house and total ruination. And she'd not been traded away by her father. She'd gone willingly to her fate, ready to sacrifice all chance at personal peace for the sake of her house. Pressing her shoulders back, Joselyn drew herself up to her full height. She inclined her chin with the loftiest tilt she could manage.

"Perhaps yours is a world where a woman has no purpose outside of breeding. But where I come from I'm worth far more than that."

"Worth so much that your father would have you marry against your"—Hollen's eyes scanned her tightened posture, a hint of appreciation twinkling in his eyes—"*considerable* will?"

Her voice went steely. "You have spectacular nerve for a man who would steal a woman into the mountains and force her to be his own."

Hollen absorbed the insult. Something hovered in his expression. Uncertainty perhaps? It was gone before she could be sure.

"And as it happens, I was on my way to marry of my own free will. Because that's what a Morhageese noblewoman does. No, I don't love Dante Viridian, but my personal feelings are irrelevant. The only thing that matters is what I am willing to sacrifice for my house."

Hollen closed what little distance was left between their bodies. Leaning heavily on his bow, he dropped his dark head low so that his face was mere inches away from hers. Joselyn could feel the warmth of his breath gliding over her pinkened nose. She met his eyes defiantly, unwilling as ever to be intimidated by his hulking presence. As she breathed in his earthy scent, fear was not the emotion that roiled within her.

"The only thing that matters to *who*?"

Joselyn's chest fluttered with the pounding of her heart. Her eyes dropped to his lips. Skies, why were they so close? Her husky voice came out in a whisper.

"You're a hypocrite. Don't pretend as though what I want matters to *you*. If it did, you'd return me home so that I may fulfill my duty."

Her breath quickened as she brought her burning eyes back to his. Contempt sharpened her focus. Her toes sunk into the snow as she arched into his challenging stare. "But then, duty isn't something I'd expect a savage like you to understand."

At her words, a haze of reserve clouded over Hollen's dark eyes. He straightened, pulling out of his intoxicating proximity. Joselyn tipped forward. She caught herself, snapping out of her daze. She studied Hollen's face, searched for a sign that he, too, had suffered some physical consequence of her nearness. Disappointment hardened in her belly when she could find none.

Joselyn's jaw tightened. She snapped her chin forward and plodded on, brushing his arm as she passed. The three-pronged tracks of the storen led her deeper into the woods. They hiked in silence a long while until the soft trilling of their quarry rose in the near distance.

Joselyn slowed her pace as she crept around the edge of a pine. The birds had settled and resumed their pecking. She crouched to the ground, her knees burrowing into the snow. Joselyn drew back the arrow just as the colorful bird skittered forward. She tracked him, lining the iron arrowhead up with his fatty breast. Behind her, Hollen, too, dropped to his knees. She stiffened as he placed a hand on the small of her back. He reached for her bow, pressing it ahead of the shot she'd been about to take.

Warm breath brushed against her ear. "Don't aim for where he is. Aim for where he's going to be." He nudged the bow along the fowl's wandering path.

With one of his hands pressing into her back and his other stretched out before her, Joselyn was encircled. Some primal instinct urged her to lean into that embrace. She stiffened, then nudged her face toward his. Was he sharing some measure of this turmoil with her? Did she want to know if he wasn't?

Beside her, Hollen also stilled. Even his breath slowed to an imperceptible rhythm. His arms fell away like feathers to the earth. Even through her furs, Joselyn felt the cold air creeping in around her, magnifying the loss. Leaning in, he whispered in her ear.

"Follow his path, *mu hamma*."

Joselyn swallowed, pursing her lips in concentration. Her nose chilled as she drew in an icy breath, harnessing all the tension in her body. Fog fanned before her face as she eased her limbs. The bird's white breast was difficult to see against the stark background of snow, but she locked onto it and edged the iron point an inch ahead. She released the arrow.

The bird squawked as the wooden shaft embedded into the center of its puffy body. The other two birds screeched their retreat. Joselyn jumped when Hollen bounced beside her, his great chest heaving with laughter.

"What did I tell you? You have aim true as any *Na Dokiri*!"

Joselyn's head snapped toward him. Had he really just compared her to one of his warriors? To a man? Before she could respond, he patted her on the shoulder with a force that rocked her off balance, then darted off his knees toward her kill.

Joselyn caught herself with a hand in the snow. She stared after Hollen, unsure what to make of his excitement. Then she, too, clambered to her feet to inspect her handiwork. Her arrow had embedded at least six inches into the bird's breast. Only a hint of blood seeped out around the edges to stain its stark feathers.

"A clean shot!" he said. "You'll have an easy time preparing it tonight."

Joselyn's eyes fell over the bird's brilliant blue plume, drawn by its magnificent beauty. The feathers, she knew, would fetch a high price at any Morhageese market. They were the sort that her father, and other wealthy nobility, used as quills in their private studies. Unable to stop herself, she gazed at the creature's face. Cool lifelessness clouded the shining black pearl of its eye.

"Did he die instantly?" she asked, keeping her voice casual.

Hollen's voice dropped to a moderate tenor. "Yes. His suffering was minimal."

She gave a stiff nod. "Can I take the arrow out?"

And his enthusiasm came rushing back. He practically leapt out of her way, dragged her by the arm up to the storen's side. "Yes. Straight back. Just like that. Be sure it all comes out."

Joselyn gripped the arrow shaft and yanked. It was harder to remove than she'd imagined. Steam rose up from the wound as she inspected the intact iron point.

Hollen held out his hand and Joselyn gave him the arrow. He rolled the shaft in his fingers, performing his own investigation. "Your first kill. The Dokiri would mark themselves on such an occasion."

Joselyn shot him a killing glare. His grin turned to a devious smirk.

"Peace, woman." He held up his hands in mock surrender. "You already bear the only mark I care about." Hollen turned again to study the bird. He chuckled, shaking his head. "Who would have guessed? My lady *hamma*, a deadly force."

He was mocking her. He had to be. The bastard. She was opening her mouth to tell him where he could put the bloodied arrow when she met his gaze. The harsh words died on her lips.

The reddish undertones of his long hair stood out in so much morning sunlight. They matched the auburn flecks in the rings of his eyes, which were all that kept them from appearing black as a clouded night sky. His broad shoulders cut an imposing figure against the backdrop of white snow, but that presence was softened by the warmth of his pleased smile. His pleasure was actually pride. And that pride, she realized with a start, was in *her*. When was the last time someone besides Tansy had looked at her that way?

Joselyn's gaze skirted away. She dusted a bit of snow off her lap. "It was only a storen. We wouldn't be going hungry without it."

"Should the mountain fall I don't think I'll ever need to fear going hungry again!" He laughed, snapping up the dead bird as he stood. "Not with you around."

He held a hand down to her. Joselyn looked at it as she brushed a red strand of hair behind her ear. Why was he so pleased with her? Why did it feel so good? She slid her palm against his. It was warm and rough, just like everything else about this savage man who'd claimed her. She felt weightless as he drew her upward in a strong, swift motion. When he released her, his fingers slackened far slower than was necessary.

Hollen heaved the heavy fowl over his shoulder and threw a wry smile in her direction. "Come, let's return and I'll show you how to prepare it. Maybe you have more talent with a butcher's knife than a sparring one."

This wasn't exactly like Tansy. There was more to his expression than the unbridled delight of a parent. There was genuine regard in his eyes, a sense of confidence. Like he knew Joselyn would bring him a better life than he could ever strive to achieve apart from her. It went beyond hope. It was joyful certainty. Joselyn's own pride glowed within her now, stoked into a searing heat by the fan of Hollen's generous praise.

She waited for him to turn before allowing a smile to tug at a corner of her own lips.

The light shone bright enough to make Joselyn squint as they stepped out of the dense tree line and into the gray tundra of the mid-mountain slope. By now the heat of the afternoon sun had melted all the snow without trees to shade it. Hollen whistled, and the sharp sound echoed all around the empty landscape. Joselyn adjusted her bow to her other shoulder, surprised how hot she'd grown during the hike back up.

A moment passed before the winged beast cast its ominous shadow over the ground. Joselyn retreated, ducking back into the tree line. As Hollen had promised, the wyvern hadn't attacked her. Still, every instinct warned it was a possibility better not put to the test. A gust of wind brushed her hood back as the serpent landed before Hollen.

Her captor strode forward, ordering the giant to drop its scaled belly to the rocky ground so that he might secure her kill to its saddle. He cast a glance in her direction and waved her forward.

She cocked her head to the side, studying him at a distance. Not for the first time, Joselyn found herself marveling that Hollen had somehow managed to bring the *gegatu* to heel. Though common among his people, a prerequisite for manhood, in fact, to her it was a feat that inspired awe.

Apparently, the dragon submits to some.

Joselyn stroked the tips of her nails across her palm, recalling the sensation of her hand in his. How strange that hands able to master a great serpent could also be so gentle.

The crisp sound of a snapping branch drew Joselyn out of her musings. She turned, inclining an ear toward the sound. She peered into the shadows which were fractured by rays of yellow sunlight stabbing through the branches. Her gaze paused on a peculiar shape, barely perceptible against the snow-streaked ground. Joselyn craned her head forward and squinted at the distant figure, trying to identify it.

The white-gray mound shifted. The movement provided temporary clarity, and the little hairs at the nape of Joselyn's neck rose on end. Not thirty yards in the distance crouched a hairless, humanoid figure with large eyes that Joselyn knew, even from so far away, were totally black.

Joselyn's breath caught in her throat. Her mouth fell open as the muscles in her knees locked. The creature stilled, going nearly invisible. Joselyn wanted to run, to call out for help, but instinct wouldn't allow her to turn her back on the unknown threat, nor draw any attention to herself. Her hand inched for the string of her bow slung across her chest. Were she not so terrified, she might have thanked the gods that she wore a quiver of a half-dozen arrows. It was one of the few items Hollen had not insisted on carrying for her.

Bit by bit, Joselyn tugged the bow down, not daring to breathe. Her hand crept up to her neck, stretching backward to finger the fletching of an arrow. Hollen called to her in the background with a question in his voice. She didn't answer. The creature was moving again.

It turned, presenting her with a stunted profile. Its bent spine sported a column of sharp spikes that seemed integrated into its skeletal structure. It stood at least as tall as she, the apex of its hunched shoulders the highest point on its jagged body. Joselyn willed her hands to be steady as she notched the arrow against her bow string, her gaze never leaving the mysterious beast.

A guttural snarl carried through the trees. The creature flashed razor-sharp teeth that seemed altogether too large for its mouth. Joselyn brought the bow up to bear and the creature quieted. Its body went stone still. Icy adrenaline shot through Joselyn's body. The monster wasn't attacking. Would that change if she fired at it? What if she missed? Where should she even aim?

Suddenly, the creature leapt forward in a full charge, its blade-like claws pounding into the frozen ground beneath it. Joselyn's heart seized in her chest.

She let the arrow fly.

14

VELIGIRI

Hollen called out to his bride. What had drawn her attention into the tree line? His gaze flitted to the trees, peering into the shaded darkness. Regna, father of the sky, had endowed the Dokiri with a keen sense of eyesight, a necessary trait for those who hunted from the backs of the *gegatu*. When down on the ground, Hollen couldn't help but wish it were his ears that had received the supernatural blessing. What good were the eyes of a hawk when the walls of a cave or a forest of trees blocked his vision?

A stiff wind kicked up the branches of the pines. Miles of green swayed in a wave that spanned across the mountain's face. The breeze sent a whiff of the storen's dripping carcass spinning into Hollen's face.

A sense of malevolence slithered its way up his spine, and his hand went instinctively to his axe. He scooted off Jagomri, and the *gegatu* growled in impatience. Hollen ignored his beast, standing to study his bride. Her back was still to him. He called out to her again, but she didn't turn. Instead, her hand crept upward as she rolled her shoulder, edging off her bow.

Panic lit his insides. She could have spotted some additional game in the woods. But, no. That wasn't right. Her posture was too stiff. Too tall. His *hamma* was afraid, and he was too far away.

He burst into a full sprint. In seconds he was halfway there. In that time, she'd drawn an arrow and taken aim into the tree line. Hollen heard the telltale snarl of one of his most common enemies.

"Joselyn! Run!" he cried, nearly upon her.

His *hamma* let an arrow fly into the trees, and he followed its path. A great, white mass bounded from the shadows. The arrow plunged into its muscle-strapped chest. The blood-seeker released another eerie howl. Hollen charged forward. He wasn't going to make it in time.

The blood-seeker, fangs glinting in the sunlight, leapt upon his bride. She hit the stony ground. Hard. Cold fury tore through Hollen's chest and rose out of his throat in a savage roar. The blood-seeker glanced up. Hollen swung his axe, missing the creature's snubbed face and slicing into its shoulder instead. The crunching of bone vibrated up Hollen's arm.

The blood-seeker screamed as it darted off Joselyn's chest. The monster locked its black gaze on Hollen. Pointed ears pressed backward as it bellowed, murky gray blood spilling out onto the ground. It squinted in the bright sun and arched its spined back toward the sky. Razor claws gave it extra height. Even crawling on its hands and feet, the seeker was taller than Hollen.

Hollen gripped his axe, prepared. Behind him, Jagomri hissed and backed farther away from the foul monster that even *gegatu* took care to avoid.

Hollen stepped over his bride, who was still lying on the ground. He wanted to look at her, to assure himself that she was well. It would have to wait. He stalked around the creature, blocking its access to the trees. If the blood-seeker could draw the fight into the shadows, it would. Its whiteless eyes were half-blind in the sun.

Hollen leaned in and thrust his axe forward, daring the creature to charge. When it shrunk back, Hollen leapt forward. As expected, the vermin pulled in its head and lashed out with its front claws. Hollen tore his axe across the row of extended talons. Ashen gray blood ripped from the seeker's hands. It screamed, rearing back on its feet.

Pain bloomed in Hollen's right arm. He ignored it, tipping his head back to watch the monster's face. It slammed its spiked elbows down, pounding rock again and again in furious agony.

Hollen darted across the puddle of gore, nearly slipping. He bellowed to cow his opponent. The beast withdrew, and once again threw out its arms in defense. With its claws removed, Hollen got even closer. He swung his axe back and heaved it over his head.

Steel split into the seeker's spike-rimmed head. This time, there was no scream. The monster's body fanned out in a spasm before crumpling to the ground.

Hollen jerked his weapon out from the fractured shards of the monster's skull. There was a pop, and fresh blood exploded from the crushed mound like bubbling spring water. He whirled, and his eyes fell upon Joselyn.

She sat up on the ground, supported by her trembling arms. Hollen scanned the area in a rapid sweep. He could spot no further threat, but then, the forest was too close to be certain. He sprinted forward, all but landing upon his pale-faced bride. Still clutching his axe in one hand, Hollen planted the other against Joselyn's narrow shoulder.

"Are you all right?"

Joselyn's wide eyes blinked once. Her gaze was locked on the fallen blood-seeker. Was she even breathing?

"Joselyn!" He gave her a shake. "Are you hurt?"

His bride flinched, gasping. She blinked up at him. Her breath suddenly came in half-finished gulps. She nodded once, and then she kept nodding. Her head pitched forward and back like a newborn babe's. She was in shock. Hollen scanned her body, taking his own account.

Sure enough, the furs of her thigh were torn open. His hands shot to her leg to stretch the leather open. Faint trails of blood welled into the soft fibers of wolf hair lining her pants. Hollen sent a prayer of thanksgiving to Helig that the talons of blood-seekers were not venomous. Still, the disgusting creatures were known for hoarding heaps of decaying carcasses within their reeking caves. The wound needed to be cleaned. Quickly.

Joselyn leaned into Hollen's chest. Her little hands clung to his coat, and her chest expanded into his as she continued struggling for air. Instinct flared. He dropped his axe and scooped Joselyn up in his arms.

"Come, *mu hamma*!"

It felt so good to hold her. If only the circumstances had been different. He clambered to his feet and snapped the axe back up. Hollen ran forward. Jagomri stood a good distance away, his great obsidian wings open. He hissed in distaste at the fallen blood-seeker. Hollen sneered in his mount's direction.

No damn help at all.

Joselyn trembled, and her blue eyes darted backward to the corpse of the monstrous creature.

"Don't look at it, *mu hamma*." No Dokiri *hamma* should have to look upon a *veligiri*. Especially not Hollen's *hamma*. She buried her face in his throat, so close he could feel her breath.

Hollen bounded up Jagomri's side, all but dropping Joselyn into the saddle. He secured his axe and thrust his legs into the leather trappings as quickly as he could. His mind reeled. What in all Helig's green earth had a blood-seeker been doing in broad daylight? He should inspect the body, investigate what would cause it to act against its nature. But, no. His only concern was protecting his bride. He couldn't do that out here.

Hollen considered Joselyn's jibe in the forest, that a 'savage' like him couldn't understand the significance of duty. She was ignorant. He didn't fault her for it. She'd only been with him for a handful of days. In truth, there was nothing more sacred to the Dokiri. Duty to his clan, the gods, his brothers, and duty to his bride. It might have been the greatest of all charges.

And he had failed.

15

DUTY FIRST

I should be dead. I should be dead.

Had it not been for Hollen, she *would* be dead. She groaned against the saddle as they landed outside Bedmeg. Her every muscle weighed heavy and cold. She was vaguely aware of her captor tearing at the fastenings of his saddle. His movements were jerky and frantic. Was he afraid? What could a man like him possibly fear?

His legs free, Hollen leapt from Jagomri's back. Joselyn tried to sit up, but her body wouldn't cooperate. Hollen caught her around the waist and pulled her into his arms. It was probably for the best.

The Dokiri chieftain shouted in his language, barking out orders to the men standing nearby who watched with wary interest. Whatever Hollen said sprung them into action. They began whistling, calling their own wyverns from the jagged cliffs above. Joselyn jumped at the sound of a blowing horn which sent even more riders pouring from outside the cave and into the open valley. Women scurried out as well, throwing their curious gazes at their *Salig* and *Saliga*.

Hollen sprinted past, darting beneath the cave's ceiling. Was the entire clan watching? Joselyn squirmed in his arms. "Put me down."

He ignored her. Erik ran to meet them as they approached the path leading to Hollen's *bok*. Hollen bit out what Joselyn assumed was another command in Dokiri. Erik's blue eyes widened. He nodded and ran outside with several other men.

Hollen wasn't going to put her down. Joselyn pressed her face into his shoulder, avoiding the stares of those around them until they were out of sight.

It was totally dark inside the *bok*. She shivered. Hollen deposited her onto the furs of his bed, and the room spun around her. Light flooded the *bok*. Joselyn's gaze floated over to where Hollen sat, hunched over the ring, feeding twigs into the kindling flame.

She glanced down at herself, only just taking stock of her condition for the first time. She appeared fine, save for her right leg. The leather of her pants had been torn open. Joselyn grimaced. It hurt.

Her eyes shot up as Hollen crossed the room in wide strides. He dropped to his knees on the ground before her. His hands darted to the top of her pants. All at once, he began tugging them downward. Joselyn gasped, barely managing to catch his wrists. She squeezed them, and his dark gaze snapped to hers.

"No!" She dug her nails into his hands.

He paused. The restraint appeared to require more than a little effort. "You're bleeding."

"No, I'm not." *Was* she bleeding? She didn't know. All she knew for certain was that she couldn't allow him to strip her. Her grip tightened and she gritted her teeth. "I'm fine."

A solid beat passed, and Hollen released her pants. His hands dropped to rest upon her upper thighs. The weight of them sent a glow of heat up her legs where it promptly ignited like a furnace within the cradle of her hips. She shuddered at the shocking sensation. Her lips parted on a gasp.

Skies! What is happening to me?

"Let me tend to you," he said, his voice a command, his expression pleading.

The pain in her leg flared, making her wince. Hollen noticed and leaned forward.

"Please, *mu hamma*," he whispered. He reached one hand up her arm, stroking her like a startled horse. "Let me see."

He *was* afraid. This hardened warrior, capable of taming wyverns and slaying demons, was afraid for *her*. Her lips parted in stunned realization.

Hollen's hands went back to her pants. Joselyn sucked in a breath as she snapped out of her thoughts. She kept her voice steady, but gentled it.

"No. Get me some water. I'll clean it myself."

Hollen stared. Indecision warred in his gaze. She met his eyes with steely daggers of her own, daring him to overstep. His intentions might be innocent, but she wouldn't budge on this. No man looked at her there, touched her there.

Hollen huffed, but backed away. She thought she heard a frustrated growl rumble in his throat. He flew to the other end of the *bok* and threw up the lid of the chest. His big hands rummaged through the contents.

He'd actually honored her request. He might easily reason to himself that cleaning her wound was paramount to her safety. What an easy justification. Yet, he'd honored her wishes. The barbarian was full of surprises.

Hollen returned and pressed a rag into her outstretched hand. He set a wooden bowl filled with water next to her, and also the pitcher he'd filled it with. Joselyn dipped the rag into the water. She glanced up at Hollen. Did he intend to watch her every move? She cleared her throat.

"I would appreciate some privacy."

He frowned, his brows knitting together. He opened his mouth, but no words came out. A moment passed, and his lips snapped shut. Hollen turned and exited the *bok*.

Silence filled the room, making Joselyn shiver. He'd actually listened. And she was . . .disappointed. How ridiculous. As she wiped at the blood, some of her anxiety returned. For the first time since being brought to Bedmeg, Joselyn's source of fear shifted away from inside this *bok*, this bed. She took a deep breath. Nothing could get to her here. There was only one way in and out. Still, her eyes drifted to the exit, waiting for an intruding demon to appear.

I am safe. Hollen is outside. Nothing will get past him.

Sighing, she wobbled to her feet. It was as though all the strength had been sapped from her body, like a day spent in full summer sun. Her knees shook under her weight as she peeled off her pants. Maybe she did need help. She was loath to ask Hollen after so stubbornly making him leave, but her pride and modesty weren't worth a fever. She bent for a better view.

Joselyn looked up to see Lavinia entering the *bok*. The older woman's full lips parted with dismay.

"*Mu Saliga*! Are you all right? What h-happened?" She hurried to Joselyn's side and pulled her down on the furs.

"Where's Hollen?" Joselyn glanced toward the *bok's* entrance. Was he not just outside after all?

"He's . . .outside. He said you wanted p-privacy." Lavinia's eyes dropped to Joselyn's lap. "He asked me to check your wound." Lavinia's hands went to Joselyn's thigh. She paused. "May I?"

Joselyn nodded, attempting a smile but falling short, her nerves too frayed. Lavinia squinted in the torchlight and ran a finger over the edges of the tear in her flesh. Joselyn stifled a shudder.

"It is n-not deep. I don't think you'll need thread t-taken to it."

Joselyn nodded. "Thank you, Lavinia."

The dark woman glanced up at her. "You m-must be terrified."

"I'm fine," she lied as she straightened. "Does this sort of thing happen often?"

Lavinia's eyes went wide and she shook her head. "Oh n-no, n-never!"

Relief eased some of the tightness in Joselyn's chest as her companion jabbered on.

"*Mu Salig* said you were attacked by a . . .blood-seeker. But that should never have h-happened in the middle of the day! Blood-seekers are . . .blind in the sun. *Atu hatu* has already ordered riders to investigate. He'll join . . .them just as soon as he's assured of your s-safety."

Joselyn gaped at the woman. A blood-seeker? No wonder he'd cut down the creature so quickly. It had not been his first time. Not even close. She thought of the marks across Hollen's biceps.

"He's going back out there? Now? Why? He was nearly killed." Surely he needed time to rest and collect himself. Joselyn was still shaking. Wasn't he suffering some ill effects as well?

Lavinia regarded her. "It's his duty, *mu . . .Saliga*. All malevolent c-creatures must be exterminated, and a blood-seeker skulking about in b-broad daylight n-necessitates immediate attention." Lavinia sighed and grabbed the rag. She wiped at the wound. "They'll be gone for a while. The f-forest blocks our men's view of the ground below. They'll have to patrol the woods . . .on foot."

Joselyn thought of Hollen and his warriors trudging through the forest without the benefit of their mounts. She imagined

Hollen being overtaken by a pack of the foul creatures, their wicked claws decapitating him. Shouldn't the idea give her hope? Without her captor, what reason did anyone have to make her stay? Surely she would be returned to her father, her promised reward collected in earnest.

Instead of hope, a surge of panic pounded through her chest. Did she truly wish to return home under any circumstances? Under *those* circumstances? If Hollen were to fall into her father's hands, he'd be summarily executed. Of that, Joselyn had no doubt. It was a fate she'd threatened him with the day he kidnapped her. At the time she'd have felt no pity for him. But now? Did she really feel the same way?

No.

One bold feat, and she was softening like a besotted little girl. Joselyn lowered her eyes to the ground, ashamed of herself.

After bandaging Joselyn's leg, Lavinia rose from the bed and crossed the *bok* toward the wooden chest. She returned with a white under-shift and helped Joselyn change.

"Thank you, Lavinia." Despite her frayed nerves, she forced herself to smile at her new friend.

Until now, she'd thought of Lavinia as well-meaning, but beneath her, as though she lacked for either grit or common sense. Like the rest of the Dokiri *hammas*, Lavinia emanated reverent awe for her captor-husband. At first, it had seemed to Joselyn like the women here had all been brainwashed. But now? After facing down her own death at the clawed hands of an unholy monster? She'd underestimated the degree of evil that resided on this mountain. And perhaps she'd misjudged the wives of the men who kept it at bay.

And what of the Dokiri men? Lavinia had said the Dokiri couldn't conceive daughters. Without brides, there would be no more Bedmeg. Was the extinction of an entire race worth the freedom of a few maidens? A race who made it their mission to protect strangers from being overrun by devils? Joselyn frowned, not caring for the direction of her thoughts.

"*Mu hamma?*"

Joselyn and Lavinia turned to see Hollen standing at the tunnel. He gripped the entrance with one hand, concern etched in his face. Lavinia patted Joselyn's arm.

"She's well, *mu Salig*. There is much blood, but the wound will c-close quickly."

Hollen's shoulders visibly relaxed. He eyed Joselyn. His mouth opened, then he glanced at Lavinia. The other woman took the hint.

"I'll be in the common area if you need me, *mu Saliga*." She strode toward the exit.

"Thank you," Joselyn called after her.

Lavinia smiled, nodding. She turned to bid her farewell to Hollen, but stopped. She caught Hollen's wrist in her hand and pulled it up near her face. A string of Dokiri words poured from her lips, and Hollen answered her in his language.

Joselyn stiffened. Irritation crept through her chest. What were they saying? Lavinia was typically so careful to use the trade tongue around her. Joselyn's eyes narrowed, falling on the place where Lavinia held Hollen's wrist.

"What is it?" Joselyn asked, her voice sharpening.

The two looked at her. Lavinia didn't release Hollen. "*Mu Salig* is hurt."

Joselyn stood.

"It's nothing," Hollen said. "Thank you for tending *mu hamma*, Lavinia."

"I'll clean and b-bandage it, *mu Salig*," Lavinia said, her stutter soft and sweet as always. For once, Joselyn didn't find it charming.

"I'll tend to it." Joselyn didn't even realize she had crossed the *bok* until she stood in front of Lavinia, with her own hand clutching Hollen's affected arm.

Both Hollen and Lavinia regarded her with surprise. Should she make up some excuse about taking up too much of Lavinia's time? She fixed Lavinia with a flat stare.

"Oh." Lavinia cleared her throat and dropped Hollen's wrist like an iron set too long in the fire. "Of . . .course. W-well, you know where t-to find me." Bobbing her head, she scurried into the tunnel.

Hollen turned to Joselyn. Just a moment before, he'd looked frantic to discuss something. Yet now he was quiet. Both their gazes fell to where Joselyn was touching him. Joselyn swallowed. Might as well embrace the awkwardness.

"Come." She drew him to the edge of the bed. He followed her like a mute little lamb. Joselyn pulled him to sit in front of her and considered how to care for him. It was only right. He'd sustained an injury in saving her life. The least she could do was tend to him.

She took him by the wrist again. A crimson line of dried blood stretched from knuckle to forearm.

It was a scratch, but it would need to be covered. Her brows knitted together.

"How did this happen? I didn't see the beast touch you."

Hollen kept his gaze on her face, watching as she examined him. "It caught me as I declawed it."

Joselyn thought of the gray blood spilling from the stubs of the seeker's severed fingers. "My arrow didn't even slow it down, but you killed it easily."

"Your aim was true. But the heart of blood-seeker is much lower down than in the chests of men. Taking off their heads is easier."

Easier? Not bloody likely. "Or crushing them."

The way Hollen's axe had cleaved into the seeker's skull. The crunching sound it had made. Joselyn shuddered. She crossed the *bok* and changed out the bowl's water. Always, she felt Hollen's eyes on her.

Breathe, Joselyn.

She returned and wrung out the rag. She lifted his hand, and he relaxed in her grip, allowing her to turn his arm this way and that as she examined him. Joselyn dabbed at his wound. "You're not really going back out there?"

"Of course I am. We have to make certain there are no other blood-seekers lurking about in broad daylight. If we find more, perhaps we'll learn what drove the last from its den."

"Surely your riders are better suited?"

Hollen's hand snapped shut at that. His eyes sparked with offense. She stuttered, only just realizing how that must have sounded.

"I only meant that . . .you are their leader. Would it not be better for you to stay where it's safe?"

If she was going to offend him, Joselyn preferred it only happen when specifically intended. Whatever else she thought of him, she hadn't meant to imply that he was too weak to handle himself. The notion was absurd. Especially after what she'd seen today.

"Is that how men lead where you come from, *mu hamma*?" Judgment thickened in his voice.

Yes, it was. It made perfect sense to her. Those with the skill and knowledge to lead couldn't be wasted on the battlefield. One look at Hollen's disdainful expression told her all she needed to know about his opinion on such matters. She supposed she could see the honor in it, leading by example, even if it did lack wisdom in some cases. No one would accuse her captor of being unwilling to follow his own commands. No one would accuse him of self-importance. Those were the sorts of judgments that could beget unwanted consequences for a ruler.

Hollen sucked in a breath. Joselyn glanced up to see him frowning at her. She was about to ask if she'd hurt him when he spoke.

"Forgive me, Joselyn."

She paused, returning his grim expression with one of her own. "For what?"

"The seeker was drawn to the scent of your kill's blood. I didn't bother to bind it up because I've never known a bloodseeker to emerge in the middle of the day. I should have been more cautious." He stilled, as though he were waiting for a well-deserved tongue-lashing.

Of all the things he might have apologized for. Kidnapping me, cutting me up, ignoring my pleas on behalf of my house.

If she weren't so damn grateful for her life, she would have rolled her eyes.

"It doesn't seem that anyone could have expected differently of you. I'm only glad that . . ." She broke off, dropping the rag back into the bowl. She sighed, then blurted, "Thank you for saving my life. Where can I find more binding cloth?"

Hollen blinked. The barest inch of a smile cracked across his lips. He withdrew more strips of cloth from his coat. He must have gathered more when sending for Lavinia. She snatched them up, ignoring his bemused expression. She'd wrap his arm *extra* tight.

"Go ahead and be rough. I'm just happy to have you touching me."

Her lips parted as she scrambled for a retort. She didn't think fast enough.

"I spend every moment after I touch you crafting excuses to do it again."

Joselyn's stomach fluttered. Did she really affect him like that? Did his skin burn like hers at every accidental brush? What did it mean? She was his captive. Surely she should feel revulsion at his touch. Fear. Anything but this...this...desire? Hollen went on.

"And when you touch me? Regna, Joselyn! It feels so good."

Without thought, she released him. She stared at his hand, still raised in front of her. Heat bloomed across her chest and up her neck. No one had ever talked to her like this, not even Lord Ellis whom she'd briefly courted. Though bold, there was a certain honesty in Hollen's declaration that seemed purer than the compliments Lord Ellis had paid her. Hollen wasn't the sort of man with whom she had to wonder if his words matched his thoughts.

He brought his wrapped hand to her face. Her gaze moved up as his fingertips paused just over her cheek. Their warmth dissolved in the blush of her own skin. His eyes scanned each detail of her face. With his other hand he brushed her braid over her shoulder.

Ever so slightly, Joselyn turned her head toward the caress.

A spark of fear flashed within her, and for once, it wasn't for what he might do to her. Rather it was for what *she* might invite. What in the name of the gods was this man trying to do to her?

Hollen leaned forward just as Joselyn was leaning back. They both stilled.

Skies above. What is wrong with me?

Hollen's fingers curled, drifting back down to the bed. He sighed. "Are you certain you're well?"

"Yes." She cleared her throat. "I'm fine."

But she wasn't. Her heart was racing so fast she could feel it in her fidgeting fingertips.

He nodded. "Good. I'll be back as soon as I can. I want you to rest."

Joselyn's head popped up. "Are you putting me to bed?"

"It would do you good." He cocked his head to the side. When Joselyn narrowed her eyes at him, he continued. "But no. Just keep to the common area until I return."

"When will that be?"

Hollen shrugged. "When I'm certain the threat has passed." He stood, flexing and stretching his wrapped hand. "How is your *tanshi* mark?"

Joselyn's eyes cooled at the mention of the scar he had inflicted upon her. "As well as it can be."

"Can you tend to it yourself if I don't return tonight?"

Joselyn crossed her arms and looked pointedly at his wrapped hand. "I think I can manage."

"Rest tonight, *mu hamma*."

Still avoiding his gaze, Joselyn inclined her chin in passive agreement.

He looked like he wanted to say something more, but in the end, he merely swallowed and disappeared into the tunnel.

Joselyn looked around the empty *bok*. Though alight with the crackling glow of the fire at its center, it felt as though Hollen had taken all the heat with him. Her eyes drifted toward the bed. Joselyn pressed the flat of a hand to her belly, grasping for composure.

She had taken care with Hollen's hand, returning the same gentleness and warmth with which he always seemed to treat her. She should have feared what her attentions might inspire within him. Yet he hadn't broken his promise. Hadn't thrown her upon the bed in animalistic lust.

A disturbing thought leapt up in her mind. She'd been wrong about Hollen in more ways than one. Her captor was no stranger to the concept of duty. Joselyn thought of him facing off with another one of the foul blood-seekers, and a thrill of fear shot up her spine. Pacing about the *bok*, Joselyn sent a fervent prayer up to the gods, asking that the Dokiri encounter no more of the frightening creatures. No one deserved to die shredded by those wicked claws. Hollen didn't deserve to die.

A few more prayers and Joselyn's panic began to abate. The bulk of her energy faded with it. Her drooping eyelids went again to the furs of the bed and she imagined how satisfying it would be to slip beneath their heavy warmth and fall into sleep as Hollen had suggested.

What's the matter with you, Joselyn? Get your head together!

A rush of shame slapped her. For the first time since arriving, she would be without her captor's constant supervision. At last, she might have a decent opportunity for making escape preparations. And what was she doing? Praying for the man who'd kidnapped her and contemplating a nap.

Not today.

Today the gods had given her a perfect opportunity to seek out how she might escape. At the very least, she would gather what supplies she'd need and put them aside for whenever an opportunity presented itself. She smoothed a hand over her ruffled hair.

The Dokiri might have need of wives, and after today, Joselyn could concede that their purpose upon this mountain entitled them to some form of recompense. But to force women to spend a lifetime upon this mountain? Without choice and with no hope of ever being reunited with their families? No. It wasn't right.

Perhaps the women of Bedmeg had led lives simple enough for such a sacrifice. Joselyn, however, could not be Hollen's reward. She had a duty as well. A gods-given purpose. She must find a way to return home, secure her father's life and the fate of her house.

A sudden image of the blood-seeker's tooth-crammed maw snapping toward her face filled Joselyn's mind, sending her heart sinking to her stomach. How was she ever going to make it down the mountain? If that were the sort of creature she could expect to come up against, what chance did she stand?

One problem at a time, Joselyn. Focus on gathering provisions.

Joselyn closed her eyes and breathed deep. She sent up one final prayer, that the gods would give her the courage not to falter. She laced up the sides of her dress and exited the *bok*, with the slightest limp in her determined stride.

16

LITTLE SISTER

Two large skins of water, a week's worth of dried meat, and a pair of flints. Joselyn stuffed the items into a rocky crevice far outside the common area. She covered it with a flat stone, just barely small enough for her to manipulate over her makeshift cache.

She had retrieved the items easily enough, though Joselyn had balked when first she saw how many women congregated within the common area. They'd rushed their *Saliga* for answers about her brush with the blood-seeker. After she regaled them with the details, the women seemed content to speculate amongst themselves about what Hollen and his warriors would discover on their patrol. For once, Joselyn was left to her own devices.

Snatching a few items at a time, Joselyn had made several trips outside the cave to "gather firewood." No one seemed to catch on that it took her a little longer than usual to carry kindling back to the cave.

The sun was beginning to lag on the horizon as Joselyn considered what other things she might need. She glanced down the snowy ravine toward the cave that served as the clan's armory. The old man who worked the forge rarely seemed to leave. Perhaps she could contrive to bring him his evening meal, and engage in light conversation as she did. Given enough time, he might eventually wander back to the common area.

Joselyn stopped at the wood stack piled slightly higher than her chest. She gathered up an armful. On the other side of the wood stack, a dull thud struck the earth. A plume of powdery snow burst into the air, causing Joselyn to jump. Across the heap, auburn hair rose into view. Sigvard grinned, mischief alight in his eyes. He'd jumped down from a nearby boulder.

Joselyn relaxed. Then she threw Hollen's youngest brother a withering scowl. "Sigvard! Skies! What are you doing?"

His impish grin grew wider and he wiggled his thick brows at her. "I could ask you the same thing."

Joselyn huffed, gesturing with her pile of logs. "I came to get firewood."

"*Mmm.* But what else are you up to?" He crossed his arms over his chest, which was not as broad as Hollen's, but still impressive for a man of his age.

Joselyn straightened. No one had seen her stowing away her supplies. She had made sure of it. And yet the expression on his face told her he knew she was up to no good. What had her mistake been?

Suddenly she realized she was standing on the wrong side of the wood pile to have come straight from the common area. She could think of no immediate excuse. Even if she could, explaining herself was worse than silence.

"Help me carry this in," she said.

Joselyn stepped around the pile and he strode across the snow to meet her halfway. She settled the logs into his waiting arms. A playful glint flashed in his eyes.

"I have a better idea." He tossed the logs back onto the pile. "Let's go do something fun."

Joselyn's eyes followed the discarded logs before shooting back to Sigvard. She cocked her head. "Fun?"

He nodded.

"What exactly do you suggest?" Her curiosity, more than anything, bid her ask.

The grin returned. He caught her about one wrist. "So glad you asked."

Joselyn yipped as Sigvard tugged her away from the wood stack and back toward the common area. Instead of entering the cave, he took her to the side of the ravine and led her up to the base of what appeared to be a narrow staircase, cut by hand into the rocky wall. It disappeared into the cliff above. It was less of a staircase and more a ladder.

Sigvard released Joselyn and turned toward her. He quirked his brows. "Still want to know more about how the *gegatu* are mastered?"

Joselyn blinked. Her eyes crept up the length of the staircase as it disappeared into the stony crags of the mountain. "I'm generally curious, yes."

He turned toward the ladder. "Then let's go. I want to show you something."

With that, the young Dokiri began his ascent. Joselyn stared after him.

When he was ten feet up, Sigvard turned back. "That little hunting trip scare all the nerve from you, lowlander?"

Joselyn's face hardened. She put one hand on the stone staircase and began climbing. Almost immediately, the wound on her leg began to burn. She continued on, and the burning grew worse. Why was she following Sigvard? The drama of the day had already sapped most of her energy. One look downward cured her of any notion to go back. Dizziness crashed through her head at the sight. She pressed the side of her face hard against the cliff. A voice in her mind warned that continuing up would only make the problem worse later, but she rationalized that she was already committed, and shoved the fear into the back of her mind.

A bit later, Sigvard turned back to offer his hand to Joselyn, who took it gratefully as she scaled the top of the cliff. The area was flat and wide, larger than the open ravine below. A great way back, the mountain wall resumed its climb into the sky above. They were on a sort of shelf. Patches of gray rock shone through where the snow had been swept away by . . .something large.

Joselyn's eyes widened.

The *gegatu* were everywhere. Her mouth dropped in horror at the sight of dozens of winged, scaly beasts. She took a hasty step back, and Sigvard's freckled hand shot out to catch her around the arm. He yanked her forward.

"Careful!" he said, pulling her away from the cliff's edge.

Joselyn skittered toward Sigvard and fell into his chest. Hollen's warnings about the *gegatu* screamed in her mind. Terror turned to anger, which spilled into her voice, "What in the name of all the gods are we doing *here*?"

"Peace, Joselyn." Sigvard was stifling laughter, as if her anger amused him. "They don't even care that we're here. Look."

The pounding in Joselyn's heart slowed as she did. Her eyes studied the wyverns as they milled about the stony ledge, oblivious to her and Sigvard's presence. They were smaller than Jagomri, but still terrifying. Even the young ones were huge. They came in an array of colors from black to gray to brown to white. The sun glinted off the glossy scales of some while it seemed to sink into the matte ones of others. Most incredible were their eyes. They came in every color she could imagine, each as rich as the jewels in her mother's many wine goblets.

The leather of their wings dragged about the ground as they moved. A few of them turned snakelike necks in her direction, those brilliant eyes sparkling in wary interest. Joselyn held her breath. They turned away in favor of whatever they'd been doing. Sunbathing, as far as Joselyn could tell.

She was just beginning to relax when Sigvard took her by the hand and pulled her along the edge of the *gegatu* pack. She hobbled after, despite the sting in her leg glowing bright from their climb. She gritted her teeth, determined not to let on she was in pain.

They were closer to the wyverns than Joselyn would have liked, though not so close as to draw further attention to themselves. She hovered against Sigvard's back, careful not to step on his heels. The Dokiri man seemed not at all discomfited to be in the presence of so many monstrous creatures. He whistled a little tune, his wide strides timed to the beat.

The *gegatu* pack thinned out. Those that remained seemed more interested in Sigvard and Joselyn. She slowed. Sigvard released her hand.

"This is where our people come to tame a mount." He cocked his head in the direction of the attentive wyverns.

"Why are we here?" Joselyn whispered. She clutched at her elbow, and her eyes skipped to the monsters at his back.

Sigvard snickered. "There's no need to whisper, little sister. They won't bother us if we don't bother them."

Little sister? Though the Dokiri often called other men of the tribe 'brother,' she hadn't heard them refer to any of the women as 'sister.' Was Sigvard even any older than she? As the youngest of five brothers, he might be eager to scoot someone beneath him in the sibling hierarchy.

Seeing that the wyverns were indeed maintaining their distance, Joselyn crossed her arms over her chest. "I'm not your sister, and I'm probably not even younger than you."

"How old are you?"

Joselyn was about to answer, then paused. "You first."

A corner of Sigvard's mouth quirked, guile thwarted. "Eighteen."

"Same."

Sigvard flattened a freckled hand over the top of his head and scanned it out over hers, keeping it at the level of his full height. His hand plummeted dramatically to land atop her red tresses. Joselyn blinked at the soft impact as Sigvard drew the flattened hand in toward his collarbone.

"The name feels right. 'Little sister' it is." He flashed a devilish grin at her. Joselyn shook her head, hiding her begrudging amusement.

Unexpected tenderness filled her as she regarded the Dokiri boy, barely a man, who was so willing to induct her into a sibling circle that from what Joselyn had seen, was remarkably close-knit. Growing up, she'd longed for a brother, but it wasn't to be. Her mother wouldn't *let* it be. An old bitterness stirred in Joselyn's chest. She bit the inside of her cheek, desperate to think of anything else. Nearby, a gray wyvern trilled at one of its nestmates.

"You still haven't explained what we're doing here." Joselyn eyed the wyverns. She searched the area for an escape should the need arise. There was nothing but the cliff edge behind her and the iron mountain wall a hundred yards past the *gegatu*.

Sigvard turned toward the pack and stretched a pointed finger in front of him. He indicated a black wyvern with a shock of white streaking from the spikes at the top of its head, all the way down the center of its back and barbed tail. The bright, yellow eyes of this *gegatu* were locked upon Sigvard with a great deal of interest.

"You see that beautiful girl?" Sigvard beamed with pride. "She's mine."

Beautiful? *If you say so, Sigvard.*

"You mean, she's tame?"

Sigvard shrugged a shoulder as though the question and its answer were inconsequential. "There's no taming a *gegatu*. One can only master them, and . . . I'm working on it."

Joselyn yanked his pointing finger downward. "Then why are you pulling her attention?"

Sigvard snorted. "She can't help herself. She's drawn to my natural charisma."

Joselyn's eyes widened. "How can you be so calm? Hollen told me not to go near the *gegatu*."

"Hollen should pull the arrow from his ass once in a while. Regna forbid anyone have fun without his supervision."

Joselyn flattened her mouth against the urge to laugh. Sigvard's copper eyes narrowed.

"Don't tell me he claimed a *hamma* as ready to bow down as everyone else around here?" He leaned forward, his voice growing conspiratorial. "That wasn't the impression you gave the morning after you arrived."

Joselyn put a hand on her hip. "Have you seen me bowing to anyone?"

"No. It's why I think you and I will get along just fine."

Sigvard drew a pound of dried meat from his pocket. The nearby *gegatu* rose its scaled head into the air and its eyes fixed upon Sigvard's hand. A forked tongue slid past its fangs to test the air. Sigvard shot Joselyn a bold look before stepping toward the wyvern.

Panic rushed through Joselyn. "No! Sigvard, don't!"

Her hands shot out to catch him, but it was too late. Joselyn sucked in a breath as she clapped a hand over her mouth.

Sigvard approached the wyvern. He stopped not twenty feet from where the scaly beast crouched, just as it let out a serpentine warning hiss. Its spine tightened, contracting as its wings stretched open. It seemed to triple in size.

Planting his feet apart, Sigvard straightened to his full

height. He waited for the *gegatu* to settle. Joselyn imagined what she would do when her guide was snapped in half between the wyvern's monstrous teeth.

Probably scream as it turns around and does the same to me.

An image of Ivan's scarred face flashed through her mind. She should have obeyed Hollen's order to stay to the common area.

Finally, the beast calmed. Its back lengthened and wings pulled in at its sides. Its cold eyes blinked, refocusing on Sigvard's offering.

Sigvard tossed the meat through the air. The wyvern cracked its skinny neck like a whip, making Joselyn jump. Sigvard backed away.

"What in all the gods' names was *that* about?" Joselyn hissed.

A dimple showed in the right corner of his mouth. "You wanted to know how the *gegatu* are mastered."

"I don't see you riding her, Dokiri."

"It's too soon. I have to keep coming back until she's prepared to be mastered."

"And if she attacks you before then?"

He shrugged. "Then I grapple with her and hope for the best."

Joselyn's mouth fell open in disbelief. *The skies is wrong with these savages?*

"Relax." Sigvard bumped her in the arm. "We survived. And now you know what it takes. Eventually she'll let me come close enough to grip her. And when she does"—eagerness lit his eyes—"it's all over."

"Grip her? You mean, beneath the jaw?"

"Yes. The *gegatu* are led by their sense of touch at key points on their bodies." He pointed beneath his own jaw, at the back of his neck and at the inner aspects of his thighs.

"It's how we direct them. It takes time, but you have to get close enough to garner their curiosity and then their trust."

"That's madness."

He scoffed. "It's hardly the most dangerous thing we do. Claiming a *hamma* is far more perilous."

He was joking. Surely. "I wonder if you'll say that after your friend here breaks your spine."

He shrugged. "Better than my spirit."

Joselyn studied him. "Well, that's easy enough to avoid. Just find a woman willing to have you. What does your lot have against courting, anyway?"

Sigvard threw back his head and laughed. "Oh, little sister, you're missing the point. Half the fun is in *making* the woman have you. When I get my chance, I'm not coming back to Bedmeg until I've searched the entire continent. I'll find the most beautiful woman and then the *real* challenge can begin."

Anger swelled in Joselyn's gut. "That's it then? We're chosen for our beauty? To heighten the conquest?"

Sigvard snorted. "That's not why Hollen chose *you*."

Joselyn cocked her head. "Oh?"

A moment passed and Sigvard's face slackened. He threw up his hands. "No no, I didn't mean . . .I meant . . . " His cheeks glowed red. "You're *very* pretty."

Joselyn laughed. "Easy, Sigvard. I'm not going to start weeping."

Sigvard ran a hand through his hair. "I just meant it's obvious why Hollen chose you."

Joselyn sobered. "Do tell."

"Let me guess, you were riding a horse when he found you?"

"Yes . . ."

"I have to know. What color was the horse?"

"White."

He grinned. "Of course it was. And were you hunting?"

"No."

"*Glanshi*. That would have been perfect."

"What are you getting at?"

"You're *exactly* like Mother. Morhageese, a noblewoman, the red hair. You even act a little like her." He paused, considering. "You don't curse as much, I guess."

"You don't think it's strange that your brother's attracted to a woman who reminds him of his mother?"

Sigvard grimaced. "It's not *that*. Hollen wants to be just like Father. No man ever loved a woman like Father loved Mother. That's what Hollen wants. To be the best in *everything*." Sigvard rolled his eyes and muttered, "Jackass."

Hollen wanted to be the best in love? Like his parents? That seemed so . . . what? Noble?

Joselyn bit her lip. "He loved your parents very much."

Sigvard nodded. "And they loved us."

Joselyn swallowed over the lump forming in her throat. Oh, to have felt even a sliver of that affection growing up. What would Hollen think of Joselyn's relationship with her own parents? A man like him would probably balk at what he'd claimed. And why not? What did a woman like her know about affection and intimacy? Love? It was a good thing she didn't care what Hollen thought of her.

So why did her neck feel so stiff? She reached a hand back and worked at the tightening muscles.

Sigvard watched her. "What do you think of Bedmeg?"

The change in subject caught Joselyn so off guard that she actually stuttered. "I-I think it's very different from my home."

"How so?"

His question almost made her laugh. Bedmeg was *nothing* like Fury Keep. Climate, terrain, and even citizens aside, there was something bigger that would always hold the two places apart. There was warmth here, a depth of loyalty so great Joselyn sensed it in each corner of the mountain. It flourished in the Dokiri people. The men, women, and children. This was the sort of place that had inspired the word *community*. Home.

"People don't fly about on *dragons* for starters."

"And Hollen? What do you think of him?"

She hesitated.

"Don't worry." He winked. "I'll keep it to myself."

Joselyn believed him. "He's a decent man."

"You think so? Even after he . . . " His gaze fell to Joselyn's chest.

She shifted and their eyes met in mutual embarrassment. His gaze darted away, and Joselyn considered his question.

Had she forgiven Hollen for marking her? No. Did she still think him a savage brute? Sometimes. But she wasn't angry anymore. Except for the fact that she still had no inkling how she'd explain it to Dante Viridian. Hollen wasn't a bad person. Him wanting her didn't make him a bad person.

"I can't afford to judge your people by my people's standards. Else I'd always be terrified."

Sigvard regarded her. "And you still want to leave?"

She nodded. "Yes."

"What will he have to do to change your mind?"

"He can't change my mind." Why did that feel like a lie? "I'm needed far too much at home. Your brother should have chosen a different woman."

Sigvard nodded, his gaze drifting. "Sometimes I worry the woman I claim will feel the same. Like there's nothing I can do."

Joselyn frowned, thinking of Sigvard being rejected by the woman he'd waited his entire life to claim. The woman that was surely on his mind every day as he scaled the snowy cliffs to risk facing wyverns. Unexpected tenderness nipped at her heart. Then she thought of Hollen, who'd waited far longer. How long had *he* dreamed of the woman who'd help him lead his people, mother his children, who'd love him? Regret tightened in her gut. Would it pain him when she escaped?

Sigvard broke the silence with a click of his tongue. "But how could that happen? One look at my handsome face and any woman would be undone. You'd be the same if you weren't claimed already." He wiggled his brows suggestively.

Joselyn narrowed her eyes. *I wonder what your brother would say to hear you speaking thusly to his bride.* The boy had nerve, that was certain. She tried for reproach but surrendered to laughter. "You're right. No woman would deny you."

Smiling, he turned back toward the staircase. But Joselyn caught the flicker of doubt in his eyes.

Again they passed the pack of wyverns, who were even less interested than they'd been before. Without a word, Sigvard crouched and started down the ladder-like staircase.

Joselyn inched toward the drop-off, barely mustering the courage to look down. A wave of vertigo rushed over her and she straightened, pulling away from the edge.

"Sigvard?" She pressed the tips of her fingers over her wounded thigh.

He stopped. "What is it?"

"I'm not certain I can go down that way." Joselyn swallowed as embarrassment welled.

Sigvard glanced at the ground below, then back up to Joselyn, incredulous. "It's the only way down. Unless you've a mind to tangle with one of the *gegatu*?"

Joselyn bit her lip. She craned her neck forward, trying to look only at where she would put her hands. Sigvard seemed to understand.

"Come. I'll stay beneath you. Just put your feet where I say."

She didn't miss the slight puffing of his chest and squaring of his shoulders. At least *he* was getting something out of this. What had she been thinking coming up here?

"We'll go slowly. I won't let you fall, little sister." Sigvard's voice was unusually sober. So, he *could* mature when the need arose.

On an inhale, Joselyn turned her back to the open drop and began her descent. True to his word, Sigvard stayed close. So close, in fact, that at one point she accidentally kicked him in the face. Joselyn called out a startled apology. His laughter was so infectious, she gave a thoughtless look downward to meet his grin. It was a mistake.

Past Sigvard's smiling face, the ground doubled. They were much too high up. Bile rose into her throat. A haze darkened the periphery of her narrowing vision. Numbness chilled her fingertips and her grip slackened.

"Joselyn?"

The cliff face tilted. Her eyelids drooped, heavy with sudden weariness. She sighed.

"*Va Kreesha!*"

The alarmed Dokiri oath was the last thing she heard before her mind plunged into total darkness.

17

STOKING FIRES

"Joselyn! Joselyn!"

White light shone in Joselyn's face around the silhouette of a man. He hovered above her.

"Sigvard?" Her voice came out in a croak.

His eyes rolled back on a sigh of relief. "Oh, thank Helig!"

"Wha-what happened?" Joselyn turned her head to the side. Her cheek pressed into the damp snow. Her mouth was filled with the taste of something tangy and metallic.

"You fainted. Has it happened before?"

The fog was dissipating from her mind. Blinking, she nodded.

"I forgot about the damned mountain sickness. I'm so sorry! You should have told me."

They were sitting on the ground at the base of the stony staircase. Her body tensed and relaxed as Joselyn tested for broken bones. All seemed well. No pain save for the burning in her thigh. She squinted. "How did we get down here?"

"I caught you when you started to slide and sort of carried you down the rest of the way." He clasped her about the wrist and tugged her into a seated position.

For once, Joselyn found herself thanking the sky god, Regna. Hollen credited him with the creation of the Dokiri race. If Sigvard had been made a smaller man, Joselyn doubted he'd have been able to save her life as he just had.

She'd forgotten about the mountain sickness too. Apart from her first night with Hollen, she'd suffered no further fainting spells. Joselyn assumed it was because she'd grown stronger over time.

Too much stress today.

Again, Hollen had been right to forbid her from leaving the cave. Irritation nipped at her. Sigvard scratched at the back of his head.

"Hollen will wallop me if he finds out I brought you here."

Joselyn regarded him. Maybe she wasn't the only one grateful for Hollen's absence. While she'd been spared his witnessing her little near-death experience, Sigvard looked like he was contemplating a near-death experience in his immediate future. A wry smile played at Joselyn's lips.

Sigvard frowned. "Promise not to tell him and I'll tell you a secret about *atu hatu*."

Joselyn had no intention of tattling on her new partner-in-crime. However, her curiosity was pricked. "Fair enough."

Sigvard breathed another sigh of relief. All apprehension vanished from his face as his expression took on a conspiratorial edge. "Hollen's ticklish."

Joselyn blinked.

"I don't mean a little ticklish, Joselyn." Sigvard shook his head. "I mean, he'd fall off his mount if someone struck him under the arm at the wrong moment."

The great *Salig* of Bedmeg? Ticklish? Joselyn arched a brow. "Why are you telling me this?"

Sigvard sat back on his heels and tapped a finger to his auburn hair. "We redheads have to stick together."

The boy was charming. Joselyn had to give him that. She returned his mischievous smile with one of her own. "Very well. But what exactly should I do with that knowledge?"

"I'm sure you'll think of something, little sister." He grabbed her around the arms and hoisted her to her feet.

HOLLEN AND RAGNAR each took hold of a paw. The slaughtered direwolf lay strewn across the ground with arrows sticking out of its rich pelt. Normally, they'd leave such creatures alone, but this one was hunting far too close to Bedmeg. Magnus and Arvid snatched the arrows away as Hollen and Ragnar hauled its body toward Jagomri. Its crimson blood streaked the snow.

They'd found no more blood-seekers, and the corpse of the one he'd killed yesterday betrayed no hint of its madness. *Glanshi*.

The morning sun was shrouded behind a blanket of gray clouds, making Hollen long for the comfort of home even more after spending all night in a cliffside camp. He wasn't the only one feeling it.

"I'm just so tired." Arvid said as he wiped at his eyes.

"Oh, I'm just so tired!" Magnus mocked, his voice a high-pitched whine. The other men laughed.

Arvid scoffed. "You don't get it! It's every night. I told her I have patrol in the morning and she said, 'Well that's fine. We can just have dinner and skip the lovemaking. And I told her, 'Whoa, whoa, whoa! That's not what I meant! I just thought maybe we could skip the gossip and go back to our *bok* a little early.'"

"*Podagi!*" Magnus smacked the back of Arvid's head.

They laughed some more as Arvid rubbed at his wild curls.

Hollen smirked. "What did you think was going to happen?"

"I don't know," Arvid muttered at the ground.

Ragnar shook his head. "Don't you understand? You answer to *her* in these matters. When she's done, you can be done. In the meantime, grit your teeth, you fool!"

Hollen snickered along with the others, ignoring the pang of jealousy hardening in his chest. Oh, to have Arvid's kind of problems. Hollen's own bride could barely tolerate his nearness, much less his touch. The day before, he'd been about to kiss her. For a moment he'd even thought she wanted him to. But then, like always, she'd tensed up. Ever afraid of him.

They tossed the wolf's body onto Jagomri's back. Hollen chucked its paw away and yanked out the rope. Together, the four men worked to lash its body to the saddle.

What was it going to take for him to convince his bride to trust him? Did all brides take so long to warm? He jerked on the rope a little harder than was necessary. *Glanshi*, he'd jump off a cliff before trading stories of the marriage *bok* with his riders. He had to do something. But what?

Perhaps he'd been too accommodating? His fear of scaring her, of rejection had kept him from pushing Joselyn. Maybe that was what she really needed. Maybe that was what she really wanted. Could he deal with the fallout if he was wrong?

Hollen thought of what might happen if he was right. His blood heated. Yes. He could take that chance. He *would* take that chance.

Tonight. Helig help him.

THE EVENING DANCING lacked the same grandeur as the night of Joselyn's welcome feast, but his clan's passion burned just as hot. His bride was sitting upon a stone bench, sipping at her malted wine. Hopefully she'd had more than one. The lilting melody of the stringed *kilds* mingled with the bounding pulse of the drums as couples took to the ring to begin dancing.

Hollen sucked the last of the storen stew from his fingers. He stared across the fire at his bride. Her skin glowed and the torchlight illuminated her beauty. Her red braid hung over her shoulder and he followed its path along the feminine curves of her body. Her eyes were fixed on the dancers. If Hollen wasn't mistaken, there was more than a hint of interest there. She was curious, wistful even. Hollen wetted his lips. He was hungry again, but not for storen. He started around the fire.

"Joselyn?"

She looked up, a brow raised. "Yes?"

There was a sultry cadence to her voice. Even her expression was soft, bereft of that tinge of hostility she usually held for him. That ever-present contempt. She tilted her head back just a little too far, exposing the creamy flesh of her throat. He swallowed.

Just do it, Hollen.

"It's getting late. I should take you to our bed. Unless..."

She stared at him without blinking. Did she know what he wanted to ask her? If she did, she could simply cut him off. Or, she could stand, take his hand in hers, and draw him towards the dancing. She could make this easier for him.

In my dreams.

Women were never simple. Or easy. Especially not his. He took a breath.

"Would you prefer to dance first?"

Hollen held his breath and waited out the ensuing silence. She just stared at him. She didn't even blink. What was she thinking? Finally, her lips cracked open.

"I'm tired." The smooth timbre was gone from her voice.

The urge to curl in on himself and die was tempting. But he wouldn't be so easily dissuaded. Not tonight. He had plans and, by the gods, he was going to make some progress with his bride.

"Come then, let's go to our *bok*." Hollen held out a hand. He forced a smile that she didn't return. Was that regret etched into her face? Why? Together they walked the path to their *bok*. Hollen made short work starting the fire as Joselyn undid her hair.

They'd established a new routine at night. Hollen would strip down, climb into bed, and shut his eyes. At which time, Joselyn would change into her nightgown and slip into bed behind him. Tonight, however, he needed her in bed before him.

"I'll be back. I need to tell Erik something."

His bride nodded at him and Hollen spent a few moments shuffling around outside their *bok* like an idiot. He prayed that she'd be dressed down by the time he returned. Helig must have heard his prayer. Her cheek was pressed into the pillow toward the center of the pallet. Were he to lay down, she'd be facing him. That in and of itself was new. It was probably the wine. Again, he hoped she'd had plenty. Hollen stripped off all but his pants.

He went around to her side and sat on the edge, sinking into the furs. His bride's blue eyes popped open. She sat up with a start.

"What are you doing?" Her fear sparked, and Hollen resolved not to take it personally. Still, some of his nerve wilted under that look.

Commit, Hollen.

"How's your leg?"

She blinked. "I-It's fine."

He pulled back the covers. "I'm going to look at it."

She snapped for the blankets. "No!"

Hollen held firm to the furs. "*Yes.*"

He uncurled her hands and pulled the blankets from them. Joselyn drew her knees into her chest and wrapped her arms around them. He'd try not to take *that* personally either. He took a breath, propping his weight up with one hand.

"Joselyn, I'm not going to rape you. Don't you think I would've done it by now?"

Her lips thinned and she said nothing. Her grip around her legs didn't ease. Hollen waited, sensing there was something she wanted to say. Now was the time for patience.

"Men don't touch me the way you touch me. None ever have."

Possessive satisfaction swelled in his chest. "Good."

Joselyn bit into the swell of her lower lip. Did she know how alluring she looked when she did that? "I know what you want, Hollen. And I can't give it to you."

Hollen reached for her right foot. She flinched when he touched her, but he held on, his hands swallowing up the cold little thing. "Really? Because all I want right now is to check your leg."

An innocent lie. What mattered were his intentions. And tonight his intention was merely to gain a measure of his bride's trust. To prove he wasn't the instinct-driven beast she apparently thought him. He began rubbing his thumbs along the sole of her foot. He could feel the tension in her body even here. He lowered his voice, infusing it with soothing tones. "Let me touch you, Joselyn."

Her hesitation was palpable. He continued his massaging, taking his time over each corded muscle. All the while her eyes remained fixed on him, as though she were waiting for him to pounce. He knew the *gneri* blade still lay under her pillow. She'd probably have her hand on it if she weren't so busy clutching her knees to herself. Hollen lightened his touch beneath her toes, "accidentally" tickling her. She jumped.

"Are you all right?" he asked, pretending not to know what

he'd done. He did it again. She started again. The corners of her mouth twitched.

"Is something wrong, *mu hamma*?" He continued tickling her.

She released her knees to kick him with her other foot. "Stop that!"

He caught her leg before she could strike him and tickled that one as well. "Stop what?"

She smiled, even as her voice buzzed with warning. "Hollen, I mean it!"

"I'm still waiting for you to tell me what's bothering you." With both her feet in his hands, he tickled her harder.

"You're tickling me!" She kicked, trying to get free.

"Oh! I'm sorry. You should have said something." He stopped, but didn't release her.

She laughed and Hollen's heart skipped a beat. He ached for that sound. He seized the moment. He stood long enough to scoop her up and lay her flat on the bed. All amusement vanished and she came up on her elbows before he'd even let her go. He put a hand on her shoulder.

"Lay down. I'm going to look at your wound." She ignored him and struggled to come up from the bed. Hollen bit the inside of his cheek. Time to man up.

"*Joselyn.*" His voice dropped low in the same tone he used when informing his riders they'd be staying out on patrol an additional day. "Be still."

She obeyed. Barely.

He pressed down on her shoulder, forcing her to rest on the bed. Her eyes blazed a hole in his flesh as he scooted down the pallet to take her right foot up in his hands. He resumed his massage, this time taking care not to tickle her. She squeezed her legs together, and her hands crossed over each other at her waist, clutching her wrists. This seemed all too familiar. He sighed. At least she wasn't fighting him. More importantly, he had no intention of hurting her this time. Thank Helig.

He waited until her foot had fully warmed to the heat of his skin before moving up to her ankle. If not for the gap between them, he might not have been able to fit his hands between her clenched legs.

"Relax, Joselyn," he murmured, circling the joint. She did. A bit. His bride was so small. Her ankle was narrower than his wrist, by a great deal. Her skin was pale and smooth. He stared at the thousands of freckles dotting her leg. Like stars in the night sky. He could spend days kissing each one. He would.

One step at a time.

He worked his way up, helping her open her legs enough to work on the muscles of her calf. As her legs parted, he could feel the slight tremor in her limbs. He stroked the back of her heel. "*Shh*. It's all right. No one's going to hurt you. *I'm* not going to hurt you."

If she felt patronized by his words, he couldn't tell. She took a shaky breath and her grip on her wrists eased, her elbows sinking deeper into the furs at her sides.

"That's it, *mu hamma*. Just rest." He took his time, brushing with the pads of his fingers in long, sweeping strokes. With each pass he pressed ever upward until he was at her knee. When he caressed the back, she twitched. It didn't seem like fear. Hollen's gaze flicked up. She was staring at the ceiling. He petted at the soft flesh again. She sighed and her eyelids slid shut.

That seemed like a good sign. Encouraged, Hollen let his own body relax. He'd been as tense as she. More so. Unfortunately, there was nothing he could do about the growing stiffness in his groin. He'd have to deal with it. Just as he had every night since bringing his bride to his bed.

When he moved up her thigh, her eyes fluttered open again. Without pausing, Hollen slid the hem of her gown up and started undoing the bandage. In his periphery, Joselyn's fingers fidgeted over her hips. He knew he was pressing the limits of her faith, but she wasn't stopping him. This was good. All things considered, the night could have gone very differently.

"Stay here," he said, rising from the bed to get a clean bandage. He returned and patted at the wound to test it for pooled fluid. "It's healing well."

He hooked a hand under her knee and pulled it up so he could slip the new bandage beneath. That tension had returned to her limbs, but she didn't resist. With extreme gentleness, Hollen rewrapped her leg and tugged the gown back down over her thigh. In one fluid motion, he moved to the other thigh.

"What are you doing?" she asked, breathless.

He resumed his massage, working his thumbs into the soft flesh. "Putting you to sleep."

"I won't sleep like this."

"Let's see."

"Hollen, I won't. I *can't*."

He moved down to her knee, showing her he'd already gone as far as he'd intended. "It will help if you stop arguing and close your eyes."

She bit her lip again but said nothing. Blue eyes remained open.

"Does any of this hurt?"

She shook her head.

"Tell me if it does."

He took his time, working all the way back down to her toes. Sure enough, her eyes slid shut again, her breath evening out. But she wasn't asleep. Perfect.

She smelled of spring water and moss. Earthen. When she'd first arrived, Joselyn had the aroma of flowers too sweet to have come from anywhere but the lowlands. The change was subtle, but unmistakable. Bedmeg suited her.

He reached up and took one of her hands. Her eyes fluttered open and she started to draw away. He firmed his grip. Perhaps it was time to back off. He'd gotten what he'd set out for. It was a square victory. And yet, he wanted more.

He'd broken down barriers, gotten a taste of her surrender, of her trust. Time to find out how far that trust extended.

How much more mountain is there to scale?

JOSELYN'S HEART thundered in her chest. Her blood had finally cooled, her nerves calmed, her lust abated. And now? Just as she'd been about to drift off to sleep, he was starting in on her hands. He was sitting closer now, so close she could smell the leather and sulfur on his skin.

He'd washed away the grime from earlier, the dirt and blood he'd been covered in from his *veligiri* hunt. He'd marched into the common area with his men, all height and power, looking like he owned the very mountain he stood on. His tooth-covered axe swung from the loop at his hip with each powerful stride. In that moment, Joselyn could almost see herself running into his arms, letting him scoop her up the way his men snatched their tittering brides for sensual 'welcome home' kisses. A flicker of passion ignited then, and she'd not been able to extinguish it all day.

It had grown hotter as she watched the couples dancing that night. She'd allowed her mind to wander, imagining what it would be like to press her feminine curves into Hollen's hard planes. Now they were in his bed, and he was stoking that flame into a roaring bonfire. How had she responded? She'd lain down in the pyre and prayed she didn't scorch.

Worse. I've melted.

Even now her body hummed with pleasure. She had to stop him. This had gone far enough. Who knew what might happen if he kept going. She peeled her tongue from the roof of her mouth.

"Hollen, I—"

"—Joselyn, I swear to Regna that I won't violate you. Do you believe me?"

Skies, he still thought she was afraid of him? Thank the gods he didn't know the truth.

Another hour of this, savage, and I might be the one violating you.

"I believe you."

He exhaled, his lips stretching in a hopeful smile. Such a beautiful smile. "Then let me do this. You can't imagine how much it pleases me."

She had an idea. A thrill of excitement skipped through her. Shame followed it. What was she doing? She had to put a stop to this. She wasn't playing with fire; she was dancing in the flames. She swallowed, mustering her resolve.

"I don't understand what you expect from me."

He held her hand in one of his and drew the rounded tips of his nails up that same arm. He left a trail of gooseflesh in his wake, and she stifled a shiver. "I know I terrified you when we met. I know you still fear me because of it." He pressed a thumb along the inside of her elbow, drawing tiny circles. Why did that feel so good? He continued his speech.

"I want to see that it's not too late. That there's still hope."

Hope? He had more *hope* than she did willpower. She said nothing as he finished with one shoulder and trailed over to the other. Curiosity flared within her. There were so many things she hadn't asked him. Did he regret having claimed her? Why *was* he called 'The Soulless'? Why hadn't he claimed her body? Rather than ask, she watched him, trying to puzzle out the answers on her own. All the while, her breaths grew shallower.

When he was done, he traced a line up her arm all the way to her throat. With feather lightness, he caressed the sides of her neck.

Don't moan!

He brushed his fingers up and around her ears, back down to the corner of her mouth. She gasped as he drew across her bottom lip and down into the dimple in her chin.

"Nothing bad's going to happen, *mu hamma*. Least of all *here*. In our bed."

Gods, his voice! The depth of it made her want to lean into him, to press her ear against his mouth just to feel the vibration.

"This place, our bed, is sacred. You will *never* suffer here. I swear it to you."

This was unfair. She was just a woman. Her lips parted on a breath and her eyelids slid downward. Just as she was about to lift her face to his, he drew back.

"I know this was hard for you."

Like settling into a rose-petaled bath.

"Thank you, Joselyn." He took a breath. "Thank you for trusting me."

He stood from the bed. Joselyn's eyes flew fully open and her mouth snapped shut. She sat up.

"Where are you going?" Had that sounded eager? She hoped not. If so, Hollen didn't seem to notice. He wasn't even looking at her as he turned from the bed and strode toward the tunnel, muttering something about "diving into a snowbank." He paused at the door.

"Get some sleep, *mu hamma*."

And he was gone.

She fell back onto the furs. What had just happened? Clarity took its sweet time creeping back.

Father would call her a whore.

This couldn't be how whores felt. Whores must feel dirty, cheap, defiled. Her body was flushed with warmth. Her limbs heavy, like she'd imbued the finest of wines. Her nerves were alight with sensitivity. She could feel the air moving over her skin, and it felt *good*.

Yes. Father would be furious.

She smiled at the ceiling and played with the ends of her hair. She thought of the day's events, of Hollen teaching her to prepare the storen he'd preserved before leaving. She'd made a mess of the poor thing, but Hollen hadn't minded. No one had. The clan had opened up to Joselyn. At least half had tasted the storen stew and been eager to congratulate her on her kill. It had all seemed so intimate. Gratifying. Could she be happy like this forever? A thousand more days like this one?

She saw herself sitting in the common area, a perfectly butchered stag lying before her. One she'd both hunted and dressed with practiced ease. Hollen, just returned from a patrol, bent down to press a gentle kiss to her temple. She tilted her head back, and the corners of her mouth curled. His hand trailed down to press against the firm round of her swollen belly.

What would Tansy think of that?

Her smile faltered. Her fingers stilled. She might as well have been the one diving into a snowbank.

He may think he's yours, but you are not his. You can never be.

A wave of guilt made her shudder. What was she doing? What sort of insanity was she entertaining? Was *that* what she wanted? To be a savage's little captive bride?

Maybe.

Joselyn's lips thinned. So what? It wasn't an option. Not for her. This world owed her nothing. She was Lady Fury, and her people depended on her. She could live without Hollen. But if she abandoned those who needed her? She couldn't live with herself. Not forever. She fingered her gold pendant, reciting the credo in her mind.

You have to do something, Joselyn. Soon.

Her duty to escape had never felt more urgent. Time was running out and, suddenly, Joselyn felt the turning of an entirely new hourglass.

18

LEANING BACK

Joselyn gasped as the air flew from her lungs for the dozenth time that day. Her braid was a mess, covered in the dust of the hard ground. Hollen hovered above her on all fours, with his hands pinning her arms to the dirt. Joselyn's knife lay a good foot away from her.

"One of these days you'll stop leaning back." His breath poured over her balmy flesh, making her shiver in the snow-flurried air.

A foot of fresh snow had collected on the ground outside the armory since they'd begun the day's lessons. They'd have to quit soon, or their trek back to the common area would leave their boots soaking. Joselyn growled through gritted teeth.

"These lessons are asinine. We both know I'll never be able to best you."

Hollen's grip on her wrists tightened as he flashed an arrogant smirk. "Not if you keep leaning back you won't."

Normally, when Hollen pinned her to the ground, he would peel himself off before she had time to fully acquaint herself with the cold earth. This time, however, the shirtless Dokiri man took his time. Fresh heat, leftover from the night before, bloomed low in her belly. His eyes brazenly trailed down the flesh of her neck, and lower.

Joselyn squirmed beneath him. "This is undignified. Get off me!"

Hollen returned his eyes to hers and his lips drew into an exasperated pout. "No one's even watching us today. Stop worrying so much about what you look like."

Joselyn fixed him with an imperious glare. "I'm a lady of Morhagen. I should always be concerned with how I appear."

Hollen rolled his eyes and reached to the side to scoop up a handful of dirt. Before she knew what he was about, he dragged his filthy fingers across her face from brow to chin.

Joselyn stared at him in openmouthed shock.

Devilish delight filled his eyes. "Now you're a lady of mud. Which is good because that's where you'll keep ending up if you don't stop leaning back."

No sound came out when she tried to speak. She could hardly believe his impudence. "Why would you do that?"

He leaned forward, stopping a scorching inch from her face. "Sport."

How *dare* he? In that moment she would have done absolutely anything to wipe that arrogant smile off his face. Without thinking, she brought her free hand up and jammed her thumb into the pit of his arm.

Hollen flinched, then froze, his face screwed up in confusion.

Joselyn poked him again, and his arm clamped down to shut her out.

A smug smile crept across Joselyn's mud-streaked face.

Hollen's eyes narrowed, his expression murderous. "Which one of them told you?"

Victory. Her smile tightened. "Does it matter?"

He regarded her, the wheels of his mind seeming to spin. "I'll kill that *podagi* runt."

Hollen withdrew and climbed to his feet. Joselyn bolted up and flung herself at him, growling as she did. The force of her attack knocked him over, and Joselyn hopped on top of him. She jabbed her fingers into any open space she could find on his scarred body.

For several moments, all Hollen did was thrash about as she attacked him. He tried to catch her darting hands.

"Stop!" he commanded. Joselyn ignored him and her assault grew even more frenzied.

"Beg for mercy!"

"Joselyn, stop!" he pleaded.

Joselyn laughed. Satisfaction dizzied her. She had him. He was at *her* mercy.

Hollen caught one of her wrists. In the time it took him to grab the other, she managed two more solid jabs. Each made his body jump. Hollen was panting, and Joselyn's body rose and fell with his chest. She shook her head.

"The mighty *Salig* of Bedmeg, bested by a lady of mud." Joselyn clucked.

Hollen's mortified expression dissolved, and mirth replaced it. He laughed. "Well Joselyn, if the men of your lands are anything like you, your father's enemies are doomed."

At the mention of her father, awareness washed over her. She was straddling her captor, practically mounting him. As if he noted her shock, his pleasured grin dissipated. He opened his mouth to speak, but no words came out.

She slid off his chest. Hollen sat up from the ground and propped his hands behind him for support. He stared at her, and the awkwardness stretched between them.

Joselyn spoke, eager to fill the silence. "My father's enemy isn't the kind one defeats with force."

Hollen cocked his head. "I thought you said his enemies were violent. That they would destroy your house."

A chill crept up Joselyn's spine as she thought of Dante Viridian's many infamous deeds. "Oh, they're violent. But it's not their nature my father fears. It's what they know."

"What do they know?"

Should she answer him honestly? Temptation nettled her. There was a bitter part of Joselyn's soul, since the moment she'd learned of them, that was desperate to divulge her father's sins. A part that longed for someone to recognize and appreciate what her sacrifice was paying for. Of course, she wasn't free to reveal her circumstances to anyone. Not even to Tansy.

Joselyn appraised her captor. What would the political intrigues of a foreign court mean to a barbarian? What did she risk by telling the chieftain of a clan so reclusive their existence bordered on legend? Joselyn sucked in her lips.

What could she say? That her father had made a mistake? No, his affair with the queen had gone on for too long. His actions had been meditated. Marcus Fury was no fool. If he'd taken such a risk, he was hoping to gain something. Something more than the release of an occasional forbidden tryst. Her father had been spinning a web of destruction for the royal House Travaran. He'd been close to entangling himself in that web.

And now I have to clean up the mess.

"My father's been having an affair with the queen." As the confession left her mouth, Joselyn felt the dark hand of secrecy slackening its grip around her chest. She sucked in a breath, the deepest she'd managed in a fortnight.

"What's an affair?"

Taken aback, Joselyn looked up into Hollen's squinting eyes. Confusion was wrought on his face. Was he being serious?

"It's . . . like when a man is with a woman who isn't his wife."

Hollen blinked back. He spoke hesitantly. "You mean bedding?"

She nodded.

A corner of Hollen's mouth turned up in disgust.

Shame suffused her. Of course he'd be repelled. Joselyn had firsthand knowledge of the respect with which the Dokiri men regarded their unions. She doubted the crime of adultery was treated lightly in Bedmeg. Would Hollen think less of her for her connection to an adulterer? For helping to cover it up?

She explained. "The king would see it as more than a betrayal of his union. He would have my father executed for treason. My entire house would suffer."

A moment passed. "What's any of that to do with you?"

She swallowed. "My father has bought his enemies silence with a marriage alliance."

Hollen's brow furrowed. He didn't understand. She continued.

"House Fury is wealthy and very powerful. Dante Viridian stands to gain far more as a blooded ally of my father than as his enemy."

Hollen stared at her. Comprehension still eluded him. How could she make this clearer? She started to speak when Hollen's face slackened as realization registered.

His next words were almost a whisper. "You mean . . .you were to be married to your father's enemy?"

Joselyn thought back, trying to understand how he'd missed that key detail. She supposed she'd never expressly stated that Dante Viridian was also the man who was threatening her house. She frowned.

"What did *you* think?" she asked.

Hollen shot to his feet, making Joselyn jump. She stared up at Hollen who stood seething above her. *What in the skies?* His volume ratcheted.

"I thought your marriage was the price your father had paid to gain allies *against* his enemies!"

What was wrong with him? Why was he raising his voice? Affronted, Joselyn scrambled to stand. She swiped at the dirt on her face.

"My father needs no allies." She shook her head as though the fact were obvious. "He's the most powerful man in Morhagen save for the king. What he *needs* is silence." She planted her hands on her hips, glaring up at him.

Hollen's eyes bled black like scorched parchment. His accent thickened. "So, to save himself from his sins he would sell his only child to a man who would turn on him?"

How nice it must be to be shocked by such things. Her hands shot out. "Yes! House Viridian is on the brink of total obscurity. Its lands are in decay, its reigning lord is a madman, and its only fame is a declining wool trade. There's nothing Dante Viridian wouldn't do to save his legacy!"

Hollen went still. His expression flattened. "What do you mean 'a madman'?"

Joselyn hesitated. The flame of her anger almost puffed out for one moment. She'd not intended to mention that. She choked on her tongue, searching for the right words. "My intended—"

"—Dante Viridian," Hollen confirmed.

"He . . . he . . . " Joselyn's heart pounded in her chest. "There were rumors." Her gaze broke away from Hollen's for the first time.

Hollen's fingers pressed into the delicate point of Joselyn's chin, drawing her face back up to his. His voice was hard as steel. "What rumors?"

Joselyn batted his hand away. Her mouth hardened into a determined glower. She wouldn't be cowed by a savage. She'd gone willingly to a monster like Dante Viridian. Hollen, of all men, wouldn't scare her. "The young Lord Viridian is plagued by bloodlust."

Tension knotted in the space between his brows, drawing them closer together. Joselyn's shoulders stiffened under the weight of his deepening scrutiny. A flash of understanding sparked across his face. Unable to stop herself, Joselyn's gaze drifted to the little stretch of ground between them.

Hollen stomped away to stand at the edge of the nearby forge. His clenched fists dangled at his sides. Joselyn stared at his bare back, and her nerve waned in the lingering silence. Now the truth was out, she needed him to respond. To react. To judge. Someone, other than she, *had* to speak their mind on the disaster that was her impending marriage

Hollen turned. His wide strides reached her in a blink. He stopped, inches from her. Joselyn could see his jaw working as he gritted his teeth.

"*That's* what you've been so desperate to leave Bedmeg for—"

'*To leave me for.*' Joselyn cringed at the subtext of his words.

"—to return to a man who harms others for morbid pleasure?"

Why was he internalizing her dilemma? Couldn't he see this wasn't about him? Why couldn't he understand she had a responsibility? One she couldn't simply set aside.

She swallowed, trying for patience. "I told you before, what I want for myself is irrelevant. What I *need* is to fulfill my duty and protect my house."

"By allowing yourself to be sold? Is that how *fathers*"—he spat the word like a curse—"treat their daughters in your country?"

Joselyn's nostrils flared. "You have some nerve to dare a comparison between our peoples. You, whose riders steal innocent women from their homes to subject them to a life of slavery."

He crossed his arms over his chest. "Perhaps you're right, Joselyn. Your people aren't to blame for your father's depravity."

Joselyn's mouth fell open and her arms slackened at her sides. "Excuse me?"

Hollen's spine straightened, increasing his towering presence. "Only a wretch would use his own kin to save himself from justice."

For a moment, Joselyn's emotions went blank. No one had ever spoken thusly of her father in her presence. Not ever. Someone had to explain things to Hollen. He didn't know the rules. Her words came out slow and deliberate.

"If Dante Viridian could be moved to such wickedness for mere sport, can you not see how far he would go to crush my house beneath his feet? It wouldn't matter to him what he stood to gain or lose."

Hollen leaned down and hissed. "That isn't your burden to bear. You aren't a price to be paid for another's misdeeds."

Her blood began to heat. She scraped for composure. "No. I'm not. I'm a lady. The only daughter of Marcus Fury. The *only* one who can save my father and our house."

"What do you think? That dying for a man who doesn't give a damn about his own blood makes you a good person?"

Damn him. Who in the skies did he think he was? "You're a barbarian! You don't know what you're talking about!"

Hollen sneered. "If I had a daughter, I would curse my soul to the deepest pit of the mountain before risking any harm to her."

Joselyn's vision blurred with a flash of white rage. "Well you'll never have a chance to prove it, savage! No woman, *especially* me, will ever bear you a daughter! Because even your meager gods know better than to entrust a woman into your cursed people's care!"

Hollen flinched as though she'd struck him. Some of the

color drained from his face. Joselyn glared, refusing to back down. Time slowed to a crawl before Hollen mustered a dry response.

"At least we have room in our hearts for love." He gave her a sweeping glance from head to toe. "And enough sense in our heads to know where to apply it."

Humiliation wracked her. "I love my father."

Her deepest deception.

Hollen scoffed. "Oh, of that, I have *no* doubt."

Joselyn's breath hitched in her throat, and her voice cracked on a more shameful lie. "My father loves *me*."

Hollen stood still as the mountain beneath him. "You're a fool."

Joselyn's body went numb. Tears, the likes of which she'd not shed in years, stung her eyes. She cocked her head, intending to throw back a retort, but her jaw went stiff. She tried to swallow but her throat was clogged.

Hollen watched as she worked to stem her tears. His black eyes chilled further as he leaned in. "If ever I had considered returning you to your father, I swear to you, no one could convince me to now. You will never leave this mountain, *mu hamma*."

A wave of nausea rolled within her. Joselyn pressed a sluggish hand to her belly. Her lip trembled as the taste of salt filled her mouth. She had to get away from him. Now.

Bumping into his side, Joselyn ducked away to run out into the curtain of snow that flurried to the earth.

She trudged up the ravine, kicking white drifts into the air like the foam of crashing waves. She had no sense for where she was going, only that she couldn't let anyone see the tears spilling down her face.

He was wrong. He didn't understand. Who was he to judge her motives? To judge her father? What did a savage know of the burden of nobility? Who was he to comment on what a lord must do to protect his house, his blood?

My father arranged my marriage to Dante Viridian because it was the only way he could protect me from total ruination.

That was what anyone would assume. And why not? It made perfect sense. But no, somehow Hollen had jumped to believing Lord Fury didn't love her.

Hollen didn't realize that no lord would have wed her after the scandal of Lord Fury's treason was made known to the world. No one would have been willing to tie themselves to the disgraced daughter of a dead traitor. This had been the *only* reasonable choice. If not for Hollen's ignorance, he would have thought of these things on his own. She could tell him. She should go back there right now and educate the cruel bastard. Then she'd tell him to go rot in oblivion.

Joselyn choked on a sob and stumbled into a snowbank. She sat up on her knees. She couldn't face him like this. She was a disaster. Before today, Joselyn had known what her father really felt for her. She'd accepted it. So why couldn't she breathe *now*? Why did it suddenly feel like the truth was crushing her from the inside out?

Because he knows. Because Hollen knows.

How could he? How could he throw that in her face?

For the first time since arriving on the mountain, she was too hot. She ripped at the tie lacing the front of her underdress, tearing it loose. Her secret was out. Marcus Fury didn't love her. Had never loved her. Old bitterness clutched at her throat with unnatural force. A strangled cry escaped her lungs, and Joselyn pressed the back of her palm against her lips.

A demand shrieked within her. A vile need for her father to feel how low this humiliation had brought her. She needed that degradation to seep so deep he could no longer bear to stand before a mirror. Just as she'd stopped doing years ago.

"Joselyn?" called a deep voice.

Joselyn froze. She swept the sleeve of her dress across her face, brushing away what she could of her tears. Her head snapped up and she fixed dagger eyes upon Ivan. He stared down at her with that scarred face of his that otherwise was so much like Hollen's.

"What?" she snapped.

Ivan glanced around the ravine. "What's wrong, *mu Saliga*?"

She hated that title. Hated these people who insisted on using it. She needed to get away from them. They wouldn't understand. No one here understood what she had to do. Sniffing, Joselyn jumped to her feet.

"Take me to the lowlands."

Ivan took a step back and dropped his head low to look into her eyes. "What did he do?"

She ignored him. "I don't belong here. Your brother doesn't see that, but maybe you do? Maybe you see a lot of things your brother doesn't see."

Joselyn had kept an eye on Ivan, waiting for a good moment to proposition him. In that time, she'd learned a few things about him. The man thought he knew better than Hollen on practically everything. Maybe he wanted to *be* better than Hollen? Well, now was his chance.

"Do you like living in a cave, Ivan? Sequestered to one small part of the world for the rest of your life? The height of your potential already realized? Wouldn't you like more for yourself, to *be* more? My father could give you that. Could give you anything you ask."

She held her breath. The gods knew, this was her best chance. Ivan studied her, his eyes narrowed in thought. After a moment, he licked his fingers and wiped away some of the dirt on her face. Before Joselyn could react, he chucked her beneath the chin.

"I'm sorry things have been so hard on you, Joselyn." A sympathetic frown crossed his face. "I swear they'll get better. One way or another."

With that, he turned and continued down the ravine, taking her hope with him. Fresh tears welled.

Joselyn turned her face up to raining snow. The season was growing later every hour. A knot twisted in her addled stomach as a thought bobbed to the surface of her mind. This was the day she'd been meant to arrive in Brance. And she was no closer to arriving than she'd been when Hollen first plucked her from her horse. She'd done *nothing*.

Enough crying. Enough begging. Enough of this. It's time to act.

She grasped at her necklace, rubbing the pendant so hard the friction warmed it.

It's time to be the dragon.

19

FOOLS RUSH IN

The common area was dark, but Joselyn carried no torch. Instead she stuck to the periphery, drawing her hand along the outer wall. Each step seemed to echo through the cavernous space, threatening to expose her. She took her time, careful not to sabotage herself.

Hollen hadn't stirred as she'd slipped from their bed, drawing the *gneri* blade out with her as she rose. Her captor was a heavy sleeper. Creeping out of their *bok* unnoticed had been no great hardship. For that, Joselyn thanked the gods. They hadn't spoken a word since their fight. When he came to bed, Joselyn heard him start to, but he'd changed his mind. It was for the best. Nothing good could have come from it.

An icy chill blew across Joselyn's face as she stepped from beneath the shelter of the common area. The nearly full moon illuminated the dead of night. Against the glare of the snow, she could easily make out the details of the downward-sloping ravine. Joselyn scurried down to the shadowy forge. Sure enough, it was empty. The elderly man, who seemed an ever-present fixture within the armory, was nowhere in sight. It appeared the gods were on her side. She snapped up the bow

Hollen had fitted for her along with a quiver of arrows, then made her way back up the slope.

Joselyn hurried to her cache and fished out her supplies. Finally, it was off to the wood stacks. Giant skids lay against the enormous pile of cut logs. The wooden pallets were used for hauling firewood up the mountain by way of mountain rams. Their bottoms were fitted with shining metal glides that helped them move up the slopes. Joselyn tipped one over.

The fresh layer of powdery snow muffled the sound of the skid hitting the ground. Her timing seemed impeccable. Even Hollen's riders had reported that no *veligiri* had been spotted on this side of the mountain today. She would never get a better chance. Joselyn stacked her supplies on the skid and tied them down with the leather trappings that were meant to secure logs. Now came the difficult part.

She grabbed on to the front of the skid and tugged. It glided with ease. Too much ease. As she dragged it backward, the slope of the ravine deepened. Joselyn dug her feet into the snow, pushing against the skid to keep it from mowing her over. It took her the better part of an hour to walk it down the ravine. A cold sweat broke out across her brow.

Finally, she made it to a safe launching point. She was already tired, but this was worth it. Instead of crossing miles of snowy terrain on foot, she'd be sledding down it in a fraction of the time. She had to disappear into the forest *before* the sun rose.

Once free of the ravine's walls, Joselyn stopped the skid. This was it. She glanced back toward Bedmeg for the last time.

She should be relieved. Yet, she couldn't shake the feeling that she was leaving something behind. Something newfound and precious. Now her anger had cooled, Joselyn could acknowledge that she didn't hate Bedmeg, didn't hate its people. In another life, she would have liked to have known them better, to have explored what kind of woman she might have become. To make a home. She closed her eyes.

I am a dragon. The dragon submits to none.

She exhaled on a sharp breath and girded her nerves against the harrowing darkness ahead.

She was Joselyn Helena Elise Fury, and Hollen the Soulless of Bedmeg wasn't the only one on this mountain who understood duty.

Joselyn crawled onto her belly, mounting the skid. It was moving even before she settled herself upon it. Just like that, she was blowing down the mountain, toward her destiny. She'd have likened it to flying, except she'd already done that. This wasn't the same, though it was still terrifying. She stifled a squeal as the skid plunged forward. It sped over a drift and she soared on a current of air, well above the sparkling ground. Joselyn's hands squeezed the wood so tightly she'd have to pick splinters from them later.

In a matter of minutes, she was miles from Bedmeg. She was free. After nearly a fortnight, Joselyn had taken hold of her destiny. So why did she feel like she was escaping one form of bondage only to rush headlong into another? She pushed the thought into the back of her mind, choosing to focus on not tumbling from the skid.

Faster than she could have hoped, the blackness of the tree line approached. She hadn't accounted for just how quickly the skid would travel. How was she going to stop it? She had little time to think. In a moment of panic, she rolled off.

Joselyn spun out of control, the wild twist of her legs carrying her far across the snowy ground. Had she not pinned it shut, her coat would have been yanked from her body as she tumbled. When she finally stopped rolling, Joselyn lay staring up at the star-studded sky. It spiraled above her. She heaved breath into her lungs, desperate to reground herself. There was a crashing sound in the distance, an explosion of lumber. Dread washed through her, and Joselyn groaned. She no longer needed the skid, but like a grim omen, its destruction unsettled her all the same.

Joselyn wobbled to her feet. The world still seemed to be spinning, and she struggled to reorient herself. She fixed her eyes upon the darkness of the tree line and trudged through the snow in the direction she'd heard the crash. It wasn't long before she found the skid tracks. Joselyn frowned. Should she be pursued, Hollen would know where to start his search. She sighed. It was unavoidable. If her luck continued to hold, the morning sun would melt most of her tracks, just as it had the morning of her hunt.

A great deal of her nerve evaporated as she stepped into the trees. An image of the blood-seeker flashed in her mind as she crept through the shadows. Would she meet a similar horror out here on her own? The question had plagued her before leaving. From the safety of Bedmeg, it had been easier to reason that Hollen and his men had just patrolled this side of the mountain. He'd assured her that they'd found no further threats. Still, their search had taken place in the daytime. Perhaps the expectations were different at night?

Focus, Joselyn.

Following the pull of gravity, she hiked her way through the forest. Instead of crashing blindly into the trunks of trees, she only scratched herself on the prickle of pine needles every other minute. Her progress was slow, and made all the slower by the amount of supplies she'd brought. It was a relief when Joselyn entered a flat clearing and was able to walk unimpeded in the light of the moon.

How long would it be before she stumbled upon one of her countrymen? A few days? A week? Joselyn had only to make herself known, and her people would do anything to assist the daughter of Lord Fury. A generous reward was all but guaranteed.

What would her father do when she returned? What would he say to the daughter who had risked her life to save their house? She ground her teeth.

He doesn't love me. But, by the gods, after this he will respect me. He'll look me in the eyes and know what his daughter did to save him from himself.

The world might owe her nothing, but Marcus Fury owed her that much.

She thought of Hollen then, thought of his excitement and unfettered pride when she shot the storen. It had required so little to please him, to elicit his praise. He'd marched through the forest *with* her, his head held high. Her own satisfaction had swelled, blazing bright by the fan of his untempered approval. How she wanted to feel that pride again. Right *now*. As she risked everything to save the life of the man who'd sold her to his enemies. Instead, all she felt was the pang of regret.

No. I don't have time for this. Focus on the task at hand.

But she couldn't. Now that she'd thought of him, she couldn't stop. She'd promised to close the lid on his memory. And yet, every detail shone in her mind. The tenor of his voice, the curve of his mouth, the warmth of his hands. Shivering against the night chill, she ached to feel that warmth now. Yearned to feel his heat around her, upon her, within her. She stopped.

She turned to look back up the way she'd come. It was just as dark as the path before her. There was no certainty there, no assurances. But there was an oath. The promise of a wild man who'd looked at her with pure eyes. Eyes filled with a depth of devotion that had never been offered to Joselyn. And it had come without condition. Without a price to be paid by her.

A swell of hot tears rose up and Joselyn let them fall. She

hadn't danced with him, hadn't kissed him. She hadn't said goodbye. Regret pulled at her chest, back up the mountain.

He could never love you. Not if he knew what you were really like.

This morning he'd guessed her secret. Her own father didn't love her. At worst that made her contemptible. At best, pathetic. And he'd only guessed the half of it. The rest was so much worse. Despite what he thought, she didn't love Lord Fury. In truth, she *despised* him. Her own father. And if she didn't continue on right now, she'd be exactly what he always thought she would be. Worthless.

Cry if you must. Shed your tears. But you are not going back.

Joselyn stood a while, her gaze darting up and down the slope of the mountain. That was it, then. She sniffed, drawing her sleeve across her face. She swallowed, calling upon a lifetime of discipline. If she was still any longer, the night's chill would set into her bones. That was what she told herself as she took a step toward her father, and away from Hollen.

A tremor wracked the ground beneath her, accompanied by a deep rumbling across the snow. Joselyn froze. A wave of fear dove down her belly. She looked down. There was nothing but fresh, gray snow sparkling in the moonlight.

Another tremor rumbled through the ground and up her knees. Her instincts wailed. Joselyn started running, her vision tunneling. She shed her water skins, desperate to be free of their weight. They struck the snow with a thud, followed by the sharp crack of shattering ice.

In Joselyn's line of sight, the tree line jumped. Before she could contemplate what it meant, her body plunged into a glacial cold that stole the breath from her lungs and seized her heart in her chest.

Hollen woke to a fist pummeling his chest.

"*Glanshi.*" He squinted, trying to see who it was against the glow of the torch. His head pounded with the ache of a fitful night's sleep.

Ivan hissed at him in their father tongue. "Get up. Your bride is gone."

What?

Hollen swept an arm out into the coolness of the furs. No Joselyn. He drew upward, feeling for the *gneri* blade. It was gone. He threw back the blankets and leapt from the bed.

"Where is she?" he demanded.

"Helig knows."

Va Kreesha. Hollen threw on his clothes.

Ivan glared at him from across the *bok*. "I saw her crying yesterday. What did you do?"

Guilt nettled at him. He *had* made her cry. A lot. Though she'd tried to hide the worst of it from him. Joselyn was nothing if not proud. He ignored his younger brother and sprinted down the tunnel.

The common area was still dark. The sun would be rising in an hour and several of the Dokiri *hammas* were already preparing the morning meal. Lavinia was among them. Hope fluttered within him. His bride had taken a liking to the woman. Hollen darted in her direction, greeting her as he approached with a jerking fall of his hand from his forehead.

Lavinia, unused to seeing him at this hour, nodded with wide eyes. She spoke in stutter-free Dokiri. "*Mu Salig*, is all well?"

"Have you seen *atu Saliga*?" He spoke loudly enough for eavesdroppers to chime an answer.

A knowing look crossed her features. "Not since last night. May I help you search?"

Hollen nodded, grateful. The woman set aside her work and

hurried in the direction of the women's springs, the one place in Bedmeg he was forbidden from entering. Ivan caught up to him and shoved an open palm into his shoulder. Hollen whipped around, ready to pummel him. The look on Ivan's face made him hesitate.

"I found skid tracks leading outside Bedmeg."

Hollen's blood went cold. "What?"

Ivan crossed his arms. "I'm not supposed to interfere. But your bride begged for my help yesterday. I figured she might do something like this. You should have been prepared."

Hollen shoved past him, racing out into the ravine. He found the skid tracks and followed them, breaking off for the forge. Hollen searched with rising urgency among the bows of his youngest clansmen. His gaze swept across the wall of hanging weapons until they fell upon the empty spot where the bow he'd outfitted for Joselyn should have been. His stomach plummeted.

Gods, woman. What madness overtook you?

He dashed back up the ravine, cursing himself with every step. His bride had made no secret of her desire to leave him. Everyone in his clan knew it. She wasn't the first Dokiri *hamma* to have entered Bedmeg an unwilling prize, but it was rare for a bride to object as staunchly as she, and so frequently.

Whose fault is that, you idiot?

Why had he yelled at her? Talked down to her? Made her cry? He growled. Because he'd been angry. Because for all he'd tried to win her, she still insisted on going back to that man. That monster. But was that really so hard to understand? She loved her father, bastard though he was, and wanted to save his life. Why had he taken that so personally?

Because I'm a bastard too.

He burst into the common area and yelled for Lavinia. She was just coming out from the springs. All around, the Dokiri *hammas* whispered to each other with widened eyes.

Lavinia ran to him. "She isn't there, *mu Salig*. The springs are empty!"

"Erik!" Hollen roared.

He didn't wait. He ran back under the open sky. It was just bluing with the threat of breaking dawn. He sent up the sharp whistle, commanding his mount to descend even as he rushed back to the armory. He gathered his weapons, his bow, his axe, knives. By the time he was yanking his saddle off its bench, *Jagomri* was trilling outside.

Hollen hoisted the leather saddle onto his *gegatu's* back, ignoring the creature's hiss. He cursed the trappings as he worked to fasten them with shaking hands. Footsteps came up behind him. It was Erik and Ivan.

Erik jumped to help with Jagomri's saddle. "*Mu Salig*, what is it?"

"I have to go. You're in command while I'm gone."

Erik worked the buckles and laces from his end, vastly speeding the process. "What's happened?"

"She's gone," Hollen said, uninclined to hide things from his second-in-command. Ivan shook his head.

Shock drenched Erik's voice. "*What*?"

"She left. Rode a lumberskid down the mountain. She's probably made it to the forest by now."

Hollen just caught his brother's expression of open horror as he swung himself up into the saddle and began binding his legs within the stirrups. The silence that ensued went thick with mounting judgment. Hollen focused on his task.

"Why would she do that, Hollen?"

Ivan scoffed. "Why do you think?"

Hollen lashed his weapons to the saddle. Erik waited, ever patient.

Finally, when there was no other task, Hollen met Erik's blue gaze. His brother and closest friend regarded him coolly. "You haven't told her. Have you?"

Hollen drew a tight breath, then released it with a downward sweep of his dark eyes. He couldn't bring himself to say it. Erik sighed, his disapproval tangible. "You're a good man, brother. But you can be a real idiot sometimes."

"And a bastard," Ivan added.

Hollen grimaced. His own sigh whirled around his face in a puff of fog. "Yeah. I know."

Empathy seeped into Erik's voice. "We would fly with you if we could."

Ivan grunted, the closest he'd come to confirmation. Maybe someday his middle brother would forgive him for perceived wrongs.

Hollen nodded. He had to go. He couldn't waste another moment in well-earned self-condemnation. If his bride was alive, she needed him. He gripped his mount, and rose into the freezing air.

20

OUT OF THE FRYING PAN

Joselyn couldn't breathe, couldn't move, couldn't think. She hadn't even realized she'd fallen through ice until the skin-peeling cold fully saturated her heavy clothes. Those clothes had nearly drowned her. She'd shed them. Now all she had was her soaking tunic, pants, and boots. Her hair was beginning to freeze as she lay panting near the jagged chasm that had swallowed her whole.

The sun hadn't yet risen, and already, she'd nearly died. She may yet. Joselyn rolled to her side. Her mind ordered her arms to support her, but they were quaking too wildly. A hoarse scream came sputtering from her throat along with a gush of freezing water. Her cry was enough to clear some of the fog from her mind. As she lay there shaking, she shamelessly hoped that Hollen had heard. That even now he was searching for her. Unlikely.

Fear shot through her. It was more likely some malevolent creature like the blood-seeker would soon find her. Joselyn craned her neck upward to scan the snow-covered ice. None of her provisions had survived, only the *gneri* blade still tucked in her pants.

She was without food, water, weapons, and most importantly, dry clothes. A wave of violent tremors wracked over her. She'd never been so cold. The frost settling on her had a bite that stung deep into her muscles. She wanted to writhe. If she weren't so consumed with shivering, she would have.

Like a dream, a vision of Hollen finding her, scooping her into his arms and taking her back to Bedmeg assailed her. She imagined him wrapping her in furs and sitting her at the fire, his warm body pressed into hers. He'd never mention her family again, and she'd forgive him for pitying her. She smiled.

Get up. A voice hissed in her mind.

She couldn't lay here still and wet in the snow. She'd be dead within the hour. She had to move, to get up! Coughing more water from her lungs, she forced her arms and legs beneath her. Joselyn bellowed as she pushed against her weight to lift herself on all fours. Every brush of the wet tunic felt like needles being dragged across her flesh. Agony. She gritted her teeth. If only she could rest.

Move now, or die.

The thought startled her. She couldn't die here. Too much was riding on her and she'd given up too much to fail now. Joselyn pressed up and stumbled back into the snow. She growled as she finally got to her numb feet.

Joselyn looked around the clearing. Which way had she come from? It should be obvious. She knew that. So why couldn't she decide which way to start walking? She looked up into the sky, searching for the moon. It wasn't there. And the stars, which had previously numbered in the millions, now looked sparse in the night sky which was shifting from black to cobalt.

How long had she been out here? Joselyn wanted to press her forehead into her palms, but she couldn't release her arms from around her trembling body. The chatter of her teeth echoed in her skull. She couldn't think. Couldn't decide what to do next. *Why* was this so difficult?

The mind-dulling fog began to regather. Before she could consider if it was the right decision, Joselyn skittered forward. Soon she was running through the clearing and toward the tree line.

With her arms still bound around her chest, Joselyn stumbled, skidding into the snow more than once. Every time the morbid hiss of warning returned.

Keep moving, or die.

No one would bury her. There would be no funeral procession, no army of mourners as was befitting a lady of her station. Her own father wouldn't know the date of her passing.

Her father.

Despite the death-whispering cold, Joselyn's body felt hot. Her father. The man who'd given her everything, and nothing. The man who'd sacrifice his only child upon the altar of self-preservation. The man who'd do so without apology for the sins that left him no other choice.

Joselyn screamed into the night with no care for what might hear her. Her tears froze on her face even as they fell. No other choice? No choice for Lord Fury? The second most powerful man in Morhagen? A man with limitless resources? Rage sliced through her stomach like a searing sword.

The only one who'd been without a choice was *her*. From her father's decision to sell her to a madman, to a savage's unrepentant abduction, Joselyn had been the victim of one man's will or another's all her life. And who had she to blame? If she'd refused her father, she wouldn't be on this gods-forsaken mountain. She wouldn't be racing against the icy fingers of death that even now were strangling the breath from her lungs.

But she hadn't refused him. She'd gone willingly. Like a little lamb. And for what? A hope that someday her father would think of the sacrifice she'd made? That he'd regret the years of contempt and neglect that preceded it? That his heart would suffer a measure of her pain? She laughed into the night.

Marcus Fury had no heart.

"I didn't do it for you!" she screamed. "I'm the only one who can save our people. Not you. Not a son. *Me!*"

She'd stopped shivering. The thought made her giddy. That meant she would survive. Right? A voice in her head cackled at her. Joselyn picked up speed as she dashed through the forest. The stinging brush of pine needles kept her weaving through an empty path. Her gaze turned up to the sky now glowing with the impending sun. Hadn't it just been night? She'd lost all sense of time. She pressed on, growing less and less aware of the cold. The pain.

Move or die. Run or die.

Out of nowhere, like a beacon on the shore, Joselyn caught the amber flicker of light creeping through a silhouette of trees. She slowed. A sound stopped her dead in her tracks. She heard voices. Human voices.

Fire.

The promise of heat started her running again. No sense of caution, no thought to investigate at a distance. She must get warm. If she didn't reach that fire soon, she would perish.

Keep moving.

The voices grew clearer. Men. And they were speaking trade tongue in perfectly accented Morhageese. Her heart melted. Her countrymen were nearby. She was safe.

She stumbled into the clearing, awash in orange light. She was vaguely aware of the fur-clad men standing around the fire, but all she could think of was the dancing flame. She lunged forward.

"Skies! What in the swiving hells is a *woman* doing here?"

A man stepped in front of the fire. Joselyn wavered, stumbling into his arms. She looked up at his weathered face, his curious eyes narrowed in suspicion.

"Please," Joselyn gritted out. "Need to get warm."

"What she sayin', Gerald?"

"The li'l snow rabbit's been drawn by the fire," the man holding her said. "Looks like she fell through ice."

The man called Gerald pulled her around to face the fire. She couldn't feel its warmth. Why couldn't she feel it? She tried to step forward but was held in place by the man standing behind her.

"Where did she come from?" someone asked from the other side of the ring. Joselyn squinted across the pit.

The speaker was a tall, spindly man whose furs seemed to swallow him up. He leered at Joselyn just like the two other men standing near him. Her shivers returned.

"Hells if I know," Gerald answered from over Joselyn's shoulder. "Maybe she be one of them dragon rider bitches?"

"You don't believe that tripe do you, Gerald?" another man said. "Next you'll be tellin' us that your wife was carried off by one of them scaly beasts instead of running off with the ferrier's son." A rumble of laughter went up around the ring.

"Shut yer mouth, Bryant," Gerald barked.

"The sun's barely risen and we've made a catch," one of the other men said. "Must be our lucky day."

Joselyn's brows knitted together. What were they talking about? Why wouldn't this man let her go to the fire? She tried again to pull out of his arms, but his fingers clamped down, puncturing her numbness. Joselyn flinched.

"My name is Joselyn Fury." She spoke as clearly as she could. "I require your aid."

The man spun Joselyn in his arms and pushed his lined face into hers. "You *require* our aid? What you mean to give us for it?"

He grinned a crooked smile and Joselyn tried to lean away. She was trapped against his arm encircling her back.

"M-my father is Marcus Fury of House Fury. He will see you rewarded."

The laughter that rose up took Joselyn aback. What had been funny? Dawning realization fell far slower than it should have. They didn't believe her. She gasped.

"I am Joselyn Helena Elise Fury, of House Fury. The only child of Marcus Fury. You will assist me." Joselyn braced a hand against the chest of the man holding her. "Release me at once!"

Gerald wrapped his other arm around her waist and crushed her to him. Her elbow bent with a snap. She cried out in pain.

"Rabbits don't tell the wolves what they will and won't do, li'l *lady*." He breathed the last word like a ridiculous joke.

Joselyn stared into his eyes. They blazed with something that took her a moment to identify. Instinct, rather than experience, put a name to it. *Lust*. She twisted against him. "Let me go!"

To his side, Joselyn caught sight of a fifth stranger. This one was far younger than the others, barely a man. He wore a bright scarlet cap. His eyes darted between Joselyn and Gerald. "What if she's tellin' the truth, Gerald? What if she really be Lord Fury's daughter?"

Gerald and the others laughed again. "Don't be daft, boy! Look at 'er. She be dressed like a savage and icy as a witch's tit!"

"She's got a witch's timing. Another hour and we'd be off on the hunt." One of the other men said.

"Put her on the ground, Gerald. Hurry up before she freezes to death," Bryant said.

Put her on the ground? She needed to stand by the fire. Before she could make sense of the words, Gerald pushed her to the snow. Her knees buckled under the force, and her back collided with the forest floor. Air rushed from her lungs. She tried to gasp, but Gerald's weight held her. He straddled her hips.

No. No. No. No.

This wasn't happening to her. Joselyn had imagined a hundred different scenarios in which she failed to return home. All had been the result of either a Dokiri's interference or her own stupidity. None had included falling victim to her own countrymen.

She'd escaped. She'd made it down the mountain and found men who were Morhageese like her. Men she could rely on. This wasn't supposed to happen. Her hand dove to her side, searching for the hilt of the *gneri* blade. Gerald's thighs molded around her waist, blocking her.

"Stop!" Her cry only seemed to intensify her attacker's excitement.

Gerald stuck his nose into Joselyn's face and breathed his foul breath over her. "Quiet li'l rabbit, do what I tell ya, and I'll be gentle while I plow ya."

Joselyn struck him across the chin. The laughter of those spectating grew as Gerald brought a hand up to his bleeding lip. A flash of hatred was all Joselyn caught before the back of Gerald's hand crashed into the side of her face. Her neck cracked. Joselyn's vision went black, her ears rang. She'd never been struck in her life.

When her sight cleared, Gerald was drawing the point of a steel knife up to her chest. Joselyn screamed. She tried to strike out again, but her wrists were caught up by one of the other hunters.

"Gerald, don't! What if someone hears her?" the boy pleaded.

"Who in the bleedin' skies is going to hear her? If you don't want a turn then shut yer mouth and finish breakin' the camp!"

With her arms pinned, Gerald lined the blade up with the

top of her collar and slashed downward. Joselyn twisted and bucked to get free. It was no use. Without her arms and with the weight of a grown man upon her, she was helpless.

Gerald dropped the knife and tore along the line he'd scored. The ripping sound made her gasp. Her pendant was pulled from her neck and tossed aside. Joselyn sobbed through gritted teeth as rough hands pinched at her naked breasts.

Gerald's body wracked with a mock shiver. "I might as well bury my cock in the snow!"

"Go ahead, I'll take over for ya!" Bryant laughed.

"Look at that scar!" another said. "Looks like someone's been 'ere already."

"Daft savages!" Gerald pawed at her *tanshi* mark, stretching it for a better look.

"No!" Joselyn choked. Somehow she was surprised when her cry went unheeded. She had to make him stop. He *must* stop. She strained to pull her arms free, earning her a bruising squeeze. Joselyn wailed even as Gerald's hands ventured lower.

"Be still, bitch. Or my cock won't be the only thing I bury inside ya."

Be still? Joselyn couldn't be still. She had to keep fighting. Had to keep moving.

Move or freeze.

Move and he'll kill me.

Tearless cries poured out of her. She was dead if she moved, dead if she didn't. Joselyn prayed first to her gods, and then to anyone who would listen.

Regna, Helig, save me!

21

HOLLEN'S WRATH

Joselyn screamed. She screamed if only to drown out the sound of the men's cruel laughter. Gerald's meaty hands thrust into her pants. Joselyn wrenched to the side, desperate to get away.

Elbows pinned her shoulders against the earth. Gerald clasped his hands around her neck and squeezed. Joselyn choked. Her eyes caught sight of the sunrise above as the corners of her vision began to fade. A dawning sense of finality heralded in her mind. This was it. For all her fear of dragons and savages, this was the way Lady Fury was to die. At the hands of her own people.

A gush of air rushed back into her lungs. Joselyn gasped. She coughed, clinging to her life these men were so determined to steal. Gerald's weight fell upon her chest in an unceremonious heap.

The men huddled around her went still. She sputtered for breath. All at once, her arms were free. Joselyn shoved against Gerald's slumped body. He was too heavy. She wailed, pushing and kicking with all her might. It was useless.

Tears blurred her vision and she blinked them away. What

was happening? She looked around. The men's leering faces were gone. Joselyn craned her head toward the firepit. There, lying in the snow beside her, was Bryant. His eyes were glassy and still. Lifeless. Joselyn tried to jerk away. She couldn't move.

She turned her face back over Gerald's limp shoulder. The shaft of an arrow protruded from his back. She knew that fletching.

Metal clanged nearby. Hope came roaring to life as she laid eyes upon the one man she'd been determined never to see again. The man she'd hoped against reason would find her.

Hollen.

Towering over the others, Hollen brought his axe to bear and drew it across the stomach of one of her assailants. The man screamed and dropped to his knees. His arms shot round his stomach as though to hold in the blood that spilled into the snow. He fell into a gory heap, and Hollen turned toward one of his comrades.

Joselyn pushed against Gerald with all her might. She braced her feet into the snow and bucked her hips against him, trying to roll him off. This shouldn't be an impossible task. Why was it so hard?

Another man screamed. Joselyn turned back to the carnage just in time to see Hollen's fourth victim collapse, and a fifth drop to his knees, pleading for mercy. Hollen spared him not a glance as he produced a knife, seemingly from nowhere, and plunged it into the man's throat. His cry was short lived. It turned to gurgling as he spurted crimson against the stark snow beneath him.

Joselyn's heart pounded at the utter violence of the scene. When her captor turned his furious gaze upon her, it froze in her chest. His eyes burned black with rage. Blood streaked his face. His giant shoulders rose and fell on heaving pants. He was every inch the savage dragon-master. In three massive strides, he reached her.

Oh, skies! He's going to punish me!

His hands plunged downward, and Joselyn's eyes squeezed shut. Her entire body rocked as Gerald's weight was yanked off her and hurled across the fire. The first full breath in what seemed like an eternity rushed into her lungs.

Joselyn's eyes flew open. Hollen hovered on his knees above her. He swept his open palms down her body, his eyes scanning her from head to toe. She shuddered. What was he thinking? Her awareness was long gone, strangled in the mire of fear and pain.

Hollen met her gaze and she saw his horror. He blurted something in Dokiri. His words tumbled from his mouth like a desperate prayer. He was trembling all over and he stroked a hand across her face, brushing the hair out of her eyes. She coughed, her throat grating.

Hollen scooped her up and lifted her over his shoulder. Her limp body hung loose around him and the world seemed to tilt. Butchered men lie sprawled about the campsite. Blood and flesh were everywhere. She groaned as Hollen's shoulder pressed into her belly.

As they raced away, Joselyn's vision went choppy. A flash of movement in the trees beyond caught her attention. It was the boy in his scarlet hat. He was sprinting in the other direction. Down the mountain.

Joselyn tried to cry out to him, but her throat was too sore. She wanted to warn the boy to keep running. She also wanted him to die alongside his companions. Confusion nauseated her. Her eyes slid back into her head. Exhaustion sank in its fangs and tore her out of all consciousness.

SHE WAS ALIVE. She was still alive. For now.

Hollen shivered against the biting cold of the gray, cloud-crowded sky. Jagomri howled and beat his wings. Joselyn didn't even twitch. Hollen had stripped himself of his coat and buried Joselyn under it. For a while her teeth had clattered so loudly he feared they might crack. Now she didn't move at all. He gave her a hard shake, relieved when she stirred.

"You stay awake!" he commanded. The whistle of air blowing past them deafened his voice.

How could he have let this happen? When he'd found the broken ice she'd fallen through, terror had struck him. He'd run across the clearing, divesting himself of clothes before seeing that her tracks led away from the fissure. He'd heard her before he saw her. The sound of her cries had led him through the woods, faster than he'd ever run before. And there, pinned to the ground, was *his* bride.

Hollen had hundreds of scars. Hundreds of kills. This morning had been different. He hadn't simply killed the men who'd forced their filthy hands on his bride. He'd murdered them. Given the chance, he'd do it again with joy in his heart.

He'd have given chase to the boy who'd fled, but it wasn't worth it. Joselyn's flesh was freezing. He knew that sting, knew what it meant. It was death. He had to get her back to Bedmeg. Fast. It may already be too late. He shook her again.

No response.

Would his last words to her be those he'd spoken in anger? Hollen pressed against Jagomri's ridges, urging him on. The beast responded with a resentful shriek. *Don't let her die, you bastard! Fly!*

The minutes stretched into what seemed like hours. Finally, Bedmeg came into sight. Hollen drove as close to the mouth of the common area as possible. He couldn't afford to lose any more time.

His riders lined the entrance; they'd been on watch for his return. Gratitude filled him at the sight. Erik would have told them what happened. They knew where their *Salig* had gone and, due to their laws, were unable to offer their assistance. This was Hollen's mess to sort out. Instead they'd stood vigilant, an unspoken demonstration of their loyalty. It was more than he deserved.

The moment Jagomri's feet touched the snow, Hollen leapt from his back. He'd forgotten to bind his legs. Hollen tugged on the mound of furs lying atop his mount. Joselyn slid into his arms like a limp pile of rags.

A path parted for him as he sprinted into the common area and charged toward the tunnels. Eyes turned down as he passed. Eerie silence echoed off the stone walls of the crowded common area. That silence had the ring of doom to it. Hollen squeezed Joselyn in his arms.

He plunged into the dark tunnel and made his way through. As Hollen rounded the final corner, light hit his eyes. A pair of torches were already notched within the little alcove he'd set his sights on.

Hollen darted to the entrance and locked upon the pair within, who eyed him with open shock. The other Dokiri man threw himself upon his *hamma*, anxious to preserve her modesty.

"Out!" Hollen bellowed, dropping to his knees.

The couple scrambled out of the water as Hollen yanked his coat from Joselyn's slackened face. He pressed his fingers to the bruised flesh of her throat. He begged Helig for signs of a pulse. Hollen held his body rigid, waiting. A sluggish rippling thrummed beneath his hand, indicating life. It was too slow. Hollen tore at the ties of his cuirass as the two interlopers retreated toward the common area.

He dropped the leather armor to the ground and ripped his

shirt over his head. Hollen's hands shook with adrenaline as he removed her pants and what remained of her tattered shirt. Under any other circumstance, he would have filled his eyes with the sight of his naked bride, satisfying his long-suffering curiosity. Passion was the furthest thing from his mind as he scooped Joselyn's unconscious form into his arms and slid into the water.

Hollen's heart jumped as they dipped below the icy surface of the pool. This alcove was the last stop couples made before concluding their visits. They would hop into successively heated pools until they reached the threshold of their tolerance. Then, while their flesh glowed red with warmth, they would plunge into the waters of this alcove which was fed by melted ice from above. The chill was invigorating and closed one's pores before redressing for the common area. In Joselyn's case, the frigid water would keep her brittle flesh from scorching as he warmed her.

Settling low in the water, Hollen found a natural seat against the edge of the pool and pulled Joselyn into his lap. He grabbed her forehead and pulled her backward to rest against his shoulder, submerging as much of her skin as he could without drowning her. He pressed his lips against her frozen ear and spoke to her in his father's language.

"You must wake, my bride, my only. You must!"

He wrapped an arm over her waist and pulled her against him, willing the gentle heat of his skin to seep into her. She was cooler than the water surrounding them. He'd give her all the heat he possessed to keep her from tumbling over the edge of death.

Hollen swallowed his fear and ran his hand down the length of Joselyn's arm, drew her hand up over the surface of the water. Her fingers were ashen gray, the tips so blue they looked black in the dim torch light. Hollen shuddered and pulled her hand back under the surface. He began kneading her palms between his fingers. All the while he spoke to her, pleaded with her, begged her.

The minutes dragged by until the temperature of Joselyn's flesh matched the water. Hollen heaved her into his arms and climbed up the bank of the pool. She was all white limbs lying ragged in the cradle of his bosom, with her head splayed backward over the crook of his elbow. Water poured off him, nearly dragging his pants from his body as he hurried to the next warmest pool. He considered removing the rest of his clothes, but then thought of his bride's inevitable horror were she to wake with her naked body pressed up against his. She *would* wake up. That thought reminded him to keep his eyes ahead as he descended into the pool, still clad in his pants and boots.

The water of this pool sent a melting surge of comfort over his own chilled flesh. He prayed the shift wouldn't harm his bride. As he settled her against him, Hollen started at the moan rising from Joselyn's parted lips. He swung her around to look at her face as he cradled her. Her freckle-dotted eyelids fluttered, but didn't open.

"Joselyn. Joselyn. Please wake up, *mu hamma*," he whispered in trade tongue, stroking his free hand over her brow. His vision went wavy with tears.

He'd done this to her. If she died, it would be his fault. And his punishment would be too high a price to bear.

"You have to live, *mu hamma*. Live and I will tell you everything. Live so that you can punish me. Live so that I may love you. Please, stay with me." His voice cracked. It was the first time he'd wept in years.

22

TWICE WRONGED

Flayed. She'd been flayed. Her skin had been cut into and peeled away from her body, exposing every nerve to the bite of icy teeth. Joselyn groaned into the darkness, her parched throat closed up.

"Tansy?" Her cracked lips split as she spoke.

"Shh, *mu hamma*," came a hushed, male voice, so close Joselyn wondered if it had come from within her own head.

She struggled to open her eyes. It was like they were sealed together, but eventually they cracked. The glow of torchlight blinded her, and she squeezed them shut again, turning her head to the side. Her nose pressed into something prickly that grated on her skin. Where was she? A weight drifted over her belly, and instinct crashed down on her. She was being attacked.

She went rigid. Her arms strained against whatever confined her. Warm water splashed over her face.

"Shh, easy! Easy!" That male voice came again, startling Joselyn enough to make her think.

The band across her waist, it was an arm. It tugged against her belly, drawing her above the sloshing water. "It's all right. You're safe."

She knew that voice. Joselyn stilled. "Hollen?"

"I'm here, *mu hamma*."

"What happened?"

"You're safe."

She opened her eyes. There he was. Her captor. Her savior. Warm water kissed her skin and tickled her shoulders as he lowered them back down into the steaming pool. "Where—?"

"We're in Bedmeg. You're safe." His bearded face was mere inches from hers. His hand brushed wet strands of hair off her brow. Her raspy voice cracked.

"There were men." Why was that significant?

Hollen's body tensed around her and an ominous echo of violence resounded in her mind. Something had happened. Something horrible. His eyes blackened. "They're dead. They'll never touch you again."

They'd touched her? Joselyn stared up at Hollen as her groggy mind tied her fragmented memories back into place. It was difficult. Her skull was throbbing.

She'd left Bedmeg, had gotten away. Then she'd fallen through ice and nearly drowned. Everything after that was hazy at best. The cold had been overwhelming. Deadly. She remembered that much. At some point she'd come across men, people she thought would help her. *Why* had she thought they would help her? Joselyn tried to swallow, but her tongue clogged up her mouth.

As if he read her mind, Hollen dragged a water skin into the pool and held it to her mouth. She let him pour the liquid over her lips. She sputtered as it sank its way down her aching throat. Hollen pressed her head forward, helping her drink.

Joselyn broke away panting. He put the skin down and raked his fingers through her scalp to massage the place behind her ear.

"That hurts," she whispered. She hurt everywhere, especially her limbs and face. Joselyn flexed her fingers and winced at the fiery burn. Hollen stilled.

"You've been snow burned. Badly." His mouth firmed into a line. "But I don't think you'll lose any flesh."

Lose any flesh? What did that mean? She looked at her arm, which was floating just beneath the surface of the water. Her skin had a blanched tint to it that grew duller closer to her hands. Her gaze skipped back to her body. She was naked except for a white sheet of wool toweling her form.

Joselyn jerked upward. The burst of energy scooted her off Hollen's knees. "Don't touch me!"

She lost contact with the pool's floor, and dipped below the surface. Hollen caught her by the arm and yanked her forward, drawing her to the rocky edge. It was shallower here. Joselyn clung to the wet rock. Her strength dissipated as she glared at her captor. He stared back at her with every muscle in his body tensed as though he were ready to catch her again.

Clarity dawned. The hunter had torn her clothes open while she screamed beneath him. Joselyn shut her eyes as the tormenting images came back in full force. Those Morhageese men hadn't helped her. They hadn't even given her a moment by their fire. Their only concern had been using her before she froze to death. Her cries for mercy had fallen on deaf ears. They'd laughed at her, enjoyed her misery. They'd violated her with their words, their eyes, their hands.

"Where are my clothes?" Fatigue dampened the betrayal in her voice.

"They're ruined. I couldn't dress you in the water." His soft voice didn't match his troubled expression.

"You let them attack me." The accusation took her by surprise. It wasn't exactly what she meant. Still, rage tossed within her. Someone was responsible for what had happened. Someone was at fault.

Hollen's mouth fell open. Could he have looked more distraught? His voice was barely a whisper. "You left."

"Because you gave me no other choice," she bit out. "This wouldn't have happened if you had just left me alone!"

"You're right."

Hollen's expression made her gut clench. He looked as though he'd lay his head upon the executioner's block if one had been lying nearby. If she'd meant to hurt him with her words, she'd succeeded. Her fury dimmed. Instinct bid her reach out, to stroke his face until those deep lines melted away. Joselyn tightened her grip on the rocky bank.

What must she look like to him? Bruised, wet, naked, and clinging to hard stone like a child afraid to drown. He'd seen her being attacked. Heard her screaming for help. Crying. Begging. Hollen had seen how very small she truly was. Worst of all, he knew the dirty truth.

Your own father wouldn't give a damn.

Shame made her want to vomit. Joselyn groaned, welcoming the fog still clouding her mind. She pressed her cheek against the darkened rocks and tried to succumb.

"I won't ask you to forgive me, *mu hamma*. I don't deserve it. I drove you out of Bedmeg. First I brought you here, and then I drove you away."

Exactly.

Wait. Joselyn's eyes narrowed. Was he apologizing for abducting her? She could hardly believe it. Not after all he'd said and done.

Hollen's gaze fell into the water between them. "I should have told you the day we met. I should have explained everything to you."

What was he talking about? She leaned away from him, bracing against whatever was about to happen.

"I've wronged you, Joselyn. I see that now. I can only beg you to believe I never meant any harm to come to you. If I'd known what would happen, I would have told you everything from the start."

Joselyn clung to the edge of the pool, certain that if she breathed she would float away. "What would you have told me?"

"...That I have no right to keep you here."

THE CONFESSION TWISTED out of Hollen like a wild hare yanked from its den. He held his breath and waited for his bride's condemnation, for her rejection. She stared. Blinked. She hadn't grasped his words.

Of course she doesn't understand. You've explained nothing. Tell her. Tell her how you kept the truth from her and how it nearly got her killed.

Dread set so heavy in his stomach he wanted to sink below the water with it. Anything to excuse himself from the explanation he owed his bride.

"I told you once that *Na Dokiri* means 'He who conquers.' Do you remember?"

Her face pressed against the edge of the pool, but her hold was lagging. Hollen had to squeeze the rocks beneath him to keep from drawing her back into his lap. His bride was exhausted, barely conscious. He might have waited until she was more alert to have this conversation, but he couldn't stomach one more moment of secrecy between them. If that meant he had to tell her more than once, so be it.

"My people take nothing. We earn what is ours. We win it. Our mounts, our kills, our brides."

"You *took* me," she interjected, her gaze tight.

Hollen nodded. "When a Dokiri claims a *hamma*, he may choose anyone he wishes. She is his by right. But—"

How to explain this? She was going to be furious. This should have been the first thing he told her. Even before carving his *tanshi* mark into her flesh.

"But, she must choose him as well."

Joselyn eyed him warily. "What do you mean by that?"

"When I carved my mark upon you, I declared to the gods that you were the only woman for me, that I would win you or die without legacy. But there's more to it than that."

Hollen thought back to the moment he'd put all his hope into one woman. When he'd given Joselyn Helena Elise Fury the power to destroy him or make his life worth living. Nothing had ever been more terrifying. Not the day he mastered Jagomri, not the time he killed his first *veligiri*, not the moment he'd been made responsible for his clan.

"What do you mean by *win* me?"

He swallowed. "A Dokiri has a year to convince his bride to stay with him, to win her heart. If he succeeds, then his *hamma* puts her mark upon him as well and the bond is complete. If not, he must let her go."

When she spoke, her voice was a whisper. "You—you have to free me?"

Hollen's breath hitched. "Eventually."

Joselyn's grip finally gave way. Hollen shot a hand out just before she slipped below the water's surface. Careful not to chafe her brittle flesh, he wrapped an arm about her waist and drew her to himself. He tucked her against his chest like a babe freshly pulled from the womb. Her dimpled chin rolled over his shoulder and red lashes fluttered over his ear.

She'd never allow this if she were well. But he couldn't let her drown. She needed him to hold her, and that was *exactly* what he would do. He tightened the wool sheet around her and ran a hand over her scalp, hugging her closer. He'd savor this nearness like it was the only chance he'd get, because, by the gods, it probably *would* be.

Hollen pressed his face into her water-darkened hair and inhaled her scent. It was distinctly Joselyn. Sweet, heady. He thought of the long nights ahead when he might be lying alone in his bed, aching for that scent. His hold on her tightened.

"What happens to the women who refuse you?" Her murmuring lips grazed the flesh below his ear. He shuddered, and his fist clenched around the strands of her floating hair.

"They're returned to wherever they were taken from and given enough ivory for a rich dowry." Hollen strained to breathe evenly as she spoke again.

"And your riders? What happens to those who are rejected?"

Hollen fixed his eyes on the wall of the alcove. "Those who can't convince their brides to stay don't get a second chance. One either wins what he's claimed, or he lives without." He prayed he wasn't prophesying his own future.

Silence. Was she still breathing? "Joselyn?"

"And then he claims someone else?"

"No, Joselyn. He lives without a *hamma*."

That seemed to startle her. She pressed a hand into his chest and tilted her head backward to gaze at him. "Forever?"

Hollen's eyes brushed over every feature, committing them to memory. "Forever, *mu hamma*."

My only.

Her lips parted on a little gasp. He held her gaze, absorbing every emotion that lingered there. Disbelief, shock, and ... was that misery? Why? *For him*? She gave a pained little moan, and Hollen reminded himself not to pet at her face.

"You are mine, *mu hamma*. As surely as I am yours. But I can't keep you against your will. Eventually, the time will come when I ... " His words went shaky. "When I must let you go."

Hollen's insides felt like ice that had been thawed and

refrozen too many times. Like at the slightest touch he might shatter.

Joselyn's fingers drew together over his chest. The tips of her nails skimmed the ridges of his *idadi* scars. His muscles tensed beneath her touch.

"Why didn't you tell me?" she asked.

Hollen's heart raced. He'd known this question was coming. Still, he dreaded answering. "I thought that you would accept me sooner if you had no thought of leaving. That it would be easier."

"You would have told me eventually?"

"Yes," he whispered.

Her gaze hardened. "Then who were you concerned with making things easier for?"

The question hit him like a blow to the gut. He'd convinced himself that his secrecy was for her benefit. But after all that had happened and with his bride looking him in the eye, the truth was plain.

He'd not been honest because he was afraid. Afraid that, knowing her options, she'd bide her time in Bedmeg whilst keeping him at arm's length. That she'd count the hours until he was forced to let her go. That she'd leave him without ever having given him a chance. Even now, the thought sent sickening dread through his body.

He'd been a coward. His eyes fell away from hers.

Joselyn braced herself against his chest and pushed back to get a better look at him. He opened his arms and rearranged her across his lap. She let him, her limbs swaying like a doll's might.

When the slosh of the water had stilled, Joselyn spoke. "You thought you could force me to stay by making me believe I had no hope. By lying to me."

Hollen said nothing. He'd not precisely lied, but he wouldn't raise a defense for himself. Not when so much of her pain rested on his shoulders. All he could do now was grasp at whatever shred of faith she might still have in him.

"I would have told you."

The words barely left his lips before she answered. "When you had to."

Hollen swallowed and nodded. He'd spent his adult life waiting for his bride, imagining what it would be like to love someone and be loved in return. The images in his head had never seemed more naive than they did in this moment. Life wasn't as simple as one of Magnus' songs. Love *didn't* come easily. Hollen was a fool and a cur to believe he could deceive his bride into offering it up.

Joselyn pressed her head into the crook of his elbow. She regarded him with bitter understanding. "So this is why you haven't touched me, then?"

Hollen blinked. His head cocked in helpless confusion. What had she just asked?

Joselyn's level gaze remained cool. "Your oath not to force yourself upon me. You made it because I'm not really yours."

"You *are* mine, Joselyn. For now, you are mine." His fists clenched beneath the water. He may not deserve her, but she was still his. No one would take her from him. Not yet.

"But if you wanted to rape me? Like those men in the forest?"

Hollen flinched. Had she truly just compared him to those rats? A lump hardened in his throat. "I could never do that."

"Because to do so would be against your laws?"

His jaw fell open. "You think the reason I haven't raped you is because of my people? Because I would be punished?"

Joselyn nodded gravely. "Why else? What man would deny himself that right?"

He huffed, too dumbfounded to be hurt. Was this what his bride expected of men where she came from? What kind of world had she been raised in?

The kind where fathers sell their daughters to madmen.

The more Hollen learned of Joselyn's world, the more convinced he was that her people were the *real* savages. Had she been prepared to tolerate rape from Dante Viridian? His temper flared. He wouldn't have been surprised to see the water boiling around him.

"I made that oath because I could never do you harm. I could never force myself upon you, could never desire to." Hollen worked to tamp down the fury in his voice. Didn't she understand? Didn't she know that he wanted her willing? Wanted her to need him the way he needed her, the way he *craved* her?

Skepticism drew over her features. Or was it confusion? Hollen's jaw clenched. If he had a soul, he'd have traded it to know what she was thinking just then. A ludicrous thought occurred to him. Did she think his restraint had been easy? A simple choice that, once made, he'd lightly put out of his mind?

His body had burned for hers every night. It had been all he could do to lie in their bed, scorching beneath his lust, instead of tearing outside and plunging naked into the nearest snow bank. *Every* night he'd lain aching, wanting, needing.

"Regna, Joselyn!" His words came out strained and breathy. "If I thought you wanted me, there's not a thing in this world that could stop me from possessing you. *All* of you. Not your father, not my riders, and by the gods, not some tradition of my people."

It was the truth. If she but breathed the word, Hollen would bury himself so deep inside her they wouldn't know where he ended and she began. He almost said as much, but he couldn't bear the thought of frightening her. And the intensity of his desire *should* frighten her. It frightened him.

Enveloped in his arms, Joselyn stared up at him. Her eyes were round and wondering. Even like this, she was so damned beautiful. Without thinking, he dropped his face low so his lips hung over hers. "The *only* thing stopping me from claiming your body, is you."

Her eyes dropped to his mouth. Hollen's whole body tensed. Her lips parted, and he could practically feel her curiosity. Or was that his own?

Taste her.

She would be sweet. Hollen knew it. Her lips, though cracked, would melt around his like warmed honey. He'd imagined it a thousand times. Had nearly willed it into existence.

Let her taste you.

Yes. Show her the touch of a man who'd ask for nothing. Nothing except what he'd already sworn in equal measure. Of one who would lay down his life for her.

Hollen pressed forward, closing the distance between their lips. Just as he would have touched her, Joselyn's eyes snapped up to meet his half-lidded ones. He'd hoped to see his own desire mirrored there. The aching longing that was stealing the breath from his lungs. There was an echo of that passion, but it wasn't pure, not refined by the flame of conviction. There was something else that danced more wildly in her gaze.

Doubt.

Hollen froze. If he spoke, if he breathed, if he did anything at all, he'd give in to the siren's call. And so he waited. There was sheer agony in the time it took for her to finally pull away.

Back off, Hollen.

Kreesha. He forced himself to straighten. His breath had gone unsteady. Now what?

He didn't want her to leave him, didn't want to be alone on this mountain. It was enough to make him want to bind her within their *bok* and horde her away until they were both old and gray. And now Hollen had more reason than ever to prevent her from leaving. Now he knew what was waiting for her. Knew what sort of man Dante Viridian was. His jaw tightened.

Eventually he'd have to let her go. He'd be damned before letting anything happen to her until then. Joselyn still needed him. For now, it was his right to keep her safe.

"*Mu hamma.*"

Joselyn returned her gaze to his. He sighed as he combed his fingers through the red locks floating in the water. He needed her attention for this. All of it. He brought out his *Salig* voice.

"You will never leave me again."

"But you said—"

"—When a year has passed, and the lowlands are again turning red, you'll tell me if you still wish to return." The words ground out of his mouth like jagged steel. "And if so . . . I *will* do my duty and return you to the plains."

Hollen didn't want to imagine making good on that oath. Setting her on Jagomri's back and flying her back to where he'd first seen her. Could he do it? Fly away knowing he would never see her again? Accept that she was somewhere else? In the arms of another man, a man who would crush her?

Don't let it come to that.

He shook his head. "But you will not leave here alone as you did last night. Swear it to me, Joselyn. Swear to me and I will swear to you."

He wouldn't let her sleep until she'd given her word. Waking in an empty bed had been terrible enough. Seeing her in that glade, her trembling body pinned beneath a man with murder in his eyes, had maddened him. It wouldn't happen again.

With her eyes locked on his, Joselyn whispered, "I swear it."

Relief swept through him. Once she'd slept, *really* slept, he would make her vow it again. Weariness might rob her memory of such an oath, and he couldn't hold her accountable for that.

He touched his forehead to hers. It pleased him she didn't

flinch away, but that might have been exhaustion. "And I swear to you that while you are in my care, I shall never harm you nor allow anyone else to. You are mine, *mu hamma*. But you are free. When the time comes, you will make your choice." He took a breath, shutting his eyes. "And we both must abide by it."

Joselyn's gaze searched his.

"What is it? What are you thinking?"

She frowned. "Why are you doing this?"

Hollen cocked his head, unsure what she meant. Joselyn swallowed hard, with her dry lips pressed together. "You know I must return. Why do you prolong our fates?"

Hollen saw her misery. He'd seen that look before. Now he understood it. She didn't *want* to return. She had no hope for a future with the Morhageese lord. No desire to be with him. And yet, she'd been willing to give all for her duty to a man who'd throw her away.

A new emotion rose in Hollen. Pity. Tender sorrow for the love his bride was so desperate to earn from a man who obviously had none to give. Hollen thought back to their argument in the armory, remembered her glassy-eyed defiance as he'd shattered her world with a few knowing words. She'd stormed into the snow. *Joselyn*, his indomitable bride, fleeing like a frightened bird. He should have known then that she would try to escape.

Hollen frowned. "You love your father?"

Joselyn stiffened in his arms. Her face hardened like ice. She didn't want to talk about this. About *him*. Too bad.

"I know you weigh all your actions against your duty to him. But, will you consider something, *mu hamma*?"

Reluctance was riddled across her freckle-strewn face, but she nodded.

"Were it not for your father, would you *want* to return to your home? To your Viridian lord?"

Joselyn's eyes sharpened. She opened her mouth to reply. Hollen drew his hand out of the water, holding it palm-out.

"Don't speak, *mu hamma*."

His bride paused, swallowing back her words.

Hollen dropped his hand. He tucked it around the small of her back. She was delicate in his arms. Strange that the Regna had breathed such an unbreakable spirit into so fragile a body. "You don't need to answer me right now. Not ever. I ask only that you consider my question. You have time."

Not nearly enough.

"We'll be together for the year to come. You've sworn not to leave. I'll demand nothing from you that you don't wish to give. You owe me nothing, Joselyn." Emotion welled in his throat. "But I *beg* of you, for once in your life, consider what you owe to yourself."

Joselyn silently fingered her pinkened *tanshi* mark. Was she aware of what she was doing? His eyes narrowed. Where was her necklace? The golden one she was always thumbing? She never took it off. He'd find it. He'd go back to the hunter's camp and dig through the snow and gore if that's what it took.

Joselyn's eyelids began to droop. Hollen hugged her against himself and pressed his lips to her brow. He lingered there, with his temple against her head. They swayed together, gently rocked by the swirling tide of the pool.

"Now you know the truth, *mu hamma*. All of it."

She wasn't his chattel. She'd never been. He had been the only captive from the start.

23

THE STRONGEST AMONG US

The flames cast warm amber light around the *bok*. At times it seemed to Joselyn like she was inside a glowing clay oven. Her mottled feet brushed across the furs as she drew her knees into her chest. The last bite of meat settled heavy in her uneasy stomach.

Across their *bok*, Hollen rose from the wooden chest to stoke the fire. Since their conversation the night before, she'd spoken hardly a word to him. He'd followed her silence, but his eyes were tidal pools of emotion. Solicitous didn't begin to cover his demeanor. He'd waited on her hand and foot, anticipating every need she could possibly have.

At first she'd ignored him purposefully, anxious to inflict hurt as some consequence for his deceit. It had been tempting to blame him for everything. The scalding ache across her snow-burned flesh, the memories of her violation. She could still feel their ravenous hands on her, palming her like ripe fruit. They'd explored her, taking liberties no man ever had. After hours of soaking in the springs, Joselyn still felt unclean.

Time and reason had begun to have their way with Joselyn's

mind. She couldn't blame Hollen for what had happened in the wilderness. He'd saved her. What was she going to do now?

His plan to set her free changed nothing. She still had a duty to her people, and that duty carried a time limit. She couldn't leave again as she had. She'd given Hollen her word. It shouldn't have taken falling through ice or being attacked by her own people to convince her. Attempting to escape had been futile. She must find another way, and soon.

She studied the planes of Hollen's face as he crouched over the fire. She could make him miserable. Make him want nothing more than to return her home and never see her again. She frowned. Was that even possible? Apparently she was his only chance for a bride. Regret nipped at her. She didn't want Hollen to spend his life alone. Didn't want him to suffer. But that couldn't be on her conscience. And, at any rate, he could very well still be lying to her.

She could hardly believe that a man who considered himself married would abstain from his husbandly rights. It seemed even more unlikely now that she knew her time here was limited. Who'd ever heard of such a thing? She'd been raised to understand that her greatest duty was to provide heirs for her husband. There was only one way to do that.

Hollen had made it unmistakably clear that he desired her, that the only thing stopping him from possessing her entirely was Joselyn's own lack of consent. If it was the truth, Joselyn had a sense that it would change something profound between them. If it was another lie, she'd suffer no more grief at the thought of leaving him forever brideless.

Joselyn threw back the furs and climbed unsteadily to her tender feet. Hollen dropped what he was doing and rushed to her side. She held up a hand to stop him from touching her, and winced as she took a few limping steps away from the bed.

"I want to speak with Lavinia."

Hollen grimaced at her feet. "I'll ask her to come."

Joselyn hadn't been outside the *bok* since yesterday when Hollen carried her unconscious from the springs. She'd spent most of her time sleeping since then. "No. I want to talk to her somewhere else."

Hollen hesitated. "If you want to speak to her alone, I'll leave."

There was more to it than that. She hadn't spoken to anyone besides Hollen in two days. She hadn't seen anyone. But they'd seen her, had seen her half-dead and possibly ravaged.

"I'm not dying, Hollen." Joselyn sighed, trying to cleanse the irritation from her tone. "I need to show them that I'm well."

Joselyn didn't delude herself into believing Hollen's people cared for her. The few connections she'd made were likely forfeit after she'd insulted them by leaving their *Salig*. She still meant to leave. It shouldn't matter to her what they thought. And yet, it *did*.

Hollen nodded and reached for her hand. Joselyn snapped it away. "The message will be clearer if you aren't hovering over me like a brood hen."

He frowned at her. "You're still weak, Joselyn."

"I am," she conceded. There was no point in denying it. "But I can walk to the springs."

Hollen bit down on the inside of his cheek, and the flesh dimpled. He scrutinized her from head to toe. What must she look like to him? She could feel the bruise where Gerald had struck her across the face. And her throat was still on fire every time she swallowed. After a long moment, Hollen sighed and nodded. "I won't touch you. But let me walk near you until we find someone to guide you to the springs."

Joselyn nodded and followed him silently out of the *bok*. If she opened her mouth, all her unasked questions might come pouring out. What if he answered them? What if his words left her unable to hold him at arm's length? She limped along the edge of the tunnel.

Too late.

THE STEAM of the springs dampened Joselyn's clothes. They stuck to her body and grated across her blistered skin. Soren's mother led her down the tunnel and through the sulfur-misted air. She seemed to know precisely where Lavinia would be.

Joselyn did her best to ignore the watchful gazes of the other women as she took a great deal longer than usual to strip off her clothing. Thank the gods there were no mirrors in Bedmeg. When there was no dancing, the women ended their evenings by washing away the day's grime in the springs. Late as it was, the cavern was crowded and loud with the echoes of feminine voices.

Joselyn nodded at those who greeted her and stepped gingerly toward the pool where Lavinia was soaking. Her curly hair was bundled high atop her head. She started to stand when she saw Joselyn.

"I'll join you." Joselyn dropped to her heels to slide into the water.

"D-don't—" Lavinia broke off as Joselyn hissed and snapped her foot back from the too hot water. Lavinia frowned and continued to stand.

"Your skin is b-badly burned." Lavinia gestured to the patchiness of Joselyn's legs. "Come, let's sit in a c-cooler pool."

Joselyn nodded and followed Lavinia. She was pleased when the Ebronian woman took them to a more secluded area of the springs. Joselyn didn't miss the tittering that was going on behind the hands of the other women as she passed. She couldn't blame them.

Lavinia slid into the water at an empty edge of a much cooler pool. Joselyn sighed and settled in next to her. The water felt far warmer than it should have, but at least she was comfortable. Lavinia smiled and said nothing, pressing the back of her head against the stony bank as though she meant only to sit with her *Saliga* in companionable silence.

Joselyn appreciated that quiet. It promised that Lavinia wouldn't press for answers. Eventually she found herself recounting the past day's events. She glazed over the bit where she'd nearly been raped, but Lavinia's averted gaze hinted that she'd already made the connection.

Ending her tale with Hollen's rushing her back to Bedmeg, Joselyn waited for a reaction. The Ebronian woman said nothing, merely pursed her lips in thoughtful silence.

"Are you my friend, Lavinia?"

Lavinia's brows furrowed. "I would like . . . to be, *mu Saliga*."

Joselyn took a breath. "Then why didn't you tell me?"

Lavinia shot her a wary gaze. "T-tell you what?"

Joselyn leveled her with a hard stare. "That they can't keep us here forever."

Lavinia sighed with a little nod. "We w-wondered how m-much longer he would keep you ignorant. Surely, after what happened, he's . . . learned better of keeping secrets from his h-hamma."

"Secrets that you all *helped* him keep." Joselyn frowned, allowing the hurt to show on her face.

Lavinia grimaced and touched a hand to Joselyn's arm. "We did. I'm sorry, but it was n-necessary."

Joselyn's skin tingled where Lavinia touched her, but she didn't move. "Necessary? How can it be necessary?"

"For anyone to interfere in the b-bonding between a *hatu* and his *hamma* would be to rob the *Na Dokiri* of his victory in winning her himself. It is a great s-sin against a man, forbidden by the g-gods. And it would be a sin against you . . .as well."

That got Joselyn's attention. "How so?"

Lavinia smiled half-heartedly as she pulled her hand away to rest on the bank. "Would you b-be content to choose or reject a *hatu* who had his true nature distorted by those around him?"

Joselyn had to think on that. It was difficult to answer because she'd never thought to seriously consider Hollen as a potential spouse. Even had she been aware that the choice was hers, she had been too focused on escaping to give Hollen any real consideration.

"It w-was up to your *hatu* to decide if he would be h-honest with you, and when. Now you may judge his . . .character for yourself."

"So he finally take her *gneri* blade away, then?" Both women jumped as Rosemary plopped down into the water on Joselyn's other side. "About damned time if you ask me."

"N-nice of you to join us, Rosemary." Lavinia eyed her friend with censure.

Unperturbed, Rosemary settled comfortably next to Joselyn, making it clear she had no intention of being left out of any further conversation.

"What do you mean, take it away? Why?" Joselyn remembered the woman's odd behavior the night of her welcoming feast when she had first mentioned Hollen giving her the knife.

"The *gneri* b-blade is a rite in and of itself." Lavinia hesitated. "Did *mu Salig* tell you what h-happens when a *hamma* chooses to stay?"

Lavinia was testing. Ensuring she wasn't overstepping her bounds. Joselyn's eyes dropped to the other woman's *tanshi* mark. "She places her mark upon him?"

Lavinia smiled, nodding. "With the same blade her *hatu*

used to mark her. The blade then becomes hers, a...symbol of her union."

Rosemary tsked. "He should never have given it to you to begin with! Cheapens the rite for the rest of us. What could he have been thinking? Probably wasn't. Men hardly do."

Lavinia shot Rosemary a reproachful look. The brunette huffed, unrepentant.

Joselyn thought of her first night in Bedmeg. How she'd stolen the blade and snuck it into their bed. She remembered how Hollen had given her the opportunity to kill him, even correcting her form. Now she knew why he hadn't permitted her to carry it outside the *bok*.

Joselyn tucked her chin and stole glances at the women on either side of her. "He did it to ease my fear. Did your *hatus*...do something similar?"

Rosemary and Lavinia exchanged looks from across the water.

"Fear of what?" Rosemary asked.

"My fear of *him*." Joselyn bit her lip. If Hollen had been lying to her, this was the surest way to find out.

"Ah," Rosemary said.

Lavinia stretched out her neck. "Well, by now you see there's n-no cause for fear. Soren slept on the ground by the fire for the first month of my y-year."

Rosemary gaped. "He didn't! Poor Soren! I let Ragnar in our bed, but I slept with so many furs wrapped around me that I needed the springs worse in the mornin's than at night. Thank Helig those days are over with!"

Lavinia laughed.

Suspicion settled hot in Joselyn's gut. How could they be so certain that Hollen hadn't taken any liberties with her? Unless there *was* a law preventing him from taking her. If that bastard had lied to her ... "So that's it then. They aren't allowed to ... to . . ."

The other women waited for Joselyn to finish. Her cheeks flushed as she trailed off.

"To plow us?" Rosemary offered.

Joselyn flinched but nodded. They didn't answer right away.

"Is that what *mu Salig* told you?" Lavinia asked in a careful tone.

"No," Joselyn admitted. She wished the women would speak more freely.

Lavinia's face softened. "P-perhaps you ought to ask him."

Joselyn gritted her teeth. "I have. He says that it's his right to have me if he wishes."

The other two women exchanged satisfied nods. Rosemary spoke. "Good, seems he's through with the lies then."

"But that makes no sense! Why wouldn't they simply take us if it's their right?"

"The same reason our boys don't throw themselves onto the backs of wild *gegatu*." Rosemary snickered. "I mean, they could do it, but they'd die for the tryin'."

Joselyn arched a brow. She thought of the hulking masses of muscle that made up the Dokiri male populace. "I doubt they fear meeting their fates at the hands of women."

Lavinia raised her dark brows. "Some fates are worse than d-death, *mu Saliga*."

"Yes, you've met Rory, haven't you?" Rosemary asked.

"Rosemary!" Lavinia hissed, shaking her head at her friend.

Joselyn wrinkled her nose, curiosity pricked. "The old man at the forge?"

Rosemary ignored Lavinia's warning. "She'll 'ear about it sooner or later. might as well be from us, and the poor girl's got a right to know."

Lavinia sighed and gave a shallow nod.

Rosemary turned and leaned into Joselyn. "It happened long before our *hatus* were born, but Rory forced himself upon his *hamma* the very day he brought her back to Bedmeg."

Joselyn stifled a gasp. She'd spoken little to the man at the forge, but had seen him often during Hollen's knife fighting instruction. It had struck her odd that the man never seemed to leave, his schedule apparently empty of pursuits outside smithing. It hadn't crossed her mind until now that he was always there because he had no family of his own.

"What happened?" Joselyn murmured.

'The whole clan could 'ear her screamin', but no one was allowed to interfere, see. He tried it again and again at the start before realizing what a fool he was. But by then it was too late. She never did warm up to him. And at the end of her year, she was beggin' anyone and everyone to stand witness when Rory took her back to the lamb pasture he'd plucked her from."

Joselyn shivered, imagining how she would have felt in the woman's place. "And Rory?"

Rosemary frowned and pressed her back against the stone bank. "Well he took her back, of course. What else could he do?"

"Was he punished?" She hoped so. But then, that would mean Hollen had lied to her. In spite of everything, Joselyn didn't want to doubt Hollen's honesty.

Rosemary's lips thinned. "For what? What he did with his *hamma* was his own business. I'll bet some of the other riders were eager to bash some sense into his head, though."

Lavinia broke in. "He *was* punished. Living without a *hamma* is a . . .sentence that lasts a lifetime and long after. Without a *hamma*, one has no legacy, no sons to ride beside him in the . . .skies beyond life."

"Unless he can get a Dokiri *gritu* to have him. 'Course, Rory's never been so lucky." Rosemary said without pity.

"A Dokiri *gritu*?" Joselyn asked.

Lavinia explained. "A w-widowed *hamma*. A rejected *hatu* may still marry the bride of a deceased...rider, but his chance to claim a bride of his own is forever forfeit. It's not an attractive alternative for our r-riders."

So it was true then. All of it. Hollen really did have the right to force her and no one would gainsay him. And yet he'd abstained, for no other reason than to win her heart. Out of hope that, when the time came, she'd choose to give herself willingly to him. Joselyn worried her lower lip. How did she feel about that?

"Do many women reject their *hatus*?"

"It d-doesn't happen often, *mu Saliga*. Most of our riders know better than to mistreat their...brides."

Joselyn shook her head. "I meant how often do women who are well treated decide to return home?"

Rosemary scoffed. "Return home to what? I don't know what Ebronian men are like, but compared to the Morhageese, Dokiri men shine like the sun on gold." She shot Joselyn a resentful look. "Well at least, *my* breed of Morhageese men."

"It's r-rare. In nine years, I've seen it h-happen once." Lavinia said.

"And their *hatus* just accept that?" Joselyn frowned, thinking of Hollen. "Why don't they try again with different women?"

Rosemary waved a dismissive hand. "Something about their silly gods. Ask your husband."

"Do you think it's right what they do? Forcing us here against our wills?"

"Yes." Gentle Lavinia was suddenly fierce. Conviction flashed in her golden eyes. Joselyn's own eyes widened.

Rosemary laughed. "Don't get her started. The ones who've been here longest are the fieriest. You'll have the stutter-stark's tongue twisted in knots."

Lavinia swallowed, looking self-conscious. Her next words

came softer. "My s-sons will bleed to protect the ones I left behind. They'll give e-everything in service to the world below. I may outlive them. My own children. If my claiming was an imposition on my f-freedom, I'll count it the lesser sacrifice."

Joselyn shifted in the pool. She forced herself not to look away from the Ebronian—no, the Dokiri *hamma*—as she spoke.

"The *Na Dokiri* are n-noble. Heroes. But even heroes need mothers. Wives. I'm both. In a way, it makes me a hero t-too."

Joselyn went still. Was that true? Was giving up one's freedom to marry and birth the men who protected the lowlands tantamount to heroism? A startling thought occurred to her. Wasn't that what Joselyn meant to do with Lord Viridian? Surrender her freedom for the sake of her people?

If only Dante Viridian were half so noble as Hollen.

Joselyn swallowed and managed a small smile for Lavinia. What a passionate heart her sweet temper concealed. Kinship bloomed in Joselyn's chest for the woman. For all the women in Bedmeg.

She looked around the torch-lit springs at the bathers communing contentedly with one another. There were no slaves here. Only women in love. Women who'd made sacrifices for those they'd left behind. By *leaving* them behind. And their husbands? Joselyn's mind whirled as she tried to absorb all she'd learned. She shook her head.

"So you mean to tell me that by choice, none of the Dokiri bed their wives for an entire year?"

Joselyn jumped when both Rosemary and Lavinia burst into laughter. Curious onlookers stared at them from across the springs. Lavinia wiped at a tear that had slid from the corner of her eye, and Rosemary slapped the surface of the water.

"Oh, sweet lady!" Rosemary said. "If you're stubborn enough to hold out for a year, then I think you'd be the strongest among us!"

24

THE SOULLESS

As Joselyn stepped into the *bok*, Hollen snapped his gaze up to her. Shirtless, he sat hunched on the edge of the bed, his elbows propped upon his knees.

"What are you doing?" Joselyn asked, fingering the dampened end of her braid.

He stood holding one of his many knives. The blade of this one was short and thin, its point needle sharp. "Considering where to mark myself." He tapped the flat of the knife thoughtfully against his palm.

Joselyn frowned. "For what?"

"For the men," he muttered. His gaze slid toward the fire.

Joselyn's breath caught. He meant her would-be-rapists. The memory of that violence made her shudder. Had killing ever given him pause? She scrutinized the web of scars on his body.

"Where did you decide?"

"My back, but—" Hollen shot her an inquisitive look. "I need help."

Joselyn blinked at him. Then her jaw dropped. "Me? You can't be serious! You saw what I did to the storen."

Hollen grimaced, but seemed undeterred. "As *Saliga* you'll

be expected to mark warriors when they master *gegatu*, and on other occasions. You might as well learn while marking me."

"No. Mark your front, or get one of your brothers to help you."

Hollen fidgeted with the hilt of his blade. Dread rolled through Joselyn's stomach. "You haven't told them, have you?"

His jaw worked, and he gave a little shake of his head.

Understanding struck her like a bolt. She swallowed hard. "Have you killed men before?"

He looked at her. "No."

Hollen had shed blood for her. *Human* blood. He was so tense, his arms plastered to his sides. Joselyn searched his face for shame, pride, for whatever a barbarian might feel after taking human life for the first time. His mouth tightened.

"I don't regret it, *mu hamma*. I just . . . I don't want to be reminded of it every day. I thought my back would be best."

Sympathy welled in her chest. She nodded. What else could she do? He'd shed the blood of five men for her. She could shed a few drops for him. Joselyn took the knife from his hand and examined the razor-sharp point.

"The Dokiri *hammas*, where do they put their marks when they decide to stay?"

Disappointment clouded his eyes. "Afraid I'll try to trick you?"

Joselyn's lips thinned. If she was wary, it was his own fault. She waited.

Hollen pointed to his *tanshi* mark. "The same place. The *hamma* only adds to what her *hatu* has already carved."

Joselyn nodded. "What image does one carve for slain men?"

Hollen leaned down and traced his finger in the furs of the bed. "Five of them."

Joselyn studied the little image. It was plain enough. Still, she doubted her ability. "I don't want to hurt you."

A corner of Hollen's mouth twitched. "I promise not to cry."

"It's going to look ugly."

Her eyes took in the relative beauty of his *idadi*. She hadn't been able to appreciate it at first. But after comparing Hollen's marks with those of his clansmen, and passively learning what each meant, Joselyn couldn't help but be impressed each time she appraised them.

"Then it will be a fitting memorial. Here." Hollen handed her a pile of rags from the bed. "Just keep the blood mopped as you work so you can see what you're doing."

Joselyn took the rags in her free hand and sighed. Fine. She put a hand on his arm and guided him to turn. As he did, Joselyn looked down at his bare feet and noticed, not for the first time, that he was missing his three outer toes on the right. She moved her focus back up to his broad back.

"Where do you want them?"

Hollen pointed over his shoulders. "Above the row of hashes across my shoulder blades."

Joselyn fingered the area. "Hollen, you're too tall for me."

Without a word, he climbed onto the furs of their bed. He lounged on his belly, resting his face against his folded arms. The muscles in his back and arms stretched beneath his skin.

Joselyn stared at him. She'd slept in his bed with him every night since arriving. But to crawl up next to him and work her fingers into his naked flesh? A thrill of excitement rushed through her.

Ridiculous.

Joselyn climbed onto the bed before she could think too much. She settled in and leaned over the center of his back. It was so broad she had to support her weight with her free arm by propping it against his ribs. It would be far easier if she were sitting astride his waist. But, no. That wasn't happening.

Joselyn lined up the blade and said a quick prayer before

pressing the tip into his skin. Blood rose and she cringed. How had she allowed herself to be talked into this?

"You need to cut deeper, *mu hamma*. They won't scar if you don't."

Joselyn took a breath and obeyed. He must be in pain, but he didn't tense. He lay perfectly still as she worked, relaxed even. More blood welled up around the knife point and Joselyn had to switch rags often to keep up with the mess.

Her progress was slow. She was so tense it wasn't long before she had to stop and strip off her overdress. She was simply too warm.

"Are you all right?" He eyed her from his place on the bed.

Joselyn swallowed, nodded, and climbed back over. If she'd known how nervous this would make her, she might have insisted on a bit of wine first.

"What happened to your foot?" she asked, eager for distraction. She might as well satisfy her curiosity.

Hollen flexed his foot, which was hanging off the edge of the bed. "During the *Veligneshi*, Jagomri cast me off his back and into a frozen lake."

"On purpose?" Then she rolled her eyes. What a stupid question.

Hollen chuckled beneath her. She drew the blade tip back, careful not to let him ruin her handiwork.

"Probably. That *raksa's* been waiting for me to die since the day I mastered him."

"How did you survive?"

"I didn't," he said flatly.

She'd been about to reapply the knife, but his words stopped her short. "What do you mean?"

Hollen pressed the side of his bearded face into his arms so he could see her from the corner of his eye. "I didn't survive. My father and Erik pulled me from the water, but I wasn't breathing, and my heart had stopped."

Joselyn narrowed her eyes. "Are you trying to be funny?"

Hollen grinned, flashing white teeth. The sight of his smile was welcome. It eased some of the tension in her chest. "No, *mu hamma*. Ask anyone. I'm speaking the truth."

Joselyn sat back on her heels. She couldn't even ask him to explain; she was so skeptical. Hollen needed no prompting.

"When the Dokiri die, their bodies are washed in the deadpools, a cold chamber set high in the mountain. The water there cleanses our souls from our bodies and returns them to Regna. My brothers carried me there to complete the rites, but while I was being washed, my body began to stir. My heart beat again, and I breathed new air into my lungs. It was the most painful experience of my life."

Joselyn blinked. Could it be possible? No. Not naturally. Nothing short of a miracle would make it so. But then, which god had blessed him? And why?

"How?" she breathed.

Hollen shrugged. "I don't know. The elders said Helig filled my veins with the sacred water. That she stayed me on this earth for a grand purpose."

"What purpose?"

"Maybe we'll find out one day."

He rolled to his side and looked at her. His eyes held searching wonder, as if she might hold the answer. Joselyn brushed a lock of hair over her ear.

Could it be true? Had he really died and been resurrected? Perhaps there was a natural explanation for what had happened. She could think of none. It was no wonder that the elders had been set on naming him their next *Salig*. They believed him the carrier of divine purpose, and surely of favor.

Joselyn had taken his men's loyalty for granted. It was

apparent to her that Hollen was a fair and devoted leader, but there was more to it than that. They expected much from their *Salig*. Did the expectation ever overwhelm him?

"So that's how you were named, then?" she asked.

"Yes." He rolled back to his stomach. "It took weeks for my flesh to heal. I was burned even worse than you. I'm only grateful I didn't lose my fingers. My toes weren't so lucky. I plan to make a sacrifice to Helig in thanks that you haven't lost any."

Joselyn didn't know what to say to that. Animal sacrifices weren't a part of her religion. Her gods weren't so bloody. They preferred gold, and lots of it. The high priest, covered from head to toe in swaths of solid gold chains and jeweled decals, was a testament to her deities' appetites. She supposed his plan was endearing, in the same crude and barbaric way the rest of Hollen was.

"Joselyn."

"Hmm?"

"Be careful where you're poking."

She was pressing the knife dully into his shoulder, far from its mark. She cleared her throat and reapplied the blade.

THE HIDE PILLOW felt warm and inviting when Joselyn pressed her cheek into it. Though she'd only been awake for a handful of hours, she was bone weary. The *bok* was dim in the fading light of the fire. Hollen extinguished the last remaining torch. Joselyn stared at the dried squares of cloth covering his fresh wounds. She'd done a better job than she'd expected.

Joselyn stretched and slid a hand beneath her pillow. She stilled when her fingers brushed cool ivory. The *gneri* blade. She drew it out from where it was tucked, as if it had never ventured outside Bedmeg with her.

Hollen stripped and climbed into bed. Joselyn sat up as he settled, and he quirked a questioning brow. She crossed her legs beneath her and pulled the hilt of the blade up between them, eyeing the images he'd carved.

"Why the heavens?" she asked, without taking her eyes off the celestial scene.

Hollen's gaze dropped to the knife. He wrapped his hand around hers and turned the blade so that the sun, with its sweeping rays, was facing her.

"For my father." He turned it back to show the crescent moon and the five tiny stars within. "My mother, and her five children."

Joselyn eyed the craftsmanship with new appreciation. She hadn't imagined the scene was so personal to him. "It's beautiful."

"That's only fitting. I made it for you."

Heat crept across Joselyn's chest. She'd been called beautiful before. Frequently, in fact. But it felt different coming from Hollen. Unlike when she'd heard it from Morhageese lords, Hollen made it feel significant and pure. She pressed the blade hilt into his palm. "Lavinia told me what this blade means."

Hollen pursed his lips. "It only means something when the *hamma* to whom it's given makes a choice to use it."

He tried to give it back, but Joselyn refused it. "It's her choice then?"

"Yes."

Joselyn bit at the inside of her cheek. Her eyes fastened to his. "You stole me from my horse, forced me down upon your altar, carved your mark into my flesh, kept me sequestered on this mountain...and still you intend to give me a choice?"

He looked disturbed but nodded solemnly.

"Why?" She couldn't make sense of it. Everything about this man confused her. A savage who would imprison her against her will, and yet would eventually chose to regard her as his equal? Worthy to accept or reject him according to her own will? He was an enigma.

"Because despite all that, if I can't win your heart, I don't deserve to keep you."

Joselyn frowned. "Why don't you simply court your brides? Trade for them?"

"Because we are *Na Dokiri*. And we conquer what is ours."

Joselyn leaned forward. "Am I free, or aren't I?"

Hollen matched her, stopping but a few inches from her face. "You *are* free." He covered her hand with one of his. "And you are mine."

Joselyn's mouth thinned. She'd never been free. Not truly. She'd ever been subject to her father's will. She'd left her home to subject herself to Dante Viridian's will. Never once had she complained, ever considered any alternative. And yet, in that moment, she knew she'd rather be Hollen's than free to choose between a thousand Morhageese lords.

"I know that doesn't make sense to you, *mu hamma*. Give me a chance to reconcile it." He touched his forehead to hers.

Joselyn sucked in a breath. Her eyes fell to his lips.

"Please," he whispered as his pine scent filled her lungs.

Joselyn's eyes fell shut. She closed the narrow distance between them and pressed her lips to his. Heat bathed her. He was soft, and solid. Calloused, but gentle. She grazed the curves of her mouth against his, reveling in the pleasure that glowed where she touched him.

Hollen drew in a haggard breath. His fingers drifted up her arm, making her shiver. The tips of his nails drew over her shoulder and played at the hollow of her neck. His other hand came up to brush away her hair. Her lips parted on a sigh, and Hollen deepened the kiss, the tip of his tongue gliding sensually over the swell of her mouth.

Good.

Too good.

Joselyn broke away with a little gasp. Her wide eyes locked upon his.

Hollen's hands fell away only to grip the furs of the bed much too tightly. He watched her, openmouthed, panting. Words caught in his throat.

Joselyn whirled in the bed, scooting her legs over the side and dropping her face into her hands. She heaved a breath, trying to regain control of her trembling nerves.

"Are you all right?" he asked.

"I'm fine." But even as she said it, her head shook in her hands.

"I—" he broke off, his voice filled with uncertainty and wanting. Joselyn ran a hand through her hair. Her heart pounded. If only it would slow so she could breathe again.

I'm going mad.

Joselyn went still and quiet, as though preparing for the consequences of her thoughtless actions to descend like a vengeful reaper. To crush her.

Nothing happened.

What exactly was she even waiting for? She flicked a glance at the empty wall ahead. Who was coming to condemn her?

Hollen's calloused hand brushed her shoulder. It was so gentle. The rumble of his voice filled the bok, covering the soft crackle of the waning fire. "Come to sleep, *mu hamma.*"

He gave her a little pull, and Joselyn forced herself to turn and look him in the eye. He regarded her with concern, his expression intense. "You're exhausted."

"Yes. I *am.*"

Hollen released her shoulder and patted a hand on her side of the bed. Joselyn lay down, but curled away from him as she did. She jumped when a heavy arm draped over her waist.

"What are you doing?" She stiffened.

He didn't answer, and he didn't move.

Joselyn twisted around to face him. He lay on his stomach and regarded her steadily. Joselyn looked at his muscled arm still lying over her. She blinked back up at him. "Let go of me."

He shut his eyes as though he meant to sleep.

She pressed a hand against his arm. "Hollen, I can't sleep like this."

His eyes popped back open. "Are you going to run off again if I let you go?"

Regret pulled at her stomach. She imagined what he must have been thinking when he woke to find her gone. Thank the gods he'd come for her. She wouldn't be here if he hadn't.

"No."

He responded immediately, "Swear it."

Joselyn hesitated, taken aback at the severity in his voice. "I've already sworn."

"Do it again," he murmured, his words half muffled by his pillow.

Joselyn sighed. "I swear not to run away from you."

His thumb brushed languid strokes over her back. The sensation tickled.

"Thank you," he mumbled.

"Now let me go."

"Why?"

"Because I swore not to leave you."

"And?" Hollen arched a brow and settled more deeply into the furs.

Joselyn hesitated. "And . . .and you said you'd let me go if I did."

He huffed and drew her in even tighter. Joselyn's belly arched into him, and her heart raced.

"I said nothing of the sort, *mu hamma.*"

25

SMALL STEPS

"*A*re you angry with me?" Hollen took his seat next to Joselyn in the common area.

Joselyn shifted on the bench. Few people remained this evening. Most had gone off to the springs for the night. As for her, she was finally feeling well enough to get around on her own.

She looked at Hollen. His hair had been freshly pulled back. The dinner fires radiated heat, and the light reflected off his perfect *idadi*. As usual, he was shirtless. Damn him.

"Of course not," she said.

"You're avoiding me."

"I'm not."

"You are," he said.

She was.

For the past five mornings, they'd eaten breakfast together and then Joselyn would determine what Hollen was up to for the day. She'd made sure her activities always took place elsewhere. If she could find absolutely no excuse to be apart from him, she'd take off to the springs with some mention of her skin and how it pained her. She hadn't thought Hollen was fooled, but he'd never pushed her. Not until now.

Joselyn crossed her arms and returned his unyielding look. "I am."

Hurt flashed over his face. "Why?"

After a moment she said, "Because you unsettle me, and I'm unsettled enough."

He was too close now. He reached out to take her hand in his. She let him, having grown accustomed to his touches. Though he'd given her a wide berth during the daytime, he'd still insisted on holding her each night. He worked a nightly balm into her snow burns and seized on every opportunity to give her a gentle caress throughout the daylight hours. Those touches made her shiver with want and, despite avoiding him, she counted the minutes between each one.

Hollen ran a thumb across her knuckles as he studied her. "I want you to come with me. I have something to show you."

She licked her lips, tasting the remains of the smoked mutton she'd just eaten. "Where?"

Hollen tilted his head toward the entrance of the common area. Joselyn looked out at the darkened sky. "Now?"

He nodded.

She hadn't left the caves since the night she'd tried to escape. She bit her lip and sent another darting gaze toward the entrance.

Hollen stood from the bench and gave her hand, still in his, a gentle tug. "Come."

His eyes glinted with a hint of excitement. There was something else on his face too. Vulnerability. Joselyn raised a brow at him. He was up to something. How familiar she'd become with him, that she could read his expressions with a quick look.

She could refuse him. She'd done plenty of that lately. Each time the sting of rejection dimmed that light in his eyes. Weariness pulled her heart apart. She was so tired of seeing that look in her wild savage, of being the cause for it.

Say no, Joselyn. You'll only cause more pain later.

She stood from the bench.

Fool.

Hollen rewarded her with a gleaming smile. They went to their *bok* for warm clothes and hurried back down through the common area. People nodded at them as they went. She sighed, her heart warming at their kind regard. Bedmeg's goodwill was a luxury she was growing attached to. There was a routine in this place, a sense of rhythm that directed the cadence of each day. It wasn't the hard-driven pace of a peasant's life, nor the strangling monotony of a noble's. Rather, it followed the cycle of both need and pleasure. It was easy, natural.

Joselyn held her head high as they drew toward the exit, but with each pace toward the darkness, a sense of foreboding grew. A shiver worked its way through her. Hand in Hollen's, Joselyn took a step out into the snow. Her eyes darted from one wall of the ravine to the other as she scanned the area. The night was clear and crisp, quiet but for the wind that never stilled in the mountains. What was she even looking for? Dread squeezed her insides together, making it hard to breathe.

Hollen squeezed her hand. She looked down at it. His thumb gave her a little stroke and he murmured, "It's all right, Joselyn."

She exhaled. Apparently, he was learning her expressions too. A tentative smile turned up the corner of her mouth. Some of her anxiety abated. Together, they started down the ravine.

He led her toward the armory. A light burned at the forge. Rory stood where he always did, hammering at some piece of metal. Knowing what she knew now, Joselyn eyed him warily. She glanced at Hollen, who regarded him as he always had, with indifference.

Hollen bit out a few words in his language to the older man.

Rory set down his work and started up the ravine. Hollen had never dismissed him before. When he looked back at her, Joselyn cocked her head.

Hollen stepped away from Joselyn and bent down behind the forge to pick up something large and bound in cloth. Even as he unwrapped it, Joselyn recognized what it was: a bow fashioned from scarlet-colored wood. It had been sanded down so that its varnish reflected the forge light. Lamb leather encased the grip, the bowstring was taut and new. What stood out most was its size.

"Come, *mu hamma*. I want to see how it fits you."

Without taking her eyes from the bow, Joselyn approached. She ran three fingers along the arch of the weapon, reveling in its smoothness. Her eyes flicked up toward Hollen's to see him watching her intently. He turned the bow vertical and motioned for her to take it. It was a perfect fit. Not just in length, but the width suited her slender hands perfectly.

"Who made this?" she asked.

"I did."

Joselyn's eyes widened.

"With some help," he added.

"I've never seen this type of wood." Joselyn studied the strong, flexible texture of the bow. It was so light. If she didn't know any better, she'd suppose it to be hollow. She'd not tire from carrying this weapon. And she'd never tire of gazing at its vivid color.

"It's wine-wood, found near the ocean shore."

Joselyn's lips parted. The closest coastline was weeks' travel on horseback from her lands. How had he managed it?

As if reading her mind, Hollen went on, "I've had the wood for years. I just never knew what to use it for until now."

Emotion welled in Joselyn's throat. In addition to the time he'd spent fashioning something for her, he'd used precious materials that he'd hoarded for years. She swallowed. "This is the finest gift I've ever received."

Hollen beamed. "Truly?"

"Truly."

It may not have been the most expensive thing, nor the loveliest, but it was indeed the finest. Of the hundreds of gifts she'd received in her life, none had ever appealed to her more. None had ever been given in such a spirit of generosity. Joselyn's throat tightened to think of how he must have been spending his time while she avoided him.

You'll never deserve him.

"Thank you, Hollen."

For a long moment they just looked at each other. The cry of an eagle punctured the air, breaking their gazes with its eerie resonance. Hollen took the bow from Joselyn, rewrapped it, and set it back behind the forge.

"There's something else," he said.

"Oh?"

A hint of Hollen's wickedness shone on his face. Without a word, he stepped out from beneath the forge's shelter and whistled loudly for Jagomri. When he came back to her, his expression had sobered. "There's something I'd like to do, *mu hamma*, but it would require you to trust me for a short time."

She eyed him. "What do you want to do?"

Hollen reached within his cloak to retrieve a thin strip of woolen cloth. He held it out to her, a sheepish look on his face. Joselyn blinked at it.

"There's something I want to show you, but much of the effect will be spoiled if you see it before we arrive."

What could he want to show her that she would see from Jagomri's back in the middle of the night? "I don't understand."

His mouth pulled into a tight line. "I was hoping you would let me cover your eyes."

Joselyn's brows shot to her hairline.

"Just until we arrive," he blurted, apology riddled across his face.

She eyed the thin strip of cloth. What harm could it do? If it would make him happy, perhaps she should allow him to blind her. Still, to be so helpless? The deep timber of Hollen's voice interrupted her thoughts.

"Do you trust me?"

It was a question, not a challenge. In the pale light of the waning moon, Joselyn breathed in.

"Yes."

26

THE GLORY OF THE GODS

The night air was frigid enough to slice skin as it whipped past them, but Joselyn didn't feel it. She was warm beneath Hollen's cloak, and more, beneath the weight of his chest. With his heat upon her and her eyes covered, she could have fallen asleep. A longer flight and she might have.

They landed with the same eerie silence they always did upon Jagomri. It was a marvel that a creature so large could move so gracefully. Joselyn lay still as she listened to the sound of Hollen unbinding his legs from the saddle. The thin air smelled fresh, and she licked her lips against the dryness of the wind. It wasn't long before he pulled her off and set her feet into the snow.

"Almost there," he said.

Joselyn squeezed his hand as he led her. After a few moments, he stopped. His arms rested heavy upon her shoulders.

"Stay right here, *mu hamma*. Don't move." The insistence of his tone gave her pause.

"May I uncover my eyes?"

The edge vanished from his voice, replaced by excitement. "Not yet. Soon."

Joselyn did as he bid. She stood, a bit awkwardly, as he rustled around before her. She shivered against the wind, which seemed especially fierce wherever they'd landed. Finally, Hollen's fingers fumbled at the back of her head. Her blindfold fell away.

An enormous valley filled her vision. She stood only paces from the precipice of a cliff. She barely caught sight of the earth below before she gasped.

She took a hurried step backward and tripped over the toe of Hollen's boot. He caught her with a large hand on her arm while the other flew protectively around her waist. How could he bring her to such a dangerous place? She was about to voice her outrage, but when she lifted her eyes, her entire body froze.

The sky was burning. Not with fire, but with every color Joselyn could imagine: aqua, fuchsia, azure, amber, and violet. The colors glowed, swirling against the backdrop of a star-studded sky. It was like a living mural painted by some celestial being on the ceiling of the world. Hollen had brought her to see The Glory of the Gods. She'd seen it before, though from Morhagen the mountain lights were but a dim whisper compared to this feast of vibrant color. Joselyn's eyes locked upon the sight, and her mouth fell open with awe.

"Why couldn't I see these lights from Bedmeg?" she asked.

"Bedmeg is too low on the mountain. Very little can be seen below the cloud banks. Also, it's on the wrong side for this time of year. In spring they can occasionally be glimpsed from Bedmeg, but it's nothing like coming to the peak."

"Are we on the peak?" Joselyn looked around, wary of losing her balance and somehow stumbling off the snow-packed edge.

"Yes."

The peak of Mount Carpe. It was the tallest point on the

earth, the closest one could come to the heavens. Or, so she'd been taught. Joselyn stared in open wonder.

Hollen stepped around her to sit on the ground. Joselyn looked down to see the bear skin he'd unrolled. So high up, Joselyn was hesitant to stand apart from him. When he gestured for her to join him, she was quick to obey. As she ducked down, Hollen grabbed her by the hips.

"Sit here, *mu hamma*." He gestured at the spot in front of him, between his slightly bent knees.

Joselyn pursed her lips.

"It's no different than when we ride on Jagomri's back," he reasoned.

You shouldn't.

She did.

Joselyn settled herself between his legs and allowed him to tuck his chest against her back. She straightened when he laced his arms around her waist and laid their weight in her lap. Eventually she relaxed, resting her head against his shoulder.

They stayed that way for a while, quietly appreciating the spectacle of light and color before them. The wind blew, but Joselyn wasn't bothered. Her clothes and her savage were of fine stock, and both enveloped her in their protective shelter. She'd not been so at ease in days. How ironic, considering her determination to avoid him.

"You're looking at Regna's love for his bride." Hollen said, leaning slightly back to give her a better view.

"Helig?" Joselyn asked, thinking of the earth goddess the Dokiri often prayed to.

His face nodded against hers. "You asked me why we only claim one bride."

Joselyn's heart quickened. Did she have the strength to discuss this tonight? The reserve? After his gift, and wrapped in his arms as she was, the last thing she wanted was to argue their impossible marriage. She didn't want to think of what would happen if she eventually succeeded in returning to Morhagen, especially what would happen to *Hollen*.

He carried on. "When time began, there were only the gods and the heavens. Regna begged Helig to be his bride, but she refused him. When Helig birthed the world, she brought forth all creatures, both good and evil."

Joselyn snuggled a bit tighter against Hollen, who gave her a little squeeze. He waited for her to settle before continuing. "Seeing his beloved's plight, Regna created a champion from his own flesh to master the earth and keep evil at bay. He sent his essence by way of a rainstorm that fell to the ground and formed a lake. From it sprung the first *Na Dokiri*. When the warrior had cleansed the earth of evil, Helig sent her daughter from the sand of that same pool to be mated to him."

The cadence of Hollen's voice was reverent as he accounted the details of his religion. Or was it his history? Perhaps it was both.

"Regna's son had but to look upon Helig's daughter to know that she was his, and that she would be his only. They were mother and father to the next generation of riders. They birthed many sons, but never any daughters, for daughters beget life, and all life belongs to Helig. After that, the goddess claimed her *hatu*, and she became his only. They were each other's reward."

Joselyn turned the side of her face into Hollen's chest as she considered his words. The story, which had started with his gods, was quickly turning into an explanation for his clan's ways. Its existence.

"Every child born of Regna's flesh can only ever reflect Regna's strength. It is our blessing and our curse. For strength, while necessary to make a place in the world, is not enough to make that place worth fighting for. For that, we need Helig's blessings. We need her daughters."

"You need lowlanders?" Joselyn asked.

He nodded. "Helig swore to Regna, while his essence remained upon the earth, protecting it from evil, that the *Na Dokiri* would always have brides, but only if, like Regna, they proved themselves worthy and true. That is why we cannot claim brides until after the *Veligneshi*. And it is why, like Regna, we must convince our brides of our worthiness."

Joselyn shook her head. "But why do you only give yourselves one chance? Why are you resigned to living brideless if you can't convince the very first woman you take to marry you?"

"We have the right to choose, but we are not entitled to the whole world. With the privilege of choosing whomever the *Na Dokiri* wishes comes the burden of ensuring that he chooses well."

"But how can you possibly know? How do you know the woman you choose will have you?"

Hollen half chuckled, half scoffed. "We don't."

Joselyn turned her face up to his. "That's an incredible risk."

Hollen looked down to meet her curious gaze. "I'd rather take the risk than never try at all."

Joselyn's cheeks heated, and she turned her gaze back out toward the sky, "But if you only have one chance, and choosing poorly means a life of solitude, how do you possibly decide? Why—"

She broke off. Swallowing, she dared the question that had been rattling in her mind for some time. "Why did you choose *me*?"

Hollen was silent for a little while. Joselyn forced herself not to press him.

"When I left Bedmeg in search of a bride, I didn't expect to come home with one. As *Salig*, my time for searching was limited, and I'd already waited so long. The first time I tried to leave, my mother hadn't woken. It seemed like the gods were set against me."

Regret welled in Joselyn's chest. Could he have ever been content? Here on this mountain without a family of his own?

"But when I saw you—" Hollen's voice took on an edge of awe. He pulled her upwards and turned her in his arms. Kneeling before him, Joselyn could just make out his features in the starlight and swirling colors of the sky. They cast an ethereal glow upon his bearded face.

"When I saw *you*, I understood that every delay, every hardship, every sorrow had been designed to bring me to you in *that* moment. You were everything I'd ever dreamed of. The most beautiful woman I'd ever seen."

Her heart quickened at his praise, even as doubt niggled her chest. "Sigvard told me I'm like your mother."

Hollen chuckled. "That *podagi* is occasionally right. You've given me trouble from the moment Jagomri released you. You can't imagine my satisfaction when you struck me with that stone."

She snorted. "Satisfaction?"

"Yes. Because I knew in that moment there was nothing that could break you. The universe could contrive any obstacle, and you would stand your ground."

Her eyes fell away from his. She traced a pattern on the shoulder of his furs. "I'm not your mother, Hollen."

Lady Colette Potrulis had been a woman apart from her breed, exceptional in many ways. Her infamous reputation had been one of wildness even before her dramatic disappearance. Joselyn's heart began to ache. She couldn't possibly live up to that standard. Upon her arrival, she'd not even been able to start a fire. And now Hollen expected her to stand among his people as their peer? Their chieftainess?

He pressed a finger up beneath her chin. "That's not why I claimed you."

She searched his eyes.

"Your beauty is what caught my attention. It seems inconsequential to me now considering all that you are, but at the time, one look was all it took. But I didn't claim you then. I kept returning to you for days. Each time I saw you I became more convinced that you were the one the gods had chosen for me. I knew you were a woman of great importance. How could you not be? With an armed escort of fifty men? And yet, where were you?"

Joselyn blinked. "On horseback."

Hollen grinned. "And set far apart from your guard. I watched you on that hilltop, your red hair blowing in the wind like a torch. You were fearless as any man, and *proud*." His hands tightened on her waist. "I wanted you. I wanted you more than I've ever wanted anything in my life."

She thought of the other thing Sigvard had told her. "You think I'll give you a love like your parents had? Some epic romance to make you feel like your father's equal?"

Hollen frowned. "My father was a great leader. The finest *Salig* in five generations. I won't deny my respect for him or the love he held for my mother. It was his love for his *hamma* that gave him strength. That's why his strength deserted him when she died."

Joselyn grimaced, regretting having brought this up. Hollen rubbed a thumb over her jaw and into the cleft of her chin.

"My desire for you isn't born of some need to succeed my father. I know that I'll love you, Joselyn. I'll love you as much as Father loved Mother."

"But *why* do you think that?"

"Because it's already started."

Joselyn's skin grew hot, and she looked away. Her throat

tightened and, to her horror, tears stung the backs of her eyes. She blinked them back. Hollen didn't seem to notice. He brushed the pads of his fingers along her jawline and down the column of her throat. She swallowed hard. She had to keep her emotions in check.

"You're not my mother. You are Joselyn Helena Elise Fury." His eyes skimmed over every detail of her face. "And you are mine."

Liar. A venom-filled voice hissed in her mind. *Your own mother didn't want you. Your own father sold you. Hollen is better than both. Why would he want you?*

"I don't belong here, Hollen. Soon you'll see that, and you'll be glad for my departure."

Hollen stared at her with denial riddled on his face. He shook his head once and opened his mouth to speak. Joselyn cut him off.

"I only regret that you may claim no one else. At least you can have a widow. A . . . *gritu*." She forced the last words through a tightened jaw.

Hollen's mouth snapped shut. "Truly? You would see me bound to another?"

"You'll grow to love one of the *gritus*, if you only give yourself the opportunity. There isn't a plain woman in of all Bedmeg." The words tasted like dirt on her own tongue. The thought of another woman sharing Hollen's bed made her stomach churn.

"You really think one of the *gritus* would have me?" he asked, irritation thick in his voice.

Joselyn cocked her head. "Of course. You're *Salig*." *And you're Hollen. What woman wouldn't want you?*

His jaw tightened. "And every woman there knows how I feel about you. They'd know that I was forever comparing them with your memory. It's hard enough being claimed as a *gritu*, knowing that the man you're with will never conquer the final rite. But to have seen how much he wanted another? To know that you're just a substitute?"

Joselyn hadn't thought of that. Even so, it couldn't be that no one would have him. It couldn't. "I think you underestimate yourself."

"No. *You* do." His arms stiffened around her and his dark eyes flashed. "You can be very sure that I won't bind myself to anyone else. And the thought of *you* with another man makes my hand itch for my axe."

He was jealous. He wanted *her* to be jealous. Joselyn tried to dismiss the wave of giddiness that swept through her. She should keep trying to reason with him, make him understand that this thing between them couldn't last.

She didn't.

Silence fell between them. For a while they just watched each other. Joselyn's hands bunched on his chest, rising and falling with each of his breaths. They grew quicker. Shallower.

"Joselyn, when you kissed me—"

She shut her eyes, unable to stop the flood of emotions that came torrenting. She'd tried to pretend that moment had never happened. Until now, he'd allowed her.

Hollen leaned forward. "—I got a taste of the future I feared was locked to me, that I'd barred myself from with my own deceit."

Joselyn remembered the feel of her lips pressed against his. Her first and only kiss. In moments like this, while she was looking at him, it didn't seem like madness that had driven her to that moment. More like inevitable impulse. Destiny.

"*Mu hamma*"—a little shiver wracked its way down Joselyn's body as he breathed that endearment— "I've never tasted anything sweeter."

Her hands had trailed up his chest, over his throat, to pet at his beard. The little hairs were warm against her pinkened fingertips. One of his hands slid behind her head, drawing her forward.

"Let me taste you again," he said.

Joselyn stiffened. Her hand went rigid against him. Their faces hovered apart by a shadow as she whispered, "It will be all the more bitter when I leave."

His eyes, black as the night around them, settled upon her. "Don't leave."

He tilted his head and closed the distance between them.

The moment their lips touched, the tension in Joselyn's body dissolved like snow in the light of summer sun. She'd cautioned him. If he wouldn't see reason, then neither would she. Not in this moment. Joselyn closed her eyes and leaned into the kiss. The warmth between them roared into burning heat within seconds.

As Hollen opened his mouth on a sigh, Joselyn's lips parted as well. She breathed in his sweet air, and didn't resist when he deepened the kiss. A shiver wracked through her as his tongue swept along her lower lip. Her nails grazed over his earlobes, and she reveled to feel his own tremor. His massive arms pulled her in. She could feel every hitch of his breath. A little moan escaped her. Joselyn felt, rather than heard, the answering rumble in his own throat. Her eyes fluttered open.

His gaze was languid. It brimmed with desire. He broke apart from her, breathing in half-finished gasps. His whole body seemed to thrum and rock with the tension of unspent energy. He brought his roughened hands to either side of her face and brushed back errant strands of hair. Joselyn shuddered as forbidden pleasure pulsed through her veins.

"I need you, *mu hamma*," he panted.

Joselyn sucked in a breath. Unable to bear the intensity of his eyes, she closed her own. She pressed a cheek into one of his palms. He was always so warm.

"We need you. Your future is here, in Bedmeg." He pressed his forehead against hers. "Stay with me."

Skies, she wanted to. She wanted it more than anything.

The voice in her mind, the terribly honest one, sneered. *You can't. And you're cruel to allow this.*

"Hollen—"

Before she could continue, he covered her mouth with his. This kiss was forceful. There was a fierceness to it, an urgency that stole the breath from her lungs along with the words she'd been about to speak. When he finally broke away, they were both panting. Joselyn brought a hand to her lips, dazedly pawing at their swollen warmth.

"Don't speak of leaving me." He grasped her face in his hands like he could commune to her very soul if only he held her close enough. "You've sworn to remain at my side for the year. And while you're here, I want *all* of you. Yourself *and* your loyalty. I would have your body and heart if you would but accept mine."

Joselyn, still trying to catch her breath, stared at him. Her lips moved, but words evaded.

Hollen's eyes dropped to her mouth. "Regna, you taste like the heavens!"

He pulled her in for another kiss. This time, Joselyn stopped him. The restraint caused a physical ache in her body.

The hateful voice whispered its ugly warning, stealing away her peace. *You don't belong here. He will realize it soon enough, and then it will be worse than if you'd never met him.*

Joselyn's heart wilted. Was she simply reserving herself for a more exquisite pain?

This can't last. I'm a fool.

She tried to swallow but her mouth had gone dry. A single tear slipped over her cheek and Joselyn swiped at it. She started to turn on her knees, determined to hide her face. Hollen caught her in his arms.

"Let me go," she demanded.

Distress creased the corners of his eyes. "Joselyn, why are you crying?"

Because she knew the truth. She'd never be a match for him. The only worthy thing about her was her willingness to serve her people, the very ones she'd have to abandon to be with him. He thought he could love her? He had no idea what a bitter, spiteful person she was. He couldn't imagine the amount of hate that filled her heart. And so much of it was for her parents, even as Hollen's own heart overflowed with adoration for his.

"You'll regret this," she said, swallowing down a sob, "you'll wish you'd claimed someone else."

He stroked her hair. "No, Joselyn. I knew I made the right choice that day. Even though you were a stranger, I was still certain. And now? I could never be surer. I think all the time about what might have happened if I hadn't claimed you. About where you'd be."

Joselyn choked on a breath. For a moment, all misery fled her body, replaced by hostile wariness. "What do you mean?"

Hollen petted at her hair. His lips thinned and sorrow filled his eyes. "The timing. It can't all be coincidence. If I hadn't claimed you that day, you'd be with *him*. I could never let that happen. Couldn't imagine your suffering."

She stared at him, knowing what that look meant.

Did he think claiming her made him her savior? Indignation stirred in her gut and rose into her throat. She wasn't a victim, some helpless casualty in the games of lords. She'd been in that procession by choice, ready to give her freedom, *everything*, for those who depended on her. Her hands balled into fists against his chest. "Who do you think you are?"

Hollen blinked. "What?"

"Do you think I would have crumbled? Broken at the earliest opportunity?"

"No. I—"

She cut him off. "I didn't ask for you to save me." Not, of all things, from her duty, the one thing that set her apart.

"Joselyn—"

She pulled out of his arms. "Don't pity me, barbarian. I have as much pride as you."

She might not be worthy of Hollen, but she'd be damned if, in his benevolence, he stole from her the one thing that gave her dignity. Her willingness to do what she must.

"I *don't* pity you," he blurted, shaking his head. "That's not what I meant."

"No?" She arched a brow.

Hollen swallowed. "I only meant . . . I can't bear the thought of you with another man."

She stared him down and saw the lie lingering in his dark eyes. Her stomach hardened. "I'm getting cold."

He took her chilled hands in his. Even as she worked to keep her emotions in check, Joselyn bristled at the thrill of want that ran through her. She couldn't think like this. Couldn't *be* like this. Couldn't let herself want him. Every minute she remained in Bedmeg her house drew closer to ultimate disaster.

She'd never expected to love the man she married and had never expected him to love her. Now her icy heart was melting for a savage who professed to be falling for her. Would there be anything left of her when the heat of his desire burned out? If she stayed in Bedmeg, it *would* burn out. Because Hollen was a good man, the kind who sacrificed for his people. If she abandoned her duty now, *she* wouldn't be. She'd be weak like her mother, self-serving like her father, the wanting half of Hollen's whole. And he'd have every right to disdain her.

Never.

"Take me back," she said.

His eyes darted between each of hers. He seemed to want to say something. In the end he helped her up and took her back to Bedmeg. Not to Morhagen. Not to her duty.

As she lay in the darkened *bok*, Joselyn blinked away another wave of tears.

She was going to have to *make* him.

27

JUDGMENT DAY

"I'm going to kill him!" Hollen roared, scanning the common area for signs of Sigvard's auburn hair. He gazed instead over his bride's red mane, and Hollen took several bounding strides in her direction. She and the women sitting with her at the breakfast fire regarded him with curious gazes.

"Have you seen Sigvard?" he asked, reducing his volume but none of his irritation.

Joselyn stood. "He ran past here a few moments ago, why?"

"Which way did he go?" he demanded.

"What's happened?"

"That *podagi* dumped fig cap in the vat where my coat was soaking!"

All around, the women burst into laughter. Thanks to Sigvard, their *Salig* would now be flying in a coat whose underside was dyed bright purple, a color that was not likely to fade any time soon.

Joselyn bit down on her lower lip with amusement lighting her eyes. "Are you certain? That it was him, I mean."

"That boy needs to grow up! If he doesn't break that damned *gegatu* soon I'm going to break *him* over my knee!"

"Perhaps one of the children was wandering about and dropped the mushroom in by mistake?"

Hollen blinked at her. "Are you protecting him?"

The women laughed even harder. Joselyn put a hand on her hip. "If you were coming for me in a similar state of rage, I hope he'd return the favor."

Hollen gaped at her. "Woman, tell me where he is!"

Joselyn nodded. A corner of her mouth pulled upward. "Of course. As soon as your temper has cooled."

Hollen was taken aback. The surrounding *hammas* broke into yet another bout of laughter, this the loudest by far. Joselyn stood tall, her calm gaze unflinching. Despite himself, Hollen's face cocked into a grin. His anger forgotten, he lunged forward to catch his bride about the wrist.

He turned toward the *bok* tunnels, just catching his *hamma's* widened eyes as he tugged her along. The laughter of the onlookers dampened to knowing giggles.

"Where are we going?" Joselyn asked, flustered.

"To have a private word." Hollen could hear her shuffling footfalls as she hurried to keep up. Pleasure suffused him. If his bride was teasing him, perhaps she'd forgiven him for the night before. What a disaster that had been. One moment he'd been kissing her, reveling in the intimacy and rising lust of the moment. The next, she was crying and demanding to be taken back. Women were perilous creatures.

He'd take her back to their *bok* now, and he'd kiss and stroke her senseless. He'd thought of little else all morning, and certainly he'd thought of nothing else as she'd slept, huddled in his arms, her face tucked against his bare chest. Regna! She was going to be the death of him, and what a sweet, agonizing death it would be.

"*Mu Salig! Mu Salig! Mu Salig!*" a woman cried.

Hollen stopped dead in his tracks, and Joselyn bumped into

him from behind. His entire body stiffened at the sound of that familiar shrieking. Where was its twin?

"Stop your bleating, you old goat!" came another shrill voice.

There it is.

Hollen cursed under his breath. He rolled his eyes as he turned back, still clutching Joselyn's hand. Perhaps if the two shrews saw that he was busy, they might stow their bickering long enough to forget the cause. One look at their wrinkled faces, each contorted with indignant fury, cured any such notion. Sighing, he released his bride's hand.

"What is it this time, Leah?" he asked, willing patience into his voice.

The two women were panting, having just raced through the common area to reach him. It was a miracle neither had fallen and broken a hip, so intent was each upon hindering the other. Leah, barely ahead, spoke first.

"She took it! She swiped it right from under my nose!" Leah shoved a damp strand of pepper-gray hair from her brow. Behind her, Briel skidded to a halt and bumped into Leah from behind. Briel's voice rose to a pitch high enough to crack stone.

"It's not true! She's so full of herself! Can't imagine I might have anything better to do than sit around looking for ways to annoy her!"

"You rarely do," Hollen muttered, quiet enough that only Joselyn would hear. It wouldn't have mattered if he'd shouted. No one could have noticed over the screeching that ensued. The two women hurled their grievances at one another, drawing every eye in the common area.

Hollen stole a glance at Joselyn. She looked astonished. He chuckled. Growing up in a royal court, his bride had probably never witnessed such antics from elderly women. For once, Hollen envied her. His thoughts were interrupted when he saw Leah's hand rise to strike her fellow Dokiri *hamma*. Hollen darted forward. He caught the errant arm before any real damage was done.

"Enough!" Hollen barked at the two of them. His booming voice just cut between their insults. The two women looked at him, their tantrum paused.

"It's too early in the morning for this nonsense." Hollen released the woman's hand. "Leah, what is the matter?"

"Why must she always speak first?" Briel whined.

Hollen ignored the outburst and turned his gaze upon the marginally more mature woman. "Well?"

"*Mu Salig*," Leah began in a tone gone woeful. "You know how my back pains me so. That's just one of the many burdens I must bear in my old age. It's been particularly bad these past days, and when I woke up this morning it ached so badly I could hardly get out of bed! My Loren had to all but carry me from our *bok*!"

"Thank Helig you've improved in so short a time," Hollen deadpanned. The old woman better have a compelling excuse for whatever had moved her to try slapping her rival. Regna! Must he govern the squabbles of women old enough to have pupped his father?

"Yes . . . well." Leah cleared her throat, and the pitiful inflection cleared from her voice. "I went to the springs, hoping the heat would ease my tension. And while I was soaking, this moxy stole my *gneri* blade!"

Hollen's brows shot up. That was a new level of pettiness, even for Briel. All around, disapproving murmurs swept through the cave. Hollen turned to Briel who was squirming, desperate to speak. That she actually waited was suspicious in and of itself.

"Briel?" Hollen asked.

Briel's chin jutted forward. "It's not true, *mu Salig*! I've been minding my business all morning. This banshee grabbed me by the hair while I was eating and started screeching and accusing."

"Because you're guilty! I've put my blade in the same place while I bathed for forty years! It didn't just get up and walk away! I knew the moment it was missing what must have happened. And sure enough, the hem of your dress is soaked." Leah pointed at the other woman's dampened dress.

Briel planted her withered hands on her hips. "It's wet because I carried in wood this morning, you mad biddy!"

Leah scowled. "If you weren't so jealous, you wouldn't feel the need to antagonize me, you lumpish hag!"

Briel gasped. At once, they were back to screaming over one another. Beside him, Joselyn did something he rarely saw her do. She fidgeted. Her fingers tugged at the end of her red braid.

"Quiet!" He had to yell to be heard over the women's howling. Reluctantly, they obeyed.

"I assume the two of you can't be bothered to come to terms on your own?"

They shot each other dirty looks and opened their mouths, each charging for the first word. Hollen raised a hand.

Was he really about to call an *idaglo*, a summit, over something so silly? Apparently.

"I thought not. Fine then." At least Joselyn's first experience helping him stand as judge would be over an insignificant matter. "Briel."

The accused woman inclined her head, still seething.

"Did anyone see you carry wood in this morning?"

"Yes," she hurried to say. "Reisha did."

Hollen scanned the crowd of onlookers for the much younger woman. His eyes fell upon her, arms crossed over her chest and looking terribly uncomfortable.

"Well, Reisha?" he asked.

The dark woman's eyes flitted between Hollen and Briel for a moment. Hollen pinned her with a heavy stare. The woman answered hesitantly. "I saw her carrying wood in, *mu Salig*. But"—she paused, licking her lips—"It was several hours ago."

Hollen wasn't the only one to steal a glance back at Briel's woolen dress, the hem of which seemed far wetter than it should have been after a jaunt through the snow in the dark hours of the morning. Briel's face reddened, and she opened her mouth to speak. Hollen cut in.

"*Mu hamma* and I will return with our ruling. In the meantime, I don't expect to hear the two of you squawking at one another from our *bok*. Is that understood?"

"*Va, mu Salig*." They nodded in unison.

Hollen took Joselyn by the hand and led her back to their *bok*. His purpose was far less enticing than it had been a few moments ago. He lit a torch, then bid her sit upon their bed. She folded her hands in her lap.

"What was that all about?" she asked. Her wide eyes flicked toward the doorway.

He sighed. "Leah and Briel squabble constantly. They always have. Usually they keep their disagreements to themselves and some of the other gossipier women. But when they get angry enough to start laying hands on one another, I'm often asked to stand judgment."

"They sound like children," his bride said, her expression incredulous.

"Yes, that's apt." Hollen scratched at the back of his neck. "And like their mother and father, we now have to settle their dispute."

Joselyn raised a brow. "Why us? Why *me*?"

Hollen quirked a brow. "You are *Saliga*. In fact, you may be asked to stand judgment even without me at such times."

"That hardly seems appropriate." She scowled.

Hollen cocked his head. "Why not?"

"Because I'm a woman."

He regarded her. "All the more reason you should govern women's affairs, don't you think?"

Joselyn was silent. Her brow wrinkled as though she were thinking very hard on something.

Hollen shot her a half-smile. "But even so, the matter was brought to me first, and you don't yet know the reputations of all your clansmen. It's good that we can discuss this together and come to a decision as one. It will strengthen our bond and please the people."

Joselyn blinked, but said nothing. Had she ever been in a position where her judgment was required by her people? His bride was a proud woman. This sort of thing might bring her pleasure someday, given enough practice.

"Will you help me decide this matter, *mu hamma*?"

"What is your opinion?" she asked.

Hollen snorted. "Briel took the blade."

Joselyn frowned. "Are you so certain?"

"Briel lives to antagonize Leah. Her schemes would make a child scoff. Though, stealing a *gneri* blade is especially bold. I can only imagine how Leah must have been tormenting Briel."

"Leah taunts her?"

Hollen grimaced. "Unfortunately. Briel is awkward and Leah is quick to remind her."

Joselyn sat quiet a moment. "I imagine Leah will demand her blade back."

"Yes, and Briel will deny she took it. *Glanshi*."

The two fell silent. Hollen wracked his brain for a solution. The *gneri* blades were a sacred symbol of one's union. If Briel was forced to produce the blade, Leah would be certain others showed her no mercy. Briel would be scorned for a long while to come. A clan-wide snub of an old woman didn't sit well with Hollen.

"What if you confiscated Briel's blade until Leah's is found?

Then you might motivate Briel to '*assist*' her rival without condemning her?"

Hollen turned the suggestion over in his mind. It could work. It could work well. Given enough time, Briel could return the blade discreetly, which would both solve the problem and allow her to save face. Briel would be furious at having her blade taken. She might even complain to her husband, but both Briel and Leah's husbands were weary of their wives' constant arguing. Hollen didn't anticipate any resistance on that account.

"*Mmm.*" He gave a slow nod, and a smile stretched across his face. "I believe I may have claimed a wise woman."

Joselyn returned the smile, but it didn't reach her eyes. Her posture remained fixed and tight.

"What is it?" he asked.

She looked away. Hollen sat on the bed beside her and ducked his head low. Perhaps she was nervous to involve herself in his people's affairs? She didn't yet feel at home here. But that would change. It was moments like this that were going to make the difference. Whether she knew it or not, she *did* belong in Bedmeg. She belonged at his side.

When, after another moment, Joselyn still hadn't answered, Hollen pulled them both to their feet. "Your solution is a good one. Everyone will see it."

She gave a little nod, glancing at the wall behind him. There was something going on behind those blue eyes. Was she thinking about last night? Hollen's stomach fluttered. He took a breath and he did what he'd been dying to do all morning.

He clasped her behind the neck and brought his lips down softly upon hers. With his other arm, he pulled her into himself, raising her onto her toes. To his delight, she kissed him back. Relief and pleasure swept through him. Regna, he could get drunk off her scent. He twisted his fingers into the hair at the nape of her neck, delighting in the silky thickness of her locks.

They were standing in front of their bed. With one step he could back her into it and lay her across the thick furs. In a breath he'd be upon her, covering every curve of her body with the weight of his own. He'd take his time, ease her along as he explored her, learning what made her breath catch and her back bow. The thought lit a fire in his blood, and he broke away, breathing a groan against her mouth.

Her lashes fluttered against his cheek. He opened his eyes only to be met with the uneasiness in her own.

"Shall we go?" Joselyn whispered as she pulled out of his arms.

Hollen's neck tightened. Had he done something wrong? Hurt her? He dropped his hands to his sides, taking a hasty step back as he did. "Are you all right?"

Joselyn smoothed her hair down. Her eyes drifted away from his and toward the exit. "Yes, I'm fine."

Hollen frowned. He suddenly felt like he'd made a major error. Was he pushing her too quickly into her new role here? Expecting too much? He hadn't thought so. Doubt niggled at him as he considered another possibility.

Perhaps she was still angry with him for last night. He'd been so careless. She wasn't a stranger anymore. He knew Joselyn. He should have considered how his words would make her feel. On top of everything else, he'd lied to her. Again. What was he going to have to do to fix this?

Joselyn shifted her weight from one hip to the other. Her voice went cool. "They're waiting for us."

Hollen stared at her, trying one last time to decipher her thoughts. Sighing, he resigned. "Come."

"LEAH, BRIEL." Hollen stood before the two women. A crowd of onlookers huddled about the open space. Normally a squabble between the two women wouldn't draw so much curiosity, but Joselyn's participation was cause for great interest. Everyone wanted to know how the new *Saliga* would handle her role. Hollen squared his shoulders. His bride wouldn't disappoint them.

"Since the two of you cannot come to terms on your own, you have agreed to submit yourselves to the judgment of your *Salig* and *Saliga*. Is this so?"

The older women shifted their gazes to Joselyn, who stood rigid at Hollen's side. Both nodded.

Hollen considered having Joselyn announce their verdict, but remembered her odd behavior in the *bok* and decided to speak instead. Perhaps his bride was rattled at the thought of passing judgment on his people, especially considering she didn't yet see them as *her* people.

"*Atu Saliga* and I have deliberated, and we have agreed that, until Leah's *gneri* blade has been found, Briel will relinquish her own."

Murmurs went up through the gathered crowd. They were mostly approving from what Hollen could sense. Leah crossed her arms, smiling, though it was likely she'd been hoping for a harsher judgment.

Beside her, Briel gasped. "But, *mu Salig*! She probably lost it in the springs! If it slipped into the pools, she might never find it!"

"Then I suggest you help her," Hollen said, curbing a grin at Briel's horrified expression. "In the meantime, hand over your blade."

Hollen held out a hand, curling his fingers inward. If she'd burst into tears or hung her head in defeat, he might have regretted their ruling, but as he'd expected, Briel reacted as a petulant child might when being corrected.

"This is unfair! She's a clumsy old woman, and now I must suffer for her empty headedness." Even as she protested, Briel unhooked her knife belt and stepped forward to give it up.

Just as Briel was about to drop it into Hollen's hand, Joselyn stepped forward and pushed his arm down. He turned toward his bride, a brow arched. The ground went silent and Briel stilled with her hand dangling in open air.

"This *is* unfair," Joselyn said, speaking loud and clear so all might hear.

Hollen stared at her, uncertain he'd understood.

"*Mu hamma?*" he asked.

Releasing his arm, Joselyn crossed both of hers and pinned him with an imperious look. "How can you justify taking one woman's blade when you have no proof of her guilt? Is Briel to suffer alongside Leah simply to satisfy her? Why should two women be without their blades?"

Hollen blinked, just starting to grasp what was happening. It seemed those around them were equally confounded. Whispers rose among the onlookers. Briel's eyes darted between Joselyn and Hollen. She snapped her blade back to her chest.

Hollen inclined his chin, and the muscles in his jaw clenched. What in Regna's name was she doing? Hadn't they just agreed how they would handle this? Hadn't he taken Joselyn's sound advice and followed it to the letter? Why was she changing her mind? And of all places, why was she doing so in front of the clan?

"I thought we'd come to a consensus." Hollen dropped his voice down low. He was turned to her now, with his arms crossed over his chest as he stared down at his bride.

Joselyn met his gaze. Confidence brimmed in her eyes. Once

again, she spoke loud and clear. "Perhaps you ought to have put a bit more thought into this decision."

Hollen's skin went hot. A rumble of disquiet rolled through the witnesses as they took in her rebuff. Had his bride really just rebuked him in front of the clan? On a matter they'd settled between them only moments before? He drew in a sharp breath, just managing to rein in his anger. He turned back toward the women.

"Briel, the blade," he snapped, shoving his hand back out.

Briel looked from Hollen to Joselyn, her eyes filled with uncertainty. Finally, she gave up her knife. The old woman took a couple of hurried steps back, as though she were getting out of range of an impending volley. Beside her, Leah looked equally concerned. Well, if nothing else, his bride had succeeded in cooling all tempers. Except his own.

Why would she do this? Hollen couldn't remember the last time he'd felt this way. Utterly humiliated. His molars ground together. He resisted the urge to saunter away from the speculative stares of his people and addressed the clan, "This matter is closed. Has it been witnessed?"

"Witnessed," came a male voice in the crowd.

"Witnessed," another said.

Hollen shot the two women a final, disapproving look. "Very well. I don't want to hear any more about it."

Most of the crowd dispersed at once. A few of the more meddlesome clan members lingered in hopes of catching some extra bits of drama. Hollen swallowed hard and attempted to rein in his anger. Just as he turned toward his bride, Joselyn stepped away from him and after Briel.

"Come, Briel. If this is the way your *Salig* would have it, let's search for Leah's blade in the springs together."

Briel and Leah both looked like startled animals. The rapid shift in their moods would have been comical. Their eyes flicked first to each other, and then to Hollen, who watched the exchange with a mixture of outrage and disbelief.

Briel spoke up. "I-I appreciate the offer, young *Saliga*, but—"

"Very well, then. Let's go now." Joselyn cut the older woman off, linked an arm under hers, and pulled her toward the women's springs. Leah followed hesitantly after.

Hollen was so stunned he could barely think until they were more than halfway across the common area. His gaze drifted to those milling about nearby, with their obvious attempts at *appearing* busy. A few of the women shook their heads. One or two men shot him pitying grimaces. Hollen growled and turned away.

The urge to stomp after his bride and demand she explain herself was strong. He actually took a few heavy steps in that direction, but by then it was too late. The gray and red-haired trio were disappearing into the tunnel. He narrowed his eyes. If his bride thought she could wait him out by hiding in there, she'd be in for a surprise.

He huffed and stormed out of the cave.

28

PLAYING GAMES

For two hours, Hollen sat waiting. After getting a moment of air, he'd camped himself by the fire outside the tunnel to the women's springs. He faced the entrance, hunched over a small piece of wood that he'd whittled beyond all practical purpose. She'd get no second chance to hide from him. In his mind, Hollen tossed over the bevy of things he was going to say when she emerged.

At last, he heard the din of feminine voices echoing through the blackened hole. Hollen's grip tightened on the wood, and his heart sped. He took his time glancing up, determined to appear fully in control. When he did, his eyes connected immediately with Joselyn's. Her expression was uneasy as she turned to say goodbye to Leah and Briel. They cast their half-hearted thanks and farewells over their shoulders, hurrying away from Hollen.

His mouth twitched. He rose and went to stand before her. Joselyn's expression went completely blank. He stopped a few feet away and waited.

"If you were hoping I'd be less angry over time, you're going to be sorely disappointed," he said.

His bride's shoulders squared and her dimpled chin raised proudly. Her eyes went flinty with challenge. In his periphery, Hollen caught a few curious glances from nearby onlookers. This wasn't the place.

"Come." For once, he didn't take her by the hand. She would follow. She would follow or he'd throw her over his shoulder and carry her to their *bok* for all to see. Wisely, his bride made no argument as they trekked up the path and through the darkness of their tunnel.

The moment they arrived, Joselyn set to work lighting first the fire, and then every torch in the room. Her movements were purposely languid. Arms crossed, Hollen watched her. She could stall for as long as she pleased. It would change nothing. After a long while, Joselyn fished her comb out of the trunk and settled on her knees across the fire pit. Without a word, she began pulling apart her red braid.

She was testing him. Toying with him. Hollen stayed frozen where he was, piling the weight of his gaze upon her as she worked. When her hair had been combed and replatted to shiny perfection, Joselyn sat fiddling with the ivory comb. She finally looked at him.

He could see her trying to call that stony wall up in her eyes, but it was far thinner this time. Mouth tightening, she spoke. "Well?"

Hollen refused to react to the flash of temper that shot through his body. "Explain yourself."

She blinked with one slow sweep of her thick lashes. "How do you mean?"

He narrowed his eyes. "So you still want to play games, then?"

She glared at him.

Hollen had convinced himself he wanted to avoid a battle of

wills with his bride. She was making it plain, however, that if he was going to have any answers, he would have to dominate her first. He realized suddenly that he was all too happy to rise to the occasion.

His mouth went flat. "Fine."

He strode across the room. Satisfaction pulsed within him as she waited until the last moment to flinch away from his outstretched arms. Too little, too late. She gave a little yip as he scooped her up off the floor. Hollen tightened his grip and plopped down at the edge of their bed. She squirmed in his arms.

"What are you—"

He covered her mouth with his, muffling her words. Shocked, she was still for a moment before craning her neck back, trying to break the kiss. Hollen pressed forward, thwarting her escape until she was shoving her hands against his chest. They broke apart on twin gasps.

"How dare y—"

Joselyn stuttered as he yanked her up in his arms. He turned her so her belly went flat against his chest. Hollen lowered her back down, hiking the hem of her dress just enough to drape her thighs evenly over his lap. His arms were laced steel behind her.

Joselyn eyes sparked wildly. "You can't—"

Another kiss, this one more savage than the last. He plunged the fingers of one hand into her silky tresses, holding her in place. Despite his anger, or perhaps because of it, Hollen's body reacted boldly to the feel of Joselyn molded over him. Heat ignited beneath his skin and a primal growl rumbled in his throat.

"Hollen"—she spoke breathily around his lips, her body stretching taught against his—"stop."

He loosened his hold and she pulled her face back a few inches. Already her cheeks were flushed, her lips swollen.

"What are you doing?" she demanded, her gaze frenzied.

"What do you mean?" he asked.

Her mouth moved, but no words came out. She blinked rapidly. Her hesitation was all the invitation he required. Hollen refastened his grip and brought his mouth down to her jaw to continue his exploration, trailing up to the hollow behind her ear.

"No, don't." Even as she said it, her fingers curled against his chest, bunching up the skin of his furs.

He checked an angry smile before breaking away to stare her fully in the face. "Why? This didn't bother you last night. What's changed?"

"I . . . I . . . " she sputtered.

Hollen could feel the furious pounding of her chest beneath his. He smirked. He'd succeeded in robbing her of her favorite weapon. Poise. He pursed his lips, allowing her to trip over her own feigned ignorance. "Yes?"

A flash of resentment danced across her face. Joselyn swallowed and her voice hardened. "You're angry."

"Am I?" He shrugged. "Why should *I* be angry?"

She regarded him with calculating eyes. When she didn't answer, he leaned in for another kiss. Joselyn jerked her head out of his path. This time, he allowed her to retreat. His point had been made.

"I opposed you in front of the clan."

"You did." The teasing vanished from his voice. "Why?"

"I'll do it again. Every chance I get."

His nostrils flared. "*Glanshi*, woman! What's wrong with you?"

"Everything. You should take me back now. Things are going to get a lot worse for you while I'm here."

Take her back? To the lowlands? His jaw slackened. "Are you serious? *That's* what this is about?"

She leveled him with a determined gaze.

"*Va kreesha*, woman. You're still trying to get away from me?" Hurt hardened in his stomach. "You humiliated us in front of our clan."

"They aren't *my* clan. This isn't *my* home."

Hollen tried to breathe, but his chest was too tight. He'd made a mistake. He'd been too eager to incorporate her into his life. He never should have included her in such a matter. It was simply too soon. And yet, he could hardly believe she'd be so spiteful.

"This *is* your home," he hissed. "These are your people and I am your husband. Has it been so bad for you? Are you so eager to inflict pain?"

Joselyn flinched as though he'd slapped her. She slammed an open palm against his chest, trying to break free. His muscles tensed, and he clamped his arms down hard over her hips. She wasn't going anywhere. Not until they'd had this out.

She raised her voice. "Me? And what about you?"

He leaned forward, nose-to-nose with her. "What about me? You were prepared to marry a madman. What's so bad about *me*?"

"Everything! You're so much worse!"

Now Hollen sprung back. His arms fell open and Joselyn scrambled off his lap. He stared at her, dumbstruck. She shoved a shaking hand through her hair then pointed at him.

"You have no idea what it's like for me. The weight of my house is on my shoulders every waking minute of the day. My own father may be executed soon, and the only one who can stop it is me!" She was shouting now, pacing barefoot around the *bok*.

Hollen watched her, unable to think. He followed her words, letting her guide him through the miserable muck of her mind.

"And you?" She spun on her heels to face him. "All you're good for is making me doubt myself. You're hells bent on appealing to my lesser nature, in making me forget everything that matters in favor of pleasing myself. You seduce me. Make me promises. Promises you could never live up to."

Hollen tried to think of what promises he'd made her. He'd promised to protect her, not to molest her, not to command her on trivial matters. He didn't think those were the ones she was referring to. More likely she meant the ones he'd taken even more seriously. The ones to keep her. Cherish her.

"And all the while you have the nerve to feel sorry for me. Well don't trouble yourself. Because I never asked for your pity, and I sure as skies never asked for you to rescue me from choices I'd already made. I'm not a victim, and you're not the only one who understands duty."

Hollen snapped out of his daze. "I never said I was."

"You think I'm useless. Selfish."

"No!"

"You think that when it counts, I'll be disloyal. That you can touch me and spoil me and . . .and . . ." She swallowed over her accusations. "And *love* me, and that eventually I'll abandon everything just to make myself happy."

Hollen was back to being stunned. How had she twisted their relationship into this? Why had she made him into an enemy? He'd been her captor, true. But wasn't he more than that now? Didn't she feel anything for him?

"Joselyn—"

She cut him off. "You bring out the worst in me."

"The worst in you?" Hollen shot to his feet. "The only regrettable thing about you, *mu hamma*, is that your will is stronger than your wits."

After all this time, she was still thinking of her wretched father. Damn that evil man.

Joselyn tilted her head up to look at him, surprise etched on her beautiful face. "What does that mean?"

"It means, you're so damned desperate for his love, you'd sooner throw yourself on a pyre than accept that your father will never have any to give. You'd throw all of this"—he gestured at the *bok*—"away, for no reason."

She made a scoffing sound that was almost a laugh. "You're not hearing a word I'm saying. You don't understand."

He took a step toward her, reaching for her arm. He barely stopped himself. He was too angry. If he touched her now he might accidentally hurt her. His fist clenched on empty air. Instead, he let raw anger bleed into his voice.

"No. *You* don't understand. You think you can throw a tantrum in front of our people and manipulate me into giving you up? After years of waiting for you? Dreaming about you? You think I'll just fly you back to the lowlands and scrub my hands? You understand *nothing* about me."

Now it was Joselyn's turn to be stunned.

"But you're going to. I *always* keep my promises, woman." His jaw was so tight he thought his teeth might crack. He pointed at her. "And I'll swear it again as I've sworn it before, nothing you do will ever make me return you to the lowlands. You're here for as long as I'm allowed to keep you. And none of your petty schemes will change that."

Joselyn's face paled. "I'll make your life miserable."

He laughed. He'd been in misery from the moment he'd seen her. She was like a perfect dream that he kept waking from the moment he got close enough to touch. "I don't care."

"I'll find a way to hurt you. I'll . . . I'll hurt the clan."

Hollen choked on a breath. Hurt the clan? Joselyn? She couldn't mean it. What could she even think to do to them? He was about to ask when he saw the widened alarm in her flickering gaze. Her hand was braced against her stomach and she sort of swayed on her feet. She was barely present, her mind racing.

She'd spoken without intent. She was bluffing. And now, desperation was making her panic. Finally, after weeks of being here, she was truly comprehending her situation. This wasn't some courtly game. This was a reality with consequences as stark as life and death. Hollen *wasn't* playing with her.

"Enough of this, Joselyn. Accept your lot."

Accept me.

She turned away. Her eyes still cast aimlessly about the room. "You have to take me back. You have to."

"It's not going to happen."

She didn't seem to be listening. "I ha—I have to get out of here."

Lunging forward, he gripped her by the arms, forcing her to look up at him. Hollen gave her a little shake. "Joselyn! Regna, you stubborn woman! What will it take to make you understand?"

She blinked. Tears spilled over her freckled cheeks. A whip of anger contorted her features, and clarity re-entered her gaze. She twisted in his grip. "Let me go!" she snarled.

The crack in her voice, like a trapped animal, sliced at him. He released her. She stumbled out of his grip and darted away, ducking into the darkness of the tunnel.

Hollen stared after her. The hum of the mountain and crackle of the fire were the only sounds left once her footsteps faded. Fury and regret boiled in his gut as he paced around the *bok*. She was *still* trying to leave him. His bride hated him and all he'd been able to do was rail at her. He scrubbed a palm over his face.

Should he chase her down? Demand that she stop crying?

Stop hurting? What would he say? What had caused her outburst in the first place? And how in the name of the gods had this situation been turned around on him?

"*Va kreesha.*"

Were all women mad, or only his?

29

CONFESSOR

Joselyn turned off into the nearest alcove of the private springs. There were no other torches around. Satisfied she was alone, she notched hers. She crept into the tiny sanctuary and took a seat on the first dry rock she spotted. Close by, a steady stream of water trickled into the pool, echoing off the smooth stone walls. The warm air was thick with moisture. It made little hairs cling to Joselyn's neck. She drew her knees up and gave in to her tears. They torrented down her face. After a while, Joselyn's head began to ache.

He's never going to take me back.

Joselyn thought she'd come to terms with that. Now she knew she hadn't. Not really. She'd always expected to get free, had known that Bedmeg would never be her ultimate fate. Her abduction had been a mere detour on her way to her true destiny. An obstacle to overcome. How wrong she'd been.

That's it. It's over.

A sense of finality crushed her from the inside. Her father would die. Her house would fall. Apart from Tansy, there would be nothing left to go back to. She'd failed. Joselyn Fury had been defeated. She reached for her pendant, but her fingers only brushed her *tanshi* mark. More tears fell. The leaking stream of water absorbed her pathetic whimpers.

What was she going to do now?

"Well, you've picked a fine spot for a cry out."

Joselyn jumped. She threw a glance toward the natural archway to see Rosemary staring in at her, torch in hand. Joselyn jerked her face in the other direction, swatting at her tears.

"Too late for that, I've seen you! Now the 'ole world will know that you're human like the rest of us."

Joselyn stiffened and turned back to glare at the brunette woman. Rosemary met her ire and chuckled. She kicked off her boots, lifted her skirts, and tiptoed through a puddle over to where Joselyn sat.

"Put your feet in the water." She sat down next to her and plunged her own legs into the steaming pool. "I didn't come all the way down 'ere just to sweat my bloody tits off."

For a moment, Joselyn forgot her misery to stare blankly at her companion. Rosemary's crassness never ceased to startle her, but she found that it no longer offended; rather, it amused her. The ladies of court would throw themselves over a hearth before allowing such words to pass their lips. Not Rosemary.

She considered asking her to leave, but realized suddenly that she no longer wanted to be alone, mired in this spirit-sucking darkness. She might have preferred Lavinia, or really *anyone* to Rosemary. But, Rosemary was here, so Rosemary it was. Joselyn dipped her feet into the water.

"Who knew you had such talent for theatrics? Do all ladies? They teach you that in your frilly schools? Alongside dancin' and curtsyin' and walkin' in ridiculous dresses?"

"What are you talking about?" Joselyn asked, trying to ignore the peasant woman's mocking tone.

"That show you put on during the *idaglo*!" Rosemary's eyes

twinkled with amusement. "If you can call it that. Leah and Briel is always fussin' about somethin' stupid."

Joselyn's skin went hot and itchy. She hadn't planned to be here for the fallout of her actions. It had been one of the perks of her plan. After embarrassing Hollen and herself so thoroughly, leaving Bedmeg wouldn't feel like such a hardship.

"I—" Joselyn stalled. What could she say? Rosemary wouldn't understand. She sighed. "I don't know what I was thinking."

Rosemary shot her a doubtful look. "Somethin' tells me a woman like you knows exactly why she does everythin', even before she does it. You're the kind of girl my mother tried to raise."

Gripping the edge of the pool with both hands, Joselyn stared into the black water as its heat soaked into her flesh. "I thought he would take me home."

She'd expected him to raise his voice to her, perhaps even a hand. It's what men in her country would have done. He was supposed to call Jagomri down and toss her back to the plains like a cursed talisman.

Rosemary scoffed. "No such luck, eh?"

Not in the least. And now, she'd hurt her savage. The one man in this world who treated her like she was worth a damn. Worth fighting for. The look of betrayal in his eyes had infuriated her. He'd pushed her to this, made her a prisoner, taken all her options. And still, she was sorry. If she could do it over again, she'd take it back in a heartbeat.

"I don't want to go home," she murmured.

But then, this had never been about what *she* wanted. Joselyn risked a sideways glance at Rosemary. The other woman looked completely unsurprised.

"Then why are you acting like the princess I'm always sayin' you are?"

"Because I *should* go. I have responsibilities."

Rosemary put a hand on her hip. "Big, important lady."

"And because . . .he'll regret me." Fresh tears welled, but Joselyn held them in. "Sooner or later."

Rosemary studied her, as if she weren't sure what to make of the statement. A few moments passed before the other woman spoke. "Doubt it. The *Salig* don't regret anythin' ever. He's like you, he is. Thinks everythin' through *too* much."

She didn't know why, but hearing Rosemary say that stole some of her despair away. Joselyn turned to look at her, noticing for the first time how young the woman was. She couldn't be but a year or two older than Joselyn, and yet, her hardness had made her seem older. Some of that hardness was gone now, as though she'd left it behind in the common area.

"I suppose everyone despises me now?" Joselyn swallowed.

Rosemary rolled her eyes. "You know, the 'ole world don't spin around you. People have other things to worry about."

The words were flippant, but her voice held no malice. Joselyn wanted to believe her. Was it possible the others hadn't condemned her? Was everyone here as forgiving as Hollen? She narrowed her eyes. "Why are you here, Rosemary?"

The brunette woman stared at her feet as she sloshed them in the water. "Cause you're a fancy thing. And fancy things need tendin.' "

Was she being kind? Specious? Joselyn's lower lip trembled. "Too fancy for you, right? Wouldn't *you* like to see me gone?"

Rosemary's legs went still as she regarded Joselyn, then shrugged. "I never met a woman who don't like fancy things."

IT WAS LATE when Joselyn went back to the *bok*. Rosemary had stayed a while in the springs, sometimes talking, sometimes sitting quietly. Joselyn had taken a surprising amount of comfort from her. Apparently, there was more to the peasant woman than drinking and crude humor.

Joselyn had remained far past dinner, unable to face the rest of the clan just yet, despite Rosemary's encouragement. When she finally crept back through the common area, it had been nearly empty. She trudged her way to the *bok*.

Hollen sat in front of the fire, shirtless, an elbow slung over one knee. He looked up when she entered. She couldn't immediately gauge his mood, and it unnerved her. She clasped her hands together and drew in a breath.

Just say it, Joselyn.

"I'm sorry."

Across the fire, Hollen blinked. He looked surprised, and for some reason that made her feel better. She'd never made an apology before. Not a real one. She hoped she'd do it well.

"I purposefully made you look foolish in front of your people, but not so foolish as I made myself. I wish I had not."

The fire popped, throwing sparks into the air. Hollen regarded her another moment before climbing to his feet. He crossed the *bok* to her.

"Where were you today?"

"I went to the springs. I needed"—she searched for the word—"time."

Joselyn looked up at him, forcing herself to meet his eyes. They were soft, but weary.

"Are you well now?" he asked.

She nodded. "Are you?"

He sighed, then nodded back.

What should she do now? Joselyn looked at her feet. They itched to turn around and walk right back out. But where could she go? At this point, she'd sleep anywhere else to avoid imposing herself on him. Her belly chose that moment to rumble its demand for food.

Mortified, she snapped her gaze back to Hollen, who regarded her with a twinge of amusement.

"Have you not eaten?"

Joselyn preferred not to admit she'd hidden all day from the entire clan, not just from him. Before she could come up with an excuse, her stomach growled again. Her face went hot.

"Here." He walked back toward the fire where he had a plate of barely touched food on the ground.

Joselyn followed. She was suddenly grateful for an inroad back to their *bok*.

Our bok?

Was she claiming it now? Joselyn looked around. Was that *their* bed, then, too?

"You must be tired. It's late for you."

Joselyn turned. He'd been watching her stare at the bed. She plopped to the ground and began picking at the food, careful not to appear famished. He sat, too.

"Tomorrow you'll begin your knife lessons again."

"Are you that eager for vengeance?" Her voice was light, but her expression betrayed her true feelings. The day's events had completely humbled her. Her failed plan, Hollen's reaction, Rosemary's compassion, and now *this*. She'd been forgiven, though surely she didn't deserve it.

Hollen's face didn't light at her jibe. "I'm not angry, *mu hamma*. Not anymore."

Joselyn had to swallow very hard to get the food into her knotted-up stomach.

"I just—" He paused, then leaned forward to prop his arms upon his bent knees. "I just don't understand you."

"How do you mean?"

He looked as though he were thinking very carefully on his next words. "Your father..."

Joselyn's hand froze over the plate of food, then retreated into her lap. Her appetite was officially gone.

"... can you not see he doesn't deserve your loyalty?"

Staring into the flames, Joselyn thought on that.

"I don't understand you, either."

Hollen's head perked up. "Me?"

She nodded. "You're a man of honor. You take your role as a leader seriously. You don't tout your power over them nor demand they serve you. You serve *them*."

He watched her, and his shoulders straightened a bit as she spoke.

"You understand duty. It's important to you?"

Hollen nodded.

Joselyn ran a tired hand down her braid, and her voice grew quiet. "And yet you say you want *me*? A woman who would have to abandon her people to be with you?"

A look of surprise crossed his features. "Are you saying it's your people who draw your heart back home?"

Joselyn tried not to scoff. The only part of her heart that remained at home was the piece that belonged to Tansy. The rest was sitting right in front of her. The thought should have panicked her, sent her sprinting back to the springs. But she was simply too exhausted to fuss. And at any rate, she had known it for a while.

"Duty is important to me, too. I have a duty to my people." She grimaced. "And to my father as well. Wouldn't you have done anything for your father? Your mother?"

She could tell Hollen was trying not to scowl. Instead, his contempt came out in his voice. "*My* parents were good to me. They deserved my respect and love."

"If you only ever gave people what they deserved, you'd have cast me out of Bedmeg tonight."

Hollen looked startled by that. He shook his head. "*Mu hamma*, you are far too hard on yourself."

"It's a trait we share, I think." She thought of how distraught he'd been when she was attacked, of how he'd managed to pile all the blame on himself. She wished now that she'd tried harder to relieve him of that guilt.

"And anyway, you'd be harder on me, too, if you really understood how my mind worked."

Warm amber flickered over him as he peered at her. "What do you mean?"

"I'm not like you, Hollen. I don't want to save my people because I have some great love for them. I don't know them. I'd never even met a Morhageese peasant before coming to Bedmeg. Helping them is an ideological imperative. One I must adhere to."

He was frowning now. "Why, then?"

Joselyn inwardly cringed. It was almost laughable. For all her attempts to bribe his men, sabotage his leadership, and outright run off, the most effective way to be sent home might well be the simplest: telling him the truth. This was it. It was time to show him who she really was.

"Because I hate my father."

Hollen cocked his head, then shook it once. "But . . . all you talk about is wanting to save him."

"A necessary evil," she said, simply.

Hollen hesitated, then shook his head. "I don't understand."

"My father is an effective lord. Those are in direly short supply in my country. Most of the land is starving for the greed and mismanagement of the privileged few that enjoy titled status. A recent plague hasn't done us any favors, either.

"In House Fury's lands, Tirvine, the serfs remain well fed.

They're treated fairly, if somewhat strictly. And our borders haven't suffered raids in decades. If my father dies, things will change. My extended family will lose their lands and titles. Governorship will go to skies know where, and none of the prospects are good."

"So you want to save him for your people's sake?"

Joselyn nodded.

"Why do you hate him?"

An old pain stirred in her chest. She'd never spoken of this to anyone. "I can't really explain that without talking about my mother."

Hollen watched as she ran a hand down her braid only to pick at the frayed ends.

"Marcus Fury had many affairs before the queen. To my knowledge, they started almost immediately after he married. Rosalie Fury was a jealous woman with few options for recourse."

Joselyn's voice was a monotone drone. She recited her family's history as though she were reading from an obscure tome. "So, she took revenge on her husband in the vilest manner she could think up." Joselyn swallowed and forced herself to meet Hollen's eyes. "She hired an apothecary to clear her womb of heirs. Every time Marcus' seed took root, she had it evacuated."

Hollen had gone still. Was he even breathing? After a moment, he seemed to peel his tongue from the roof of his mouth. "And...what about you?"

"You mean, why did I survive?"

Some of the color drained from his face. Joselyn scowled, disgusted to be talking about this. But it was too late to stop now. She pressed on.

"I asked my mother the same question. I saw her once, heard her talking to the apothecarist. I'd thought my birth had made her barren. That's what she told everyone. When I confronted her about it and asked why she hadn't done the same to me, she scoffed and said she would have, if she'd had the presence of mind." She glanced away from him. "My mother was in love with her cups. Apparently, she'd been too drunk to call for the apothecarist in time."

After a moment, "How old were you?"

"When I learned of this? Eleven."

Hollen glanced toward the fire, as though looking at her burned his eyes. She couldn't fault him.

Joselyn scooted the food around on the plate. "I didn't understand why she did it, couldn't appreciate what having a son meant to my father. That realization came later. And then my mother's words to me that night finally made sense."

Hollen was silent, though she felt his gaze return to her.

"She said, 'It was a trivial oversight, sweet girl. You'll never be enough for Marcus anyway."

Sick misery curled around her heart at the recollection. Hollen drew in a sharp breath, as though the memory had struck him. Joselyn plunged on, determined to get this over with.

"I spent the next seven years determined to prove her wrong. I did everything I could imagine to endear myself to my father. At first, I did it for love. But eventually I grew up and, as you said, I realized that love wasn't something my father was capable of giving. After that I worked to make myself useful. To prove I could be as loyal and self-sacrificing as any son he might have had."

She ground her molars together. It had never meant a damn thing to Lord Fury.

"When I learned I was to be married to the Viridian lord, a part of me was happy. For the first time in my life, I had the chance to serve my house in the sort of way that's unique to a woman. A way my father's heir could never have done. Most ladies would have refused. I probably could have as well."

"But you didn't," Hollen murmured. She still wasn't looking at him.

"No. And even that wasn't good enough for my father. He didn't care. In his mind I was merely obeying orders, ceding to his wisdom."

"Then why...were you still so determined?"

She shrugged. "Because it didn't matter if he acknowledged what I did. I knew the truth. I was willing to sacrifice for my house. To do what he couldn't. What my mother wouldn't."

At last, she met his gaze. "And that gave me every right in the world to hate them both."

The fire crackled, and Hollen swallowed. His lips parted as though to speak, but his words must have caught in his throat. He looked stricken. Probably still reeling from the news that he'd worked so hard for so little. Joselyn dipped her chin.

"So, that's it, savage. All my wild deeds, boiled down to hateful spite." She shot him a wretched smile and gestured at herself. "Thirty-six generations of highborn blood. And the only noble one in this *bok* is you."

"Joselyn, I'm sorry," he sounded like he had that night in the springs. Horrified.

"Don't be." She flipped her hair over her shoulder. "Feel sorry for yourself, if anyone. Now you know what sort of woman you've claimed. Now you know what a favor I was doing you in trying to leave."

Hollen leaned forward, frowning. "What do you think's changed after telling me this? Did you think to make me regret you?"

She blinked. "Don't you?"

He gave an incredulous huff. "No."

She stopped breathing. "But you love *your* parents."

His frown deepened. "My parents were nothing like yours."

Clearly, she'd shocked him. She hadn't given him enough time to think this through. She spoke a bit slower, even gesturing with her hands as if to guide him through her logic. "Your people love you. I don't even know mine. I don't do what I do because I care about them. I do it because I should."

He raised a brow. "What's wrong with that?"

"Hollen, the only good thing about me is what I'm willing to do for my house. And now you've made it clear that I'll never be able to help my people. You've taken my purpose away. What's left? Just bitterness. Resentment."

His lips thinned as he listened to her. Joselyn's throat began to tighten. She cursed every god she could think of as yet another round of tears welled in her eyes. She'd cried more in the last fortnight than she had in all her grown life.

She swiped at a falling tear and her voice cracked. "I'm worthless."

Hollen rose up on his knees and shuffled over to her. She sat there sniffling, trying to regain control of herself. In one swift movement, he scooped her into his arms and settled her over his crossed legs. Joselyn didn't even try to stop him. She was just too tired.

"You're wrong, *mu hamma*. Last night, when I said I didn't pity you, I lied. It didn't make sense to me, what you've been doing. I didn't understand why. But now I do." He batted her hands away to wipe her tears himself. His rough fingers seemed to absorb them. "Joselyn, pity is the furthest thing from my mind." He took her by the chin and forced her to meet his eyes. "I'm in awe of you."

That made her cry harder. She barely kept from whimpering like a babe even as more tears spilled down her temples and into her hair. Hollen kept up with them, petting each one dry as it fell. He didn't really seem to notice them, though. He was staring into her eyes like the only thing that mattered was making his thoughts known to her. He went on.

"You never had the opportunity to know your people. You don't love them. They can't love you. And *still*, you've put your life on the line to get back to them, because in your mind, it's the right thing to do. No one was going to thank you for it. No one would ever have known why it was so important. But that didn't stop you. Don't you see how incredible that is?"

Joselyn shook her head. Was this really happening? Had she truly just exposed the darkest part of herself to this man, only to have him wax on about how worthy he thought her? He leaned down and brushed a kiss on her forehead. His lips were warm on her skin, his beard soft. Joselyn closed her eyes as a ripple of comfort spread through her.

"I don't care that you hate your father, Joselyn. If it helps, I hate him too. And I don't care that your motives for helping your people revolve around spiting him. Most people wouldn't do what you did. If their parents treated them as yours treated you, they'd find other ways to reconcile it. They'd shirk their duties, destroy their family's reputation, *glanshi*, they might even destroy themselves. And here you are confessing to me like some blasphemer? All because, instead of rolling around in the muck with your parents, you chose to rise above them?"

Joselyn forced her gaze to his. She had to see if he was being serious. He was looking at her with a mixture of admiration and compassion. Had anyone ever looked at her quite like that? He raked his fingers through her hair.

"Did you have no one to guide you, growing up?"

Joselyn thought of Tansy. Though the old woman had been paid, no amount of money could have purchased her love. That had been a free gift. "My nurse. Tansy."

Hollen nodded once. "I'm grateful. No child should have been raised the way you were. And I'm certain no other child could have grown into the kind of person you've become. You're the strongest woman I've ever met."

For the first time, Joselyn allowed herself to entertain his words. Maybe he really meant them. Of course, that didn't make them true.

"I don't feel strong when I'm with you," she said. "You make me want to be selfish and wanton. You make me want to give in to you and forget everything else."

Suddenly, Hollen's demeanor seemed to shift. Though his hold on her remained gentle, every muscle in his body tightened. The soothing cadence dropped from his voice, an edge of challenge replacing it. Like he was going to battle. "You want to give in to me?"

"If I did, would you still think me strong? Willingness to serve, loyalty, is true strength. As a leader of men, surely you can understand that."

He wrapped a hand around her upper arm and gave her a light squeeze. "Loyalty is only a strength when it's placed in a good man."

It was true; Joselyn knew it. Yet somehow she'd spent her life convinced otherwise. Or rather, convinced she was in no position to judge her father's worthiness. It was a mindset integral to a society where leaders were born, not chosen, as Hollen had been. For a moment, Joselyn allowed herself to explore the idea of a world where she could pick and choose her own loyalties. What would that be like?

"*You* are a good man," she murmured.

Hollen's lips parted on a ragged breath. He was so beautiful. Everything about him appealed to her, as though he'd been designed by some god who understood her inmost desires. Even his scent made her blood warm. Being this close to him was intoxicating. She reached up to run a palm over his beard. Her heart sped up when his eyes went heavy lidded with pleasure.

"You're attentive, and loyal, and selfless." She smiled sadly. "You're too good for me."

His eyes popped back open. "No, *mu hamma*. I know who you are. I think I might know it better than you know yourself."

She continued stroking at him and suppressed a shiver when he covered her hand with his own. His voice was throaty again. "We have time. I'm going to convince you."

They *did* have time. Joselyn could finally acknowledge that fact. She'd exhausted all her options. She was out of ideas. Leaving on her own was too dangerous and, Hollen had proven his own will was as great as hers. It was out of her hands.

In that moment, an invisible weight lifted from her shoulders. She breathed deep in Hollen's arms. Her heart raced with newfound freedom as the claws of guilt eased their grip.

A year would be too late to save her father's life. If not for her people's good, what reason did she have to leave?

She could think of a thousand reasons to stay.

What would it be like to stay in Bedmeg forever? She'd wondered before, of course, but it had never seemed real. She'd never allowed her mind to revel in all the possibilities. The pain would have been too great. But now?

She thought of her father's favorite rebuke: *"this world owes you nothing."*

She looked into Hollen's dark eyes, and saw her own hope reflected back at her.

The world may not. But maybe, *just maybe*, Joselyn owed something to herself.

30

GEGATUDOK

"Hollen! Hollen!"

Joselyn's ears perked up at male voices. It was rare to hear people using her savage's name rather than his title. She and Hollen both paused from their sparring to look into the ravine at Erik and Magnus, who were rushing down toward the armory, their faces alight with excitement.

Hollen called out to them in his language with concern carved into his features. His tone turned up in question at the end. Magnus plowed past Erik; his massive strides outpaced his older brother and propelled him toward she and Hollen. Thankfully, it was trade tongue that poured from his lips.

"He's done it! The little runt's finally done it!" Magnus' sandy hair whipped wildly as he spun around to race back up the ravine.

Joselyn blinked. He hadn't even paused. Erik, too, was already making his way back toward the caves. Joselyn jumped when Hollen slapped the dust off his palms and laughed.

"Looks like lessons are over for today, *mu hamma*."

That was a stroke of good fortune. Hollen had resumed her instruction a fortnight ago and, though he did so gradually, he wasn't shy about increasing the length and intensity with each passing day. Of course, he'd been making up for his ruthlessness with no small number of kisses and caresses in the evenings. Those little interludes had been growing more and more passionate with each passing day.

Before Joselyn could ask what was going on, Hollen rushed shirtless into the snow. He slowed just enough to throw his hand back to her in invitation. She darted out from the cover of the cave and slipped her hand in his, allowing him to half pull her up the ravine. She hiked up her skirts, trying not to trip. Up ahead, Joselyn could see people pouring out of the common area. The buzz of their voices echoed off the canyon walls.

"What's happened?" she asked, though she thought she already knew.

Hollen answered without slowing, "Sigvard. He's mastered a *gegatu*!"

Joselyn grinned as they trekked up to the same shelf where she'd made the sacrifice on the night of her feast. She and Hollen had to push their way through and around the frenzied crowd to join Erik, Ivan, and Magnus a good way back from the ledge.

Joselyn was just about to ask what they were doing when a collective cheer rose up from the crowd below. Their faces were turned up to the gray sky. A black *gegatu* burst through the cloud bank and circled a rapid descent.

On either side of her, Hollen and his brothers punched their fists into the air and whooped their praise of their youngest brother. Joselyn couldn't see Sigvard, but she assumed he was on the beast's back. The collective cheers were all in Dokiri, even those spoken by the women.

Sigvard's new mount spiraled toward the ground, and Joselyn realized it meant to land before them, upon the platform. Energy hummed through the crowd. To the side, Magnus' deep voice began booming a Dokiri song that was instantly taken up by the people. Their volume intensified as the winged beast drew closer. If only she knew more of Hollen's language, she could join in. The urge surprised her.

At last, a flash of auburn hair showed over the shoulder of the scaly beast. Sigvard was sitting proudly up even before his steed's clawed feet touched the ground. His excited eyes fixed on the clan below him. Joselyn recognized his wyvern by the white streak of spikes running down her neck and back. He had done it after all. A twinge of disappointment prickled. She'd hoped to witness the mastering herself. Then again, she thought of nearly falling to her death the last time and decided she was better off this way.

Amidst the fervor, Joselyn felt warm hands upon her upper arms. She turned her head back to see Hollen pulling her into his chest. Joselyn leaned into his bare skin, inhaling his salty pine scent. Was he never cold? It seemed not, a fact that suited her just fine these days.

"The *Gegatudok* is concluded with a rite." Hollen said into her ear. "Tell me now if you don't wish to participate."

Participate? Anxiety made her heart clench.

Joselyn tried to steal a look into his eyes, but Hollen's attention was torn away. Sigvard's mount landed gingerly in the snow and shrieked at the gathered crowd. Joselyn shrunk at the horrifying sound, but no one else seemed bothered. They hollered further approval as Sigvard sat fully forward to pound his chest in salutation to the gathered onlookers. He was triumphant, gloriously pleased.

Despite herself, Joselyn clapped for him. He'd long been working himself up to this monumental task, and she couldn't contain the overwhelming sense of joy that filled her at his success. The corners of her mouth pulled into a wide grin as Sigvard jumped down from his mount's back and strode toward his family. Behind him, his *gegatu* hissed at the crowd, but remained where she was, her eye upon her new master.

The noise died down as Sigvard addressed his brothers in Dokiri, his gaze particularly upon Hollen, who stepped out from behind Joselyn to face the younger man head on. Some of Joselyn's enthusiasm dampened at being left out of the conversation. People here were usually very careful to use trade tongue around her, so she had the distinct impression that whatever was being said was meant to be said in the father tongue.

At the end of Sigvard's speech, his gaze slid to Joselyn. His usual impishness was gone. His eyes danced with manly pride, and Joselyn had to smile. Hollen answered Sigvard with a string of Dokiri words, followed by the other three brothers' confirmation.

"*Va!*" They said in unison the Dokiri word for 'yes.'

The crowd resumed their cheers as the men echoed '*va,*' and the women trilled and ululated alongside them. Hollen's hand brushed Joselyn's lower back. He stepped toward Sigvard. The auburn-haired boy, no, man, eagerly shed his furs and wool shirt. His pale, freckled skin seemed to reflect the winter light. His *idadi* was nearly nonexistent. That was about to change.

Hollen stepped around Sigvard and put his back to the crowd so they could watch as he performed the rite. Anticipation lit Sigvard's face as he turned to face the clan. Did no one here fear having their skin carved? Sigvard stood stone still with his hands at his sides as Hollen brought the knife up to the right side of his chest. Beside her, Erik sidled up to Joselyn and began murmuring a translation of Hollen's words as he worked the blade into their brother's skin.

"Son of my mother."

Sigvard's head inclined an inch as Hollen spoke.

"Today Regna sees you, just as I see you standing before me."

"*Elsa Regna!*" the men cried.

"The sons of the sky acknowledge your strength."

The men in the crowd saluted, pounding their fists upon their chests.

"The sky itself bears witness to your deeds, and may your flesh recount the tale for all your days."

The crowd cheered. Hollen was smiling. For all the grief Sigvard gave him, it was clear he was proud of his brother. Hollen lowered the knife, cupped his hand to Sigvard's chest, and waited. After a moment, he turned to the crowd and flicked Sigvard's blood over the people's heads. They roared their approval. Joselyn swallowed hard as her savage drew a damp thumb from the center of his hairline, down his forehead and along the ridge of his nose. A crimson streak trailed behind.

Once he turned to face his family again, her savage's eyes glided past Sigvard's freckled shoulder and rested upon her. There was a question there.

"The next part of the rite falls to the clan's *Saliga*." Erik supplied, speaking discreetly from the corner of his mouth. "If she should accept."

The crowd's volume diminished as all eyes fell upon her. Joselyn's stomach tightened. She'd only just recently gained the confidence to stand straight again after the scene she'd caused before. Was this something she was willing to be a part of? She had no idea what to do. Hollen's ever-patient eyes rested on her. Slowly, her feet carried her to the edge of the platform.

She caught the smiles upon the faces of those below. This, she knew, was an honor, not a duty to be borne. Coming up beside Sigvard, she caught the wash of bright blood streaming down his body from where her savage had worked him over. She sucked a breath in through her nose. She'd never appreciate the Dokiri's fascination with blood rites.

Hollen pressed the hilt of his knife into her hand. He was

glowing. Joselyn's heart fluttered. Her anxiety evaporated. She'd do this for no other reason than to please him.

She turned to Sigvard and brought the knife tip up to the bleeding mark. Looking at him, she could guess what was expected. Over the many nights spent huddled in Hollen's arms, Joselyn had become intimately familiar with the designs covering his upper body. The bloodied mark on Sigvard looked just like the one adjacent to Hollen's *tanshi* mark, save for a few missing lines. Those must be the ones for her. Hollen's hands warmed her waist as he leaned down to whisper into her ear.

"Repeat after me, *mu hamma*."

With her eyes on Sigvard, she nodded.

"*Selska ri mu hatu*."

Joselyn recognized the word 'husband' in the line she was to speak. She wasn't certain of the context, and there was no time to ask. She repeated the words so all could hear, trying to mimic the guttural accent. Sigvard's coppery gaze dropped down to hers, and Joselyn saw the anticipation there. Excitement radiated off him, encouraging her. She forced a smile as she put the first of four lines on his skin. He didn't even tense.

Hollen whispered the next line into her ear, and when she repeated it, the women in the crowd cheered, "*Elsa Helig!*"

Sigvard looked out at the assembled clan as Joselyn drew the next mark on him. Hollen gave her another line, and it was followed by the frenzied trilling of all the clanswomen. Joselyn stole a glance outward to see them practically dancing their enthusiasm.

Make it good, Joselyn.

After Hollen whispered the final line, Joselyn completed the mark and recited the words. Sigvard's flesh glowed pink, but he didn't seem to care. He was looking with wonder at his wyvern, as though he'd like to climb onto her back and experience the thrill of flying again.

"You don't have to paint yourself, Joselyn. You've done enough."

Joselyn tensed, thinking of how Hollen had drawn Sigvard's blood over his face. Was that expected of *her*? Joselyn's mouth firmed into a line. She had come this far. She pressed a cupped palm into Sigvard's chest and waited for the blood to pool. Sigvard looked down at her with a brow arched in a dare. Taking a breath, she smirked back.

When she had enough, Joselyn turned toward the throng of people. A hush fell over them as she met their hopeful gazes. She steeled herself, then flicked the blood over the people who raised their open hands joyfully to her. Before she could overthink it, she brought a thumb up to her face.

Joselyn felt a little squeeze at her elbow. Hollen was guiding her hand downward several inches. Instead of starting at her hairline, she pressed her thumb into her lower lip, and drew it wetly down over her chin, along her neck, and stopped just below the hollow of her throat. The clan erupted.

Whatever you do, don't lick your lips.

Behind her, Hollen's brothers took up the song again. The people joined in, though many simply shouted blessings. Hollen drew her away from the ledge, and Sigvard smiled at them both as he passed, with thanks bright in his eyes. Joselyn's chest swelled in the relief and thrill of having done something right for these people with whom she was falling in love.

Sigvard approached his mount. He gripped her beneath the jaw and drew her nose into his bloodied chest. The creature sniffed at him. Her black pupils widened as he massaged her. That went on a moment before Sigvard released her and bounded down the length of her body to throw himself onto her back. Joselyn sent a quick prayer to her gods that he wouldn't fall since he had no saddle. The young man whooped in triumph. He and his mount were gone in a heartbeat, leaving a whirl of powdery snow in their wake.

Joselyn joined in with the cries of the clan. She extended her bloodied palm into the air. It felt natural. Right. And with everyone around her doing the same, it was suddenly like she was doing exactly what she was meant for. Exactly where she was meant to do it. The hairs on the back of her neck rose.

Hollen stood a few feet away. Unlike his brothers, who were still focused on Sigvard, the *Salig* of Bedmeg watched Joselyn. There was a depth of emotion in his eyes. Gratitude and affection simmered there, along with something else. Joselyn's heart raced.

Desire.

He wasn't the only one burning with it. She turned toward him and inclined her chin. He lowered his, the thoughts on his mind clear as the sun. Her blood heated.

She wasn't going home in time to save her father. Joselyn had accepted that. And since then, she'd lived every moment in Bedmeg with an ever-growing peace and contentment. Her role as *Saliga* hadn't felt natural at first, but she was settling into it. And Hollen? She hadn't imagined a man could be so pleased with her for so very little. Despite all odds, Joselyn had never been so happy. She pressed her lips together.

Perhaps it was time to be Hollen's *Saliga* in *all* ways.

31

THE SHOULDERS OF THE MOUNTAIN

"You were magnificent, *mu Saliga*! Magnificent!"

Joselyn nodded her head, acknowledging the women who blew past her out of the springs. Everyone was heading back to the common area, eager to begin the feast that was to be held in honor of Sigvard's newfound manhood. As she looked forward to it herself, Joselyn was quick to exit the steaming water. She didn't want to be left behind.

"You've made quite an...impression upon the clan," came a familiar tinkling voice.

Joselyn turned to see Lavinia coming up alongside her. Damp as it was, the woman's curly hair was already bouncing back up. Her fawn eyes were soft and approving. Joselyn swallowed, a little self-conscious.

"I had no idea it would be received as such a grand gesture." She looked about the cave, catching the appreciative smiles of several onlookers as they marched toward the exit.

"It was no s-small thing. It has been many years since Bedmeg has had a *Saliga* to properly complete the rites. *Atu hatu* has had to fill...both roles since the day he took l-leadership."

"What did I say? During the rite?" Joselyn leaned in toward her friend.

Lavinia pressed her head into Joselyn's. "B-blood of my *hatu*, today Helig sees you, just as I see you standing before me. The daughters of the earth acknowledge your . . .worthiness. The earth itself bears witness to your deeds, and m-may your flesh recount the tale for all your d-days."

Joselyn realized then why her actions had been so strongly received by not only Hollen, but by all his people. For every mention of the sky god Regna, there was a feminine acknowledgement to his earth bride, Helig. From what Joselyn could tell, neither was held in greater esteem than the other, though the role of each was distinct. For Hollen to stand in for both sides of the rite diminished the occasion for everyone.

They walked into the common area together, and already the dinner fires filled the cave with their heady scent. Joselyn's stomach rumbled. Hollen's sparring had worked her into a ravenous appetite. She was about to take a turn toward the smoking mutton when Lavinia took her by the hand.

"C-come with me, *mu Saliga*. I have something to g-give you."

WHEN HOLLEN SAW HER, Joselyn immediately sensed his wonder and attraction. He looked at her as if she were Helig herself, and indeed, Joselyn felt that way.

Lavinia had presented her with a dress the clanswomen had made for her. It was called a *hala*, traditional Dokiri garb meant to be worn on special occasions. It was dyed a brilliant amaranth. Unlike the purple one she already owned, this one was embroidered with stark diamond patterns around the hem. Bright crimson highlights provided accents to the gorgeous details. It fit her figure perfectly, and she'd never felt more like a Dokiri *hamma* than she did in that moment.

She'd owned gowns of far finer quality, but none was so unique as this and, like the bow Hollen had made, none had been given in such a spirit of generosity. What had she done to deserve such consideration?

Nothing. This speaks of their honor, not mine.

Dozens of eyes rested on her as she crossed the common area to her savage. She didn't mind this sort of attention; this was something she understood. Clothed in full Dokiri regalia, Joselyn was not merely herself tonight. Rather, she represented the clan. Raising her chin, she made certain to do them justice.

"*Salig.*" She stopped a few feet from Hollen and allowed him to continue his appraisal. Her body warmed to feel his dark eyes scan the length of her body. He was unabashed, and she loved it.

"*Mu Saliga,*" he said, drawing his gaze back to hers. He greeted her with a downward sweep of his hand. Joselyn smiled, feeling very much like she was at a feast and her escort had just given her a courtly bow. Of course, this was no grand foyer and Hollen was no lord. Somehow, she preferred it this way.

Joselyn inhaled as she took in the sight of her savage. His hair was pulled back and up into a high braid. It had tiny loops of bone weaved in and out of the strands, the vertebrae of some bird. His beard had been trimmed, and he wore his finest wool tunic. The sleeves were rolled up, and the deep 'v' in the front showed off much of his *idadi*. Like the other men, he'd washed, and Joselyn had the sudden desire to press her face into his flesh and inhale his scent. Time enough for that later, when she was curled beneath the blankets of their bed.

Hollen reached out and ran the backs of his fingers over the smooth embroidery of her dress. "*I* have something for you as well."

More gifts? What more could she have wanted? Hollen

walked to a nearby bench and bent to retrieve something. When he returned, Joselyn leaned forward to see what was in his hand. He held it up. A long, rich blue feather, flanked by shorter curly ones, hung by an ivory bead.

"From the storen you killed." He drew up the bauble. "For your hair."

Joselyn ran the pad of one finger along the spine of the velvety quill. It dangled by a leather cord, which Joselyn took and tied at the base of her scalp. It contrasted vividly against her red hair, and Joselyn wished she had a looking glass to help her more fully appreciate it. Strange. She hadn't desired a mirror in years.

"It's beautiful," she murmured.

"*You* are beautiful," he corrected, smiling devilishly at her. "I wanted you to have a memory of our first hunt, and, I thought you'd find this more agreeable than a scar."

Joselyn brushed her hand along the decorative piece, pleased that its length was even with her long mane. "Quite."

His thoughtfulness was stunning. Everything about him dazzled her. His easy dismissal of the drama she'd created before had been especially moving. After their conversation in the *bok*, Hollen hadn't brought the matter up again. It was as if it had never happened. Would there come a time when he no longer surprised her? She was beginning to wonder.

I could spend a lifetime finding out.

Hollen took her by the hand and pulled her toward the fire pit that roasted the slaughtered ram. They ate standing up. There was no time to sit. Joselyn was too distracted by the men, women, and even children who approached them, offering their compliments and blessings. Hollen addressed those who spoke in his language, with a hand pressed at the small of her back.

Sometimes he would pull her to stand in front of him and ask her to specifically greet one of his riders. She did so with every grace she'd been trained in. At one point, she noticed a strange twinkle in Hollen's eye as he watched one of the men he'd bid her speak to. A corner of his mouth was curled up, his shoulders square, stance wide.

He was showing her off.

Feminine pride bloomed in her chest, and Joselyn tried even harder to present herself well, to make *him* proud, too.

An air of joy surrounded the clan that Joselyn hadn't sensed before. It was as though something in them had shifted, a darkness removed. She could feel it in the energy around her. When Sigvard entered the firelight of the common area, the people cheered so loudly Joselyn's own voice was drowned out.

He leapt through the crowds, reveling in the attention. The blood on his chest had dried, and Joselyn tried not to cringe as she thought of all the dirt that might have gotten into the wound. She wasn't the only one concerned. When the noise died down, two older women came up alongside him and drew him to the water trough like a pair of plow oxen. Sigvard threw his head back on a laugh and said something Joselyn couldn't hear over the din of voices echoing through the cave.

It wasn't long before the wine started flowing, and spilling. Joselyn was just finishing her first horn when the drums began to beat. The center of the common area was lit by a roaring fire, the space around it empty of benches. As they had on the night of her feast, the men took to the dancing first.

They performed their traditional dance with Hollen chanting his challenges, and the riders shouting back with their answering doxologies. Her savage joined the throng of dancers and Joselyn watched with no less fascination than she had that first time. His body pulsed with the thrum of the music, rhythm guiding every step. Dark hair would have flown wildly about him had it not been pulled so tightly back. She itched to release his hair, wanted to witness his reckless abandon. Joselyn took a seat and pressed a hand against her thigh, relaxing in the glow of the wine, even as she sipped more.

"There's a sight for dreamin', eh?" came a familiar voice.

Joselyn turned a smile up toward Rosemary, who took her seat to the right, along with two other women Joselyn didn't know well. One of them tried to sit on Joselyn's left, but Rosemary snapped that the seat was already taken. The woman begrudgingly scooted a small distance to the side. Joselyn arched a brow at Rosemary.

"Lavinia will be 'ere in a minute. She be takin' care of the youngins."

Turning her attention back to the men, Joselyn saw that Hollen was staring at her from where he danced. His focus broke as he turned and dropped in time to the music, but his gaze always returned to hers. His expression made her want to squirm. Joselyn held his gaze as she rose her horn to her lips. No one moved like her savage. No one else was worth looking at.

Time rushed by, and Joselyn found herself bursting into laughter, along with her companions, at Rosemary. Somehow she'd managed to spill her entire drink down the front of her dress. Luckily, it was dyed the same deep purple as Joselyn's.

"Bleedin' skies!" Rosemary cursed, jumping to her feet.

Joselyn and Lavinia rose to help their friend strip off her outer gown before the wine had time to sink into her white under-shift.

"Right. Off with yours, then! I'm not about to be the only woman 'ere half-dressed!"

Lavinia began to unlace the cords at her sides. The other women seemed to take this as a sign that their turn for dancing had come. All around the fire, women rose and shed their clothing.

"I'm going to keep mine on, Rosemary." Joselyn laughed,

plopping down harder than she'd intended. She might switch to water for a while.

"Oh no!" Rosemary cried, far louder than was necessary, "Don't tell me you're sitting out again! I thought for sure you'd grown some nerve since you arrived!" She clamped a hand around the cords of Joselyn's *hala* and began tugging.

Joselyn stood without a fuss, flicking the brunette's hands away. "Stop it, you lush. I didn't say I wouldn't dance."

Rosemary's face wasn't the only one to light up with hope. "Truly?" Several of the women asked.

Joselyn tilted the last of her wine back and gulped it down. In Bedmeg it was considered bad luck to leave a horn of wine unfinished. The women clapped and giggled. Joselyn slipped her hands into her companions' and walked with them toward the fire. A wave of excitement swept through the cave, echoing off the walls. Joselyn looked around to see dozens of faces light up as she approached the fire. Apparently her friends weren't the only ones pleased to see her participating. A twinge of regret made her swallow. How often had she offended the clan with her uptight refusals?

The men shuffled away from the fire and took their places on the benches. Joselyn watched Hollen as she passed. Her shoulder just brushed into his side. In her periphery, she saw him slow and turn ever so slightly rearward. Now her back was to him, she smiled.

Linking arms with the other women, Joselyn listened as the lilting melody of stringed instruments joined the revelry. The beat of the drums evolved, and suddenly she was skipping along with her dance mates, back and forth around the fire. Joselyn surprised herself when she managed to break away at just the right moment, clapping as she spun to face the gathered crowd of onlooking men. Joselyn rejoined arms and laughed freely with the other women as they leapt across the stony floor.

The second song hadn't finished before Joselyn was desperate to remove her overdress. She'd been intent on wearing the *hala*, eager to show her appreciation to the women who'd made it, but it was just too hot. Breaking away, she approached the bench where Hollen was sitting. Her savage extended his cup of water to her. Instead of taking the cup, Joselyn leaned forward and took greedy gulps as he held it. She caught the look of surprise on his face, but he quickly recovered, tipping the cup back over her lips until she'd had her fill. She straightened back, panting.

"Had enough dancing?" Hollen asked, his voice teasing.

She paused, then fixed him with a look so brazen she should have blushed. With her eyes still on him, she began unlacing the cords of her dress. The men sitting at Hollen's sides suddenly became very interested in the crowd, the dancing, even the floor. But, their *Salig* only had eyes for the woman standing before him. They narrowed to slits as Joselyn yanked the wool *hala* over her head and her red hair spilled out around her. Without thinking, she tossed the garment into Hollen's lap, then retreated back toward the circle.

She rejoined arms with the dancing women. Perhaps she should have taken care to fold the dress, especially in front of the clan who'd given it to her. Joselyn tried, but couldn't quite muster up any regret. The look on her barbarian's face had been worth it. When she thought it was safe, Joselyn risked a glance back at Hollen. He was leaning forward, his attention fixed solely upon her. The *hala* remained conspicuously wadded up in his lap. Surely it was too hot for that. Looking away, she grinned.

Joselyn was gasping for breath when the music changed. She found herself without a partner as her companions broke off to pair with their *hatus*. Her panting slowed when she saw Hollen standing a few paces away. His bare feet were drawn apart, his arms crossed about his chest. His gaze ran over her, exploring, suggesting all manner of impropriety. Joselyn, who'd been swaying with the beat of the drums, went suddenly still.

He closed the distance between them. Joselyn tilted her head back. He was magnificent. He towered above her like a god, all strength and power. In that moment, she wanted to match him. Wanted to appear to him as he appeared to her, the image of desire.

From the corner of her eye, she caught sight of the other women, and their bodies pressed tightly against their *hatus'*. They wore the necklines of their shifts precariously open, venting the heat from their bodies, their *tanshi* marks visible. Joselyn's fingers trailed up to her collar, and began yanking at the threads which held it closed.

Hollen's eyes locked upon her hand as she moved, and she watched with deep satisfaction when his lips parted. Pressing her shoulders back, Joselyn sighed at the kiss of cool air that drifted over the valley between her breasts. Hollen looked at her then, the fire reflected in his dark eyes. Or was that simply him?

His hands reached out and took her by the waist. He dragged her across the narrow space that remained between them. She went willingly. Her own hands glided over the soft hairs at his chest as her stomach settled against his body. He was all muscle. All man. Her fingers grazed over the ridges of his *idadi* marks, appreciating, for the thousandth time, how plentiful they were.

The music played on around them, but they were in no hurry. Hollen's hands went to her shoulder blades, ran down her back in a firm stroke, only to settle at the swell of her hips. His fingers massaged her through her under-shift. With a shock, she realized that she wanted to feel his hands there, without the barrier of clothing.

He began moving, or rather he was moving her, his heavy palms rocking her in time with the drums. Joselyn let him lead her, falling into the rhythm he set. He swayed in tandem.

They danced like that for what seemed like hours, each learning the other through sheer motion. The stringed melody of kilds accompanied the drums now, and it added a sensual cadence to the revelry that was echoed by soft pants and murmured promises throughout the common area.

All at once, Hollen was standing behind her. He drew her rear against his hips. Joselyn gasped at the intimacy, but put up no resistance. He might have groaned, but it was impossible to say over the pounding of the drums. She continued to rock, allowing the music to carry her even as she pressed her head against Hollen's chest. One of his hands slid over her belly and pulled into her navel. Fire swelled beneath his palm, and Joselyn closed her eyes.

Hot breath caressed her ear, lips trailed down her neck. The music was either fading or it was her senses. All sense that wasn't the rising tide of lust that was trying to sweep her away. She shivered, melting when he pressed his mouth into the place where her throat met her shoulder. Her eyes flew open, but her vision remained hazy, blurred completely at the edges. She brought her hands over his and gripped him for dear life. His fingers bunched the wool of her dress together, pricking the skin beneath them. His kiss at her neck turned to the softest of nips. She could take no more.

She broke away.

The music still played, but already the ring was cleared of half its couples. They had gone back to their *boks*, or perhaps to the springs. Joselyn looked over her shoulder at Hollen. He was tense, his entire body leaning toward her, like she possessed some magnetic pull. Tentatively, she held out a hand to her savage.

He slid his palm against hers. Though excitement blazed in his eyes, he looked uncertain. Joselyn smiled at him and mustered up all her courage. She hoped it would be enough for both of them.

Joselyn handed him a torch and led them up the stony path to their *bok*. She glanced back once or twice, catching his simmering eyes upon her, the firm set of his jaw. It was clear he was thinking very hard on something. Joselyn could empathize.

They crept through the tunnel. Joselyn sighed on the coolness of the air as they entered their *bok*. She'd been to Lavinia's today, and, unlike hers and Hollen's, it was clear a woman had been living there. It was softer, warmer. Joselyn resolved to put her own mark on their home as soon as possible. Hollen ignored the torches and lit the firepit, setting the room in a dim amber glow. He tossed the torch onto the pile.

When he turned toward her, Joselyn inhaled, at once aware of just how indecent she must appear. Her hair hung in tousled locks over her shoulder and about her waist. Her shift was still open, baring her freckled chest. She could feel the sensual flush of her own cheeks. She lifted hazy eyes to his, a question lingering in her mind. As though he'd heard it, Hollen stepped toward her and took her in his arms.

"*Mu hamma*." He was breathless. Closing his eyes, he skimmed his lips along the curve of her brow.

Desire swelled in the cradle of her hips and stretched up into her chest and throat. She pressed her nose into his chest and inhaled his scent. She felt weak, like her knees would give out from want. Was it the wine? No, she hadn't drunk enough. In any case, her need had kept growing long after she'd stopped drinking.

Joselyn leaned into him. He was ever a pillar of strength. Her fingers trailed up his jaw, and she brought his face down to hers. She stood on her toes and explored him with her mouth, running the swell of her lip along the edge of his beard, relishing the soft prickles. She heard him sigh and felt the tremor that wracked down his body. He squeezed her to him. She moaned as he kissed her.

That little sound seemed to light a fire in her savage, and one of his hands seized her by the hair. She shuddered as his tongue slid between her lips, begging, no, *demanding*, entrance. She acquiesced, endorsing his exploration.

Curiosity burned at her, begging for satisfaction. What would it be like to give herself to a man? To *this* man? He, who was so foreign, so wild. One whom she'd feared, and loved? Joselyn had to know. Whatever else happened, she could not live her life wondering.

Joselyn remembered his words to her in the springs. *"If I thought you wanted me, there's not a thing in this world that could stop me from possessing you."*

When Hollen broke the kiss to gasp for air, Joselyn went stiff against him. His eyes, which had gone half-lidded with paassion, sobered, instantly attentive. Joselyn took a step back, but didn't break the visual connection between them. A quiet moment passed, and she brought her hands up to the wide collar of her shift. She pulled it apart, allowing it to slip off her shoulders and fall into a puddle on the ground.

I want you, savage.

Hollen's chest expanded as his eyes gazed over her bare body. "Joselyn."

She pressed her lips together and closed her eyes, stealing herself against the shame that tried to rear its ugly head. This was her savage. She was his *hamma*. And there was no room for guilt here. When her lashes fluttered open, Joselyn saw the need in him. The craving. She smiled.

He stepped toward her, a shaking hand extended. He didn't touch her. Instead, he dropped his palms so they hovered at her sides. His face hung inches above hers. She ran a hand up his naked chest where his heart pounded furiously.

"Is this what *you* want?" he whispered, his body still as the mountain they stood on. He wasn't even breathing as he waited for her answer.

Joselyn considered his question, considered what all she may be giving up if her words followed where her body was leading. With her virtue gone, relinquished to this savage, she may never acquire remittance into her household.

She didn't care.

"Yes." And she meant it. With everything in her, she meant it.

Hollen needed no further encouragement. He gathered her up in his arms and carried her to the plush furs of their bed.

Joselyn sighed and wrapped her arms around his neck. She wasn't going anywhere. She was Joselyn Helena Elise Fury. *Saliga* of Bedmeg.

Hamma of Hollen the Soulless.

32

A FEAST FOR THE GODS

"You've conquered *me*, woman."

Hollen lay panting on his back at Joselyn's side. A thin sheen of sweat made his *idadi* glow in the firelight. She knew now those scars extended even beyond where his pants covered. It was inevitable, for a man as fierce as her savage. There was only so much space on one's arms and chest, giant or no.

Joselyn lie curled into his side, a bare leg stretched over his hips. She sighed, still caught up in the swell of lust that had prompted her reckless abandon. She brought a hand up to his beard and pulled his chin down to her face. She gave him a light peck on the lips, but Hollen brushed a hand over her ear and tangled his fingers into her red locks. He pulled her forward to deepen the kiss.

Finally, they broke apart, and Hollen looked her in the eyes. His expression lost some of its haziness. "Did I hurt you?"

Joselyn's womb clenched automatically, and she felt the rawness there, as well as the moisture on her thighs that was surely in part blood. He'd been so careful with her, so gentle. But, as Tansy had explained, some things couldn't be helped.

"I'm all right," she breathed.

He studied her as his thumb stroked at her scalp. His other arm, the one she was lying on, curled around her. He kissed her brow. Once, twice, caressing her with his lips. She lifted her chin, reveling in his tenderness. He smelled so good.

She felt as though she'd spent the night sipping on the strongest of wines, but she hadn't. This feeling was all Hollen's doing. Her limbs were bathed in warm fatigue and her head swum with dizzy passion. Indeed, she was intoxicated. *He* intoxicated her senses.

Hollen rolled onto his side so that he was facing her. One of his knees wedged between hers. The fur blanket slid down her arm. Joselyn looked. He was pulling it away from their bodies. She snapped for it.

"No," he pleaded. He propped himself up on one elbow and stared down at her. "Let me see you, *mu hamma*."

Joselyn started to speak, but he dipped his head down to hers and kissed away her words. She never wanted him to stop. She sighed as he pressed his tongue between her lips. The blanket slipped the rest of the way down her body.

Hollen pulled back, and his dark eyes scanned the freckled expanse of her skin. Did he think she had too many? Joselyn pressed the side of her face into the furs. His appraisal scorched her, and it was the most delectable kind of burn. That heat intensified as he drew a fingertip down the curve of her waist and over the swell of her hip. He stopped at her mid-thigh and gave her a little squeeze. His gaze crept back to her face.

"You are *perfect*," he said, his tone worshipful.

Joselyn dared to meet his eyes. He'd seen *all* of her now. More than any other man. If he was pleased, then she was satisfied.

"Flawless." He kneaded her thigh, nearly swallowing it with his massive hand.

Joselyn brought her gaze forward and performed her own assessment. His body was every bit as imposing as the rest of him, though she knew now that her savage had a generous side as well. He'd shared that part of himself with her, lavishing her with every bit of his attention and affection.

"Tell me," Hollen said, "was it Sigvard taming his *gegatu* that got us here?"

Joselyn blinked at him, then snorted.

"Because I'll toss his skinny ass up to their nest every night if that's what it takes."

She burst into laughter, and her hands bunched into fists at his chest.

Hollen's face lit. "I love that sound. I love it more when I'm the cause of it."

She quieted, smiling up at him.

He brought the calloused fingers of one hand up to the hollow of her throat. "Though it's no longer my favorite sound of yours."

Joselyn sucked in a breath, her cheeks warming. She'd been wanton with him. Succumbed to the basest of instincts. She should be mortified. But as she looked at him, at his utter fascination, a thrill of boldness rippled through her.

She slid a hand down his body, past his waist, and grinned with satisfaction as his eyes rolled back into his head and a rumble rose in his throat.

"You are quite expressive, yourself, *Salig*."

His eyes cracked open, looking at her like she was a feast for the gods, and he, a starving man. "Are you happy, Joselyn?"

Behind his thin veil of humor, he was vulnerable. He wanted to know if she regretted what had just happened. If she regretted *him*. She brought her wandering hand back up to his chest and stroked an absent pattern there, allowing her eyes to retreat to the same spot.

"I am happy," she muttered.

It was true. Joselyn was certain she'd never felt such contentment in all her life than she did in that moment, gathered in Hollen's arms, no barrier between them.

As for regrets . . . What had really changed? It was a truth she'd long been ignoring. Even if she were to return to Morhagen, no one would assume her still a maiden. She'd been carried off by a man, a *wild* man. The conclusion would be drawn that Joselyn was despoiled. What had she really sacrificed in giving herself to him?

He ran his fingers through her hair. She'd sacrificed nothing, and gained everything. This man had held nothing back from her since the moment she'd arrived. His love was free and bountiful, given with an open hand and never running dry. Had she ever felt so cherished? So desirable? She didn't want it to end.

Joselyn curled into him. He pulled her closer until the lengths of their bodies were flat against each other. Hollen sighed. His massive lungs caused his chest to rise and fall heavily. He pressed a kiss to her forehead.

"You can't imagine my thoughts when you dropped your shift for me."

Joselyn's mouth firmed into a line. Tansy's jaw would have dropped. Had she really done that? *She*? The Lady Fury, brazenly baring her body before a man?

Only this man. Only ever for him.

A sneaky sense of pride began to well in her chest. Now more than ever, Joselyn felt like a woman fully grown. Powerful.

"What were your thoughts?" she asked, dismissing her lingering embarrassment.

He scoffed, as though there were so many he could hardly select one or two. "Aside from being utterly devastated by your beauty?" His voice was full of mirth but not at all unserious. "I was wondering what on Helig's green earth I had done right, and praying to Regna that I wouldn't ruin it in the next hour."

He pressed himself backward and devoured her mouth with rapid kisses. "I should have prayed for a lifetime. Now that I've had you, I'll think of nothing else until I have you again."

He continued pressing his lips to her mouth, at the corners and even into her dimpled chin. He moved so quickly Joselyn had a hard time catching her breath. She giggled, pressing against him, trying to get out of his mouth's path. He didn't let up.

"You've ruined me, *mu hamma*."

He kissed her.

"It's hopeless!"

Another kiss.

"You'll never get another moment's peace!"

He pressed his mouth hard against hers. Joselyn's giggles turned to outright laughter around their melded lips. Loosening his grip, he finally allowed her to break away. His grin matched hers, wide and full of wonder. A quiet moment passed, and his eyes softened. "Say you won't leave."

Joselyn's smile faltered. "I swore to you I wouldn't."

He shook his head. "I mean *ever*. Say you won't *ever* leave me."

Could she do it? Skies, she wanted to. She wanted to promise him everything. And why not? Even if she eventually left, what would it change? It would be too late. Who would she save? Her father would still be dead, her house in ruins. She opened her mouth, ready to make the vow.

Something stopped her. Would he still want her in the same way if she pledged herself to him? She'd been Joselyn of Bedmeg for a matter of weeks. She'd been Lady Fury her entire life. What would change if she gave that up? Would *he* change? Would he eventually come to see things as she had? That giving up all hope for her house was a selfish and cowardly thing to do? Fear tightened in her chest. "I can't, Hollen."

Not yet.

His face fell, and his fingers stopped petting. He stared hard into her eyes, his breath the only sound save for the crackling of the fire.

"Then I will," he whispered. "I'll say it until the words become yours. I won't ever leave you, *mu hamma*. You are my bride, my only, my mated one. I will always come for you."

He cupped her head and pressed his forehead against hers. "I love you, Joselyn."

Her heart stuttered in her chest.

Love? He *loved* her? No one had ever declared such a thing, no one except for Tansy. But that was different. Tansy's love was that of a mother. And even Tansy received payment for her services. Joselyn's own parents had never declared such an emotion as love for her.

What did that word mean to Hollen? Hadn't he just said? He'd promised that he'd stand with her, never to leave, always to come. And there had been no reservations in that vow. No price that she must first pay.

Emotion swelled. Joselyn tasted salt in her mouth, and her eyes began to sting. She started to turn away, to hide herself. Hollen's arms went tight around her, holding her in place.

"No, don't," he said, trying to catch her gaze, which was wildly skipping across the stone ceiling. He gave her a gentle shake. "Joselyn."

She forced her eyes to his and swallowed hard against the lump forming in her throat. He waited to speak until she was focused on him. "Nothing has changed. I'll never demand anything of you that you don't freely wish to give me."

He ran a hand over her shoulder and down the length of her arm. "Not your body, not your heart."

She held her breath, considering his words. His next were whispered.

"I only want you to know that you have mine."

Her heart shattered. Tears filled her eyes. Who was this man? *What* was he? Was it his mission to humble her? Strip her of all dignity and strength? To peel away the layers of prejudice and creed she wore like armor? Reduce her to a creature of base desire and instinct? Would he not rest until he proved she'd been wrong about everything in life?

Joselyn looked at him. *Really* looked at him. Listened to the steadiness of his breath. Inhaled his smoky musk. She absorbed his heat, his warmth. Brushing her fingers over his *tanshi* mark, she felt the steady pulse of his heart. *Her* heart.

Joselyn rose to her knees and pushed Hollen to his back. She draped herself over his body. Her fiery hair fell like a curtain around his face as she kissed him, long and slow. Her hands roamed over him, stroking, caressing. In time they began to rock against one another, lulled into the natural rhythm set by their mutual need.

Joselyn let her body say the words that her lips had not.

33

BROTHER OF MY HEART

The steady rise and fall of her savage's chest was soothing. Whatever strength he'd retained, Joselyn had drawn every last bit until he'd collapsed into a sated pile of slumbering man beside her. Joselyn watched him now, propped on her elbow, mind alert as his was dormant. She traced the patterns of his *idadi*, humming. When had she become the sort of woman to hum to herself? She smiled. Her answer lay before her.

Her stomach growled, interrupting her tuneless melody.

How late was it? She scoffed. It was likely morning, or would be soon. If Hollen woke to a plate of food, would he be ready to resume their evening's activities? Her skin warmed at the appealing idea, even as her thighs clenched in disapproval. Perhaps she and Hollen could devise a more creative form of distraction. One that wouldn't put further strain on her recently deflowered body. The private springs, perhaps? In anticipation of that, she rose from the bed, careful not to disturb Hollen.

Outside the common area, Joselyn could see the deep blue of predawn painting the sky. Much as it had been the morning after her welcoming feast, the cave floor was littered with the reclining figures of boys who'd not made it back to their beds before passing out. She stepped over and around them, shaking her head at their purple-stained lips.

By now, several of the women were typically up, preparing the morning meal. As it was, only two old widows milled about, far less careful than Joselyn to avoid disturbing the sleeping boys. They even occasionally "tripped" over their lounging bodies. Joselyn smirked. She gathered a plate full of meat and cheese and turned to make her way back to the *bok*.

"Good morning, little sister."

Joselyn started and nearly dropped the food. Her hand flew to her chest.

"Sigvard!" She hissed. She glared up at his mischievous face, then dissolved into a fit of giggles.

"You have to be the sneakiest boy *man* I've ever met."

His eyes flashed as she corrected herself, and his chest puffed out. Joselyn smoothed back her hair. "I thought surely you'd be indisposed after your own feast."

Sigvard scoffed. "So recently after gaining my wings? Where's the fun in that? I slept just long enough to give *Grelka* a rest."

"*Grelka*?"

"My *gegatu*." He said, shining with pride.

"A fine name."

"I suppose I shouldn't be surprised to see you awake, after you and my brother *both* retired *so* early."

Joselyn started to respond, but he cut her off. "Perhaps you found something more exciting to do than celebrate my victory?" He wiggled a brow.

Joselyn's mouth hung open. Had it been so obvious? Had everyone noticed? Or was Sigvard simply toying with her? She wanted to say something clever, but only stuttered.

"I know how you can make it up to me!" he declared, grabbing her food and setting it aside. Before she could protest, he grabbed her by the hand and tugged her toward the cave's entrance. She rolled her eyes, but followed, her curiosity piqued. Just before exiting, Sigvard snatched up a discarded fur cloak and handed it to Joselyn.

They trudged down the ravine through the freshly fallen snow. All the way around the edge, well out of sight of the common area. The sky was softening to lavender now, not quite heralding the sun. Joselyn shivered in the crisp morning air.

"You know, the last time I followed you somewhere, I nearly died."

"Ah, but not before having a little fun, eh?" He glanced back at her with a smirk on his freckled face.

Joselyn scoffed. "I could think of far better words to describe that experience."

"Yes. Dramatic, intriguing"—his smirk deepened—"provocative?"

She snickered, unable to maintain the facade of censure. "What are we sneaking off to do, Sigvard?"

He turned toward the cliff face and performed a rapid series of whistles. The piercing sounds echoed off the stone walls. A moment passed, and then Joselyn could hear it before she saw it. His *gegatu* shrieked from the ledge above them. Grelka dropped off the side, opening her black wings to glide gently toward the ground where Joselyn and Sigvard stood.

Joselyn took several hasty steps backward. Instinct dredged up the desire to bolt like a wild hare from a descending eagle. Sigvard seemed not to notice. His appreciative face remained fixed upon his new mount. The beast, now saddled, landed softly in the snow and hissed at Joselyn.

"*Eh!*" Sigvard waved an arm and bit out a series of commands in his father tongue, intent on gaining his mount's full attention. With what seemed to Joselyn like a great deal of reluctance, the creature obeyed.

Joselyn planted her feet into the snow, willing herself not to run. She'd only mark herself as prey. It was one thing to stand so close to this creature while the entire clan was also there. But with none but Sigvard, Joselyn felt like the obvious target should the wyvern decide it was hungry.

"Sigvard?" she asked, trying to keep her voice low.

Hollen's brother held his steed beneath the jaw. He turned to look at her. "It's all right Joselyn. She's not going to attack you."

Joselyn eyed the creature warily, remembering how Hollen had warned her never to approach a *gegatu* without its rider present. Did that mean she was safe so long as its rider *was* present?

"How do you know?" she asked.

"Because I told her not to," he said, as though it really were as simple as that. "Come here."

"I'd rather not," She said flatly. She didn't like the *gegatu* as a species, not even Jagomri. She could think of no reason to approach the creature.

"Come now, Joselyn. Don't tell me you can't appreciate beauty in all its forms. Does looking at gold all one's life do that to a person?"

Despite her nerves, Joselyn managed to shoot Sigvard a wicked glare. He was goading her. She ought not take him seriously. The auburn-haired man laughed, pleased to have riled her. His easy demeanor drained some of her fear away.

Flicking a glance at the skinny-necked beast, Joselyn sighed and crept forward. She stopped just behind Sigvard, and managed not to flinch when he drew her hand up to rub Grelka in the space between her nostrils. It was surprisingly soft, and Joselyn's flesh warmed as the beast blew out a puff of hot breath. It made no move, and after a few moments, appeared to lose interest in Joselyn, looking instead at the glowing horizon as though it longed to fly.

"See, nothing to fear." Sigvard looked down at her. Pleasure emanated from him.

Joselyn drew her hand slowly away, with a hint of self-satisfaction rising at her own daring. "She *is* beautiful, Sigvard. I'm glad she didn't kill you."

Sigvard laughed, freely stroking a hand up the center of Grelka's face. "She couldn't possibly. Just the thought of a life without me would destroy her."

Joselyn's brow wrinkled doubtfully. "I suppose you're in a hurry to complete the *veligneshi* now? Anxious to claim a bride of your own?"

Some of Sigvard's pleasure seemed to dissipate at that. "What's the point? I have three brothers ahead of me. It will be a long while before I get *my* chance."

Joselyn considered him. "You're still young."

He huffed, then released Grelka to turn toward Joselyn. He studied her, an odd expression on his face. "Got any adventure left in you this morning?"

"Why?" She'd already been on the adventure of her lifetime just hours ago.

"What do you say to a morning flight? I've never seen the sunrise from the sky. Have you?"

Joselyn blinked at him, then realized what he was suggesting. "You want me to ride with you?"

He grinned sheepishly. "Why not?"

"Why not?" she sputtered. "Because it's dangerous!"

He waved a hand, clucking dismissively. "Hardly. Come on, we can be back in half an hour. I *assume* Hollen won't be waking for a good while yet?" He looked as though he were holding in a laugh at those last words.

The tightness in Joselyn's face slackened, replaced by the

heat of a blush. Sigvard *indeed* knew exactly what she and Hollen had been up to the night before. Desperate to change the subject, she shook her head solemnly.

"I'm sorry Sigvard, but no."

Sigvard's shoulders slumped and he physically deflated. His coppery eyes dropped to the snowy ground between them. "Oh."

There was an awkward silence, and Joselyn found herself regretting her quick refusal. Couldn't she have shown just the slightest interest in his idea? Her eyes scanned the length of the wyvern's white streak of scales that disappeared under the saddle.

Grelka looked docile, or at least, as docile as any mastered *gegatu*. They reminded her of cats in a way, generally foul tempered, but ultimately harmless if approached correctly. She wrinkled her nose at her own comparison. She'd never seen a cat large enough to swallow a man. Still, Sigvard's new beast didn't appear hungry. It only seemed like it wished to be off, away in the sky.

She glanced back at Sigvard's defeated expression and fidgeted with the edge of her cloak. He'd wanted her to fly with him, demonstrate to her the speed and power of his mount, a subtle hint at his own masculine prowess. Fresh off the high of his victory, what he probably really wanted was to claim his own *hamma*, and show *her* what he'd accomplished. Just how long would it be before he got that opportunity?

"We'll be back just after the sun rises? No longer?"

Sigvard's face lit up like a torch. "Yes! We could be back long before the clan begins to rouse."

"And we won't land *anywhere* but back here?" Joselyn looked hard at him, remembering the trauma she'd nearly experienced the last time she'd left Bedmeg.

"I swear it." He sobered a bit, as though he understood why that particular detail was important to her.

Taking one last look at the wyvern's disinterested eyes, Joselyn sighed and nodded her consent. The dimples in Sigvard's face appeared with his smile. That look almost made this madness worth it. Joselyn had gone her whole life wishing for a brother. Now she had four. He took her by the hand and led her toward the beast's back.

He all but lifted her to the saddle, reminding her of just how strong these Dokiri men were, even young ones such as Sigvard. When she'd settled, Sigvard leapt up behind her and set to binding his legs in the saddle. They swayed several feet to the side as Grelka shifted and growled, shaking her head like a dog in the rain. Joselyn tensed.

"Don't fear, Joselyn. She's just preparing for glory." The edge of teasing humor was back in his voice.

Joselyn rolled her eyes, mostly to distract herself from her jittering nerves as Sigvard finished his preparations.

"I, uh—are you ready?" he asked, a strange hitch to his voice.

She nodded. Joselyn understood the reason for his hesitancy when he slid his arms past her waist and leaned over her, pressing his chest into her back.

"Sorry." Sigvard mumbled, his tone so sheepish Joselyn had to laugh.

She settled her belly against the leather of the saddle, instantly deciding she would never mention this little lapse in judgment to Hollen. Not that she'd planned to before.

Sigvard grasped the ridges on Grelka's back and urged his mount forward. The wyvern jolted, and Joselyn was glad to have the weight of a grown man upon her. However awkward, it was better than falling to her death. After a brief running start, *Grelka* opened her wings and beat against the frigid morning air. She leapt up and, after a slight dip, they were free of the white earth below.

Sigvard's infectious laugh of triumph rang loud before the

piercing wind swallowed the sound. Joselyn shivered, happy she'd only agreed to a short flight. They soared down the mountain, streaking across the sky like a falling star. It was obvious Sigvard was particularly proud of his mount's speed, and he intended to make it clear to Joselyn just how much of it *Grelka* possessed. Joselyn would give him an earful when they finally landed. For now, she held on.

The sky was now going blush, a remnant of purple just visible to the west. To the east, a ray of golden light beamed like a beacon into the cloudy heavens above. Joselyn stared, transfixed by the spectacle. Indeed, a sunrise from the sky was an experience all its own. Nothing obstructed this visual feast, no trees, no mountains, nothing. She was free to marvel at it in its full majesty.

The first shred of daylight blue was just peaking over the horizon when Joselyn glanced downward, curious where they'd flown. Below them, the ground had turned a deep green, covered by a fir pine forest. The trees reached toward the heavens like snow-dusted spires. Joselyn glanced back. She was shocked to see the mountain a good way behind them, looking again like the imposing monument it was rather than her new home.

She laced her hand around Sigvard's arm and tapped at him until his chin pointed in the direction of her extremity. She jabbed a finger backward in silent demand that they return. He nodded, his chin bumping into the top of her head, and pulled hard on one side of *Grelka's* shoulders. The creature crowed, loud enough to be heard over the wind. She banked right and circled back toward Bedmeg.

Joselyn breathed a sigh of relief, wondering at her own need to return to the place she'd once thought of as a prison. To the man she had once thought her jailer. Despite the icy air, Joselyn warmed to think of slipping back beneath the furs of their bed and wrapping her bare body around his once again. They couldn't get back fast enough.

Above her, Sigvard stiffened. Joselyn tried to crane her head backward to see what the matter was. As she did, one of his arms released *Grelka* to jerk against Joselyn's shoulder and face.

Something hit them. Hard.

Terror ripped through her chest. Joselyn couldn't see what caused their mount's body to jolt, nor the reason for its abrupt, wild screeching. Her vision was blocked by Sigvard's body curling in around her. Panic overtook her, and she screamed as the wind around them began to slow. They were falling.

The snapping of branches sounded like cracking thunder as they tore through the canopy of trees. Sigvard's body folded heavily over Joselyn as they hit the powdery ground and skidded across the snow. She could see nothing but white as they slid, and felt the icy spray on her hands and face until they finally halted against the trunk of a pine.

There was a brief moment of stillness before Sigvard tore himself off her back and set to working his right leg from the saddle.

"Joselyn...Joselyn...Joselyn!"

Sigvard's screaming voice finally got through to her, and she jumped. Leaning, she looked backward to see Sigvard frantically scanning her body, even as he continued to attempt to free himself. Joselyn tried to relax, as if doing so would make her more aware of herself. Was she injured? She didn't think so. What about Sigvard? He seemed intact.

Way out to the side, Joselyn saw what had caused them to crash. The arm of *Grelka's* wing was wound in a thick, triple corded rope, weighed down by three, heavy metal balls. The leather of the massive wing was fanned out against the snow, still, like the rest of the wyvern's body. Joselyn glanced back at Sigvard, hoping he could make sense of what had just happened. His eyes were wild with fear as he finished releasing one leg. He whipped around to free the other.

In the distance, Joselyn thought she could hear voices shouting. Male voices.

Just then, *Grelka* woke from whatever stupor she'd been in. The creature reared, causing Sigvard and Joselyn to lurch forward. The *gegatu* bucked and tossed, trying to free its entangled wing, all the while shrieking loud and high.

Joselyn's head whipped forward and back, causing her to bite down hard on her tongue. Fresh panic rose in her and, as Sigvard rose off her back, she tried to swing a leg around and jump free of the spooked creature. She fell more than leapt off its back, landing heavily in the blanket of snow. Before she could think, she was rolling, trying to get out of the way of the enormous beast's jagged talons.

When she finally stopped spinning, Joselyn rose to a sitting position to see Sigvard being thrown back and forth. One of his legs was still caught in the saddle. He was trying to reach the leg, trying to pull himself out, but he couldn't grasp the straps.

"Sigvard!" She cried, utterly helpless.

Grelka's wing was beginning to unwind, which was miraculous considering. Would the creature still when it was free? Give Sigvard a chance to unbind himself? What if he was seriously injured? Joselyn scrambled to her feet and jumped back even further as Grelka swung round and nearly into her.

The voices grew louder. Closer. She barely noticed them, unable to take her eyes off Sigvard. Invoking the name of every god she knew, Joselyn begged them for mercy, fearing she was about to watch something horrific. Sigvard went diving out of the saddle, tossed forward by a particularly powerful buck. His leg caught and, even in the commotion, Joselyn heard a sickening popping sound. Sigvard wailed in pain.

Tears streamed down Joselyn's face. Before she could stop

herself, her legs went sprinting toward the wild creature.

She made it all of three paces before an arm shot round her waist and hauled her off her feet. Joselyn screamed, more from instinct than actual fear. Her arms flailed as she was swung face to face with a handful of men clad in scarlet and gold winter armor.

"Milady! You're safe!" Her attacker yelled, his hot breath pouring into her ear.

Joselyn froze. Her mind raced to make sense of what was happening. Those were House Fury's colors. *Her* colors. These were her men. Not Morhageese peasants. Knights. Soldiers from her own, ancient lands of Tirvine. She stopped crying.

What were they doing *here*?

"Get her back! To safety!" A different man yelled to the one still holding her at the waist. They were carrying bows, arrows already notched.

Joselyn gasped. She threw a look over her shoulder at Sigvard, who still hung upside down. The bolas had just fallen free of Grelka's wing, and the wicked creature turned its attention on the group of men approaching her. She roared in rage.

The knights paused; they drew backward a moment before letting their arrows fly.

"No!" Joselyn cried in horror, just before the knight tossed her bodily over his shoulder.

She kicked at him, screamed, pounded her fists on his back, demanded to be released. Her father's men ignored all and ran through the trees. A pair of soldiers followed, bows in hand, frequently tossing their eyes backward as if to ensure they were not being pursued.

Joselyn's gaze lifted to the sky when she heard *Grelka's* shriek rising above the trees. She was flying clumsily away, back toward the mountain.

Sigvard dangled in tow. An arrow jutted from his limp body.

34

HARD CHOICES

The blast of the horn from the common area had shaken the stone walls of Hollen's *bok*. The sound, which was a call to arms for every available Dokiri man, should have ignited dread in his stomach. Instead, all Hollen could feel was the fierce pounding of his heart, as he woke to find his bed empty. Joselyn was gone.

He sprinted to the common area half-dressed. She was nowhere in sight. Erik was at his side in an instant, recounting the details of a *veligiri* sighting unlike any ever before. Hollen barely listened, too intent upon finding his bride.

Had she fled? Left him just as before? Had he hurt her somehow?

A darker, more sinister side of Hollen whispered, *perhaps she intended to leave all along, just when you'd not expect.*

Hollen crushed those thoughts as quickly as they arose. His fear for his bride's well-being overshadowed all.

All around him, his riders spilled out of the cave and into the ravine, calling down their mounts as they did. The women and children made their way up to the floating caves, inner pockets which could only be reached by rope ladders descending from the ceiling. They'd stay there until their husbands and sons returned. With no one left to guard them, it was the only way to ensure their safety when all men were required at once.

"*Mu Salig!*" Erik cried, grabbing Hollen by the arm. "Did you hear what I said?"

He hadn't.

"She's gone," Hollen said in Dokiri, unable to stamp the panic from his voice. "I can't find her anywhere."

Erik's face paled, "Are you certain? Would she really leave after . . . " Erik trailed off, his question answered by the terror on Hollen's face.

"I can't leave."

Uncertainty crossed Erik's features before he nodded. "I'll lead the men. Soren says the *veligiri* pack was sighted on the north face, near the throat."

"I'll come to you when she's found," Hollen said, grateful.

Erik nodded and pounded a fist to his chest before racing to join the others.

It was a hateful choice, his duty to his bride over his duty as *Salig*, but in that moment, there was no contest. He must find Joselyn and get her back to Bedmeg where it was safe. If the report about the *veligiri* was true, the danger had never been more real than it was this morning.

"*Mu Salig.*"

Hollen froze, and turned to see the wrinkled face of Ginny, a Dokiri *gritu*. Her husband had died of fever a decade ago.

"Get to the floating caves." He barked and started to turn away.

"*Mu Salig!*" She repeated, her voice far more insistent, her mouth drawn into a disapproving scowl.

Hollen sucked in a breath, forcing patience. "What is it, wise one?"

"It's your bride," she said.

Hollen stiffened, his attention rapt.

"She's with Sigvard."

His face slackened. "Sigvard?"

She nodded solemnly. "I saw him take her outside early this morning. Later I saw him flying away on his new mount."

Hollen's voice went flat. "Was she with him?"

The woman looked uncertain. "These eyes don't see so clearly anymore. But I believe so."

"And they've not returned?"

She shook her head.

Hollen called his thanks and sprinted from the cave, catching up to the few remaining men who were still mounting their *gegatu*.

"*Mu Salig?*" they called, curiosity and concern plain.

"Forgive me, brothers. Erik will lead you." Hollen didn't slow to assess their reactions. He called for Jagomri.

HOLLEN HAD SET out hoping to find his bride. Now, the day nearly gone, he prayed he'd return to Bedmeg to find her and Sigvard already arrived. Once he'd taken to the air, his mind had tormented him with grim possibilities.

He relied on the idea that Sigvard, idiotic as he was, had merely convinced Joselyn to ride with him. He'd want to brag on his new mount's speed or grace. There were other explanations, each less palatable than the last. That she'd convinced him to take her to the lowlands. Hollen couldn't believe that Sigvard would do so knowingly. But his bride was clever. Perhaps she'd found a subtle way to manipulate him. The idea would have sickened him, but it wasn't convincing enough. It didn't speak of the Joselyn he'd come to love and trust.

In the fading daylight, Hollen was making his final pass over the north side when something caught his sharpened vision. A break in the canopy of trees ahead, like something had fallen from the sky. Lightning? His blood ran cold. A *gegatu*? Hollen urged Jagomri forward, praying for the former.

He circled over the broken branches. With every foot closer to the ground, Hollen's horror grew until they glided but a man's height over the accident. His stomach threatened to upend itself then and there.

Sigvard dangled heels-over-head by his mount's torn stirrups. His mount lay lax in a tangle of trees, caught by the leather bindings of her saddle. Her wings were spread wide, torn in several places, as though she'd batted at the branches, trying to free herself. Her eyes were closed, her breathing slow yet steady. What Hollen couldn't see was whether or not his little brother was alive.

He urged Jagomri down, having to convince the beast to land in such a densely packed area. Even so, once he'd freed himself from his saddle, he had to backtrack a short distance to reach the place where Sigvard hung suspended, perhaps forty feet in the air. Joselyn was nowhere in sight. He thought of calling for her, but it was growing late, and he dare not attract the attention of any nefarious creatures roaming about.

"Sigvard!" he hissed. Horror threatened to turn his low call into a bellow.

Sigvard didn't stir.

The broken shaft of an arrow stuck out of the right side of his brother's chest. Had it pierced his lung? Hollen couldn't tell. Terror seized him as he set to climbing the tree, desperate to reach him.

He was panting when he reached the level of Sigvard's head, but the auburn-haired man hung too far from the center for

Hollen to reach him. Taking hold of the trunk, he crept out to the periphery of the branch, mindful his weight didn't snap the limb beneath him. It groaned precariously.

"Sigvard," he hissed. His fingers just brushed his brother's coat. He swatted at him, catching him just enough to spin him around. Deep scrapes and bright purple bruises covered his face. From the tree, maybe?

Sigvard moaned low. His eyes didn't even flutter. He was breathing. Alive. Hollen breathed his thanks to Helig.

What had happened? Had Sigvard been conscious, Hollen would have demanded answers. Where was Joselyn? Had she been with Sigvard when this happened? Had she ever been with him at all? Hollen cursed, drawing his knife to work at the leather which bound his brother in the tree.

Hollen cut the first cord, and Sigvard's mount began thrashing. So erratic were her movements that Hollen had to withdraw, afraid he'd be knocked from his perch and fall to his death. He bit out a few Dokiri words, ordering the newly tamed creature to stand down. He resheathed the knife and extended an open palm, mindful to keep it out of reach of her snapping jaws. He shushed the creature, tried to ease her wild fear.

It was useless. Even were he Sigvard, the beast was too frightened to calm herself. She shrieked, warning him to keep his distance. Her yellow eyes locked on him and dilated. White teeth flashed.

Hollen swore. He needed Erik. His second-born brother could make short work of this situation and free both Sigvard and the creature. Hollen could return to Bedmeg, hope that Erik was there, and return with him. But what if he wasn't? Even if he were, could Sigvard wait that long? Could Joselyn?

"Sigvard!" Hollen whispered loudly, trying to rouse his brother.

Nothing.

Hollen gritted his teeth and made a decision. He climbed down, jumped the last several feet, and sprinted back to Jagomri. He withdrew his bow and quiver and returned. There was barely enough light to see through the trees. Hollen nocked an arrow and took aim.

The beast screamed when the iron point lodged in her throat. Dark blood fanned onto the white ground below. He drew another arrow, muttering a word of pity for the dying beast as he fired at her again. Her body thrashed, desperate for life. A third and final arrow bled the creature of its strength. Her rage-filled cries grew dim and muted as her jerky movements stilled. *Glanshi*. If only there had been a way to kill her quickly.

Determined not to make the creature's sacrifice a vain one, Hollen threw down his bow and scurried back up the tree. This time, after what seemed like hours of careful toil, he was able to free Sigvard. They nearly fell as his brother's heavy weight settled with Hollen's onto the branch. It cracked, and they slipped to a stronger one below.

The sky was almost dark, and Hollen was covered in a mixture of his own sweat and the *gegatu's* blood when he finally lowered Sigvard to the snowy ground. His pulse was rapid and thready. Hollen shook his brother by the shoulders, calling his name. After several moments, Sigvard's orange eyes cracked open. They rolled sluggishly in his head.

"Hollen," he croaked, his voice full of gravel.

"Brother," Hollen said. Relief flooded him. His voice took on a tone of command. "Tell me what happened."

"Lowlanders. They ensnared *Grelka*, brought us down."

"Was Joselyn with you?" Hollen's voice was low and even, not betraying the anxiety pulsing in his veins.

Sigvard nodded, squeezing his eyes shut in pain, or guilt.

"Where is she, Sigvard?" Hollen squeezed Sigvard's shoulder, willing him conscious.

Sigvard looked Hollen in the eye. "They took her."

"Who?"

"Soldiers. Red and gold."

The colors of House Fury. Hollen wanted to know why. Why had Sigvard taken his bride traipsing about the skies? Why had she agreed to go with him? But there were more important things. Hollen had to work his jaw loose to speak. "Was she hurt?"

Sigvard hesitated. "I don't know. I think not."

Hollen breathed, trying to still his racing heart as his mind projected images of every dire possibility. Sigvard coughed, bringing Hollen back to the present.

"Hollen, I'm sorry. I—" Sigvard broke off with a scream as Hollen snapped the shaft of the arrow in his chest. The healers could remove the head. For now, they needed the shaft out of their way.

"Come." Hollen planted his hands beneath Sigvard's arms and hoisted him upward. "We have to get you to Bedmeg."

"But, Joselyn—"

"Home first. You'll die if I leave you here."

"Set me on my mount. I'll fly back myself."

Hollen grimaced as he swung one of Sigvard's arms over his neck and pulled him toward Jagomri.

"Your mount is dead."

A part of Hollen wanted Sigvard to suffer at those words, to feel the pain brought about by his own stupidity. But as he watched his younger brother's gaze turn up to the tree above them and lock upon his newly mastered steed's dangling body, Hollen only wished for the power to turn back time. To stop this nightmare from occurring.

Sigvard's face seized with horror as he choked on whatever words he'd been about to say. He looked back at Hollen, seeming to just now notice the flecks of blood that covered him.

Devastation filled his eyes, along with tears. Instead of speaking, he made a little whimpering sound as his gaze fell into the snowy ground they limped across.

"Come on," Hollen said. Sympathy leaked into his voice. "You need a healer, and Joselyn needs me."

35

THE GAMEBOARD OF LORDS

Five hundred men. Ten times the number Lord Fury had sent with Joselyn on her way to Brance. Apparently, her father was taking no chances. She'd been locked in a carriage. Her "bodyguard" was a gruff man who spoke almost as rarely as he smiled. He'd insisted on keeping the shutters closed and the door barred as "precautions."

Her demands for a report on what had become of Sigvard had gone ignored, dismissed with a curt apology. Was he still alive? Had he been captured? Joselyn could only pray his mount had taken him back to Bedmeg. Pray, and curse herself for her foolishness. If Sigvard died, it would be on her conscience. Of course, she might never find out.

They'd moved with all haste. The men were anxious to get to safety before any "dragon riders" had the opportunity to give chase. She'd been told they were headed to Castle Arland, home to a neutral family between Houses Fury and Viridian at the southeast edge of Morhagen. It was the closest keep to the Crookspine Range, a day's journey from the foot of Mount Carpe.

"My father is there?" she'd asked her sullen carriage mate.

He nodded grimly. "He, and the Viridian lord."

Joselyn had to turn her face to the wall to hide her dismay. Dante Viridian? Here? With her father? The thrum of her heart picked up. She'd be facing not only her father, but also her intended. Her stomach churned.

"How long have they been there?" she asked.

"Since your father was informed of your whereabouts by a young hunter."

Joselyn's fingers went icy as a vague memory flashed across her mind. A young man, nearly a boy, running away. The one Hollen let escape from the clearing. He'd been the only one to consider her claim of the Fury name. It seemed he'd taken her seriously. Her father had probably made him rich enough to never need to hunt again.

The carriage hummed as it rolled onto a cobbled pathway. A few moments passed, and it came to a stop. Joselyn swayed forward. Someone outside threw the door open, and her bodyguard leapt out. Behind him, the sky burned orange with the setting sun. Joselyn took her escort's hand as he helped her down to the paved ground.

Castle Arland had no walls. The Crookspine Range was more than enough protection from rival kingdoms. What money the Arland family had saved for lack of defensive structures, they'd made up for in ornate details. The castle's exterior was inlaid with swirling streaks of silver granite that formed ostentatious patterns that could be seen from miles away. Every corner of the structure boasted exquisitely carved statues of fantastic creatures, ranging from sleeping dryads to roaring wyverns. The latter were eerily close to life.

The courtyard teemed with soldiers. Where were Arland's residents? Perhaps, for security's sake, they'd been cleared prior to her arrival. Whatever the reason, Joselyn was grateful. Still clad in furs, she was a feast for gossiping tongues. Joselyn took her escort's arms and was led between two columns of men up to the giant doors of the castle. Sir Richard burst through, likely straight from her father's side. He gave her a breathless bow.

"My lady, Joselyn!"

Genuine pleasure sparked in Joselyn's chest at the sight of her father's steward, a man who'd been like an uncle to her. She extended her hands toward him, and some of the tension left her body when he bent to kiss the backs of them. His scarred face rose up and stared down at her. Relief warred with anxiety in his features.

"Praise the gods, you're safe. Safe, and returned to us."

"I *have* returned." She let her expression go blank. Safety was another matter.

Sir Richard's eyes sharpened. He had questions. He glanced at the small horde of men behind her. One of the captains stepped forward to whisper in his ear. Joselyn's neck heated as she imagined what sort of report was being passed.

With a grim smile, Sir Richard extended an arm and Joselyn was quick to take it in favor of her bodyguard's. He felt solid. Steady. As they walked into the marble foyer, Joselyn tried to draw those sensations into herself. The smell of bread and lacquered wood hit her. The scents of civilization. A bough of pine was laid over the mantle of a vast hearth. She could smell it, too, and wanting for Hollen made her throat swell.

Don't. Not now. Get through this first.

"Your father awaits you," Sir Richard muttered, leading her to a massive, winding staircase.

Joselyn nodded, willing the appearance of confidence. "Kindly call me a maid, and I'll attend him as soon as I've been appropriately dressed."

As they climbed the first few steps, Sir Richard turned a pitying glance toward her. "He requires your *immediate* presence, my lady."

She swallowed, not returning his gaze. So, this was how it was to be? Joselyn would be presented to her father like an errant child, still covered in the mire of mischief.

"He's most anxious to assure himself of your safety."

"Indeed. *Nearly* as anxious as his steward." She kept her gaze ahead.

Their steps faltered. In her periphery, Joselyn caught the shocked look Sir Richard shot her. Never had he heard her speak even a hint of reproach for his master. Joselyn inclined her chin and pressed on to the interior balcony.

A pair of guards stood outside a heavy door. It was gilded in the same silver granite which adorned the outer walls. Surely Sir Richard had taken her to the master's suite. Joselyn sucked in a breath. Lord Arland had likely relinquished his own chambers for a guest such as Marcus Fury. Truly, there seemed no limit to what men would do to win her father's favor.

The door swung open with a groan. Joselyn squinted against the last red rays of setting sun that poured through towering stained-glass windows. Sir Richard drew her forward, and the doors shut behind them. Her eyes adjusted, and Joselyn's gaze fell upon the man she'd nearly died trying to return to.

He sat on a satin settee, an arm draped over the back. His other hand held a golden goblet. Steeling herself, Joselyn looked into his eyes. Cold and gray as the day she'd departed. The only things different were the lines over his brow and about his eyes. They were longer. Deeper.

Beside her, Sir Richard released Joselyn's arm and straightened on a bow. "My Lord Fury. Captain Royce sends your daughter."

There was silence.

Joselyn held her breath as her father's eyes wandered up and down her furs. She clasped her hands together and waited. An eternity passed, and Marcus looked away.

"Where was she found?"

"North of where the boy reported, in the company of a dragon rider."

"Where is this rider?"

Sir Richard cleared his throat. "He wasn't recovered, my lord."

"A pity." Marcus lifted the goblet to his lips and took a long sip.

Joselyn watched him. An old bitterness curled in her stomach with each passing moment. Would he not greet her? Acknowledge her in any fashion? She drew in a breath. No. Not until it suited him.

"You are dismissed, Sir Richard," Marcus finally said.

Nodding, Sir Richard pounded on the door and made his exit. Joselyn barely caught the flicker of sympathy in his eyes as the doors shut behind him.

"I confided in you."

Joselyn's shoulders stiffened. She turned her attention back to the man who'd sired her. He set his goblet on the nearby table with a crisp clank, then stood. His gaze was wintry, accusing, as he crossed the room.

"I explained to you what this alliance with Viridian meant for our house. Explained what fate awaited us if you failed to meet your duty."

As he drew closer, Joselyn had to tilt her chin upward to hold his gaze.

"And yet, barely on the eve of meeting your sole obligation in life"—he paused, staring hard down his nose at her—"you vanished."

She didn't respond. Knew better. He meant to punish her with shame. Her participation wasn't required. Only her endurance.

"For what purpose were you taken?" he asked.

Joselyn stared through him. "He desired a bride."

Marcus' lips thinned. "And you became his bride? Spread your legs for him?"

"No." Joselyn didn't know which question she was answering. She was a liar regardless.

"No?" Marcus stepped to Joselyn's side and looked her over head to toe. She stood tall, refusing to flinch.

Marcus spoke from behind her, "You've been gone for six weeks, Daughter. Surely the barbarian made use of you."

"I wasn't harmed."

A moment.

Another.

Finally, Marcus circled back into Joselyn's line of sight. He was grinding his teeth. "My carriage was returned to me intact, as was the maid accompanying you. One would wonder how the fiend managed to get ahold of you. But I've been told you were on horseback, riding *away* from the procession no less."

Joselyn turned her head toward him. Even now, after all she'd done, he sought to blame her for his troubles. It had been that way since the day she was born, intolerably female. It would never change.

"Yes."

"You put the future of your house in jeopardy. You put the life of your lord father in the utmost peril. Answer me truly, Daughter, are you still loyal?"

Disgust bubbled in Joselyn's gut. His question was a slap in the face. No daughter had ever been more loyal, and where had it gotten her? Here. As ever, she stood before her lord father like a wayward dog, awaiting a whipping and the next command. She squared her shoulders.

"I am ever loyal to House Fury."

Relief crossed his features. The tension in his muscles eased. That's what it had taken, her assurance that she still planned to fulfill her role. That she was alive and unharmed had done nothing for him.

Marcus sighed, a rare gesture. "By some miracle, Dante Viridian is still willing to have you despite the indignity you've called upon yourself."

Joselyn fought the urge to grimace. Like she'd been an adolescent girl, sneaking out her window at night. She bit her tongue.

"You cannot begin to comprehend what your indiscretion has cost our house. Placating Viridian has been absurdly expensive. Your dowry has doubled. Twice."

Joselyn raised a brow. She might have been marrying a prince for such a sum, not a backwater lord. How much suspicion had *that* raised?

Lord Fury continued. "The money wasn't half so troublesome as convincing Viridian that your disappearance wasn't some fancy trick. How do you think he responded when informed that the price for his silence had been carried off by a reclusive creature of the mountaintops?"

This conversation was getting tedious. She forced herself to go along. "I imagine he was most unaccommodating."

"Were it not for the peasant who spotted you whilst you traipsed about on the mountain, you might never have been recovered. House Fury would have suffered the consequences of your indiscretions."

Joselyn looked to the floor, an outward sign of submission. Inside she burned to remind her father that House Fury wouldn't be in this position were it not for *his* indiscretions.

"You will marry Dante Viridian the night after tomorrow."

Joselyn's gaze snapped up. "So soon? Here?"

Marcus scrutinized her as though he'd been ready for her reaction and was prepared to make something of it. Joselyn dug her nails into her own palms.

"Yes. It would be sooner if the priest were amenable to a ceremony outside of Soulday. The Viridians are anxious to receive payment for their end of the deal. And after the events of these past weeks, I'm inclined to oblige them."

"But... surely the other lords will whisper of scandal."

"Indeed." Marcus began to pace. "It's unavoidable."

"And Lord Arland? He has agreed to host a wedding?" The nearest keep was several days away in any direction.

"All the arrangements have been made. I regret that your wedding will not be a formal affair. Though it will be legal, and that shall be enough for you."

Joselyn might have scoffed were her mind not rising into a full state of panic. Her father hadn't even planned on attending her original wedding, a slight meant to insult her bridegroom. It wasn't the unorthodox nature of her nuptials that distressed her. It was the rapidly approaching date. It could be counted down by hours.

"Surely, this can be gone about another way. Father, think of my reputation." She poured every bit of feminine duress into her voice.

Marcus' whirled on her. "Your reputation is near irreparable as things stand. Be grateful, Daughter, that Viridian still desires an alliance more than he desires a virtuous bride."

How had her circumstances changed so much, so quickly? Hours ago, she'd been bathing in the afterglow of the best night she'd ever experienced. Like an impossible dream, the sunrise had woken her to the nightmare that was her true life. The tingling of pins flushed down Joselyn's arms. She shook her head once. "I nearly died on that mountain, Father."

Marcus Fury stiffened, and his face went momentarily blank. He looked startled, as though he'd never imagined she might try to tell him of what she'd been through.

"I tried to escape. My fear for our house drove me to take

risks. Ones I paid for. I nearly lost my life many times over." She paused, swallowing hard. "I would have done anything to uphold my duty to House Fury. To *you*."

Marcus regarded her. "And you think you're entitled to some thanks now, is that it?"

For the first time in years, Joselyn let slip her mask. Her father would see her raw, a creature of his own making. She tilted her head back, presenting him with a full view. "Did you ever love me, Father?"

A long moment passed. When he finally spoke, his voice was measured for effectiveness rather than sincerity. "I don't doubt your loyalty, Joselyn. It's because you are loyal that you will marry Viridian. It will serve my will and preserve our house."

Joselyn let her gaze float to the floor. That was it. The extent of his regard for her. She inhaled a deep breath and was surprised at how easily it came.

A flash of gold shimmered at the edge of her vision. She blinked back up. Lord Fury held out her pendant. It spun on the chain, reflecting the firelight.

"You've been an admirable daughter, Joselyn. Don't fail me now."

SHE WAS a guest in a stranger's home on the nigh-eve of her wedding to a madman. Bone weariness assailed her every step. She'd not slept since the night before last and now? Even her furs were too heavy.

A servant led Joselyn down the plush-rugged corridor to her chamber. As the young girl cracked open the door, Joselyn plowed through without waiting for a formal welcome. She needed the sanctuary of four walls. Solitude.

The servant girl began her explanation of the many amenities the room had to offer, but Joselyn waved her off. She couldn't care less if it was rude. Mercifully, the girl tripped over a curtsy and hurried out.

When the door clicked shut, Joselyn leaned into the wall. She pressed a hand to the cool stone and ran it downward. The bricks were rough beneath her fingertips. Not like at Bedmeg, where the walls of her *bok* were naturally smooth.

Hollen.

Tears filled her eyes.

Hollen.

Now, more than ever, she wanted to feel his arms around her, to hear him whisper the words she hadn't returned. *I love you.* Her lip trembled, and she slid to the floor.

Where was he? Where did he think *she* was? She'd sworn not to leave him. Would he know that something had happened to her? Would he think she'd tricked Sigvard into taking her home? Was Sigvard even alive?

It was too much. The tears spilled over. Joselyn reached for her *tanshi* mark. Her fingers bumped into her pendant, the symbol of her house, first. The chain hung like a collar around her neck. She choked on a whimper.

There was a pounding at the door. Joselyn jumped up. She swept her hands under her eyes, whisking away the tears. She was just opening her mouth to shoo away the visitor when a familiar voice called her name.

Joselyn leapt to the door and threw up the latch. Yanking it open, she saw the one face she'd missed most.

Tansy.

Her curly-haired nurse stared up at her, eyes puffy with emotion. Joselyn took one look at the old woman and practically fell into her arms. Tansy's warm body was round and soft, the definition of comfort.

"Oh child. I was so worried, I was! I thought you'd been taken forever. That I'd never see you again."

Joselyn's shoulders heaved on a sob and Tansy immediately pressed her backward into the chamber. The door latched behind them with an audible click.

With unexpected strength, Tansy pulled Joselyn off her shoulder and held her at arm's length. Joselyn's tears seemed to have inspired her nurse's. Now they were both crying. Tansy's plump face pinched with concern as she swept a gaze up and down Joselyn's body.

"Are you all right? You've not been harmed, have you?"

Joselyn realized her weeping was half of what had her nurse so terrified. Even Tansy was unaccustomed to witnessing such outbursts from her. Joselyn tried to swallow, but only succeeded in temporarily choking herself and heightening her nurse's anxiety. Tansy's eyes widened, and she dragged Joselyn to the velvety bed at the back of the room. They sat together as Joselyn struggled to compose herself.

"Now, now, hush child. It will be all right. You're safe." Tansy used both hands to brush Joselyn's hair back.

"Oh Tansy!"

"What's wrong, child? Tell me!"

Joselyn shook her head, lip quivering. "*Everything.*"

Tansy listened with a stroking hand as Joselyn lay in her lap and poured out the details of her captivity. All of them. From the terrifying day she was taken to the night just before. She'd slowed as she recounted the evening of passion she and Hollen had shared, but she didn't withhold the truth. Not from Tansy. She needed someone to understand, and her nurse was the only one who would try.

"Why did you want to return, my girl?"

Joselyn ceased crying with a start. She sat up from Tansy's lap to look her in the eye. "What do you mean?"

"I mean, why in the skies did you think to come back here? Knowing all you could have had elsewhere?"

How could she answer? Why was Tansy even asking? What did it matter what she could have in Bedmeg when her duty lay here? But then, Tansy didn't know what she knew. She didn't realize what would have happened to their people if she hadn't returned.

"Do you love him, child?" Tansy scrutinized her hard.

She wouldn't lie. Not to Tansy. She had spent enough time lying to herself.

"Yes. I love him."

Tansy humphed with no trace of surprise. "And you say he loves you."

Joselyn nodded.

The old nurse inclined her chin. "Then nothing else matters."

"I"—she swallowed hard—"I didn't mean to return."

"Good."

Joselyn shook her head. "How can you say that? You know that I am to marry Lord Viridian. Surely you . . . " She trailed off, uncertain how much to say. "You must have guessed how important this is."

"Important to who? Your father?" Tansy scowled.

"My father, House Fury, our people. You and Horace."

A look of pain crossed Tansy's face. Joselyn saw it then. The grief. Much like her father, her nurse had aged in the time since Joselyn had disappeared. The effect was far more devastating on Tansy.

"Tansy?" Fear saturated her voice.

"Horace passed two weeks after your disappearance, child."

Joselyn's throat went dry even as a bevy of fresh tears began to rise. "Dead?"

Tansy nodded. "It was a long time coming."

"Oh, Tansy, I'm so sorry!" Joselyn cried, forgetting her own troubles. She covered her nurse's withered hands with her own. Misery ripped through her chest on behalf of her nurse.

Tansy nodded, but no tears fell. It was as though her husband's passing were a distant grief, one she didn't intend to carry with her much longer. Something about it made Joselyn's heart speed up. She squeezed her nurse's hand.

"You'll stay with me, then. Allow me to ensure your remaining years are lived out in comfort."

"I'll see him again, child. That's the only comfort I need. That, and the assurance of your safety and happiness. You must not marry that creature."

Joselyn stared at her nurse. "You cannot mean it. Would you have me abandon my duty?"

Darkness like a thundercloud filled Tansy's usually kind eyes. "I would have you live. And live life fully. Not to slip out from under the boot of one man who would use you only to fall beneath the next."

Joselyn's lips parted. Her nurse had never spoken so plainly her opinion of Marcus Fury. Joselyn had never allowed it. But with the pain in her nurse's eyes came a new energy, a determination of sorts. Joselyn blinked, amazed.

"You're only thinking of me. But what will happen to our people if my father is removed? Who will stand in his place? Morhagen is falling apart. Lord Fury is the only one keeping our lands from unraveling."

Tansy cocked her head, and her lips pulled into a sad smile. "Oh child, you're so young." She brushed a lock of hair over Joselyn's ear. "So sweetly naive."

Despite her overwhelming misery, Joselyn still managed to bristle at the hint of benign contempt in her nurse's expression. She frowned. "What do you mean?"

Tansy squeezed one of her hands. "You're loyal and fierce as the day is long, my girl. And no one ever dared speak plainly in front of you, especially not about your father."

Joselyn searched Tansy's eyes. For some reason, Joselyn held her breath.

"Your father isn't the grand leader you think he is. He's not a bad lord, but this image you've crafted in your mind is just that. A fancy idea."

"But, I've poured over our account books. I know how well-fed our people are. What of House Brandor? And Myron, and a dozen others? Their serfs decay with hunger."

Tansy nodded like she was trying to ease Joselyn into a bitter understanding. "Yes. But that's circumstance, child, not your father's leadership. The plague those years ago barely touched our lands, and we've not suffered drought as much as others. Of course your father claimed ownership of those fortunes. And of course you believed it. You've always clung to what little good you could find in his black soul."

Could this be true? Had she gone her whole life not realizing her firmly held beliefs were little more than her father's own propaganda? Joselyn shook her head as her mind tried to put the possibility into perspective. What did this mean?

"Are you saying any man could run our lands as my father does?"

Tansy didn't answer, only pinned her with a contemptuous gaze. Joselyn's cheeks burned.

"But, what of House Fury? What of duty?"

"When last I checked, Marcus Fury was Lord of Tirvine, not you, Joselyn. Whatever evil your father is hoping to dodge by marrying you to a monster, me thinks it's his burden to bear."

Shame sunk low in her belly even as a great burden lifted from her shoulders. Tansy was a peasant, uneducated, and led by her heart more than her mind. But she was also wise from the gut and her very soul was gilded in platinum. Her nurse was holding nothing back, and Joselyn would be a fool to ignore her.

"As for duty, don't you have a duty to the man you love? What of your heart, child? Would you bind yourself to another? Body and spirit? Even knowing that what you give belongs to someone else?"

Joselyn began to look away, but Tansy stopped her with a soft hand on either cheek.

"I know you didn't ask for this, child. None of us ask for our fates. But the gods dole them out all the same. Perhaps you should consider the possibility that Joselyn Helena Elise Fury is destined to be more than a pawn on the gameboard of lords."

Joselyn's brow furrowed even as her lips thinned. She wanted to believe what her nurse was saying, wanted to live it. But there was so much at stake. Her duties aside, she was now a relative prisoner of her father, locked in a pretty cage.

"Tansy," Joselyn's voice quaked with the fragile hope swirling in her chest, "I'm to be married the night after next. And my . . .Hollen, he has no idea where to find me. Nor have I any idea how to return to him."

Tansy released Joselyn's face only to clasp her by the hand. She smiled then, as though every obstacle had already been removed. And, perhaps, the only one that really mattered already had.

"Faith, child."

36

KEPT VOWS

The previous night's clouds had made it difficult for Hollen to scout ahead. Even so, he knew retrieving his bride would be no simple feat. She was guarded by hundreds of armed and trained soldiers. Perhaps worse, she'd been confined to the inner walls of a castle, her exact location a mystery. That was his first obstacle.

Hollen had waited the remainder of the night and several hours into the morning for an opportunity. He'd shed his armor and furs for the inconspicuous wool garments beneath them. Winter had come early to the lowlands, but he wasn't cold. Not here in this soft world. He'd torn the bones from his hair and covered his scars. With luck, he'd look like an overly large vagrant in search of work.

The village streets bustled with movement. Hundreds of people were here, more than Hollen had ever seen in one place. Everything smelled strange. Things that seemed fantastic to him, like great iron carts being wheeled through the square, elicited no response from others. He swallowed and remembered to keep his eyes down. He had to blend in for now.

Finally, the castle guard exchanged shifts with the daytime

patrol. Those who'd stood watch through the night took their leisure in the village surrounding the castle. Hollen had spent the morning occupying himself with whatever menial tasks he could convince someone to pay him for. He was helping a lumberjack unload his wagon when Hollen's opportunity walked by.

Two pairs of laughing guards and a silent, solitary one were making their way for the nearby tavern. Hollen insisted on half his pay before hurrying in the direction of the alehouse. The solitary guard, short and thin, looked despondent. Perfect.

"Friend, have you no one to drink with?" Hollen was suddenly very aware of his guttural accent. He tamed it as best he could, but there was only so much to be done. At least no one outside Bedmeg would be able to place its origin.

The young soldier stopped and looked around, as though he were surprised to be addressed. Hollen met his eyes and smiled. The guard looked him up and down. At least there was no disdain on his face.

"How could you tell?" the man asked, gesturing to the pair of men walking on ahead of him.

Hollen shrugged. "You look how I feel. Come, let's keep each other company."

The man pursed his lips. "Aye. Though one drink is all I'll be having on a guard's wages."

"A lumberjack earns just enough to buy for a friend."

The soldier regarded Hollen with an hint of surprise that morphed into delight. Hollen clapped a hand over his shoulder and led him into the alehouse.

Hollen had to steady his new "friend," Harris, by the time they left. It had become increasingly difficult for Hollen to play the charming companion once Harris began relaying the details of Lady Fury's recapture. *And* impending marriage. Hollen hadn't even needed to raise the subject. It seemed nothing was more interesting to the townsfolk here.

"Stay with me, today, Harris. I'm renting a room from an old widow that's bound to be warmer than whatever barn they have you lot holed up in." They stepped into the street and blinked against the midday sun.

Harris grimaced. "Tents! They put us in tents. Bloody things don't even keep you dry when it starts to rain. I never thought I'd miss the swiving barracks."

Harris staggered hard, and Hollen had to grab him to keep him from falling. Hollen didn't look forward to getting this pitiful man alone and making him answer questions. He'd try for the easy way first. Glancing back, he nodded at the castle.

"Where do they keep a noble woman in a place like that? The lower level? Can't imagine ladies are keen to climb stairs with their tiny little feet."

Harris snorted. "You'd think so. But no, only the best for the fancy folk. Including the views. Gotta stay up high where they can look down on us common-folk like the ants we are."

Harris swung an arm back toward Castle Arland and pointed at the third highest tower. "There. That's where they be keeping the fiery wench."

Hollen raised a brow. That was easy. He'd anticipated having to lure Harris into a secluded area and use an aggressive brand of persuasion to get answers. His heart leapt at his good fortune. Not only did he know exactly where to find Joselyn, but she was held in a room with an exterior window. His mind was already working out how he would extract her when Harris stumbled to his knees.

Hollen pulled him to his feet. "I've had too much to drink, my friend." It was a lie of course. Hollen had barely touched his drink, focusing instead on keeping Harris' full. "I forgot that the old woman said no guests were permitted. She probably meant whores, but..."

"Eh!" Harris half shouted, tearing his arm out of Hollen's hand in mock outrage. "You should be so lucky to afford me!"

Hollen forced a laugh, ignoring every instinct to take off running toward Joselyn. There was nothing he could do for the time being anyway. "I'll be out cutting trees the next two days. If you're still here when I return, meet me back at the alehouse? Good company is hard to come by."

In truth, Harris was terrible company. The man did little more than grumble about every detail of his miserable life. But he smiled broadly at Hollen's suggestion and vowed to do exactly that before stumbling his way back toward the temporary encampment for House Fury's men.

Hollen watched him go, then strolled out of town. He and Jagomri would have to wait for their opportunity. When he reached the woods, his mount's hiding place, Hollen regarded the obsidian wyvern with a flash of determined hope.

"We found her."

THE PREPARATIONS HAD BEEN MADE. Joselyn was ready. She sat on the bed across from a silver-polished looking glass, pointedly avoiding her reflection. She swept her braid over the front of her shoulder. Waning sunlight filtered in through the window and made her hair glow as though it were truly made of fire. She was warmly dressed, clad in finely woven wool that reflected the rapidly approaching winter.

Who had she become? In a handful of weeks, she'd gone from Lady Fury, dutiful daughter of Marcus Fury, to what?

I am the Saliga of Bedmeg. I am the Saliga of Bedmeg.

She closed her eyes and repeated the internal affirmation. Perhaps if she thought it often enough, her actions would make more sense. This was it. After tonight, she'd prove her parents right. Justified or not, Joselyn was always destined to choose herself over House Fury.

The impulse to look into the mirror tempted her.

There was a knock at the door, and Joselyn called her nurse in, turning to face her as she entered.

"Are you ready child?"

Joselyn inhaled and relaxed her shoulders as she breathed out. "All went well?"

Tansy grabbed her by the hand and gave her a gentle squeeze. "Yes, child. I've sent word to my nephew in Wind Slope. He'll be waiting for you. Now, we just need to get you to the stables. I paid off one of the boys with your broach."

Joselyn smiled at her nurse. Tansy was a force to be reckoned with. Joselyn had always known it, but had never experienced the extent of her deviousness until now. That she would risk all to see her charge to happiness was a testament of love. Joselyn's heart swelled.

"Tansy, if your role in this is discovered, I—"

"Hush." She was already turning to the door, pulling Joselyn with her. "It won't happen. And if it does, what can they take from an old, childless widow?"

Joselyn planted her feet and tugged on her nurse's arm. "Your life."

A bitter smile caused her plump cheeks to dimple. "My life has been lived, child." She ran a hand down the length of Joselyn's braid. "And it's been a full one. Don't fear for me. All will be well."

Embracing her, Joselyn attempted to return some measure of the love Tansy had always given. Joselyn realized then that, thanks to Tansy, she'd not been a true pauper for affection nor regard. Despite whatever her parents had denied her. And now? She would return to the man who had made her richer than any queen.

"I love you, Tansy." She breathed in the scent of tallow and buttermilk.

The old woman returned the embrace, her fierceness tempered by the softness of her plump body. "And I, you, child. More than anything."

They were still a moment before Tansy broke the hug. "Come now, let us be away, before our man in the stables loses his nerve."

Directed by Tansy, Joselyn made her way to the grand foyer. Joselyn wouldn't have ventured out of her room for any other reason. She was too afraid she might run into her intended groom. She had yet to meet the man. If all went well tonight, she never would.

A pretty, young lady's maid from Fury Keep approached, along with a pair of guards. They stopped before Joselyn as Tansy helped her shrug into a heavy cloak.

"My lady," The first guard asked, scrutinizing her, "you intend to leave the castle?"

"Hardly. I wish to visit my white. My nurse tells me he was recovered after I was taken."

Tansy nodded with nauseating enthusiasm, "Indeed, milady! He's just outside in the stables. Old Tansy's been looking after him for you in your absence, sneaking him apples and oats. He'll stomp the gate down when he sees you, he will!"

A corner of Joselyn's mouth flicked up at Tansy's performance. Few things were harder for men to manage than excited women.

"Indeed," Joselyn returned, ignoring the perturbed expressions on the guard's faces. "Let us go now, while I'm still an unmarried woman. The stablemaster tells me his breed is partial to maidens."

The lady's maid rushed to collect her own cloak while the two guards frowned at one another. The older of the two men spoke first.

"Milady, I think—"

But Joselyn was already walking away. "Come along, then. I'll not set foot outside without an escort! Not after all that's happened."

From the corner of her eye, Joselyn caught Tansy's smile as the guards followed, their heads bowed in resignation. It didn't take long for the maid to catch up. A pang of sadness stabbed at Joselyn's heart for what would come next.

Joselyn turned to Tansy and put a hand on her nurse's shoulder. "Surely you wish to remain, Tansy. The air outside is frigid. I have a maid for propriety."

Tansy made a show of her disappointment, but then muttered something about old lungs before giving Joselyn's hand a parting squeeze. Of anything she might regret about her decision, leaving Tansy behind would be the greatest.

There was no choice. Hollen had explained that women were forbidden from the upper reaches of the mountain unless claimed by a *Na Dokiri*. Her *tanshi* mark ensured her own acceptability in the eyes of their gods. Tansy would never be permitted at Bedmeg. All of that aside, Tansy had scoffed at the idea of leaving Morhagen.

"I'm an old woman, and old women don't live on mountain tops." She'd said, as though it were the most obvious thing in the world.

As her nurse walked away, Joselyn resisted the urge to clutch at her arm. If all went according to plan, this would be the last time she saw Tansy. Joselyn forced herself to turn toward the door, reminding herself that they'd said their true farewells in her chamber. Now was the time for action.

Steeling herself, Joselyn linked arms with the young maid and strode out the massive wooden doors that were opened for her as she passed. Two more guards joined them.

The winter air swirled with a smattering of dry snowflakes. Torches lit the courtyard and led a path to the stables and other outbuildings. The smell of straw and manure drew Joselyn forward.

"Surely your steed must be a marvel, indeed, to coax you out in this weather, milady." The maid said, her tone not at all approving.

Joselyn ignored her and strode forward as though to sanctuary. The handsome stablemaster bowed low as she stepped over the threshold. Yellow lanterns illuminated the inside of the wooden structure, and the flesh on Joselyn's hands and face warmed. Now, for the difficult part. She turned toward her guards.

"You men will remain."

"I beg your pardon, milady, but I insist we attend you," the oldest of the guards said.

Instead of arguing, Joselyn turned to the stablemaster. "You there, tell my guards that their presence will agitate the horses."

The stablemaster was a surprisingly young man, perhaps twenty-five years. Joselyn's maid seemed keenly aware of his dark hair and pleasing physique. She stifled a giggle at his look of nervousness to be addressed by the Lady of House Fury. The stablemaster flicked an uncertain glance at the imposing men behind her.

"As milady says, fewer men are better," the young man stuttered.

Joselyn smiled brightly. "An honest man. And obliging too." She shot her guards a disapproving glare. "How gratifying."

The stablemaster managed a wobbly smile. Joselyn threw a dismissal over her shoulder. "If you wish to guard me, secure the entrances. I'll not have you upsetting my white."

Joselyn walked away with the confidence of a woman who fully expected to be obeyed. It was an easy thing. She was Lady Fury after all. Still, she sent a hasty prayer up to the gods as she went.

The guards didn't follow. One less obstacle. One step closer to Hollen. The dry straw crunched beneath her boots as she stepped under cover of the roof. The stablemaster led her and the maid down one of the many narrow rows of individual pens where the pampered steeds nickered from their stalls.

Joselyn pretended to appreciate their superb beauty and breeding, nodding in acknowledgement at the many enthusiastic compliments the young man paid House Fury's own stablemaster. Her lack of interest was easy to hide amidst her maid's bubbling chatter. Apparently the girl had developed an intense appreciation for horses in the time it had taken her to cross the courtyard. Joselyn spotted Morningstar's flickering ears over the glossy wooden gate that housed him.

"Here he is, milady. A fine animal. He's hardy. But he's retained all the grace his breed is known for."

Joselyn nodded and reached a hand to stroke Morningstar's soft muzzle. The horse's warm lips nibbled at the flat of her palm, searching for treats. Joselyn's lips curled.

"Hello, boy."

"Tell me!" The maid clutched the stablemaster's arm, startling him. "Which horse in this stable is the finest?"

"I . . . well, that would be Lord Fury's white. Never seen a more highly bred creature this far from the capital."

"Indeed! Oh, do you know that I've never had a good look at the master's horse? Of course, a girl silly as me wouldn't know what to look at first. I'll bet you could point out all the finest details."

Pressing her face into her mount's forehead, Joselyn covered her smile. Her chaperone was proving to be a most helpful ally, if unwitting. She turned to them. "The man speaks truly. There is no finer mount than my father's white. Go and see for yourself."

Silence ensured. "Milady? Shall you attend us?"

Joselyn shook her head. "I desire a moment alone with my mount."

The stablemaster spoke. "Surely you'll want to retain an escort."

Joselyn went back to casually stroking her horse. "Have no fear, young man. The entrances are guarded."

More silence. Joselyn turned abruptly to the stablemaster. "Or should a few moments alone make me fear for my maid's virtue?"

The man's face paled and he shook his head hard enough to make his brain rattle. He seemed all too relieved when Joselyn's giggling maid took him by the hand and urged him to lead the way.

Joselyn looked up and down the straw-covered aisle. A sense of urgency took over her body, and she had to force herself to breathe steadily. Tansy had bribed a stable boy, but Joselyn had no idea which one. The boy would find her at the opportune moment. Now was the time for faith.

A minute passed.

Three more.

Despite the coolness of the stable, Joselyn started to sweat. Where was her man? Had he double crossed her? Been found out, gods forbid?

All manner of dire possibilities were cycling through her mind when a brown head of hair moved at the back end of the stable. She looked up. A boy, no more than thirteen, watched her with purposeful green eyes. Joselyn inhaled and nodded once. The boy nodded back. Joselyn looked around. The maid and stablemaster were still gone. Joselyn released Morningstar and went to the stable boy.

"Milady," the boy said, with more courage in his voice than Joselyn felt, "Fancy a look at the stars?"

Joselyn nodded. She followed the boy through the stable, somehow avoiding all other workers. Perhaps that was by design. They shuffled into a dark corner near a supply entrance. The boy turned back and held a silencing finger to his lips. Joselyn nodded in understanding. There were guards about. Possibly, just outside the latched gate.

The next vital task: slip out of the stables without being caught. The boy pulled back the leather tarp that covered the bed of the wagon. Joselyn's hand flew over her face. The cart was filled with chilly manure. The stink was enough to put down an elephant. The boy twisted up his face in an expression that was half mocking, half anxious.

"If you can't stand the smell now, you'll never make it out the village. You still want to go through with this, lady?"

Joselyn squared her shoulders and dropped her hand to her side. Her mouth hardened into a determined line. This did not even approach the limit of what Joselyn was willing to do to escape this place and get back to Hollen. No one would think to search a dung cart for Lady Fury. It was an abysmally small price to pay for her freedom.

The boy regarded her with an impish grin that reminded her of Sigvard. "Right, then, time to swallow the shite." He jumped up into the back of the cart.

Joselyn frowned at the indelicate idiom, but stepped toward the cart. This was it. She was almost there. Joselyn reached for the boy's open hand.

She froze.

Shouts rose up from outside the stable. Dozens of them. More terrifying was the pounding of soldiers' boots on hard stone. Horror whipped through Joselyn like a flash of lightning.

The boy's head perked up in alarm. Their wide gazes met. Feminine screams joined the pandemonium before a heartbeat of total silence. The doors at the front of the stable burst open. Joselyn whirled just as a snarling roar blasted from outside. Guards came pouring into the stable, their eyes frantically searching.

Behind her, the stable boy hopped off the back edge of the cart and disappeared. Joselyn didn't care. She was running. Running toward the sound that could only mean one thing.

Hollen.

He'd come for her.

Ahead, Joselyn sensed more than saw the wall of guards rushing toward her from the opposite end of the aisle. In the last moment, she tried to dodge them. One of them seized her against his armored body. Her breath left her in a scream.

She demanded to be released. The cacophony of panicked horses and shouting guards drowned out her voice. Joselyn was pushed to the packed-dirt floor of the stable. A guard practically straddled her hunched figure. In the time it took to blink, guards filled in the space behind her, circling around from the other end of the aisle.

Joselyn continued to struggle, to issue demands, to do anything that would get her out of this stable and into Hollen's reach. It was useless. She couldn't move.

Minutes seemed like hours until she was finally allowed to rise. More like yanked from the dusty ground. She tried to speak, but was silenced by a guard who clutched her arm like his own was a vice. Dragged to the front of the stable, Joselyn jumped when a dome of clanging shields was raised above her head and all around her sides.

Joselyn tripped over the feet of the shield-bearing men. They were so close she could smell the gruel they'd just been eating. The men ushered her out of the stable and through the cobbled courtyard.

Joselyn was desperate to break out of the mobile prison, to see what was going on. He'd come for her. She *knew* it. She had to see it. To see *him*.

"Hollen!" She cried, her voice turned up to the shield-blocked sky.

An arm encircled her chest and slid roughly over her mouth. "Quiet, milady!"

The smell of leather and unwashed man gagged her. Joselyn struggled as a guard dragged her the rest of the way toward the castle entrance.

When they stepped onto marble-carved floors, the mobile fortress broke off all around her. Joselyn threw the assailing guard's arm off her face and spun just as the deep creak of the entry doors began droning.

There, in the courtyard, lying motionless on the icy ground, was her savage.

37

MARK OF THE CAPTIVE

If Joselyn had first entered Castle Arland feeling like a war prize, she now felt a condemned criminal. Huge, armed guards flanked her on either side. Each had a meaty hand on her shoulder. They pushed her up the massive staircase of the grand foyer. Normally she might have reprimanded them for their outrageous handling of a noblewoman, but all she could think of was Hollen.

He'd come for her. Just as he'd promised. And it would likely cost him his life. Unless Joselyn could change it.

Lord Arland, a short, balding man, stood at the inner balcony, surrounded by his bodyguards. He directed the commotion in his household with all the finesse of a child attempting to herd frightened cats. He contrasted steeply with the cold, still figure standing just behind him. Lord Fury.

Her father's gaze landed upon her. At that look, her stomach felt like a shattering ball of ice. Indignation saved her from flinching. She met his gaze full on, chin raised. The captain of House Fury's guard brought Joselyn to her father.

"We have her, milord. She's safe."

"The rider?" Marcus growled.

"Apprehended."

Marcus' eyes didn't leave Joselyn. "Take her to my chamber. Secure the castle."

Joselyn knew better than to speak just now. She needed a moment alone with her father. For better or for worse, she was about to get exactly that. She was shoved into the empty room. The doors slammed behind her before she could turn.

Joselyn flew across the room and pressed her hands against the windowpane. Though it faced the courtyard, it was too dark, and she was too high up to see what was going on below. All she could make out were the scurrying shapes of men on the ground. Her gaze searched frantically for Hollen. The whine of the door pulled her mind back into the room.

Her father strode in, scarlet robes swaying behind him. As the door swung closed, Joselyn pushed off the windowsill and walked toward him.

"Father, please!"

Marcus' spine went straight as a sword. His eyes flashed with warning. "You called that barbarian here?"

Joselyn stopped in her tracks. "No. Of course not." She'd never have called Hollen here. "How could I, Father?"

Marcus' furious eyes searched hers. Despite her pulsing fear for Hollen, Joselyn shrunk a bit. She was unaccustomed to seeing so much emotion on her father's face. He bared his teeth.

"And yet he's come for you. Rode his foul beast to the roof. Made his way to your window. Gods know how he knew where to look."

Joselyn didn't have to fake her confusion. It was genuine and wild. Marcus must have sensed it, because his accusatory tone shifted to conspiracy.

"We've been inordinately fortunate. He's the one who took you, no?"

Stuttering, Joselyn wondered how to answer. Would she seal

his fate to speak truly? Would she condemn him if her father sensed she was lying? In the end, she didn't need to speak. Marcus nodded. Her hesitation was confirmation enough.

"Good. His presence here proves the truth of your ordeal. We can expect no further suspicion from House Viridian once he's been executed."

Joselyn's vision narrowed. Trying not to sway, she pressed a hand to her stomach. "Father, you can't."

"Can't I?" Marcus cocked his head, his voice full of challenge.

Joselyn scrambled to form an argument. "There must be a trial. What of the proper channels?"

Marcus scoffed. "As if the king's justice could be extended to savages."

Joselyn shook her head and did her best to still her trembling knees. "Justice applies to all. That's what makes it just."

Marcus' expression darkened. "You would defend your captor? Or is he your lover, after all?"

Joselyn's limbs went numb as a sense of impending disaster overtook her. "Father, I beg of you. Have mercy. Spare his life."

The distance between them evaporated. He floated toward her like a vengeful specter. Joselyn tilted her pleading face back and made no attempt to hide her desperation.

"No."

No.

Eighteen years, and *still* it was the only word her father had for her. The old bitterness reared to life with frightening vigor. This time, however, instead of tearing at *her* insides, Joselyn turned the demon outward. Wielding it.

She took an abrupt step backward. "You *will* spare his life. You will spare him, or I swear on the gods I will refuse to marry Dante Viridian."

Marcus drew back, aghast. Never had she defied her father. Not once. And now she was giving him an ultimatum of the direst variety. Surely he was wondering what had happened to his daughter on that mountain.

I outgrew you.

When he'd recovered, Lord Fury's face went neutral. "You will marry Dante Viridian tomorrow. If I have to order you bound, you *will* appear before the marriage altar."

Joselyn shook her head. "No. I think not."

Without giving him a chance to respond, Joselyn's hands went to her broach. Unpinning it, she let the heavy cloak fall to the ground in a pile behind her. Whatever Marcus had been about to say, he held his tongue, too confused to speak.

Joselyn let fear and anger fuel her boldness as she reached for the neckline of her bodice. She gave it a tug until her *tanshi* mark was on glaring display.

Her father's eyes fixed on the darkened ridges of the intricate carving.

Joselyn flashed a scornful smile. "No legitimate priest would marry a sullied noblewoman. Not for all the gold in Ebron."

His gaze came up to meet Joselyn's. Hatred. His eyes blazed with it.

"So," he said. Every muscle in his body went still. "My daughter is a slut *and* a heathen."

A month ago, she would have been crushed by those words. Not anymore. Now she knew who she was, and his vitriol only fueled her daring. She narrowed her eyes in defiance.

Marcus glared back. "*One* of those can be rectified."

A shimmer of uncertainty made her release her dress. The neckline popped back over her chest. Marcus turned only his head to shout for the guards. The doors cracked open.

"Two men. Now," he ordered.

He looked back at her. "Breathe one word to them or anyone else, and that nurse of yours will serve my hounds their breakfast."

The blood drained out of her face and pooled into her feet. The guards appeared in an instant. They hovered near the door as if they sensed the maelstrom of tension hanging in the air and were reluctant to come close. Marcus turned toward them. "You are sworn to silence."

They nodded their understanding without hesitation.

"Bring her to the hearth."

Joselyn stepped back in alarm as the men approached. She made it all of two steps before their large hands were upon her. She tried to bat them away, but they had their order. They would carry it out, no matter what it was. That truth went screaming into the front of her mind as they tugged her toward the large hearth alight with flame.

The guards turned her so her back was to the heat and faced her father, who crossed the room to retrieve a jewel-encrusted knife. The weapon was meant for show rather than any practical purpose. Still, the filed steel glinted in the light. Instinctively, Joselyn began to struggle.

On either side, the guard's grip tightened. Joselyn thought she could see trepidation in her assailant's eyes. Confusion, certainly. But there was no yielding in their wary glances.

Marcus stopped inches away, bringing the knife up between them. Joselyn's gaze widened with horror when he brought the shining tip to her neckline.

"Look away, you idiots," Marcus barked at the men holding her. "She's a lady, not one of your village whores."

The men jumped to obey, turning their entire faces out to either side. Despite the blade's showiness, it made short work of the delicate material encasing Joselyn's panting ribcage. Tears of shock ran down her cheeks.

"Father?" she gasped, unable to make sense of what was happening. Lord Fury's cold gray eyes met hers.

"In all your life, you'd never made a fool of yourself." He

frowned as though with genuine disappointment. "Tonight you've made fools of us both."

Joselyn's heart pounded against her naked chest. She could hear its frantic beating in her ears as her father chucked the knife aside and turned toward the fire. From it, he pulled a glowing red iron.

The guard's hold on her tightened so severely she might have heard her own bones cracking, were it not for the sound of her screams.

Joselyn's chest blazed with pain. Still, the searing ache above her skin wasn't half so potent as the agony beating just beneath it. The man who'd been her father branded her. Her *tanshi* mark was gone. Replaced instead with a searing, scarlet burn.

She'd been locked in a new chamber. One without windows. It was impossible to know the precise hour, but she guessed it was sometime in the early morning. The night before, her wounds had been tended by a wrinkled old chambermaid. She'd pinned Joselyn with questions. When it was clear no answer was forthcoming, the maid resorted to offering long, pitying glances. That had been the extent of Joselyn's comfort. When finished, she'd been left completely alone.

The solace of sleep evaded her.

Where was Hollen? Was he alive? In pain? Afraid?

Joselyn had seen Hollen afraid once. The day he took her hunting, and she'd nearly been destroyed by the blood-seeker. He'd been afraid then. Now, she fully understood what it was to be afraid for someone else. He was here because of *her*. Because of her foolishness. Because of his duty to her.

Sitting on the bed, Joselyn scoffed through her silent tears.

What had duty accomplished for either of them? Her love

awaited a death sentence and she was hours away from marrying a monster. A new, bitter conviction rose up. Hollen had been right all along. Duty to the unworthy was no strength at all.

The door's iron lock scraped from the outside. Stiffening, Joselyn wiped at her face and called up a steel wall of composure for whatever she was about to endure.

A guard crowded the opening of the doorway before stepping aside, revealing Lord Fury. Joselyn's hands bunched up the bed's coverlet. She stared him down. It was possible he'd not slept either. Beneath his robes he wore the same clothing as the night prior. His red-streaked hair, while not wild, was unkempt. He entered the room, his gait proud and steady despite the fatigue that hung around him.

"Daughter," he said when the door had shut behind him.

Joselyn blinked.

Silence.

Lord Fury regarded her. His gaze dipped down to her bound chest before jumping back up. "I've come seeking your forgiveness."

Joselyn would have fallen over at those words had she not already been sitting. Forgiveness? Lord Marcus Fury? Regretful? Never.

"I acted rashly," he said.

You acted as the beast you are. That you'll always be.

"Surely a woman as sensible as you can understand why. What with so much at stake, and the rampant chaos last night."

Joselyn had to force her head to stop shaking. That he would try to justify his actions brought on a fresh wave of incredulous rage.

Lord Fury went on. "All we must do now is decide how we will proceed."

"Proceed?" Joselyn's mouth stretched into a miserable smirk.

Darkness eclipsed Lord Fury's expression. "Yes, Daughter. You're to be wed at sunset. Or have you completely forsaken your duty?"

Joselyn went to her feet and laughed, a dark, sharp sound. "*My* duty? What of *your* duty, Lord Fury? What of your oaths of fealty sworn to our king? What of your vows to forsake all interests to protect and prosper the lands of Tirvine?"

As Joselyn stepped forward, the man who had been her father seemed to rise in height. It was no matter. After last night, there was little he could do to frighten her.

"What of your duty to *me*?" she asked, stopping when she could feel the heat of his body. "What of your duty to your only child?"

Lord Fury stared down at her. His eyes took on the cool calculation years of use had made natural on him. "You believe I don't care for you."

Joselyn's gaze could have frozen him solid. "You care for no one."

He arched a brow. "Oh? And do you mean to throw your loyalty away along with your virtue?"

Loyalty was an illusion to Lord Fury, a fine trick he performed to suit his own ends. At last, she'd seen the sleight of hand. Joselyn reached up and ripped the clasp of her pendant's chain. Like a candle in the rain, she let the flame of her hatred snuff out. There was a reason Lord Fury had always been the victor. Her spite had never mattered to him. Instead, it had been one more means with which she'd let him control her.

Never again.

All her life, her need to prove him wrong had been a chain around her neck. With empty eyes, she dropped the pendant at his feet. Let the charlatan have his gold.

Lord Fury stared at the pendant. Slowly, he looked back up. His eyes flashed steel. "Indeed."

The drums of war echoed in that one word. The hairs at the nape of Joselyn's neck prickled.

"Then there's only one more matter between us." He straightened. "I'm prepared to spare your lover's life."

Joselyn's lips parted. Her hand flew instinctively to her chest, to the place where her *tanshi* mark had been. Pain made her wince even through the bandages.

Joselyn didn't miss the spark of triumph that flickered across Lord Fury's face, and she didn't care. If there was any chance he was speaking truly, she must do everything in her power to make it so.

"You will free him?"

"Life, Daughter. What I'm offering is *life*. Your filthy savage will never fly again."

Joselyn's hope broke apart in uncertainty. "What will become of him?"

"Imprisonment. Indefinitely."

Joselyn's mind scoured the possibilities. A life in prison was no life at all for Hollen. But given enough time, who knew what was possible? She could petition the king, bribe a guard, and who could say what else?

Lord Fury seemed to watch her run through the myriad of scenarios. A corner of his mouth curled upward. No doubt, he'd considered each of them himself and knew they'd give her hope. For Marcus Fury, hope was a double-edged sword, and he wielded it masterfully.

"And the price for your *mercy*?" Joselyn already knew the answer.

"Your oath. You will marry Dante Viridian, and keep to him."

The weight of Hollen's life slumped over her narrow shoulders. The burden was enough to crush her. And yet, bearing up under it, Joselyn only felt relief. Her spine straightened.

"Is that all?" she asked.

"It's more than you deserve. Remember what I taught you, Daughter. This world owes you nothing."

"No. But *you* did."

The man who'd been her father had cheated her. And now, Joselyn must cheat herself.

"I swear it."

38

THE BUTCHER OF BRANCE

Joselyn sat upon the white linens of the turned down bed. Waiting.

Dressed in a fine, gossamer gown, she might as well have been naked. She was almost grateful for the bandages which covered her burn and bound her breasts. Fallen into a hearth. Fainted from exhaustion upon her recent rescue. That was what she was to tell her new husband when he asked about her wound. The thought of Dante Viridian becoming intimate enough to make such an inquiry sickened her.

The small horde of candles flickering in the chamber gave the richly designed room a nauseating effect. Joselyn's eyes searched along the tapestry-covered walls for a chamber pot, or anything else that might hold the limited contents of her choppy stomach. They grazed over the small pile of artfully wrapped gifts that were meant to enhance the wedding night. Negligee, most likely. She grimaced.

The metallic groan of the door's iron hinges drew Joselyn's immediate and complete attention. She straightened, sucking in a breath. Too fast.

Steady Joselyn. Breathe. Just breathe.

No longer a maiden, Joselyn had something just as precious to lose. After tonight, gods help her, her body would no longer belong to *only* Hollen. Never again. Yet another price she must pay.

With thudding footfalls, Dante Viridian entered the room. Joselyn looked up at the man she'd married just hours ago. Like the other Viridians, Dante was tall and thin. He had sharp cheekbones and an aquiline nose. His long hair shined black as a scavenging raven. His skin was pale, more so than even hers. He didn't look fragile, though. The eerie nature of his chilling expression saved him from that.

His dark robes swayed behind him as he moved. Stopping several feet across the room, he drove his green eyes hard into her. He tsked. "No, no. This is all wrong."

Joselyn inclined her chin, wary.

"They should have brought you to me." He looked around the elegantly furnished chamber. "Though indeed, our host seems to have given you the preferential accommodations. Do you know much of livestock?"

She blinked.

Dante tilted his head to the side and went on, stepping closer as he did. "Doubtful. House Fury has long since risen above such things. No matter, I'll share with you something I've learned over the years."

Joselyn bristled as he closed the remaining distance between them. He moved just before her knees and stared down at her.

"When rabbits are bred—"

Ice spread through her veins at the word *bred*. She sensed that whatever comparison he was about to make, she would not care for it. Not in the least.

"—they put the doe into the *buck's* hutch."

He reached down, took her folded hands, and drew her up. Joselyn stood smoothly, holding his gaze. She fought the urge to pull away when he didn't release her. His hands were soft, narrow, and cold as winter stone.

"Do you know why?"

"No." Her eyes remained willfully dull.

"Because"—he quieted a moment. The man seemed to delight in long pauses between his points, as though the suspense might provoke his audience to cheer for the next word—"the reverse makes the female feel threatened. Enough to turn on the buck. Kill him outright...or die trying."

Dante gave her hands a gentle squeeze and leaned down until his face was but inches from hers.

"Do you feel threatened?" His breath was cool on her face and hinted of sour wine.

Joselyn held his gaze and kept her voice even as she lied. "No."

An easy smile crossed his face. "Shall we take a walk?"

She blinked, cocking her head. "Now?"

His black brows rose. "Indeed."

Joselyn glanced awkwardly down at her nightgown as if to say *you can't be serious*.

Dante snickered. "Surely our host has provided you with a robe?"

When Joselyn didn't immediately respond, Dante lifted his hands to either side of her face and swept up thick sections of her cascading, flame-colored tresses. He drew them in front of her shoulders. Joselyn stiffened.

"Do not worry, my little candlestick. The guests are surely abed by now."

She didn't want to go anywhere with this man, but she wanted to stay *here* with him even less. She nodded her agreement.

Quiet, Joselyn and Dante made their way down the stairs and across the grand foyer. She didn't know where he was leading her, and she didn't ask. Settling on a destination might end their diversion that much sooner.

They walked down a carpeted corridor, passing several of the intricately carved statues which littered the estate's halls. Dante kept his gaze focused straight ahead, and Joselyn followed suit. It wasn't until they were passing the stone likeness of a wyvern that Dante's interest was piqued. He slowed, drawing them both to a halt.

Regarding the carving, he said, "As you can imagine, I took an intense interest in your family's history once our engagement was finalized. Your family crest is a dragon."

He nodded at the statue with appreciation. Joselyn stared at the open-mouthed figure, wishing it were alive and could fly her away, back to Bedmeg. Dante continued his monologue.

"A fine sigil. A great deal mightier than a thornless rose. It seems your ancestors were richer than mine in wealth *and* imagination."

Joselyn turned and stared at him. She didn't care for the contrast he kept drawing between their houses. Though he esteemed hers over his, the comparison felt bitter. Dangerous.

Not meeting her gaze, Dante continued to look pointedly at the carved *gegatu*. "Remarkable! To think that a mere man might master such a creature."

As Dante shook his head, the hairs on Joselyn's arms stood on end.

He tsked, "Do you know, I heard talk a dragon appeared at Castle Arland just last night, if you can believe it."

He released her hand then and turned to face her.

"That's not half so fascinating as this, reportedly it was being ridden by a man. What madness!" He laughed, but the sound didn't match his stiff posture.

Misery tightened through Joselyn's chest, making it harder to breathe. Her body tensed as he twisted a finger into a strand of her hair and wound it around.

"It makes me think of your family's words: 'The Dragon Submits to None.' A powerful statement."

He released her hair, holding her instead with his eyes. "What say you?" He batted an absent hand toward the statue. "Has this dragon been mastered? Tamed?"

He took one of her hands and leaned down. His skin put off no heat. His deep voice dropped to a lower timbre.

"Ridden?"

Bastard.

Joselyn gave a slow blink and cocked her head. "You've made an error, Lord Viridian." Her voice remained cool as ice as she swept her free hand toward the statue "This is a *wyvern*"—she paused, mimicking his style of speech—"not a dragon."

Dante's eyes darkened even as his lips slithered into a smile. "Please, call me 'husband.' "

Joselyn didn't respond.

They were moving again, a bit faster than before. He clutched her arm so high, Joselyn had to rise to her toes to keep from leaning into him.

Her ambivalence began to fade as they walked deeper, and lower into the castle. They passed a pair of guards and descended a flight of stairs until they were presumably below the ground. The air was cool and musty. There were no windows. Perhaps just as disconcerting was the lack of tapestries, carpet, embellishments of any kind. Wherever they were, it was not meant for the likes of a noblewoman.

Joselyn's gaze flitted around the bare halls. Anxiety was beginning to overcome her stubbornness. She was just about to ask where they were going when Dante turned them around a sharp corner and stopped at an iron-plated door.

There was a little window at the top, covered with a grate of metal bars.

Joselyn opened her mouth to speak just as Dante reached into the pocket of his robe and withdrew a long key. Words caught in her throat. He winked at her before shoving the key into the lock and turning it loose with a metal scrape. The door swung open with a low creak as Dante gestured for her to enter.

Joselyn eyed him, with his casual posture and easy smile, so out of place in this dark corridor. Her rising fear leapt to anger. She opened her mouth to demand that they return above ground, but as she did, Dante jerked his head inward, as if pointing something out. Without thought, Joselyn's eyes skipped through the doorway and fell instantly to the back of the room.

There, behind bars and pasted against a stone wall, was Hollen.

Lightning shot through her body. He didn't appear conscious. His head slumped against one arm which, like its twin, was locked against the wall in an iron cuff. Dark bruises covered his shirtless body. Thin streaks of dried blood seemed to have come from his unkempt hair. Was he alive? Every urge, every instinct, bid her run to him. Joselyn's will to preserve his life, if he still breathed, was the one thing that kept her feet planted to the ground. She couldn't disguise her shocked expression as she turned her head toward Dante.

He grimaced as though in apology. "I know. I know. A grisly venue for our wedding night. I promise, we won't tarry long. But—"

Still holding the door back, Dante glanced at Hollen.

"—humor me."

Before Joselyn could respond, Dante brought an arm around her back. His hand crawled across her shoulders like a venomous serpent. He nudged her forward.

With knees locked, Joselyn nearly tipped forward before

she took the barest of steps into what she now recognized was a dungeon. One step. Two. A third. Soon she was striding steadily into the dingy room. Within the swooping sleeves of her robe, Joselyn's nails dug into the backs of her clasped hands.

Beyond the bars, Joselyn assessed the dusky pallor of savage's hands and bare feet. He'd been left secured to the wall for quite some time. The dungeon door slammed loudly behind them, and Hollen stirred. Suddenly, Joselyn could breathe again. His head lulled to the opposite shoulder, and his dark lashes fluttered, but didn't open. A pain-filled groan rumbled in his throat.

Dante's voice snuck up behind her. "They spotted him on the roof, his winged beast crouched upon the highest tower."

Joselyn didn't take her eyes off Hollen. She was waiting for him to rouse. To give her another sign he wasn't mortally injured.

"Do you know *precisely* where this savage was spotted?"

Pale fingers gripped her by the arm before swinging her gently round to face Dante. Joselyn's hands broke apart and she looked up into her husband's cruel, green eyes.

"Outside *your* window."

Joselyn sneered and pushed his hand off her arm. "Are you responsible for this brutality?" She demanded, gesturing to Hollen.

Dante's hand flew over his chest, and his face twisted with affront. "Of course not, dear wife! Little candlestick. You insult me."

Joselyn scrutinized him, measuring his words. She sensed no lie in them. There was something far more insidious lurking there.

"This man has given me no cause to harm him." His brow furrowed. "Or *has* he?"

She'd been thrust into a deadly game, one where she still had much left to lose.

The ghost of a smile played at Dante's lips as he turned away, pulling open the gate of Hollen's cell. He entered like a wolf into a pen of lambs. It wasn't until he shut the door behind him with a click that she realized she should have followed.

Reaching into the pocket of his robe, Dante plucked out what looked like a crude, metal spoon with a long wooden handle. He set its curved end into a nearby ensconced torch.

Joselyn took a halting step forward, just close enough to rest a tentative hand on the bars of the cell. She breathed in, trying to gain control of herself. She dare not let on how much Hollen meant to her. Something told her that doing so would end poorly for both of them.

Dante regarded her. "Your father's made a gift of this creature to House Viridian. A gift . . . with a most curious caveat. He says the prisoner must not be sentenced to death."

Her mind went alight. Frantic. What had she thought? That Lord Fury would see personally to his humane treatment? She'd expected him to keep Hollen close, within the dungeons of Fury Keep. There, at least, he'd be at the mercy of men who weren't given to madness. She looked on in thinly veiled horror as Dante walked toward her. Joselyn's very soul began to tremble. She would soon learn if the rumors about her new husband were true.

"It's so very odd since I also hear this barbarian is the reason our nuptials were delayed. I have little patience for idle gossip, so I hoped you would confirm the whispers."

He already knew. *Of course* he did. His question was a trap. A cruel trick. Joselyn's mind raced through a myriad of possible responses until Hollen's voice claimed both hers and Viridian's attention.

"It's true," he rasped.

Hollen was staring at Viridian from across the cell. No longer hanging limp, he'd risen to his full height, which was equal to Dante's.

His words, though they spared her from answering, ignited her heart into a frenzied panic. Her gaze snapped back to Dante. He wasn't looking at her. His interest had shifted totally to Hollen.

"He awakens. Providential timing. I sensed my new *wife* was about to lie to me."

Hollen's gaze flicked to Joselyn's just long enough for her to see the misery there. A misery that had nothing to do with the abuse littering his body.

Dante stopped a mere two feet away from Hollen. He seemed to be scanning the expanse of her savage's body, lingering on his *idadi*. Dante crossed his arms and huffed. "You *are* an impressive specimen."

Somehow, Hollen managed to smirk. "Don't tell me you came all the way down here just to stroke your cock."

If Viridian was vexed, he showed no sign. "Tell me, for what purpose did you steal my wife away?" His tone was easy, passive, as if the question were being asked merely to scratch an itch of curiosity.

Hollen wasted no time in answering. "I had need of a bride."

"So you simply"—he shrugged—"took her? Plucked her up and flew away? Must all savages resort to stealing their brides?"

"No. Some men *buy* them." He stared hard into Dante's eyes.

There was a moment of tension when Joselyn thought her stomach would implode. All at once, Dante broke into genuine laughter. "I admit, you *are* entertaining."

He leaned forward and lowered his voice as if to impart some secret, though Joselyn heard every word. "More so than she."

Hollen's expression was empty, blank.

Dante straightened and his voice rose once again. "A pity. I have a lifetime to share with her, whereas *you*, on the other hand, will be here only until you've outlived your usefulness."

Joselyn's fingers went from touching to clutching the bars of the cell. With Dante's back turned, she looked pointedly at Hollen, trying to speak without words. She wanted to beg him for forgiveness. To swear to him this hadn't been her intention. He didn't look her way again.

"Fear not. I sense my bride is a compassionate woman. Fortunately for you, it's upon *her* shoulders that your fate resides." He stepped away from Hollen and turned to Joselyn.

Too quickly, Joselyn released the bar. Her hand dropped to her side. "What do you want?"

He approached the bars until he was standing only inches away, keeping his body turned so that Hollen wasn't left out of the conversation. "*You*, my little candlestick. Only you."

Of course. The only thing she had left to give.

"Though legal, and thus, effective, I regret that the execution of our wedding was met with little enthusiasm by our guests. I can't help but wonder if an enthusiastic *bride* would have changed that."

He was offended that she'd not danced her way into the sanctum? It was true, she'd approached their altar like a widow approached her lover's casket. She'd regurgitated their vows like acid bile bubbling out of her throat. No one had cheered. No one had even smiled.

"You've an iron spirit. I sensed it the moment you looked into my eyes as we were joined." He glanced at Hollen, a hint of smugness evident on his face.

Hollen watched the two of them with a passive expression, but Joselyn didn't miss the clenching of his bound fists.

"I respect that," Dante murmured. He shook his head. "But I have no time for it. House Viridian is on the rise, and you are going to do everything in your power to help me see it climb above all others."

Reaching through the bars, he traced an icy fingertip along the sweep of her jaw to pause at the point of her chin.

"You will, or each night, when I've finished amusing myself with you, I shall amuse myself with *him*. Am I clearly understood, dear wife?"

No. He was not. Joselyn's mind spun with morbid possibilities. What sort of amusement might Dante Viridian derive from a bound and broken Hollen? Despite what he'd said, her imagination was likely not so grand as Dante's.

"Yes," she whispered. Her shoulders slumped.

"Good." His voice was low and even. Joselyn jumped when the casual lilt of his voice resumed. "Now, I've one final matter to settle."

As Dante stepped away from the bars and back toward Hollen, Joselyn's breath caught. Her eyes skipped between Dante and her savage.

"Fear not, little candlestick," Viridian called over his shoulder. "My dealings with you are done."

He directed all his attention to Hollen.

"You've robbed me of something precious. My wife's maidenhead. It's a pleasure I'll spend many nights regretting." He pointed at Hollen and casually added, "But you won't have the last word."

Joselyn flinched as soundly as if she'd been slapped. She put both hands on the bar and called out, "Lord Viridian, I—"

Without glancing at her, Dante held up a hand. "Please, wife. Don't bother to deny it. Rest assured that I hold nothing against you."

Joselyn swallowed heavily as Dante refocused on Hollen. "In Morhagen, thieves lose their hands."

A whimper caught in Joselyn's throat. She started looking around the dark room, uncertain what precisely she was searching for. Nothing appeared. No weapon. No help. No escape.

"But seeing as how you'll be spending the rest of your life in chains, that hardly makes an impact. No. I think your eyes are more practical."

Joselyn stopped breathing. He couldn't. He wouldn't.

Wouldn't he? Every rumor about Dante Viridian sparked in her mind.

From within the cell, Hollen glared at Dante. Unflinching. Defiant.

Returning to the ensconced torch, Dante retrieved the little spoon he had placed in the flames.

Joselyn could keep still no longer. She spoke in a shaking voice. "Lord Viridian, please, this isn't necessary. You've been deprived of nothing. I have not been touched by this man."

Dante continued to approach Hollen. "You know, the more often you lie to me, the easier it becomes to recognize when you're doing it. We've many long years ahead of us, wife—"

Viridian cast a vicious glance in her direction.

"—You ought to slow down."

Dante gripped a handful of Hollen's dark hair and yanked his head against the wall. Hollen grunted from the impact.

"Lord Viridian, I beg you, don't do this!" Joselyn threw herself to her knees and all but screamed, "Please!"

A pause.

Dante released Hollen and turned, approaching the place where she knelt clutching the bars.

He stared down at her. "Please . . . *what*?"

Joselyn knew what he wanted.

"Husband," she sobbed, as tears cascaded down her face.

Dante regarded her long and hard as she wept. "Compassionate to a fault. Very well, Wife. You should know early on that I'm not incapable of mercy."

Joselyn choked on her tears, trying, and failing, to regain her composure.

"I shall take only *one* of his eyes."

Joselyn blinked as his words sunk in. As he walked away, Joselyn clutched at the bars and hauled herself to her feet.

"No, stop!" she cried.

Dante ignored her. Hollen didn't flinch as he was gripped by the scalp and forced once more against the wall.

Joselyn flew to the dungeon entrance and threw all of her weight backward against the handle. The door didn't budge. It had been locked. She'd been too distracted by Hollen's presence to notice. She jumped up to the little window and screamed through the bars for help. No one came. She screamed anyway.

She was distracted from her efforts by the sound of Hollen's muffled cry. She whirled around and froze against the dungeon door. She watched in mute horror as Dante scooped the glowing spoon into the left hollow of her savage's skull.

Joselyn could hear his flesh singing, even around his sounds of excruciating agony. A puff of steam rose into the air above Hollen's face. Every muscle in his body was clenched, his veins standing out beneath his skin. As she watched, Joselyn's own fresh brand roared to tortured life. Seconds passed, but time seemed to stretch into one terrifying eternity.

When Dante finally released him, Hollen was panting. His arms pulled straight again and his chin hung so far down into his chest that Joselyn couldn't see his face. Part of her didn't want to see it. The rest of her *needed* to. She raced across the room and crashed against the bars of his cell.

"Hollen!"

He didn't move. Didn't answer. He seemed only intent on breathing.

"Hollen, look at me!"

Nothing.

"Be reasonable, dear Wife. The man's just been through hell. Let us give him a night to recover before we go making demands of him." Dante chucked an arm forward, and something hit the floor with a dull thud. It was Hollen's eye.

Joselyn looked up. Icy rage needled beneath every inch of her skin, and her fingers flexed. Red clouded the corners of her vision as her instincts cried out to attack.

Dante looked not the least bit threatened. Unlocking the cell, he strode casually through the gate and extended a pale arm in her direction. "Come, Wife, we've a marriage to consummate."

She knew now, *truly* understood why Dante Viridian was called 'The Butcher of Brance.'

39

WINGS IN A SNARE

"Still yourself, Wife! Or you'll get your wish and we shall *both* return to his cell."

Dante's words turned her blood to ice. She went half limp as he ushered her back up the stairs leading to the castle's main level. She'd been twisting wildly against him, desperate to free herself, to go back to Hollen, to save him. It was a mad need. She had no plan, no options, no allies.

Her new husband had taken Hollen's eye. He'd threatened to take the other should she not obey his every command. That Hollen was here, that his fate rested in the hands of a madman, was her fault. Hers, and Marcus Fury's.

Damn you! Damn you, Father!

Rage had moved her beyond the point of tears. She passed the guards at the top of the stairs with a dry face. She twisted her head toward the closest one, trying to catch his eye.

Dante clenched her arm with bone-crushing force. A warning. Joselyn turned her gaze to the floor. Would they see the blood on Dante's hand? Hollen's blood? Pain seized her stomach. Surely they'd heard her screams. Stone halls carried sound an eerie distance. If that hadn't been enough to draw their aid, nothing would.

The halls of Castle Arland were hauntingly empty, save for the guards, whose number had been reduced after Hollen's capture. Joselyn's feet scraped their way up the carpeted stairs that led from the grand foyer to her temporary chamber. The higher they climbed, the harder Dante had to work to pull her with him. They crested the top and then made their way down the narrow corridor. She couldn't do this, couldn't let this happen. Without thought, Joselyn pulled against Dante's grip.

"You're dismissed." He hissed at the pair of guards who'd been stationed outside their room.

He was sending them away? Joselyn could only think of one reason why he'd bother. She wanted to faint.

The guards wasted no time in obeying, though one of them seemed to take note of Joselyn's frantic expression. His step faltered only a moment before Dante's wicked glare sent him jogging after his watchmate.

Instead of barging straight into the chamber, as Joselyn had expected, Dante swung her around to face him. His nails dug into the pale fabric of her robe and gouged her upper arms. He pressed the end of his nose into her face and crushed his lips onto hers.

Joselyn whimpered as her teeth cut into the flesh of her own mouth. Was this his idea of a kiss? This violent imposition? Her body went rigid against him. Dante only pulled her closer. It wasn't until she was nearly suffocating that he finally pulled his mouth off hers.

Joselyn gasped and jolted backward. Dante gave her not an inch. He slid an arm around her back and pulled her up against himself until she was all but dangling on her toes. His cool breath chilled her ear. "Compose yourself, dear wife. I anticipate a willing bride. Anything less would leave me sorely vexed. Do I make myself clear?"

Joselyn was about to respond when she caught a wisp of movement in her periphery. Dante must have seen it too. They both turned their heads. A wrinkled old Arland maid, the same one who'd dressed Joselyn's brand, stood at the end of the hall. She must have turned the corner at precisely the wrong moment. Joselyn couldn't stop herself. She poured every drop of wretched, pitiful emotion into her eyes, begging for help.

"Be gone, crone." Dante snarled.

The old woman didn't move right away. She seemed to take in the sight of Joselyn before her aged gaze slid to Dante. Her mouth went flat. Eyes flinty. Dante's grip tightened on Joselyn's waist, and she whimpered.

A moment passed. Finally, the old woman turned and ambled back around the corner from where she'd come. Joselyn's heart went dark. Above her, Dante scoffed. "Did you think to be rescued? I wonder how long that optimism will survive."

He released her. Leaning forward, Dante opened the chamber door and nudged Joselyn inside. She swallowed back a sob and entered the dimly lit chamber. The click and barring of the door behind them smothered what remained of her faith.

Joselyn whipped around. The predator lurked forward. Dante's gaze hovered over the ground by her feet. Joselyn glanced down. The wedding gifts. Her eyes jumped back to Dante. He was smiling.

"Though few, it appears our guests were quite generous. Come, let's see what they've brought us."

Joselyn scowled. She had a strong sense for what Dante had in mind. Most of the gifts would be clothing meant for a bride. Clothing meant to be appreciated only by her new husband.

Wood scraped across stone. Dante pulled up the single chair in the room. He set it a few paces in front of Joselyn, between her and the door. As he took his seat, Joselyn stepped back to avoid his foot as he crossed it over one knee. He stretched his arms out as though making himself comfortable for a long night ahead. Threading his fingers together, he rested the back of his head against his folded hands.

He grinned. "Well?"

Joselyn shook her head, not so much refusing as trying to understand how her life had led up to this moment. Dante's smile faltered.

"My dear, you seem intent on spoiling the night by requiring me to make constant threats. I've decided to make no more."

Every trace of mad amusement vanished. Uncrossing his legs, Dante dropped his elbows to his knees and leaned forward. "Open the gifts."

Do it. Or he'll hurt Hollen.

A voice spoke out in her mind as though from another person. One who didn't feel, only reasoned. Numbly, Joselyn knelt and picked up the nearest box. She took a breath as she wobbled to her feet.

Exquisitely wrapped, it was small and heavy. Joselyn tore off the emerald-colored paper to reveal a wooden box. Inside was a cylindrical glass bottle. Candlelight filtered through clear, yellow fluid inside.

"Open it." Dante said, his voice softer than it had been.

When she uncorked the top, a briny scent wafted to her. Her nose wrinkled up. Dante chuckled.

"Torrin oil. Very expensive. It seems you've more allies than you thought."

Joselyn didn't respond. She stood there awkwardly with the bottle in one hand and the cork in the other.

"Do you know what it's for?" Dante asked.

Joselyn kept her eyes on the bottle and shook her head.

"It's to help your body receive mine."

The bottle slipped from her fingers and shattered on the floor. Joselyn jumped, one of her slippered feet coming off the ground. Her eyes shot up to Dante, who was staring at the ground with pursed lips.

"Well," he said, meeting her gaze, "so much for that." He stifled a laugh.

Joselyn looked at the glassy mess on the floor and bit her tongue hard. She searched for a clean spot to stand on and caught her balance. If she stepped on a broken shard, it would be the least terrible thing that had happened this day.

"Let's try another," Dante said, already sounding bored.

Joselyn selected another box, this one larger and a good deal lighter. It took her a few moments to untie the ostentatious ribbon sitting atop it. She lifted the lid and her stomach lurched. It was a gown, or something like one. There was not nearly enough material to give it a practical use. Joselyn plucked out the sheer, blue garment like a soiled rag.

Dante's eyes glowed with pleasure. "Mmm. Very nice. I think it will look much better *on* you."

Joselyn didn't move, and he quirked an impatient brow. "Go on."

Closing her eyes, she sucked in a breath. *You have no choice. You must.*

She pulled off her robe, then reached to gather up the hem of her white gown.

"Wait," Dante said. He closed his eyes. "Tell me when you've finished."

Joselyn glared. Her skin felt like it was melting away from her bones. This was all a game to him. A pleasurable pastime. And somehow, Joselyn knew what she was witnessing was the very best of him, and that it carried an unbearably brief expiration date. She pulled on the blue gown.

When Dante opened his eyes, he gazed at her with interest

similar to a farmer selecting which hen to slaughter next. A frown crossed his face when his eyes landed on the bandages covering her breasts. "What's this, then?"

Lacking the will to regurgitate the lie she'd been supplied with, Joselyn answered plainly. "A wound."

Dante seemed satisfied with that answer, though his enthusiasm had dampened. "A shame. It does spoil much of the effect."

Joselyn shuddered as his eyes appraised her other curves which were on full display through the near translucent material. She fought the urge to cover herself with her hands, knowing it would only prompt him to 'ask' her to remove them. One more opportunity to demonstrate his power over her.

"I've changed my mind," he said. "It will look much better on the floor."

Joselyn kept her expression neutral, refusing to entertain him with her shock. Part of her wanted to tear the gown off and march directly to the bed, to have done with this horrific experience.

"Shall I remove it?" she asked with all the passion of a man paying his taxes.

Dante hesitated, perhaps surprised by her forwardness. For full effect, Joselyn lifted her hands to her shoulders and made to peel back the thin, lacy straps.

"No," he spat. "Open another."

Joselyn made sure the next box she chose was small and heavy. Perfume. Dante bid her apply some then and there. The floral scent nauseated her, but it was better than undressing again.

Her eyes searched for a fourth gift, favoring the small packages. They paused on a narrow, rectangular box wrapped in brown paper with a crimson ribbon. It was the tie of the bow that caught her attention.

Tansy.

Joselyn's nurse was the only one she'd ever seen tie a knot that way. The plain red color of the ribbon and simple brown paper was as good as a signature. Joselyn hadn't seen her nurse since just before her failed escape attempt. After learning that she and Tansy had made arrangements to go out to the stables, Marcus Fury had prevented any further contact between them. The threat of death dangled over her nurse's neck like a hangman's noose.

Joselyn bent down and brought up the package. It was heavy. Thank the gods. Gently, Joselyn untied the bow and tore off the paper. A wooden box with a slide top lid. What would her nurse give her for a night like this? More torrin oil? Joselyn swallowed and slid back the cover. A glint of light reflected the candles, and Joselyn froze.

It was a plain, unsheathed, dagger.

Joselyn's heart raced, sending a rush of blood down her limbs and back to her heart. Every nerve in her body lit up.

"Well?" Dante asked.

His voice startled her. Joselyn's gaze flew to his. He was looking straight back. Joselyn watched realization creep up on him.

He lunged from the chair.

Joselyn's hand was already around the knife's hilt. The box fell away. Lord Viridian flew toward her, and every instinct told Joselyn to flee. She didn't.

She leaned forward.

A wall of black robes crashed into her body, taking her to the floor.

Her vision went white as all the air rushed from her lungs. The ceiling was just coming back into view when Dante's face moved over hers. His full weight was upon her. She knew he was shouting, but Joselyn couldn't make out his words over the ringing in her ears. His hands went around her throat and clamped down hard.

She gagged.

Her hands tried to go to his wrists, to pull them off her neck. They didn't move. They were still plastered to the blade hilt buried in Dante's gut.

Pull it out.

The voice rang in her mind, but it wasn't hers. It was Hollen's. Suddenly she was back at Bedmeg, standing at the forge. Hollen had a knife at his own stomach, and he was explaining to her that blood loss was what ultimately killed men. *"Pull out the knife, mu hamma, and he'll be dead in moments".*

Joselyn ignored her throat and, with all her might, yanked back on the blade hilt. Its descent was sluggish against the weight of Dante's body bearing down upon her. Shaking, he cried out. Joselyn could barely hear him. Her head felt like it would burst as he crushed the edges of her throat together.

She was going numb. Her feet. Her hands. Her mind.

Darkness. Soon there was only darkness.

A KNOCK AT THE DOOR.

Joselyn's eyes grated open. She felt as though the mountain itself had fallen on her chest. She tried to scream, but could only cough. She kicked out her limbs, and the tinkling of glass drew her gaze out to the side. Something had shattered, and she was laying in it. Or it was laying on her. Her body was heavy and wet.

A wave of vertigo hit her as she lifted her head. When the room stopped spinning, she saw him. Dante Viridian was lying atop her. Dead. His lifeless green eyes stared up at the wall behind her.

She jolted, flying the rest of the way up and shoving to roll him off. He slid off her with a sticky thud, and Joselyn whipped over to vomit. The bite of jagged glass dug into her open palms as she heaved onto carpeted stone.

Another knock, this one much louder.

"Milord? Milady?" A voice called from the other side of the chamber door.

A sob escaped her lips as Joselyn pulled her knees up to her chest. She tried to rise. The smell of salt and iron hit her like a slap, and she had to wait until her stomach relaxed to try again. From throat to toe, Joselyn was covered in Dante Viridian's blood.

Another knock.

Her knife lay a foot away. Joselyn snapped it up. The leather-wrapped hilt almost slipped from her blood-soaked hand. She stumbled to her feet.

She was just straightening when the metallic scrape of a key turned in the door lock.

The wooden door cracked open.

Joselyn brought the knife up to bear, not thinking through what she would do with it. A white head of hair popped through the door.

The old maid who'd walked away earlier peered in from the narrow opening. Her gaze fell to where Dante lay curled on the blood-stained floor. Her eyes narrowed, then skirted up to Joselyn.

Joselyn opened her mouth, but words evaded her. She coughed instead, aware of how loud the rattling was. A splash of cold panic coated her insides. Beads of sweat broke out across her body.

The old woman blinked once, then took a step into the room and closed the door behind her.

"Well little bird, you've certainly got your wings in a snare."

Joselyn stared back, dubious. The old woman's scrutiny

caused Joselyn to look down at her own blood-drenched figure. The fine blue fabric of the gown was totally shredded. Joselyn's hair stuck to her body, redder than ever. She looked back up.

"Please. Help me." Her voice was hoarse, broken.

The maid pursed her lips and put a wrinkled hand on her hip. "It appears I must," she said, with a shake of her head.

Joselyn stood there, small and helpless. She would have fallen to the ground weeping if Dante's corpse hadn't claimed the area.

The woman took a step toward Dante and spat on his lifeless face. With a mild look she held a wrinkled hand to Joselyn. "Why don't you put the knife down, and Old Bess will see what she can do for you."

40

FOR THE LOVE OF A SAVAGE

Old Bess was the former nursemaid to the father of Lord Arland himself. As such, she knew more about Castle Arland and enjoyed more privileges than any other member of the household staff. On their way out the door, she'd kicked Dante's corpse and muttered, "Reap what you sow, Viridian spawn."

Clad in the garb of a kitchen wench, Joselyn followed the old woman through a darkened corridor at what she imagined was the periphery of the castle. A candle was all that lit their way as they descended a narrow staircase obviously intended only for servants.

Bess held up a hand, bidding Joselyn to wait as she tapped open the door at the bottom of the stairwell. After confirming no one was about, she took Joselyn by the hand and they crept into the same hall Dante had led her through just an hour before. They were about to round the corner that led to the lower level stairs when Bess pulled her into a darkened alcove.

"Now, you wait here while I send the guards off. You remember the way out?"

Joselyn nodded. She was panting, and the sound of her own pulse seemed loud enough to give them away.

"What will happen if they discover you helped me?"

Bess scoffed. "They won't."

Joselyn blinked, amazed by the old woman's confidence. By her courage.

"I can't repay you."

"Hush, child, I'm not doing this for you."

Joselyn didn't know what to make of that and didn't have time to ask.

Drawing a deep breath, Bess sighed. Her shoulders slumped as she stepped away from Joselyn and rounded the corner.

The old woman spoke to the two guards who kept post at the stairs. Her words were hushed and unclear. Joselyn jumped when the two men walked right past her hiding spot, back toward the grand foyer.

Silence. Joselyn closed her eyes and peeked around the corner. There were the stairs, but no one was in the hall. No guards. No Bess.

Joselyn tiptoed her way along the wall. The hairs on the back of her neck stood on end and Joselyn glanced back the way she'd come. Nothing. She swung her head back toward the stairs but hesitated.

Across the corridor, Joselyn caught her reflection in a wall-mounted looking glass.

She and Bess had done their best to scrub the blood from her skin and hair, but in their rush, they'd done a poor job. Patches of crimson still caked her hairline. A smudge or two crossed her deeply bruised neck.

She gave herself a good look, the first she'd had in years. What a sight.

No matter. It wasn't the first time she'd been covered in blood. As *Saliga* of Bedmeg, it wouldn't be the last.

THE FIRE WAS INSIDE HIM. Inside his head. In the brief moments he'd been conscious, Hollen hadn't been able to escape it.

He opened his eyes. His *eye*.

The single remaining torch was close to burning out. When it did, he'd be in total darkness. Hollen welcomed it. Perhaps he could fool himself into believing he was in his *bok*. That Joselyn was safe in his arms instead of the clutches of a sadistic demon.

The sight of that man brushing his fingers along Joselyn's cheek, his cruel threats. Hollen wanted to kill him. Unlike that bastard, Hollen would do so quickly, whether he deserved it or not. Every moment he breathed was a moment Joselyn would suffer.

She was suffering now. Lying beneath him, or bent before him while he did whatever he wanted with her body. He tried not to, but Hollen's mind imagined her crying out, struggling, trying to get free. Or worse, quietly withstanding whatever she was given, knowing it would be Hollen who paid the price if she didn't.

The Viridian lord was the man Joselyn had been so desperate to leave him for. What irony. She'd escaped Bedmeg, only to end up with both of them. For as long as he lived, she'd endure one husband using the other against her. Fate could be cruel.

He'd failed. Failed his clan, his brothers, his bride, himself. Now the only thing left was the misery. And there was plenty to be had.

Every muscle in his body ached. He'd been cuffed to this wall for a day and a night, taken down only intermittently by the guards to keep his arms from dying for lack of blood. His throat was hoarse with thirst. Regna, he was thirsty. And cold. Hollen could almost laugh. Atop his snow-blown mountain, he'd never been cold.

Through the bars and past the door, Hollen heard the sound of footsteps. His head came up, waiting to see what fresh hell would enter the room. The door needed straightening. It scraped loudly against the cobblestone floor.

Hollen squinted with his remaining eye, trying to focus in the dim light.

How?

His bride squeezed past the door, her gaze stuck on the floor. She winced at the noise she'd made. She'd changed into a simple brown dress.

Hollen tensed as he looked past her. Was *he* with her?

"Joselyn?" he murmured.

"I'm coming," came her whispered sob. She sprinted up to his cell door and began working at the lock.

Hollen's breathing picked up. Adrenaline poured into his deadened limbs. Without thought, he strained against his cuffs. The helplessness was painful. He glanced back at the cracked door. He needed to know what was happening. If she was in danger or not. "Joselyn."

"Shh! Hollen," she hissed. Her voice bordered on frantic.

After another moment, the door swung open. Joselyn slipped into his cell. At once, her hands were upon him.

"Hollen!" She choked, pressing her mouth into his throat. Her hot tears ran down his skin.

"*Mu hamma*," he whispered, wanting more than anything to wrap his arms around her. "What's happening?"

She pulled away, and Hollen's stomach clenched. There was dried blood in her hair, on her face, and who knew where else? "What did he do?"

Joselyn sucked in a breath "Nothing. He'll never do *anything* again."

He was dead. Hollen knew it. He didn't have to ask. Later, when they were both safe, he would find out what had happened after she'd been dragged away. For now, Hollen only knew he must get Joselyn free of this wretched place.

"Can you open it?" Hollen looked at the cuffs.

He had no word for the metal stick she pulled out of her dress, but Hollen knew it was what opened doors and cuffs. She freed his right arm first. It fell limply to his side, and the weight of it jerked him downward. The next one sent him sliding to the ground.

He tried to get up, but his arms wouldn't move. He couldn't even use one hand to rub life into the other. They were useless.

Joselyn fell to her knees before him. Taking his face in her hands, she pressed her mouth to his. Hollen tasted the salty tears on her lips.

"Hollen I'm sorry. I'm so sorry!" She was trembling.

"There's nothing to forgive, *mu hamma*."

"I didn't leave you. I swear I didn't. I never meant for any of this to happen."

"Shh." He leaned his face into hers.

Sniffing, Joselyn drew back and regarded him with agonizing emotion. "I have to get you out of here. Come. Come on."

Joselyn pulled up on his arm. She seemed to notice the dusky pallor. At once, she was massaging up and down his arms, trying to revive them. He groaned. He'd be little use if they were attacked. They didn't have time for this. *She* didn't have time.

"You must go, Joselyn. Leave now, before someone finds us."

"I'm not going anywhere without you," she hissed.

"I can't . . . I can't protect you. You have to—"

"Be quiet!" Even whispering, her voice was forceful. He couldn't sit here and do nothing.

Inhaling, he mustered all his will. With his knees, Hollen pushed backward, trying to walk himself up the stone wall. He managed, just as the first flashes of agony seared in his wakening arms.

"I know a way out. Can you walk?"

Hollen gritted his teeth and pressed an arm against the wall to push himself forward. His first step nearly sent him to the floor. His second and third were more promising. "I can walk."

And that's likely all I can do.

Joselyn took his hand. He looked at her, and was disturbed at how far he had to turn his head to do so. The left field of his vision was gone. Hollen couldn't imagine what he looked like, but his bride wasn't gaping in horror at him. Something far more painful was etched in her eyes.

Shame.

They may have only moments, but Hollen used his free hand to pull her clumsily into himself. She was no bigger than before, but Hollen could feel something had changed in his bride. She was at once stronger and more vulnerable than she'd ever been. He buried his face in her hair. A strong floral scent, not at all like his Joselyn, filled his nose. He remembered where they were.

"We have to get out of here, *mu hamma*."

Joselyn stiffened, then pulled away. "Follow me."

They both cringed as she eased the dungeon door wide enough to let Hollen through. The scraping boomed and echoed down the stone corridors. When no footsteps could be heard, they crept out of the room Hollen had thought never to leave.

They had no torch. The halls, which felt more like tunnels, were completely dark. Hollen kept one hand on Joselyn and another on the wall as they went. All the while, he listened to his bride counting under her breath.

"...three, four, left."

They turned a corner.

"One, two, three..."

Who'd given her directions? How had she escaped to begin with? He hated walking behind her. Instinct told him to push her aside and take the lead, so that he might protect her from any attack. At least his body would provide some cover. But he had no idea where they were going. At the moment, time was their most precious resource.

Finally, they came to a stop.

"This is it." Her hand felt along the wall for something.

Hollen stuck out his own arm. They were at a door. "You're sure?"

There was a pause. "I'm sure."

Helig, let her be right.

Joselyn grunted as though she were pulling hard on something.

"It's stuck!" Panic filled her hushed voice. "Or maybe . . . locked?"

Hollen followed her arm to where she was holding the door. He brushed her aside. With all his remaining strength, he yanked backward. The door popped open, and a whistle of air blew past them into wherever the door led, sucking it shut. Hollen just barely managed to keep it from slamming closed again.

"Go!" he said, and Joselyn slipped through.

The sound of an opening door made Hollen whip right. A torch-carrying guard peeked out. His eyes scanned the opposite end of the hall. Hollen strained against the weight of the door. If he tried to slip through, the alarm would be raised before he and Joselyn could make their full escape. There was only one choice. He released it.

The door slammed shut and the guard jerked around just in time to see Hollen barreling toward him. He opened his mouth to scream, but Hollen wrapped his arms around the smaller man's head. The torch clattered to the ground, and the guard's arms went wild. He tried to punch and scratch, but he was blind against his assailant's chest. Hollen gave a sharp twist against the man's flailing body. The guard continued to squirm. Hollen had failed to break his neck.

With a curse, he changed tactics and slammed the guard hard into the brick wall. He threw his entire weight into the attack, hopeful at the crunching sound the other man's bones made. At last, the guard went limp. Hollen released him and he crumpled to the floor. The guard might still be alive. Regardless, he wouldn't be raising any alarms.

Hollen wanted to rest, but knew better than to slow down now, while his panicky instincts were still lending him strength. He leapt back to the door and hauled it open just wide enough to squeeze through. Though it might have been too late for stealth, Hollen applied counterpressure to keep the door from slamming. With every muscle in his body flexed, he allowed the door to gently reseal itself.

"Hollen!" Joselyn threw her arms around him.

Hollen leaned panting into the door as a wave of lightheadedness crashed over him. Praise Helig his bride hadn't seen what he just did. He never wanted Joselyn to see him like that. Never again. His body was screaming in pain. They were running out of time. He was working on pure adrenaline and, very soon, he would collapse. He had to get Joselyn out before then.

Dirt.

Hollen flexed his numb toes. They weren't walking on sanded stone anymore. Wherever his *hamma* had taken them, it was a good deal more primitive. Hope surged to life within him. Perhaps they wouldn't meet their ends in this cursed place after all.

They hurried along the narrow path. Some places were so tight Hollen had to turn sideways to squeeze through. He managed. The temperature remained steady, so it was a shock when they made their way up a steep incline only to find themselves beneath the open, autumn stars.

Joselyn started to walk on, but Hollen caught her by the wrist and pulled back. His voice came out labored. "Do you know where we are?"

Joselyn turned and regarded him with worried eyes. "In the forest, just north of the castle."

Hollen shut his eye with relief. Jagomri would be nearby. He hoped. His mount had fled from the volleys of arrows the soldiers had fired in his direction. In their minds, Hollen had been a mere secondary threat. For once, Hollen couldn't blame his steed for his uselessness.

"I'm taking you back to Bedmeg."

"How?" she asked with disbelief.

Despite everything, part of him still wondered if this was where his bride wanted to be. Not here, exactly, but was she really ready to call Bedmeg her home?

Just focus on getting her to safety.

"We have to get away, somewhere they won't hear me calling Jagomri."

"He survived?"

Hollen grimaced. "What was your plan if not?"

"To get to the next village." By the light of the stars, Hollen could see her head shaking. "But now I doubt you'd make it."

She could tell how weak he was. Hollen cursed. If she could sense it, others could, too. They had to get out of here. Fast.

"Let's go." He stepped barefoot into the snow.

His bride, at least, was properly clothed. She led him by the hand. The force of her pulling kept him focused. He was Hollen the Soulless, and it would take more than cold to kill him. That didn't stop his legs from going numb.

When they'd been walking for the better part of an hour, she turned and asked, "Is this far enough?"

"Let's hope." Hollen put his head back to the sky and pursed his frozen lips together. His whistle echoed through the forest and off the distant mountain wall, causing them both to cringe.

The sound of a hooting owl broke the ensuing silence.

"Come on," he said through chattering teeth.

They kept moving. They went on for so long Hollen wasn't certain if they still moved to find Jagomri, or if it was to keep from dying. At least his head didn't pain him anymore, though his throat was drier than ever. He was slowing down. Joselyn was supporting him now, or trying to. To be of any true help, he'd have to give her more of his weight than she was capable of carrying. They went on like that. with Hollen occasionally whistling for his mount. The bastard was probably sleeping. The idea held significant appeal.

His leg caught on something, and Hollen folded to the ground, taking Joselyn with him.

"No!" she cried out, as though she'd been expecting this to happen.

Hollen tried to bring himself back up, but the momentum of his fall continued, dragging him the rest of the way down. He turned his eye upward, and the stars began to spin. He squinted, trying to slow them down. It didn't help.

"Joselyn. Do you know where we are?"

"I can guess," she said. She seemed further away than she'd been only moments ago. He searched, but he couldn't find her face.

"You have to get somewhere safe, *mu hamma*."

"We will."

He swallowed dryly. "Now. Without me."

Silence. Had she gone already?

After what seemed like many long minutes. "Yes, Hollen."

Those words gave him hope and crushed his spirit. He should say something else. An apology? For failing her. For pulling her off her horse and away from her life only to lead her here. To this.

A declaration? That he loved her. That she was the culmination of all his dreams. His every hope. That, despite it all, he'd have chosen no other.

Perhaps a simple goodbye.

"*Loragi, mu hamma.*"

Farewell, my only.

Silence filled his ears. His body was limp, paralyzed by the cold. Time stretched out in a warped daze around him. She hadn't said goodbye. Or had she, and he was simply too cold to remember?

It made no difference. The only thing that mattered was that Joselyn was free. For that, Hollen would die grateful.

Helig, protect her.

Though he was sure he hadn't closed his eye, the sky above went totally black.

41

A BEACON OF HOPE

"Erik!"

Joselyn would have run weeping to Hollen's brother if the man were not still atop his stark white *gegatu*. She stayed where she was, draped over Hollen's half-naked body and squeezing his hands beneath her breasts. He was cold as death. His breathing had grown shallow and slow. Joselyn had lent him her heat, done everything she could to preserve him. All the while she'd filled every second of silence with fevered prayer. The gods had heard.

She looked up into the sky as another dark figure descended through the opening of trees.

Jagomri.

Joselyn had never been so happy to see the wicked creature. As he landed, he fixed yellow eyes upon her, or rather, upon his master. His forked tongue slithered past his lips as he hissed.

Erik, free of his saddle, leapt to the ground. He dashed across the clearing and skidded to his knees, kicking up snow beside them.

"Joselyn!" The blond man's voice cracked with fear. "Is he alive?"

"Yes, but Erik, he's so cold!"

Erik unpinned his coat as Joselyn scrambled off Hollen. She could feel the heat of Erik's body radiating from the fur garment when he swung it over his brother. He pressed a hand into Hollen's throat. Checking for a pulse? Erik's gaze locked on the blackened area where Hollen's eye had been.

"You have to take him to Bedmeg." Panic gripped her insides. Every second felt like another hour, pulling her savage closer to his doom.

Erik grabbed Hollen under the arms and hauled him off the melted ground. Grunting, he threw his older brother over one shoulder. It was a good thing Erik was larger, if only slightly.

Instead of taking Hollen to his own mount, Erik approached Jagomri. Joselyn watched with a mixture of suspense and fascination as Erik slowed and calmly navigated the *gegatu's* space. With easy grace, he managed to get Hollen properly lashed into the saddle, throwing an extra leather cord over his back for good measure.

Erik jumped down and hurried to his own mount. He extended an arm toward Joselyn, a question in his eyes.

Joselyn didn't hesitate. She darted across the snow, grabbed onto his hand, and let him lift her onto his mount's back.

"Jagomri will follow?" she asked. What if they'd come this far only for the stubborn beast to fly elsewhere with his master freezing upon his back?

"He will," Erik confirmed, fastening his legs into the stirrups.

Sitting upon someone else's *gegatu* sent dreadful recollection through her mind. "Sigvard?"

"He's fine."

Joselyn listened to Erik work as his mount shifted its weight from one foot to the other, causing them to sway. They'd made it. *Almost.* Gratitude ached in her heart.

"Erik?" Joselyn asked, her voice so quiet he might not have heard.

He grunted in response.

"I thought the Dokiri were forbidden from interfering in matters between a *hatu* and his *hamma*." Hollen had explained the reason none of his men had accompanied when he'd rescued her from the hunters.

When the last tie had been secured, Erik swung forward to press her into the leather of his saddle. His weight, that of an ally, was like a blanket of relief over her soul.

"*Va*, it's not the first sacrament I've broken," he muttered, raw bitterness in his words.

Joselyn's brow furrowed, trying to make sense of him. His arms slid past her and he took hold of his steed's ridges.

"Regna help me; it won't be the last."

THE FIRES of the common area burned hot and bright. The glow stretched outside like a beacon of hope. It was too late at night for such, but Joselyn quickly discarded the thought as she tumbled from Erik's mount only to race through the snow toward Jagomri.

"Joselyn, wait!" Erik called after her.

The black beast hissed in warning, and instinct stopped her dead in her tracks. Her heart was pounding. She needed to go to Hollen, to assure herself that he was still alive. Erik blew past her with his long strides.

Joselyn watched as Erik worked at Hollen's saddle. In moments, other Dokiri men stood by her, all watching and calling out in their language to Erik, probably pelting him with questions.

Within minutes, Erik had Hollen down and was rushing him

toward the caves. As soon as he was away from Jagomri, Erik was swarmed by other riders who helped carry Hollen in. Joselyn jogged to keep up with them, never letting herself be crowded too far out. There were so many people awake for this hour. What had been going on before they arrived?

As they stepped under cover of the common area, the sudden heat sent a chill up Joselyn's spine. Hollen was brought to the ground near a fire, and Joselyn had to elbow her way through the gathered men.

"Joselyn," Erik called. His blue gaze landed upon her as she fell to her knees at Hollen's side. "Where all has he been injured?"

"I don't know." Joselyn fought hard against the edge of hysteria growing in her mind. "He was walking before. But he was badly beaten. And—" Her gaze fell to the singed crater in his skull, unable to speak the words.

"He's just cold then." Magnus said, pushing into the ring.

Ivan, was there too, his scarred face grim but calm. "And exhausted. Let's get him to the springs."

"The *private* springs." Joselyn said, her voice full of command. Women were forbidden from the men's springs, and she'd be damned if Hollen were taken somewhere she couldn't go.

A few of the men shot questioning glances in her direction, but Hollen's brothers were already carrying him off in the direction she'd indicated. Women hovered at the edges of the crowd, and more roused from their *boks* by the minute. Where was Lavinia? Joselyn craved the older woman's calming presence. There was no time to go searching.

They were at the springs in minutes. Joselyn paced as Magnus and Ivan lowered Hollen down to a shirtless Erik, who was waiting for him in the first pool. Only Hollen's brothers had come. There was too little space to navigate the narrow tunnels and tight alcoves. That suited her just fine, as she began shedding all but her wool under-shift. A month ago, she'd have paled at the thought of doing such a thing, but now?

The water wasn't as cold as she'd anticipated. Perhaps because her own skin was teetering at the edge of snow burn. Still, she gasped as she waded her way over to Hollen and took his head in her arms. Erik was supporting the rest of him on his knees, much as Hollen had done for her when she'd nearly died.

"Will he live?" Joselyn demanded of no one in particular. Her gaze was fixed on Hollen as she brushed blood-dried strands of hair from his face.

Ivan spoke from where he crouched at the pool's edge. "The cold tried to take him once, and Helig sent the bastard back. He'll be fine."

"I don't like the look of those knots on his head," Magnus cut in, his voice *far* less reassuring.

"And what of our *Saliga*?" came a feminine voice from the tunnels.

They all turned. It was Rosemary, her expression soberly fixed on Joselyn. "She's not going to drop on us now, is she?"

Joselyn's grip on Hollen's face firmed as all three men suddenly focused on her. It was clear by their stunned and somewhat flustered expressions that they'd not noticed the blood on her body, nor the bruises around her throat. She hurried to reassure them.

"I'm well." It didn't feel like a lie. Compared to what her savage had suffered, her injuries were inconsequential.

"Maybe you should go with Rosemary?" Magnus suggested.

Beside him, Ivan nodded. He reached across the water and wrapped a hand around her arm to tug her away. Joselyn snapped out of his grip. "I'm not going anywhere."

"Leave her be," Erik said, adjusting his hold on Hollen. "I'll watch over them both."

Joselyn stared at Erik as more gratitude swelled in the form of tears. She blinked them back and resumed stroking Hollen's hair.

"We need to get back out there," Magnus said.

Ivan stood. "Joselyn, will anyone try to follow you?"

Joselyn froze. *Would* anyone follow? Attempt to recover Lord Fury's daughter? A gory image of Dante's lifeless body flashed. Lord Fury hadn't been able to assassinate his blackmailer since Dante had arranged for his secret to be sent to every corner of the kingdom in the event of his untimely death. After tonight, there would be hell to pay, and the price would undoubtedly be charged to Marcus Fury.

Faced with the thought of her Lord Fury's execution, Joselyn felt nothing but the satisfaction of divine justice.

She ran a thumb along the edge of Hollen's jaw. "No."

HER SAVAGE WAS WARM AGAIN. Under the furs of their bed, Hollen glowed like the summer sun. He wasn't fevered. That was just Hollen. She'd finished rewrapping his head, and was curling into his side. She'd chosen the one with less bruises, careful not to bump into them as she settled herself against him.

He'd yet to waken, and fear was an ever-present vermin, gnawing deeper and deeper into her mind. After spending the night and half the morning in the springs, Erik had assured her he *would* wake, but it wasn't enough. It was evening again, and still, he'd barely stirred.

Joselyn traced her fingertips along the edges of his *tanshi* mark, humming a song that Tansy would sing to her when she was ill. They'd largely been left alone, though Rosemary periodically checked in on them. Joselyn had requested to see Lavinia, and it was then that she'd learned the reason for the unrest last night. Her and Hollen's ordeal hadn't been the only tragedy suffered these past days.

Lavinia was now a Dokiri *gritu*. In mourning for her husband, Soren. The day of Joselyn's disappearance, every rider had been called out to answer a *veligiri* threat. It had been so unusual, the men were still arguing over what to make of it.

A multi-species pack of underdwellers, at least five different varieties, had descended the mountain in a group, as though drawn together by some common purpose. With one exception, the *veligiri* didn't travel together nor form alliances. The *Na Dokiri* hadn't been prepared, and they'd suffered the consequences.

Five riders had been washed in Helig's pool. Five riders had been burned. Joselyn prayed Hollen wouldn't be the sixth. Her heart ached for Lavinia. For Volo and Brodie, her young sons. When Hollen finally woke, she'd go to them.

"Joselyn?" a male voice called from the tunnel of their *bok*.

She sat up, shifting her gown to ensure she was covered. "Yes?"

At the entrance, Sigvard limped into view. Joselyn tensed. A jumble of emotions cascaded through her. She'd been told he was alive and that he'd heal from his injuries. But seeing him up and walking released a knot of worry in her chest.

"Sigvard," she gasped.

Joselyn threw back the furs, climbed out of the bed, and rushed across the room. Standing on her toes, she threw her arms around his neck and squeezed.

Despite his wavering balance, likely owed to his bad leg, Sigvard went rigid. He didn't return her embrace. Joselyn released him and took a small step back, searching his eyes.

He wasn't looking at her, not directly anyway. "I came to see that you were as well as Erik says. *Both* of you."

Joselyn glanced backward at Hollen. "He hasn't woken yet,

but his body's warmed and we've managed to get some water into him."

Turning back to Sigvard, Joselyn caught the auburn man's eyes on her throat before they skittered away. He swallowed hard. Joselyn lifted a hand to her neck. How terrible must she appear?

"As for me," she said, "I'm not any worse for wear."

Sigvard's coppery gaze flashed, meeting Joselyn's. All at once she wished he'd go back to avoiding her eyes. His expression was so livid, she took a tentative step back. This was not the silly, carefree Sigvard she'd known only a few days ago.

"No worse?" He scanned her up and down, making Joselyn wish she had a robe, or maybe Hollen's coat, to hide herself in.

Joselyn crossed her arms over her chest. Her shoulders came up a bit closer to her ears. Sigvard seemed to notice, and suddenly his expression morphed from one of rage to one of anguish.

"You both nearly died. Hollen might still—" he broke off. "It's my fault. All of it."

Joselyn blinked, then forced her shoulders to relax. "Sigvard, what happened down there, it wasn't your fault."

"Wasn't it?" he countered. His eyes bored into hers.

Joselyn opened her mouth to speak, but he cut her off.

"Can you tell me that any of it would have happened if I'd left you alone that morning?"

Joselyn stuttered, uncertain how to answer.

Sigvard gave the smallest of nods, and his gaze slid down to the floor.

Joselyn bristled. Sigvard was barely more than a boy. He couldn't shoulder the evil of Morhageese lords. Neither of them could have anticipated what was to come. Even so, flying out that morning had been a lapse in *both* their judgments. The responsibility was not entirely on him. She started to tell him so, but Sigvard held up a hand.

"Don't, Joselyn. *Please.*"

The grief in his voice made Joselyn's heart clench. Her words caught in her aching throat.

"I can't make things right. I *know* that. I won't ask you to forgive me. I don't deserve it and I never could."

Joselyn shook her head. "Sigvard, we're alive. We're safe."

Sigvard's expression darkened. Tears welled in his swollen eyes. "Not everyone."

Grelka. Erik told her what had happened. Sympathy curled in Joselyn's chest. Sigvard was looking at Hollen again, and Joselyn knew he was studying the bandages over Hollen's missing eye.

"It should have been me," he murmured.

Hand outstretched, Joselyn took a step forward. "Sigvard—"

He spun, wobbling hard on his right leg. "Just have someone tell me when he wakes."

He was gone before she could think of words to stop him.

42

KNITTING SCARS

Joselyn.

Hollen could hear her voice, could feel her presence.

"No," he groaned through cracked lips.

She wasn't supposed to be here. Not with *him*. She was supposed to be somewhere safe. Somewhere warm. But then, Hollen was warm now. His body was heavy, like the weight of the mountain was pinning him down. And yet, he was in total comfort.

His eyes scraped open. Or at least, one did. The other was still shut. Was he lying on his side? He didn't think so. Hollen scanned his surroundings. The flicker of firelight caressed the smooth, rounded walls. He was in a *bok*. His *bok*. He tried to sit up. His muscles tensed, but didn't respond. Something stirred beside him.

"Hollen?" It was *her* voice.

"Joselyn." Could it be? Was she here? Were they *both* in Bedmeg? Together?

"Oh Hollen!"

She came into view, and her red hair spilled down around

him as she lowered herself to cover his mouth with her own. Her hands went to his beard, stroking him like he were made of fashioned ice.

She was alive. She was here. And so was he.

"Joselyn," he choked.

Sensation eased back to his limbs. He swung an arm over her, and pulled her body to his. It hurt, but he didn't care. She was soft and warm and everything that was good in the world.

They lay like that for a long while, tangled up in each other's arms, their tears mingling with their lips. They reveled in the feel of one another's bodies, their joint presence. They'd escaped. They *had* survived.

Hollen slipped in and out of consciousness several times before he gathered the awareness to ask questions. He'd slept a night, a day, and another night. They'd been recovered by Erik. Sigvard had survived his wounds and Hollen had lost five riders in the time he'd been gone.

Those were the easy questions.

"Joselyn, what happened?"

She lay curled in his arms, her forehead laid against his. "I didn't go with Sigvard to leave you. It was supposed to be a quick flight. He'd been so excited."

He'd wondered. A part of him had feared she'd gone gladly with Sigvard, hoping to get away. Now, after seeing what his bride was capable of, what she was willing to do for him, Hollen couldn't believe he'd ever doubted her.

"That's not what I meant." Swallowing, he mustered the will to learn what he must. "I meant, what happened to *you*?"

She stiffened in his arms. Her eyes fluttered shut. Hollen used the hand of the arm she was lying on to stroke her back. He waited with painful anticipation to absorb what she would say.

"I killed him."

He'd guessed as much. "How?"

Joselyn's eyes cracked open, but she didn't focus on him. "My nurse slipped me a knife. He wasn't prepared for it."

After a moment, "Does this mean?" He stared hard at her. "Am I not a hopeless teacher after all?"

There was a pause, then they both smiled. She giggled. It was the sweetest sound he'd heard since waking. He wanted to hear it again, to make her laugh.

He couldn't. Not yet.

Hollen thought of how she'd looked when she'd slipped into his cell. He remembered the blood she'd been covered in. Even now, he could see the bright remnants of the bruises covering her throat. Hand-shaped bruises.

"Did he hurt you?" Hollen forced himself to look her in the eye.

Joselyn's gaze went cold as her voice. "He tried. He failed."

Hollen's body shook as he exhaled. He put a hand at the base of her neck and pressed a kiss to her forehead.

Thank you, Helig.

Hollen could have found a way to live with his shame if she'd been violated under his protection. Eventually. But, could Joselyn? Even so, there was so much he had to atone for.

"Hollen, I'm so sorry."

Her words jerked him out of his own thoughts. "What are *you* sorry for, *mu hamma*?"

Her mouth flattened, regret darkening her gaze. "Your eye. For everything."

Hollen squeezed her a little more. "That wasn't your fault, Joselyn. I should never have been captured. I should have found another way to rescue you. *Before.*"

Joselyn shook her head. "It all happened because of me. Because you came for me."

"I told you I would always come for you." Hollen nudged the end of his nose into hers. "That wasn't an empty promise."

Her lip trembled. "I need you to know . . .that I never meant for any of it to happen. I never meant to leave you."

"I know," he whispered.

Joselyn watched him. Some of the sorrow eased out of her features. She stroked at his chest, and her fingers traced along the edges of his *tanshi* mark. It felt good. Hollen ran his hands down the edge of her collarbone and dropped low to do the same. Joselyn hissed in startled pain.

Hollen jumped. "What's wrong?"

Pulling away, Joselyn curled into herself. She covered her breasts with folded up arms. Why was she looking away?

Hollen pushed himself up on one elbow. Alarm rose in his chest. "Joselyn? What is it?"

Tears filled her eyes. His bride didn't cry easily. Fear shot through him. He tried to examine the place he'd touched her, but she was hiding it from him. He sat the rest of the way up.

"Let me see." Rolling her onto her back, Hollen had to pry her hands away from her chest. What he saw turned his blood cold. His voice came out strangled. "You said he didn't hurt you."

Joselyn choked through a sob. "He didn't."

Hollen had to remind himself not to clench his fists. He was still holding Joselyn's hands apart from her chest. "Who?"

Silence.

Joselyn swallowed hard. "My father."

There were no words.

Hollen wrestled with twin urges to destroy and protect. To maim and comfort. He released Joselyn's hands. Lord Fury wasn't here. His daughter was.

Hollen lay back down and gathered Joselyn into his arms. He held her as she wept.

A long time had passed with Joselyn falling in and out of sleep. Hollen remained awake. He'd done enough sleeping. Now it was his turn to watch over her.

Joselyn stirred in his grasp. Her voice barely rose above a whisper. "Does this mean I can't stay?"

Hollen loosened his hold and pulled back to see her face. "What?"

"The day you claimed me, you said the mark was necessary to avoid a curse. That your gods demanded it."

He put a finger under her chin. He waited until her gaze wandered up to his before speaking. "Joselyn, Helig herself couldn't command us apart. You understand that, don't you?"

She blinked, her expression unreadable. "I was so afraid of you that day you marked me. All I wanted was the scar removed. But now?" She drew in a shaking breath. "I never imagined I could feel this way. Like I'd die if you sent me away."

Hollen leaned down and brushed the softest of kisses against her chest, just above where her *tanshi* mark had been. "I'll never send you away, *mu hamma*. Only you have that power."

Joselyn threaded her fingers into his hair. The sensation of her nails drawing against his scalp made him groan. She pulled his head upward until they were face to face. "Do I also have the power to command us together, then?"

Hollen shook his head, amazed at the force of will this woman held over him. "For as long as you'll have me."

"Forever, Hollen. I want you, forever."

43

MU HATU

Every man, woman, and child in Bedmeg made their way outside, a song on their tongues. This one was bright and cheerful, full of wonder and promise. They were heading for the ledge where sacrifices were made and rites performed.

The sun shone bright, glittering off the snow. Joselyn shivered as she stepped into the cold. It was late winter, and a wool shift wasn't enough to keep her warm in this weather. Hollen was shirtless and unaffected as ever. He squeezed her hand in his, urging her forward.

"Not having second thoughts are you?" He grinned.

Joselyn pursed her lips. "Are you?"

He laughed, and Joselyn marveled for the thousandth time that losing an eye had not robbed him of his beauty.

"Not a chance."

This was the day. The one she'd been looking forward to every moment since returning to Bedmeg. Today, she would become Hollen's. Or perhaps, more accurately, he would become *hers*.

She would have insisted on this as soon as Hollen was strong enough to come outside. But her brand had needed time to heal. It wasn't the only thing. Hollen's balance had suffered, but he'd made adjustments and his aim was improving daily with both his axe and his bow.

For all the strides their bodies had made, the nightmares still plagued them both. When one of them would wake in a cold sweat, the other was always there. And really, that was the only thing either of them needed.

"You sure you want to do this, little sister?" Erik asked, sidling up alongside Hollen.

"There's still time to change your mind!" Ivan added from behind.

"Blink twice if you need us to hide you!" Magnus piped in.

Hollen directed an obscene gesture at all of them, and the surrounding crowd roared with laughter.

Joselyn shook her head in mock dismay, certain she'd never been happier than she was just then. The only thing that could have made the moment more perfect was if Sigvard had joined in. Joselyn was certain he was present in the crowd, but it was rare to find him in the thick of things these days. He preferred instead to stick to the edges. Along with Hollen, she hoped someday soon the Sigvard they all knew and loved would return.

A new song started, and Joselyn understood just enough Dokiri to make out some of the words. They were singing of bonding, of the gods, and of love. Joselyn squeezed Hollen's hand as he led her up onto the ledge. The people filed in around the front, pressing forward to get a good view. They were smiling at her, and their open regard infused her with pride.

She'd learned much in the past months. Not the least of which was how to be a Dokiri *Saliga*. Joselyn hadn't yet mastered the role. She still made mistakes. But she knew in her heart she was grasping something far more important. A sense of her own goodness. That virtue didn't come from blind duty. It came from deciding daily who she would be, and why. That mastery was what would make her into the leader her people deserved. One day. For now, she was Joselyn of Bedmeg. And it was enough.

She remembered the moment just before Hollen had stolen her away, as she sat upon Morningstar's back. She'd been watching the mountain. *This* mountain. She'd marveled at how something so large was so still and made no sound. Glancing around now, Joselyn realized that the mountain was not what she'd believed. This was a place for singing. A place for dancing. A place for life.

Home.

Hollen took her by the hands and turned her toward himself. She looked up at him and drank in his sheer magnitude. He was the wildest thing she'd ever seen, and he was *all* hers. Her Hollen. Her savage. *Hers.*

Hollen reached to his side and produced the *gneri* blade he'd given her on her first night in Bedmeg. The sun carved into its ivory hilt reflected the light. The rays seemed to glow with a light of their own.

She accepted the gift.

As the crowd roared their approval, Joselyn brought the tip of the blade up to Hollen's chest. She met his gaze then. It blazed with an intensity she knew to be completely for her. He grinned, and bent toward her ear.

"Don't lean back," he whispered.

She would always love Hollen, because he would always do the same. That was loyalty. *That* was strength.

Joselyn pressed the knife into his skin. "Never, *mu hatu.*"

The End

WANT MORE?

Curious about Hollen's parents?

Get their love story for **FREE** by signing up for Denali Day's newsletter at...

www.subscribepage.com/sven-the-collector

...AND MORE?

Get a **FREE** ebook full of cut scenes and alternative point-of-view chapters by visiting Denali Day's website at...

www.denaliday.com/extras

ALSO BY DENALI DAY

Sven the Collector
Erik the Tempered
Ivan the Bold
Magnus the Vast
Sigvard the Nameless

ABOUT THE AUTHOR

When Denali Day was trying to figure out "what to be when she grew up" she noticed all her written stories featured a scene where the beautiful heroine patched up the wounds of a gallant hero. So she decided to become a nurse. Twelve years and two degrees later, she realized all she ever really wanted was to be a writer.

Now she lives in the midwest with her adoring husband, a real life gallant hero, and their two wicked goblins (children). When she isn't writing she's reading and when she's not doing either of those things she's probably plundering the fridge for something she can smother in whipped cream.

www.denaliday.com

GLOSSARY

atu (ah-too): your/yours (Dokiri language)

bedmeg (Bed-meg): one of six Dokiri clans along the Crook-Spine mountain range

bok (boh-k): a smooth-walled cave hollowed out by ancient volcanic creatures (Dokiri language)

dokiri (doh-ki-ree): a race of peoples who dwell in cold places, large bodied, hardy, unable to produce female offspring

ebron (eb-ron): desert lands to the south west of the Crook-Spine mountain range

gegatu (ge-gah-too): wyvern (Dokiri language)

gegatudok (gegah-too-dock): a rite in which Dokiri boys become men by taming a wyvern (Dokiri language)

glanshi (gla-n-shee): an expletive (Dokiri language)

gneri (ner-ee): rite (Dokiri language)

gritu (gri-too): a widowed Dokiri hamma (Dokiri language)

hala (ha-la): a traditional dress worn by Dokiri hammas on special occasions

hamma (ha-ma): only/mated woman (Dokiri language)

hatu (ha-too): only/mated man (Dokiri language)

helig (he-lee-g): one of two Dokiri deities, the 'earth mother'

idadi (id-ady): a collection of bodily scars the Dokiri use to denote their deeds and clan-status

idaglo (id-ah-glow): a summit among the Dokiri in which the Salig is asked to stand as judge (Dokiri language)

kild (kild): a stringed instrument made of wood. Rectangular, flat, uses a bow

kreesha (kree-sha): an expletive (Dokiri language)

lagi (la-gee): peace (Dokiri language)

loragi (lor-a-gee): farewell (Dokiri language)

morhagen (mor-hey-gahn): temperate lands to the north of the Crook-Spine mountain range

mu (moo): my/mine (Dokiri language)

na dokiri (nah-doh-ki-ree): he who conquers (Dokiri language)

podagi (poh-dah-gee): idiot/moron (Dokiri language)

sestoria (sess-tor-ee-ah): the planet on which the Dokiri Brides Series takes place

salig (sa-lee-g): chieftain (Dokiri language)

saliga (sa-lee-gah): chieftainess (Dokiri language)

selska (sel-sk-ah): blood/body (Dokiri language)

tanshi (tah-n-shee): bonding (Dokiri language)

veligiri (vel-eh-gee-ri): under-creature (Dokiri language)

veligneshi (vel-eh-g-neh-shee): a rite in which Dokiri riders become full citizens by killing a veligiri (Dokiri language)

velsa (vel-sah): a word of command (Dokiri language)

vokmadi (vah-k-mah-dee): a game similar to tug of war, played by the Dokiri peoples

ACKNOWLEDGMENTS

While this wasn't the first book I've ever published, it's the first book I ever ever wrote. The year and a half surrounding its publication has been the most trying and incredible time of my life as a writer. Of course I've had significant help from people who want nothing more from me than to see me succeed. Each of them is worth their weight in gold.

AJ, my husband, I doubt there is a better model for that of the "supportive lover". You've helped me in so many ways I could take up a chapter mentioning them. Paramount among them has been your steadfast commitment to seeing me achieve my goals if for no other reason than my own happiness. You've made countless sacrifices on that altar and I'll always be grateful.

Hollee Mands, my critique partner, I'm convinced God put you in my path right from the beginning of this journey by design. I honestly don't know if I would have made it this far apart from your constant encouragement and willingness to come alongside me every step of the way. Thank you for being a friend as much as a teacher.

Kelley Luna, my line-editor (and also cheerleader), your enthusiasm cannot be matched. Your joy is infectious and was occasionally the only thing that kept me from hating my work and everything about it. Thank you for puffing up my ego while still managing to teach me how quotation marks work.

Ivy Williams, occasionally you've supplied me with some of the most creative solutions to story problems I've had and it blows my mind. Thank you for your "outside the box" thinking.

Justena White, if there's an award for fastest reader on the planet, I think you should apply. Thanks for always being an instant message away.

Isla Cristeon, one of my very first beta readers, thank you for your endless supply of positivity and clever marketing tips. You've been there for me even when I haven't been around for you. You're the best sort of friend a writer could ask for.

Jacie Lennon, I met you a little later in the game, and yet you somehow were one of the first people to convince me I might actually end up with decent number of readers who actually cared to read Book #2. Thank you for never being sparing with your praise.

Courtney Kelly, finding you was a god-send. Thank you for providing the highest quality service anyone could ask for, with a price tag that this stay-at-home-mom could afford without crying. Your constant communication and willingness to go the extra-mile has been an absolute pleasure throughout my journey.

Eliza Raine, you came out of nowhere and have been a steadfast source of encouragement since. You're kind of like a beacon on the shoreline overlooking what can sometimes feel like the perilous seas of publishing. I know exactly where to look for guidance and support. Thank you for being big enough to, with the tenderness of a child, ask "want to be friends"?

Grace Draven, your incredible books served as a foundational source of my love for this niche (along with a few others, of course). In addition to that, your infectious sense of humor can only be bested by your generosity in lending a hand to an unknown author who asked for a free favor. I got a lot of traction from it when I needed it most. Thank you.

Miranda Bridges, I still can't understand why someone as unbelievably successful as you has gone out of her way to make me feel so valued and respected, but you keep doing it and I'm starting to walk a little taller (a real thrill considering my 5' 2" frame). Your beauty obviously started on the inside and only grew outward from there.

Lee Savino, you're a shark in the water and I want to hold onto your tail fin while you conquer the ocean! Every time I see you've posted something on your Facebook group I get excited because you just bring that energy. And girl, I *need* that fire. Thank you for inspiring the rest of us and plowing the way forward.

Philippians 4:13 I can do all things through Christ who strengthens me.

Printed in Great Britain
by Amazon